Mortal Touch

To Suzanne

Thanks and to
sure you watch
for the next me!

Inanna Arth

The Vampires of New England Series

Mortal Touch

Inanna Arthen

By Light Unseen Media
Pepperell, Massachusetts

Mortal Touch
The Vampires of New England Series

Cover and interior design by Vyrdolak, By Light Unseen Media.

This is a work of fiction. Names, characters, places and incidents are either the products of the author's imagination or are used fictitiously, and any resemblance to actual persons, living or dead, business establishments, events or locales is entirely coincidental.

ISBN-10: 0-9793028-0-3
ISBN-13: 978-0-9793028-0-0
LCCN: 2007902580

Published by
By Light Unseen Media
PO Box 1233
Pepperell, Massachusetts 01463-3233

Our Mission:
By Light Unseen Media presents the best of quality fiction and non-fiction on the theme of vampires and vampirism. We offer fictional works with original imagination and style, as well as non-fiction of academic calibre.

For additional information, visit:
http://bylightunseenmedia.com/

Printed in the United States of America

0 9 8 7 6 5 4 3 2 1

Chapter One

On April 16, 2004, only four people in the small town of Sheridan, Massachusetts were aware of the strange events that had been occurring in its vicinity for the past several months. This was about to change.

It was Friday of the Patriots Day holiday weekend, midway through one of the rainiest Aprils on record. The last of the snow from an interminable winter was finally washing away, leaving only a few dirt-encrusted icy mounds where the highest plow piles had stood. Rivulets of glittering water ran along the gutters of every street, and spring peepers sang from small ponds and boggy areas, which at the moment described every low-lying piece of ground in town. This included a waterlogged third of the unpaved parking area of the store, Regan Calloway noticed as she arrived for work. But it was the first holiday weekend of spring, and Regan was glad it wasn't raining for a change—or worse, snowing.

In several respects, Borrowed and Blue and its manager were alike. Both had been around for a little more than thirty years, both had a tidy but unexciting exterior, and both had far more interesting stories to tell than first impressions conveyed. The store occupied one of those sturdy one story buildings that line the older stretches of mixed-zoned neighborhoods in every New England town. The original wood frame and cinderblock construction had been spruced up twenty years ago with white vinyl siding, with the store's name on a tasteful painted signboard over the front window. Before Regan unlocked the front door, she paused a moment, as she did nearly every morning, to peer south down the long straight stretch of Swansea Road. Small strip malls and commercial buildings bumped elbows with stretches of houses, both growing older and more closely packed until they blended with the town center about two miles away. Looming over the downtown on the southern horizon were the blocky brick shapes of the community's economic mainstay and biggest employer, the Standish Mills. If you stood on the roof of the tallest mill building and threw a Frisbee southwest, it might, with a good tail wind, clear the river and land in Rhode Island.

As Regan gripped the front door handle, she paused, frowning. Someone, she felt, had grasped the handle and shaken it, not too long ago. She closed her eyes, her fingers curled around the cool metal, trying to identify who the door rattler had been. As often happened, no clarification came and Regan was left mystified. It wasn't an attempted break-in, and many people knew that she was sometimes at the store early. Regan gave her hand a shake, to get rid of the impressions, checked the empty mailbox by the door for notes or messages, and went inside.

She reached down and opened the window shade that covered the glass door, so morning sunshine lit up the central aisle of the store. The long rays gleamed on the immaculate shoulder-high shelves, which were filled with a colorful and eclectic mixture of second hand ephemera, popular gift shop items and unusual hand-crafted wares. Regan had taken over a moribund antique store and over the past seven years, had built up a loyal customer base and a reputation that attracted vacationers and day-trippers all summer long. But it had been a slow winter, with the war and the post-9/11 economy. Every year, Regan hoped to increase profits enough to hire a part-time assistant, but every year, the books balanced out just barely in the black.

She turned on the credit card machine and electronic cash register at the cashier's counter by the door, then unlocked the tiny office at the back of the store. The cordless phone base was blinking its message light, and she picked up the phone and dialed in the access number and code with her thumb, setting her vintage lunch pail on the scarred wooden desk as she listened to the phone's trills and beeps. "You have two new messages..." began the automated voice, and Regan punched 1 and reached for a square of scrap paper. She paused when she recognized the voice of Dr. Hiram Clauson, a psychology professor at Bridgewater State.

"Regan," he said, his words clipped and urgent, "Can you get free tonight? We can see another one, and this could be a breakthrough. Just happened last night. Give me a call, I'll be in my office after two."

Tonight, tonight, what's happening tonight, Regan thought vaguely—for some reason, she felt that there was something she was supposed to be doing. But she couldn't recall anything specific, and there was nothing penciled in on the desk calendar. Her stomach had tightened into a sudden knot at the words, "happened last night." *Weren't these things ever going to stop?* But her thoughts were cut off by the next message.

"Hi, Regan! I stopped by in case you were early but I guess I missed you. I'll come in later today, I know you hate me bugging you when you're working. Hope you're not doing anything tonight, because I really need you! Tell you later, bye."

That explained the door rattler—and the feeling that she was committed somewhere. "Oh, Veronica," Regan sighed aloud as she punched 3 to erase the message. Veronica Standish was her best friend. After her own parents, Regan had known Veronica longer, and on a deep level, trusted her more, than anyone else in the world. But she was fairly certain she knew what Veronica needed her for so badly, and it was a toss-up which made her more apprehensive, that or Hiram Clauson's proposition. Watching Veronica career through life was like watching video of a toddler on the edge of a swimming pool. You knew there was a disaster ahead, but there wasn't a thing you could do about it.

Regan gave herself the usual quick check in the little mirror by the office door to make sure she was completely presentable. There was little to fuss over: Regan regarded herself as thoroughly average and made no efforts to gild a dandelion, as she saw it. Medium height, medium weight, plain brown hair just below her shoulders, gray-green eyes, a face that was neither homely nor pretty and looked exactly its age. Her hair had a natural wave when she let it out of its ubiquitous loose ponytail, but that happened seldom. Regan had a few qualities that were anything but average, but they weren't tangible assets.

Abruptly, she realized that it was 9:59 a.m. Satisfied that she was ready to greet her customers, she hurried to the front of the store to turn over the CLOSED sign, taking the cordless phone with her to keep at the counter. It was going to be a long, and she hoped, a very busy day. She was expecting a substantial UPS delivery from a crafter in North Adams, it was the beginning of the first big holiday weekend since Presidents' Day, and schools were letting out for spring break. She'd zeroed out the winter advertising budget putting block ads into Sheridan's weekly newspaper and had even gotten one into the Fall River *Herald*. As she rearranged a few items in the larger window display, she wished that she still had one of those red, white and blue OPEN flags to put out front. The store used to have a vintage one, but last fall somebody had made her a premium offer for it, and any legitimate offer involving money was an offer Regan couldn't refuse.

The front door had a set of little copper bells on a spring steel coil that jingled cheerfully when the door was opened. These freed Regan to work around the store or in the office between customers. She went up and down the aisles checking merchandize tags and flicking a sixty-year-old feather duster (for sale, if anyone wanted it) unnecessarily here and there. When the bells jingled for the first time at 10:23, Regan hastened to the counter. "Hi, Ellen," she said somewhat breathlessly. Ellen Hayes, about fifty-five with tightly curled gray and brown hair, was one of her regular customers. She stood staring around the store with a lost expression, as though she was trying to figure out where she was and how she'd gotten here. But Ellen always looked like that. When Regan spoke, her face suddenly became alert.

"Good morning Regan, I need something for a wedding, one of Roy's nieces, I was wondering if you had anything like those leaf plates you had at Christmas?"

Regan put the duster on the counter. "Today's your lucky day. That artist just brought me a whole batch of new stuff last week. Come on back here and have a look." That artist was a rather capricious soul, but her wares sold like Toscanini's ice cream in August. As Ellen exclaimed over hand-painted poppy bowls, the bells jingled, and Regan glanced quickly at the door. This customer, short and stocky with close-cropped dark hair, was a new one, and the brief eye contact she made before pointing her gaze intently at one of the shelves telegraphed a browser who didn't want to be asked if she needed help. Regan knew to wait until she seemed to be wandering at a loss and heaved a little sigh—then she wanted to be asked.

Ellen was a deliberate shopper, so Regan started back toward the counter. An elaborate series of jingles and some thumps of rubber wheels against glass announced the entrance of two young women and a stroller. Regan suppressed a wince. She tried to keep the lower shelves filled with heavy items, boxes and non-breakable knick-knacks up to stroller and toddler level, but there was just so much you could do with limited space. The mother, ash blond hair pulled back in a ponytail, was talking earnestly into a cell phone while her friend, iPod buds in ears, was humming and bouncing her upper body side to side in rhythm to her MP3's. To ratchet the worry factor up even more, three heavy plastic bags swung from the handle of the stroller. But the women didn't want to be pestered, so Regan tried to keep the stroller in her peripheral vision. The cordless phone buzzed. "Borrowed and Blue...we're open until seven. You're welcome." iPod lady, buds unplugged, had come up to the counter.

"Do you have two of these?"

"No, that came from an estate sale, there was just the one. If you looking for a pair like that, let me show you these—"

"No, that's okay, I'll just look around some more." The customer set the brass candleholder on the counter and followed the stroller back down the main aisle. Regan picked up the candleholder, grimacing a little—she wished someone would buy this piece. Every time she picked it up, a pain ran from her chest down her left arm. The original owner had died suddenly of a heart attack, not while holding this knick-knack as far as she knew, but she could never analyze why some possessions held impressions and others didn't. The new customer came up to the counter, her mouth set in a tight line.

"Excuse me," she said, as though she had been waiting for hours and was now being ignored. Regan smiled pleasantly—not too brightly, that would make this customer feel offended.

"Yes, what can I help you with?"

"This is the fifth place I've tried." The customer sounded as if each establishment had turned her away out of spite. "I'm looking for something unique for my daughter's tenth anniversary."

"Well," Regan said carefully, "maybe if I knew a little bit about your daughter's personal style, we could find something she'd like. You wouldn't happen to carry a picture of her, would you?" The customer looked annoyed, but she put her large purse on the counter, dug out her thick wallet and after some searching, pulled out a snapshot, which she handed to Regan. "What a pretty woman," Regan said, although she was only pretending to look at the photograph. Her fingers were lightly tracing patterns on the back of it, and her attention was on the visions that were coming to her mind's eye. After a moment, she looked up and smiled. "I think I have just the thing." In fact, Regan had six different things to offer, which was fortunate because the customer agonized over every one of them before she decided on an expensive 1920s silver tea set. But she departed with a much more relaxed expression, and even smiled and accepted a business card. The stroller mom and iPod lady had left without buying anything, but at least the baby had fallen asleep. The only customers Regan hoped to bore into a coma were the ones under five.

The day went on to exceed Regan's most optimistic hopes. The UPS delivery failed to appear, and it was after 3:00 before the store was empty long enough for Regan to risk eating her lunch, a sandwich and thermos of coffee from home. But she had logged sixteen purchases, twenty-three browsers, and eleven phone calls by the time the door bells jingled and Regan looked up to see Veronica smiling uncertainly from the door.

"I hope it's not too early."

Regan glanced toward the back of the store, where there was one browser examining a display of pewter. "No, come on in." Veronica came inside, the door sighing shut behind her. She wore very high-heeled boots, and her legs were so long and thin that she always reminded Regan of a fawn when she walked, stepping not so much gracefully as carefully. Veronica was tall enough to be a fashion model, but her face, under its flawless Clinique makeup, had a strained tautness. Regan knew too much about what Veronica did to keep her figure to be envious. She would have given a lot for the natural hair color Veronica despised, the shade of warm honey, but there was no denying that her friend's waist-length platinum blonde waves had a dramatic effect.

"Did you get my phone message?"

"I did, but it was almost ten and you said you'd be stopping in."

"Oh, that's okay, I know you don't like to make personal calls from work." Veronica ran her tongue along her perfectly outlined lower lip. She seemed barely able to restrain her excitement about something. "So...are you free tonight?"

Regan hesitated. She hadn't called Hiram Clauson back, for several different reasons. "I'm...just not sure."

"You're not *sure?* Why not?" The browsing customer came up to the counter at that point, glancing from Veronica to Regan with a disapproving frown.

"Excuse me," Regan said to Veronica, trying to sound as if Veronica was just another customer. She rang up the small sale, half a dozen Yankee Candle votives and a small carved teak box from India, circa 1972. When the shopper was gone, Regan and Veronica were left in privacy, at least for the moment. "I can't make any promises about tonight, Ver. I might have to go do something. What's up, anyway?"

Veronica bridled like a game show host working up to the jackpot announcement. "Well. You remember Theo, Karen's stepbrother? You know that band he started up last year?"

"Yeah, I do. They're good."

"They've gotten a huge break. They're playing a big job at this private club up in Taunton. Karen's trying to get everyone who knows Theo to come. It's semi-private, but she's gotten some passes."

"That's great! For Theo, I mean, but god, I'd feel like a crasher."

"No, it's okay! There'll be hundreds of people there, it's some big corporate bash, for their IPO—Akins Biotech or something, it's on the passes. Karen's heard that they're getting big funding from the Krafts. A couple of the Patriots might be there. Not Brady or anyone like that, but a couple of the second string."

"Holy shit." Regan blinked. "And we can get into *that*? Are you serious?"

Veronica plopped her Gucci handbag on the counter and pulled out an envelope with a flourish. "Here's the passes."

"My god. A corporate party, huh? I could—"

"Yeah, you could work the room, pass out some business cards—see, business and pleasure! Come *on*, Regan..."

For one dazzling second a mini-daydream flashed through Regan's mind, involving a sign in the front window announcing the Official Thrift Store of the New England Patriots, and she almost giggled. But reality abruptly took over, and Regan's shoulders sagged. "I just don't know, Ver—I'm going to be open every day this weekend. It's a big holiday."

"I know...but you wouldn't have to stay late. You deserve a night out."

"Well..."

"It'll be fun. And it's really important to me that you come."

"It is? Why is it that important to you?"

"Well..." Veronica hesitated, glancing around as though she thought someone might still be in the store listening to their conversation. She leaned toward Regan, lowering her voice. "Because I've managed to persuade Jonathan to come along, and I want you to meet him."

For a moment, Regan had to search her memory for this reference. "Jonathan...oh. Right. This guy you met a couple of weeks ago. Jonathan Vaughn. The writer."

"Don't say 'writer' in that tone of voice. You make it sound like he was some kind of slacker. It's not like that at all."

Regan realized she was right, and felt chastened. "I'm sorry, I didn't mean it that way. It's just that...well, you're not the only person who's mentioned him lately. Everyone seems to know that he's a writer, but no one can name anything he's published, and he doesn't seem to want to talk about what he's writing now. It does sound just a little dubious."

"He told me he doesn't like to talk about his work, he's writing about a sensitive subject." Veronica sounded defensive. "Something political, I think. He's paid his rent for the next six months in advance. Doesn't that sound responsible?"

"Yeah, I'll bet his landlord thinks he's very responsible." Regan frowned thoughtfully, considering this detail. Paying that much rent in advance didn't sound like something a fly-by-night would do. That was considerably more committed than Regan's own housing arrangement. "So, is this the kind of thing you two talk about when you get together, his rent?"

"No, of course not." Veronica's cheeks reddened underneath the pale pink blusher. "I...well, it was Derek who mentioned the rent."

"Um-hm. How indiscreet of Derek to gossip about his clients. You must be spending a lot of time with this Jonathan Vaughn."

The last statement was disingenuous, and Regan wasn't surprised when

Veronica hesitated, looking a bit shifty.

"Um...no, not really. I mean, not more than anyone would..."

"Just going out for coffee and doughnuts every now and then?"

Veronica looked a little desperate. "He's very busy, you know—writers have to be disciplined." As Regan leaned back against the rear of the counter, giving her friend a skeptical smile, Veronica blurted out, "Well *you're* the one who's always telling me not to rush into anything! Besides, I'm not going to chase a guy, that would look pathetic."

"Not even coffee and doughnuts, then."

Veronica glowered down at the countertop for a moment. "Not even coffee. I just don't *get* it!" She slapped the counter with her hand so hard that the soft leather handbag fell over, and her voice was rising steadily, like the whistle of an approaching train. "I've been as respectful of his space as hell, wouldn't you think that any normal guy would love the attention? All this *Cosmo* bullshit about men not wanting to be rejected and hoping women make the first move, and then when you do, all they do is stand there and stare at you. If he's not interested, fine, he should *say* so, but he never acts like he's unhappy to see me! Oh, hello Veronica, how are you, but ask him if he wants to go *do* something and he's got every excuse ever written. And Jesus, Regan, you're supposed to be my friend and you're asking me all these questions and looking at me like that, don't you think—"

"Whoa, whoa, whoa, Ver," Regan said, making a time-out sign with her hands. "Stop that. Take...a deep...breath." Veronica complied, her eyes squeezed shut and her mouth curled like she was eight and swallowing a spoon of cough syrup. "Again," Regan said, and this time the breath turned into a deep sigh.

"Okay, I'm sorry," Veronica muttered as she opened her eyes. "But I don't do that with him, Regan, really."

"I know, Ver. Love's a bitch." *And you hold it all in until you can come vent all over me, where it's safe.* But she understood why, and Veronica had listened to more than a few rants herself. "So, does this Jonathan call you?"

"Well, he returns my calls."

"He gave you his number?"

"Yes! That's why I thought—god, it's so confusing, Regan."

Regan was beginning to see why. "And he agreed to go to this big club date with you."

"Probably because there will be so many other people there," Veronica said cynically. "That's what seemed to interest him about it, a chance to meet people. He said he needed to get out. You know what he said? He said he'd *escort* me. Escort me, like it was the prom! I feel like I should hire a chaperone." Veronica started laughing, and then abruptly stopped.

"Now I see where I come in," Regan said, smiling.

"No, no, no! I'd have asked you anyway, I swear! Karen was going to ask you, and I told her I'd take care of it."

"Should I bring a date, then?" Regan said lightly.

"Oh, you mean there's someone you'd—" Veronica broke off at the look Regan gave her, and this time the flush extended to her forehead. "I only meant... I didn't think you were seeing anybody."

"It's okay," Regan said, turning away and picking up a pewter ashtray the last customer had decided not to buy and stuffing it savagely into a box of items to reshelve. "We all know I don't have a life, no breaking news there."

"I didn't *mean* that, Regan—everyone we know is already going, that's all. Derek's going, stag, I'm sure of it."

At the thought of being paired up with Derek, Regan couldn't help smiling. "I'll just bet." She straightened up with a sigh. "Look, Veronica—I think I'm pretty clear about why you want me to meet Jonathan Vaughn tonight." She leaned against the counter and folded her arms, looking at her friend narrowly. "You want me to read him. Right?"

Veronica look flustered for a moment, then spluttered, "Well, that's what you do, isn't it?"

"Veronica..."

"Please, Regan. I need you for this."

"I *hate* doing this kind of reading. It goes against all my principles—it's like going through someone's wallet. I don't even shake hands with people because of that, you know that."

"You told me after Terence that I should check out anyone new I meet. And that was damn good advice. I said so then."

"Yeah, but not like this! Ver, I've told you over and over, I'm not that reliable—especially when I have a personal connection. You're my friend, I'd be liable to think I was picking up all kinds of crap that's not true, because I want to protect you. Especially after I met Terence and totally missed little details like the fact that he was kiting checks from your checkbook."

"That wasn't your fault."

"But it gives you an idea of how fallible I am. I don't want to be responsible for your life like that. Run him up on PublicData.com, or hire a private detective. God knows your father can afford it—he probably has one on retainer."

Veronica looked sullenly down at the floor. "I don't want Jonathan to find out that I'm trying to check up on him. If he's not hiding anything, he'll be offended, and he'll probably never speak to me again."

"These days, people understand. Anyway, what do you call this? 'Hi, meet my friend Regan, she's psychic.'"

"It's not the same thing. People are fascinated by psychics."

The phone buzzed and Regan picked it up. "Borrowed and Blue...yes, we are. Sunday and Monday. You're welcome. Veronica," she put down the phone, "People are fascinated by psychics when they're on TV. It's a whole other story in real life. Don't do this to me, Ver, please."

"Oh, Regan..." Veronica leaned her elbows on the counter, resting her forehead on her hands for a moment, as if she was suddenly exhausted. "I wouldn't ask this if I wasn't completely baffled by this guy," she said, looking up dejectedly. "Does he like me, does he not, does he want to see me, does he not, is he gay, is he straight, did he fall out of a UFO! He won't tell me to get lost, he returns my calls, but he won't let me close—I can't figure it out."

"So drop it, Ver. Don't put up with someone who's just going to mess with your head."

"But I *like* him, Regan. He's the nicest guy I've ever met—ever. I hate to just throw that away because he's, I don't know, maybe he's just shy, or went through a horrible divorce—"

"You'd know about that."

"No shit!"

"What if there are kids?"

Veronica straightened up. "You see? That's exactly the kind of thing I need to find out."

"You should find out from him."

Veronica flung her hands heavenward, where they probably heard her. "I can't! That's the problem!"

"Breathe..." Regan said.

Veronica dropped her hands to her sides. "You're going to get customers, I better go." She picked up her handbag and extracted a pass from the envelope with her long fingernails as though she was picking up evidence with a pair of tweezers. "Here's your pass," she said, placing it on the counter. "They're comps, so Karen says it's no biggie if you can't make it." She turned to go, and Regan held up one hand.

"Wait. Just wait a minute." Veronica turned to look at her glumly. "I do want to meet him. God knows you've piqued my curiosity. I just can't promise it will be tonight. If I don't see you, bring him into the store sometime."

"You'll do it?"

"I'll *try*. There are a lot of problems, Ver. I have to touch him, you know. It's pretty hard to do that without making people suspicious. And I might not get anything from him, anyway. Some people can't be read, and almost everyone can block if they want to."

"I know, you've told me that." Veronica looked incredulous that Regan was agreeing.

"And you have to promise me—*promise* me—that you'll treat anything I get with skepticism. No one's died and made me god."

Veronica's lips curved in a knowing smile. "I will. But you're *good*, Regan. No matter what you say." Her smile broadened. "And I trust you. Deal with it."

Regan looked down at the counter for a moment, her face sober. "Right," she said quietly. To stop this line of discussion, she picked up the pass and read the name of the venue. "Hey, I know this place, it's right off 138. Theo's playing *here*? Holy crap! They're going to be recording an album next."

Veronica shrugged her Versace jacket closed. "There's been talk."

"Seriously?"

"Yeah. I'm curious, what's going on tonight that you might have to miss this?"

Regan glanced uneasily back at the office door, where the phone message still waited on the answering machine. "Well…Hiram Clauson left a message this morning. He wants us to interview someone tonight."

Veronica's expression changed instantly. "You mean—there's been another one of those weird…things?"

"Apparently. He didn't say much in the message and…" Regan swallowed. "I just haven't wanted to call him back."

"So don't."

"I can't just drop it now, Ver."

"Yes, you can. It's not like he's paying you or anything."

"I want to know the explanation as much as Hiram does. It's just that it's getting so—" she stopped as reflected sunlight suddenly flickered across the walls and ceiling. Both women turned sharply to watch a minivan pull into the parking area next to Veronica's little silver Mazda. Regan realized that her knees were suddenly shaking. *Yes*, she thought, *this has gone far enough when just thinking about it has both me and Veronica going to code red at a stray flash of light.*

"I better go." Veronica hunched her shoulders and almost shuddered. "I hope I'll see you tonight, Regan. Good luck with Dr. Clauson." She hurried out the door, almost bumping into the customer coming in.

By 7:00, when Regan locked the front door and cashed out the register, all she really wanted to do was go home and take a hot bath. She had been on her feet more or less continuously since 10:00 that morning. But 7:00 was closing time, not quitting time. She put together the daily deposit to drop off at the bank, before locking the register cash drawer into the small office safe. Today's total was rather refreshing, and she started to think that the club party didn't sound too bad. All she'd need to do was stop by her apartment and change. *Theo's band, a couple of margaritas and the mysterious Mr. Vaughn.* She tapped the computer out of screensaver mode, her first chance since lunch, to check the status of the missing UPS delivery. She was about to get the small vacuum cleaner from the corner and quickly vacuum the carpet runners in the main aisles, when the cordless phone buzzed. She hesitated before picking it up, thinking, *we're closed, damn it!* "Borrowed and Blue."

"Regan?"

Regan caught her breath. "Yes, Hiram, I got your message," she said after a moment. "I'm sorry I didn't call back, it's been really busy today. Made lots of money, though."

"I'm glad to hear it. I was waiting until after business hours to try you again. Are you free tonight?"

Regan grimaced. "Well, I...I sort of promised that I'd be somewhere...can you fill me in a bit?"

Hiram's voice sharpened. "This could be very important, Regan. We've never been able to interview a subject so soon after reporting. There's far less danger of contamination, there might be more memory intact—"

"With what I do, Hiram, those things don't tend to make a lot of difference. I'm not depending on the subject's memory, in fact, that can be a distraction."

"She might change her mind if she has time to think about it, too. Please, Regan—there's got to be a break sometime."

"Where are we going?"

"Fairhaven. It will take about thirty minutes to get there from Sheridan."

Regan was silent for a moment, torn between her ambivalence and the urgency she could hear in Hiram's voice. "Could we go tomorrow night? I mean, would it make such a difference?"

"I had to do some very delicate negotiating to get the family to agree—it would be unforgivable to call her up now and postpone, and bad for our credibility to cancel. We won't take all night, I promise you. Can you push your other plans up a bit?"

"I don't want a late night. The store is open tomorrow, and it's going to be a very busy weekend—at least I hope so."

"Then we can do our follow-up work later this week, it doesn't have to be tonight. I can be there by eight to pick you up."

Regan could feel her heart pounding. *Damn, damn, damn...* "Can we just swing by the bank's deposit drop on the way?"

"Of course."

Regan sagged back in the creaking desk chair, looking over at the vacuum cleaner with a wistfulness it rarely evoked from her. "All right...I'll be ready." In every sense but the superficial one, that was a lie.

Chapter 2

Regan leaned back against the passenger's seat of Hiram's Corolla, watching the steady sweep of trees past the car. If she hadn't been so uneasy, she would have been half asleep by now. Behind the wheel, Hiram's eyeglasses kept catching reflections from the dash console. Oncoming headlights gave him glowing round eyes like something out of J.K. Rowling. Indeed, with his short graying beard, hair that could have used a trim, and stooped shoulders, all he needed to fit in at a magic academy was wizard's robes and a wand.

"I appreciate your coming along on such short notice," he said, as Regan yawned. "I know how hard you work, but this subject reported early this morning, just before dawn. We'll be able to see her within twenty-four hours of the event."

"That's a nice vague word. Event. Whatever that means."

He glanced over at her. "You know, you still haven't told me much about what you think."

"I don't want premature conclusions to influence—"

"—influence future readings, yes, so you've said. But after four weeks, I don't think the word 'premature' applies. And you're deluding yourself if you think you can collect information and not form any conclusions. You don't even want to discuss possibilities. My speculations wouldn't affect your readings, would they?"

"Of course they would, you know better than that." She fidgeted against the shoulder belt, which was perfectly comfortable. "Hiram, I honestly haven't formed any definite conclusions. There are just too many missing pieces of information. The only reason I'm still going along with this is that I keep hoping I'll finally pick up something that will make all the different facets come together. At this point, I'm not very optimistic. By the way, I'm assuming there's nothing obviously different here than the others?"

"No, it's exactly the same. Loss of consciousness, contusion, mild shock—and no memory about what happened. I hope that this time you might be able to get more detail."

Regan sighed. "We'll see. You know, eventually one of those cable shows is going to get wind of this, Hiram, and come in and do a segment on it, and then the whole thing will just blow up with hoaxes and hysterical delusions in all directions."

"I know." Hiram sounded grim at the prospect.

"And when that happens, Hiram, you've never heard my name. If you want to give expert interviews, fine. You're on your own. I don't want to be quoted, and I'm not talking to anyone from the media. We *are* clear about that, aren't we?"

"Yes. I understand why you feel that way. I just think that—"

She cut him off. "Good."

Following penciled directions, Hiram turned off the main road onto a bumpy country lane and followed it about a half mile until he saw the mailbox with the number 137 and the name "Stockard" picked out with reflective block letters. He turned into the driveway of the saltbox house and parked behind a large pickup truck with a contractor's tool box built into the bed. Next to it sat a nondescript little hatchback with a badly rusted rear fender and several "Support Our Troops" magnets. The house windows were all lighted and a bright floodlight starkly illuminated purple and white crocuses scattered through the flattened yellow grass of the front yard. There was a floodlight on over the low deck in back, too. Regan saw two of the Venetian blind slats in one window pull apart briefly as they got out of the car.

The door opened quickly when Hiram knocked, and a thin woman of about forty looked warily out at them. "Good evening, Mrs. Stockard," Hiram said with a cordiality that was almost unctuous. "I spoke to you and your husband this morning. I'm Dr. Hiram Clauson, from Bridgewater State, and this is Regan Calloway." He had identification ready in his hand, but Evelyn Stockard only glanced at it as she pushed open the storm door to let them in.

"You're very punctual." She had the husky voice and worn, drawn look of a life-long smoker, but Regan guessed that her appearance was not usually as haggard as it was tonight. Her eyes had dark circles under them and her face had an unhealthy pallor. As she ushered them into the small living room, she tamped out the cigarette she was holding in an ashtray that was choked with butts, and immediately reached for the pack next to it. The air in the room was thick with smoke. A heavyset man of her own age with a weathered, guarded face appeared in the kitchen door, and Evelyn introduced him as her husband, Jim. Hiram shook hands, but Regan kept her hands firmly in her pockets. She heard a small sound from the hallway and glanced over to see a teenage girl craning her neck around a doorway, wavy blond hair pulled into a perky topknot. When the girl saw Regan looking, she ducked hastily out of sight, and Regan was sure she heard the peeping of a cell phone being dialed.

Introductions having been completed, Jim Stockard said, "You people will forgive me, if I don't hold with all this psychic stuff. If it'll make Evie feel better then that's her business. I'll be in the den if you need me, Evie." He turned and walked off down the hall.

"Please don't mind him," Evelyn said.

"I'm glad that he trusts us alone with you." Regan was relieved, since readings were more difficult with anxious or suspicious family members hovering nearby.

"We'll try not to take much of your time," Hiram said. "We don't want to impose on your family any more than we have to." He and Regan sat as Evelyn waved them perfunctorily to a pair of worn armchairs.

"You couldn't impose much more than this whole thing already has." Evelyn perched herself on a sofa that didn't match the chairs or the grayed pink 1970s shag carpet.

"How are you feeling, Mrs. Stockard, are you up to this?" Regan asked.

Evelyn took a drag on her cigarette. "I'm fine. I don't really know what all is involved. Dr. Clauson said that you'd be doing a psychic reading?"

"I'll need to just hold your hand or something like that, Mrs. Stockard, but that's all. If you're uncomfortable with that, I'll understand, but..." she hesitated, but Evelyn appeared unsurprised.

"No, Dr. Clauson said you'd need to. I've seen those TV shows where they do that. It's not much after all the poking and probing I just went through at the hospital. Anything that helps me find out what happened—" she broke off, and took another hasty drag on the cigarette, her eyelashes fluttering. Regan and Hiram glanced at each other.

"I don't know how much I'm going to be able to help with that," Regan said. "I'll be quite honest. I never know what I'll see."

With a thin smile, Evelyn exhaled a long stream of smoke. "Yes, well, that's what you people usually say, isn't it?"

Hiram glanced at Regan. "Perhaps you'd like to see a demonstration of what Regan does."

Evelyn's smile disappeared. "What do you mean by a demonstration?"

"Usually I read inanimate objects, Mrs. Stockard—jewelry, watches, keys— things people have worn or made or handled a lot. It's kind of an old-fashioned talent, it used to be called psychometry." Evelyn's brow creased at this suspiciously technical word. "The jargon's not important, it changes every decade or so. Now I think it's just called 'psychic touch.' But if you'd like to test me, pick out an object for me to read. You can try and trick me if you want."

"Oh, I wouldn't want to trick you on purpose, what would be the point of that?"

Regan smiled. *I wish more psychic investigators would have that attitude,* she thought wryly.

Evelyn got up from the couch and went over to a wall-mounted wood veneer shelf unit in one corner—pretty enough, although Regan recognized it as one sold from the Spencer discount catalogs. She poked around among the items on the shelves and returned holding a small china figurine, which she handed to Regan. "Is this the kind of thing you mean?"

"Exactly the kind of thing." Regan closed her hand around the piece quickly, deliberately avoiding looking at it. "No," she said, as Evelyn started to speak, "don't tell me anything about it. Just give me a minute or so." Evelyn resumed her seat on the sofa and watched expectantly. Regan closed her eyes, letting her breathing slow and her conscious awareness of everything else in the room but the little figurine fade into the background. Evelyn had chosen an ideal piece. As Regan turned the cool china in her hands, it seemed to buzz with energy that prickled her fingers. Then Regan felt echoes of sharp pain through her hands, which for a moment felt clumsy and stiff. She cupped both her hands because it had become hard to hold the figurine and she didn't want to drop it. Pushing past the pain, she seemed to see an image of a boxy wood frame house with a large red barn behind it. The landscape all around was wide open and flat, with a great arching blue sky and clear views to every horizon. It was a dizzying sensation, this openness, and Regan felt that by contrast New England's woods and hills were claustrophobic and confined. She felt a pang of such desperate loss that it brought tears to her eyes. Children laughing...a group of girls in simple print dresses *oh thank you Rosie I'll keep this forever and ever...* Regan didn't even realize she'd spoken aloud until she heard Evelyn gasp. While the images and emotions flicked past, their story had been filling her mind, and she had to stop because too much was piling up and becoming confused. She opened her eyes, still not quite seeing the Stockards' living room, and began to talk rapidly.

"This belonged to someone very close to you—I think it was your mother, but it might have been one of her sisters, she had very bad arthritis in her hands. She kept this with her when she was hospitalized...no, nursing home, she used to hold it in her hands and dream about her childhood. She grew up out in the Midwest, Nebraska, she hated New England, she always wanted to go back, she didn't like the land here, closed in, she used to say, it feels so closed in. This piece was a gift from someone who died young named Rosie—not a relative, more like her best friend, best friend in all the world...the woman who owned this had something wrong with her heart and lungs, she died...she died of congestive heart failure, she couldn't breathe." Regan looked down at the figurine for the first time now—it was a little shepherdess with a wide pink skirt, body tilted forward and one hand cupped by her mouth, calling her sheep. "You keep this to remember her by, but she didn't give it to you. Her name was...not Linda. Belinda." The impressions were blurring together now, like a watercolor painting under a running faucet. Regan sighed, suddenly tired. She looked up at Evelyn. "How did I do?"

Evelyn was staring at her, one hand over her mouth. After a moment, she lowered her hand, and said "All of that...was absolutely correct. Even the names. Even little things she said. She used to sit and hold that in her cupped hands, so she wouldn't drop it, just like you—how do you *do* that?"

Regan almost laughed—she was always asked that question, as though there were some trick to what she did, or a set of directions. "Mrs. Stockard—what can I say? I'm psychic."

"Yes, but—do you get that much from everything you touch?"

"Oh my god, no. I'd be a padded room someplace if that happened. I never know what I'm going to read from something. I can block it out to a certain degree. It's hard to live a normal life otherwise." She handed the figurine back to Evelyn. "That's a very nice little piece. If you ever want to sell it—"

"What? I don't think so," Evelyn said, startled.

"Regan," Hiram said reprovingly.

Regan, who still wasn't quite back to reality, flushed. "Sorry, I didn't mean to be offensive."

"Regan runs a second hand store," Hiram said.

"Oh." Evelyn replaced the figurine on the shelf. "I'm flattered, but I don't think this is worth anything."

"Umm...you might want to have it appraised sometime. Just a thought."

"Really?"

Hiram cleared his throat. "Perhaps we should stay focused on our reason for being here. It is getting a bit late in the evening."

Evelyn returned to her seat on the couch and picked up her cigarette, which had almost burned out in the ashtray. "Well, you've certainly made a believer out of me. But you're right, you came down here to talk about what happened last night. I guess there's no point in putting it off. What do you want to start with?"

Hiram leaned toward her slightly, his hands relaxed and open on his knees. "We already have a general idea of what happened, Mrs. Stockard. You were leaving work last night around midnight, the Seatech warehouse, isn't that right?"

"Yes, I'm an assistant supervisor for the second shift, five years now."

"And you left work later than usual. Were there any other employees still in the building by then?"

"At least fifteen, we're a twenty-four hour operation. But it was an hour past the usual shift change, so there was nobody outside."

Regan said, "All right, that's all we want to know right now. The whole point is to see if I can read what you *don't* remember. I don't want any more details or I'll just be extrapolating from what you've told me."

"Well, that makes sense," Evelyn said, "Let's try this reading, then. That is what you came for." She tamped out her cigarette and tugged down the hem of her sweater. "So what do we do? Do I need to be lying down?"

"No, but why don't you come over and sit in this chair, and I'll sit on the hassock in front of you." Regan got up and turned off the two lamps nearest to the chair as Evelyn crossed the room and sat down. Regan sat on the hassock facing her, careful not to let her knees bump into Evelyn's shins. "Now you don't have to do anything at all, I do all the work. Just lean back in the chair and relax, and try to blank out your thoughts. Think of something very neutral. Like this, try to visualize a big long, completely empty wall, and you're painting it beige. Can you try that?"

"Okay," Evelyn said with a crooked smile. It didn't take a psychic to read her thoughts: *this is just silly.* But she leaned back and closed her eyes, and sighed a couple of times. After a minute, her muscles began to relax.

"That's good. Now, Evelyn, I'm just going to hold your hands in mine. Just stay relaxed. Keep painting the wall." Evelyn smiled, but her clasped hands uncurled in her lap. Regan took both of Evelyn's hands, and closed her own eyes, quietly breathing herself into a light trance. A mental image of a paintbrush sweeping by with beige paint on it flickered past. Then she opened herself to deeper impressions. A myriad random images passed through her mind, as though she was fanning the pages of a book full of vivid photographs: Jim, the teenage girl she had seen, a cluttered, mostly green room that Regan supposed was Evelyn's office at the warehouse, and many more, but Regan tightened her focus, consciously attempting to home in on the night before and the moment at which Evelyn had left work. Then she had locked on to it, seeing through Evelyn's eyes, coat on, purse over her shoulder, shoving open a heavy steel door and stepping out into chilly night air. The bitter, musty smell of nearby ocean water filled her nostrils. She was walking briskly through a large paved parking lot with woods on both sides, cars scattered through it, a bright red pickup truck standing alone just ahead. The truck grew closer and larger, bright, shiny red... red like a fire truck...then it was an ambulance. Flashing lights reflecting off of painted metal, a mask over her face...someone patting her cheeks and saying her name, *Mrs. Stockard...can you hear me?...Mrs. Stockard*...the red truck again. Back to the red truck. Regan pushed harder, trying to see past this image. Was there someone behind the red truck? Or in it? Back to the ambulance lights. She sighed and let go of Evelyn's hands, and opened her eyes.

Evelyn sat up, looking a little disappointed. "That was fast. Did you see anything?"

Without focusing her eyes on anything, Regan nodded. "You left the building through a heavy solid metal door, painted rust-brown. You started across the parking lot. It was brightly lighted, with those mercury vapor lights, so it almost looked like day. There were cars scattered around the parking lot, but yours was near the entrance, about a hundred feet away. Do you always park so far away?"

"I have to. The lot's filled with the day shift's cars when I get to work at three-thirty. I suppose I could move my car later on, but I never worried about it before."

"You didn't see anyone else anywhere in the parking lot. About halfway to your car, you had to walk right by a very large, red pickup truck. Just as you were getting near the truck...that's when everything stopped."

"Everything stopped?" Hiram said.

"There's a blip, or a gap...then there's an ambulance, flashing lights, looked like a group of people standing around. You were on the ground...with your back against something, you were sitting up. Against that same truck, I think. Anyway, I saw a lot of red. Was there a lot of blood, were you bleeding everywhere?"

"No," Evelyn said, "But the hospital—" Regan raised her hand to stop her.

"You were hurt." Regan touched the side of her neck as she spoke. "You knew that as soon as you woke up...you were unconscious, and you'd been there a while. Several hours. You were stiff and cold from sitting there on the ground, god, it was close to freezing last night, no wonder."

"They put me under one of those heating blankets at the E.R., they said I nearly had hypothermia."

"One of the employees found you, young, reddish hair, mustache, blue eyes? I think his name is Dustin?"

"Yes." Evelyn sounded amazed. "I must have looked awful, because he called the ambulance on his cell, and he kept telling me not to move. I thought he was going pass out himself, he was so white."

Regan sighed deeply and sat back on the hassock. "Well..." she said unhappily. "That's all I got. I doubt that's any more than you remember."

"You didn't see what happened to me?"

"I'm sorry, Mrs. Stockard." Regan shrugged helplessly. "From what I'm reading here, all I can see is that you passed out and fell against that red truck."

Evelyn sank back in the chair, looking almost angry. "Then what's the point of all this?"

"We're not necessarily done yet, Mrs. Stockard," Hiram said in a placating tone. "Could you tell us what they said at the E.R.? The hospital won't give out any details without your permission. What do they think happened?"

"They think the same thing."

"And you don't?"

Evelyn shook her head grimly. "Just like she said, I was hurt. I knew that the minute I woke up. My neck was very painful, and when I touched it, I could feel that it was all hard, like my skin was all swollen up. At the hospital, at first they said that it looked like I'd lost a lot of blood. They said my blood pressure was low and I was in shock. But there wasn't a drop of blood on my clothes, or anywhere in the parking lot, according to the police. The hospital checked me for internal bleeding, but they didn't find any. They did some more tests that haven't come back yet, but I could tell that they didn't know what to think. The doctor sent me home about nine this morning, and all they could say was that it looked like I'd lost consciousness and fell and hurt myself that way. But that doesn't make any sense at all. I don't take any medications that would make me pass out, and I've always been perfectly healthy. They're sending me to see some neurologist, though."

Evelyn got up from the chair, returned to the couch, and started to light a fresh cigarette. "All right, now it's my turn. Dr. Clauson, you said on the phone that there had been other things like this. I haven't seen anything like this on the news." She sounded as though she was reproaching the news for dereliction of duty. "Could you explain what you meant?" Regan got up off the hassock, feeling dejected, and walked over to the window, trying to center herself a little.

"There's not that much to tell," Hiram said. "This past January one of my colleagues told me about a patient he counseled at the local emergency room one night. The patient was a man about thirty years old, homeless, and he'd been found unconscious and brought in. He claimed he'd been clean and sober for six months, but he couldn't remember anything for a space of about four hours—missing time, is the technical term. The hospital staff assumed he'd been using, but his tox screen came back negative, and...well, he had a very strange-looking injury. Mild symptoms of shock, but no signs of internal or external bleeding. The patient was very distressed about his loss of memory. My colleague asked me to try hypnotic regression on him, which I am certified to do. But the results were negative—that is, the patient couldn't remember anything more under hypnosis. He was physically cleared and the hospital discharged him."

"What happened to him?"

"I had no opportunity for follow-up, because he wasn't my patient. As far as I know, nothing happened to him—at least, I didn't hear anything more.

"A couple of weeks later, I had a call from a friend of mine who works in the Fall River police department. They'd had a very strange case come in, he said, and he wanted to hear my opinion, off the record. This was a complete coincidence—if you believe in coincidence. My friend went on to describe a call in which a young man, about twenty years old, had been found by his neighbors sitting on the steps of his apartment building. Not unconscious, this time, but it seemed that he had been, and was just recovering himself. He had a very strange-looking injury. He told the responding officer that he'd be fine, he didn't want any medical treatment, and he didn't want to make any complaints. He claimed he didn't remember what happened. He didn't seem to realize that he was injured. When the officer asked him about it, he said he must have fallen. He wasn't very cooperative, and the officer inferred that he probably had reasons for not wanting to talk to the police. He told the man to call emergency services if he needed medical attention and that was the end of it. And no, I didn't hear that anything more ever happened to him."

Evelyn was staring at Hiram blankly. "It doesn't make any sense."

"That's what I thought. But I wondered if there were any more cases like these. So, I started to make calls to police departments and emergency rooms, and private ambulance services, to find out if there had been any similar complaints, and whether I could talk to the affected persons, if so. Well, I met with a lot of resistance. I heard about cases, but no one was willing to give me names or details because of confidentiality laws. However, I managed to gain the trust of some police departments and two hospitals, and they've been willing to give my name and number to anyone who has made a similar complaint, so the reporting people themselves can call me if they want to talk about what happened. I've collected fifteen cases, going back to November—"

"Fifteen!" Evelyn said. "All around here?"

"Southeastern Massachusetts and Rhode Island, yes. But then, that's as far as I've been looking. I do have a day job."

"And you've interviewed all those people?"

"Well—no. Only eight of them called me, and of those, only five consented to be interviewed. And even then, I immediately ran into a problem. They all suffered total memory loss, and hypnosis didn't get us anywhere. So, about a month ago, I called Regan."

Evelyn pivoted around to look at Regan. "Yes, he brought me out of retirement," Regan said wryly.

"But...how did you two know each other?"

"Oh, I didn't know Hiram from a hole in the wall. But I'm notorious, unfortunately—or I was, about eight years ago."

"Why?"

Regan looked away. "I'd rather not get into it."

"Regan worked with the police on a criminal case," Hiram said. "Very successfully. That's how I knew her name. Of course, I was rather skeptical about psychics, but the police department she assisted spoke very highly of her. I was completely stonewalled in my own investigation, so I decided to give her a call."

"He's very persuasive."

"I didn't hold a gun on you, Regan. You were interested."

"Yeah, I love a mystery." Regan went over to the vacant armchair and sat down heavily. "The trouble is, after six interviews, that's still all we've got."

Evelyn said slowly, "So, all fifteen of these people...had memory loss, and...an injury?" She reached up and touched her neck, which was covered by a loosely tied silk scarf. Regan had noticed it immediately when Evelyn answered the door.

"It's a very distinctive injury," Hiram said. "And yes, all the same, at least the ones we've seen. Not all in the same location, but they all look the same."

Evelyn licked her lips, as though her mouth was dry. "But you said these were all men."

"No, there's no pattern," Hiram said. "Of the fifteen, there are both men and women, ranging from a seventeen-year-old male high school student to a fifty-five year old housewife. It doesn't fit any profile at all. Except that none of them have been children."

There was a silence in the room. Regan leaned forward from her seat on the couch. "Could we see your injury, Mrs. Stockard?"

Evelyn looked at her for a few moments. Then she nodded. She untied the scarf, revealing a wide flesh-colored bandage. As she carefully worked the edge of the bandage loose with her fingers in order to peel it off, Regan went and sat on the couch next to Evelyn. She winced as the bandage came away and she saw the injury—this was the most recent one she had seen so far. In the center of a black and purple contusion about the size of fifty cent piece was what appeared to be a deep cut that had been sealed over. Like the others, Evelyn's injury had an unnatural appearance. The cut appeared more healed than the bruise, and its edges curled under so that the effect was of a mouth held tightly closed, rather than a wound made by any instrument. The injury was directly over the jugular vein. "Looks awful, doesn't it?" Evelyn said, and Regan realized she'd been staring.

"Yes, it does." She let out her breath in a huff—she hadn't realized she'd been holding it.

"Is it like those other ones?"

After a moment, Regan said, "Yes, it is."

Evelyn looked at Hiram, and he nodded. "And I saw photographs, of some of the cases where I didn't actually meet the patients. That's exactly like them. And I've never seen anything similar, anywhere else. I admit, I'm not a forensic pathologist—wounds aren't my field of expertise."

"The emergency room doctor said it looked like I'd been hurt at least three days ago. I told him no, that it wasn't there before. He said I should have bled to death. And then—" her eyes narrowed with sudden anger. "Some social worker actually came in and started asking me questions about whether my husband ever hurt me. They thought *Jim* did this! Can you imagine the nerve?"

Regan grimaced sympathetically. "I think they're required to ask that now, Mrs. Stockard."

"Even *so!* They were trying to make out that Jim hit me or something three days ago and that's why I passed out last night. I told them to go straight to hell. You two know Jim couldn't have done this."

"It wouldn't be my first assumption," Hiram said diplomatically.

"Yes, but—" Evelyn sat up straight. "What do you suppose would happen if you did one of your readings on this?" she asked Regan, indicating the injury. "If you touched this, maybe you'd be able to read what caused it? At least you could say it wasn't my husband's fault."

Regan froze, a sudden chill in the pit of her stomach. "I'd hate to...to be that invasive, Mrs. Stockard..."

"Oh, go ahead. You've come all this way, see what happens."

Regan glanced at Hiram, who was almost quivering with eagerness, like a terrier who'd just spotted a squirrel. Her mouth had gone dry. She didn't want to directly read an injury that looked like that. All her instincts told her that neither an animal nor an accident had made that ugly wound, and she sensed that by touching it, she would cross a boundary that was protecting her from more information than it was safe for her to know. But she couldn't think of a way to refuse. "I better go wash my hands," she said. It was one way to procrastinate. In the tiny bathroom, she ran hot water for almost half a minute, trying to warm her cold fingers and stop them from shaking. When she returned to the living room, Evelyn was sitting again in the armchair. She and Hiram were both watching the hallway, waiting for Regan attentively.

"Are you okay?" Evelyn asked.

"Yes, I'm fine. Are you ready?"

"Yes. Should I do the same as before?"

Regan walked over to stand next to the armchair, rubbing her hands together. "That's just fine. Now if you feel uncomfortable at any time—suppose my touching you brings back any feelings, or memories, or whatever—just indicate that to Hiram, and he'll stop me. I may get pretty tranced out, and not be aware of what you're doing."

"I understand," Evelyn said.

Evelyn leaned back in the chair, closed her eyes and took a couple of deep breaths. When her hands began to relax in her lap, Regan moved to half-sit on the arm of the chair. She reached over and very gently rested her hand on Evelyn's shoulder, her fingers barely brushing the surface of the injury. She could feel the heat of the contusion, and the roughness of the strange cut. She closed her eyes and opened her awareness to whatever impressions might be available... and they came. Almost immediately, there was a flood of images, empty streets and dark woods at night, although strangely visible, as though the buildings and trees were glowing. She pushed back, consciously focusing on keying in to an earlier time, and there was a dizzying feeling that she was standing on the verge of a long tunnel of memory, decades long, longer than one lifetime. Confused, she tried to narrow the mass of images to the beginning, to wherever these memories started. Abruptly, she seemed to have been dropped into a vivid, fully sensual scene, streets crowded with people and traffic, streets that were somehow very familiar, as if this was someplace she knew. But the traffic was not modern but horse drawn, carriages and heavily loaded carts and small wagons. The people wore the clothing of a century ago, long skirts on the women, frock coats and beaver hats on the men, and boys were running everywhere, working, not playing. Thick smoke rose from compact red brick buildings, and there was a pungent, almost overwhelming, impression of mingled smells: sulfur, manure, rotting vegetables, cooking odors, sweat. Unable to find any obvious relevance to this scene, Regan pulled back from it. She collected herself and consciously directed her attention to the previous night, when Evelyn left the warehouse... and then she was there.

"I see you," she said aloud, softly, and she heard Hiram shift in his creaking armchair. But now the whole scene had engulfed her, and she no longer had any awareness of the living room or the people in it. It was though she had locked her hand onto a live electrical wire. She was standing by the red truck, she had been there for a few minutes, looking at the building, and she'd actually been about to leave, when she saw Evelyn come out of the door. She watched Evelyn cross the parking lot, and then she stepped out and spoke to her. *I'm looking for a Mr. Singleton, there's a family emergency.* Her voice was low-pitched. She was taller than Evelyn, but not a great deal taller. Evelyn slowed, her face wary and suspicious. *Rob Singleton's on the floor, you want to go on in and ask for him at the supervisor's station.* She answered Evelyn, *thank you.* She turned away and started to walk toward the building, hearing Evelyn's footsteps clipping smartly in the crisp night air. Evelyn was walking rapidly and fumbling in her handbag for her car keys because she was afraid of the stranger in the parking lot. She turned around, aware that she would know if anyone else was in the lot—that she'd be able to hear them, see their bodies glowing with warmth, *smell* them. She took several rapid, almost running steps, making no sound, Evelyn heard no one coming up behind her, and then...Regan tried to pull back. *I don't want to see this, I don't want to do this, let me go back let me go back* but she couldn't break loose. She could feel, see, *taste* herself stepping up behind Evelyn and reaching around, putting a hand over Evelyn's mouth and pulling her back against herself, free hand yanking down the collars of Evelyn's coat and blouse and then gripping her shoulder as Evelyn twisted and kicked, back arching, trying to escape, as her attacker bent down and...

With a guttural sound Regan wrenched herself away from the chair, so violently that she lost her balance and fell onto the floor between the two armchairs, setting one of the floor lamps swaying precariously. She was aware that Hiram and Evelyn were both on their feet, making exclamations, but she couldn't understand what they were saying. She thought she was going to vomit onto the shag carpet, which would certainly be a precedent in her career. She clutched both hands tightly against her mouth, shuddering, trying to convince herself that her mouth wasn't filled with blood. The salty metallic taste of it was so strong and persistent, she thought she must have bitten her lip when she fell. Hiram knelt down beside her. "Regan? Are you all right?"

"I'll get a glass of water," she heard Evelyn say. Regan took deep breaths, trying hard to recover her equilibrium. Her nausea faded, and finally she was able to rise to her knees and, shaking, move to sit in the armchair that Hiram had vacated. She wiped at her face with her hands. Her skin felt cold and clammy to the touch. *That can't be good.* She realized that Evelyn was standing by the chair and offering her the glass of water.

"Thank you," Regan said, taking it. She glimpsed shapes in her peripheral vision and turned to see Jim and the teenage girl standing in the entrance to the hallway, staring at her. Regan looked away, mortified, and took a gulp of water. She felt like she was inside one of her recurring nightmares, the one in which she had collapsed, hysterically raving nonsense words while a crowd of people stood around gawking at the...*nut job, psycho, fruitcake, freak...*

"Does this happen very often?" she heard Evelyn whisper to Hiram, but she couldn't hear Hiram's response.

She was feeling more normal now, aside from the shaking, and she drank more water, to drive the memory of the taste of blood from her mouth. But she kept her head lowered, unwilling to look at Evelyn or Hiram, because they would certainly want to know what had just happened. *Now what do I say?* she thought desperately. *Do I lie? Do I tell Evelyn that she was assaulted by a stranger in the parking lot, make her live in fear from now on? Do I tell her what he did? Can it possibly be true?* But she had to say something. Taking a deep breath, she straightened up fully in the chair. "I'm really sorry. I don't know what happened."

"No, *I'm* sorry," Evelyn said quickly. "Touching the injury was my idea and obviously it was too much." Regan saw that Evelyn had put the bandage back into place.

"What are you talking about, mom?" the teenage girl said.

"Angie, go back to the den," Evelyn said sharply. "There's too many people here. We can talk about it later."

"Mom!"

"Now. Go on."

Angie stomped down the hallway, grumbling audibly, "Stupid crazy lady, the house could burn down and nobody would tell me anything..." until the den door slammed resoundingly and cut her off. Jim stayed in the doorway, silent but watching Hiram, rather than Regan, with a cold look.

Regan stood up. "I think we've overstayed our welcome, Hiram."

"I'm afraid so," Hiram said immediately. "Mrs. Stockard, let me apologize profusely for any unnecessary concern we've caused you and your family. It was very generous of you to meet with us and I'm sorry that we haven't been more helpful." He picked up Regan's coat from the back of the chair and handed it to her.

"Wait a moment," Evelyn said. "Aren't you going to tell me what you saw? After all that? You can't just leave. What did you see, what happened?"

Regan braced herself and met Evelyn's eyes. "Nothing. I'm sorry. I just...went into overload. It happens sometimes. I've been doing too many of these, and I guess I was just too tired tonight. I didn't see anything." Evelyn's brow creased, and Regan could see that she wasn't convinced. "Did I say anything?"

"No. I mean, you just said, 'I see you.' Then you didn't move at all for a couple of minutes, until you...had that sort of fit. What did you mean when you said, 'I see you?'"

"I saw you, leaving the building last night. It was the same thing that I saw in the first reading, the same thing you remembered. That's all."

"But you didn't see—" Evelyn broke off.

"I didn't see what happened." Regan repeated firmly. She put her coat on. Hiram was already standing by the door, waiting for her. As Regan was about to follow Hiram outside, Evelyn suddenly hurried across the room and caught Regan's arm. Regan gasped at what she felt.

"Just tell me one thing. Is it safe for me to go back to work? Jim doesn't want me to work nights anymore."

Regan turned and looked steadily into Evelyn's anxious eyes for a few moments. If what she had seen had really happened, then she also was sure of one fact—the assailant would not come back. "I think you'll be safe going back to work, Mrs. Stockard. This won't happen again. And I'm sure Seatech is going to put in some increased security. It's your decision to make. But..." she reached over and put her hand on Evelyn's shoulder, "if I were you, I'd get a chest x-ray done as soon as possible. I'm not a doctor. I'm just saying you might be glad you did. Good night, and, I'm sorry again." She turned away from Evelyn's stunned expression and ducked out the door into the chilly night air.

Chapter 3

The car was back on I-195 before Hiram said anything. "Why did you tell her that? Just to distract her from what happened?"

Regan opened her eyes. "I wouldn't be that cruel, Hiram. Yes, I wanted to distract her. But she needed to be warned. I knew that when she took hold of my arm." She sighed heavily. "It doesn't matter. She's going to be dead in a year."

"How do you know that?"

"Because she's not going to go for that x-ray. She'll be too afraid." Regan was silent, staring unseeing at the road ahead. "This is it, Hiram," she said finally. "I quit."

Hiram sighed heavily. He sounded, Regan thought, rather irritated, as if she was being irrational and unreasonable and now he was in the position of persuading her to come around. "I wish you would at least tell me what you saw."

"I didn't see anything."

"I don't believe that for a moment, Regan. I talked to them up in Gardner, you know."

"Then you know why I moved back here."

"Regan, I'm trying to say that I have faith in you. I don't believe you just had a psychotic episode or ischemic attack. I've been working with you now for weeks. I've known all along that eventually we'd break through to something, and I didn't think it would be pleasant. I won't say that I anticipated it hitting you this hard. But whatever it was...Regan, you can't keep it to yourself. Nothing could be worse for your own mental health, never mind the possible safety of others. What did you see? Please, tell me." After a short silence, he said, "I've been expecting it to be something...out of the ordinary. I thought that would have been obvious. Don't be afraid that I'll rationalize or laugh at you."

"You're a psychologist, Hiram. I don't have a great history with psychologists."

"But I've been working with you. I called you. I'm not narrow-minded, Regan. If you don't know that by now..."

"I can't have seen anything real, Hiram. It...it can't be. I must have been projecting, or hallucinating—or I've finally gone completely around the bend."

"After that reading you did on the figurine, I'd have said you were in top form tonight. Have you ever done a reading that turned out to be totally without veracity at all? A complete fantasy?"

"Well...no."

"I didn't think so. You're too hard-headed about your gift. Hell, you're more hard-headed about psychic work than some psychologists, Regan. Whatever you've seen, I don't care what it is, alien abductions, demon possession, poltergeists—tell me what you saw. We'll sort it out. I thought we were work-ing as a team here."

Regan closed her eyes and sighed heavily. "You sound just a little bit obsessed, Hiram, do you know that?"

"People are being hurt, Regan. There's something very strange going on that is impacting human beings and causing them pain and distress, and we're the only ones who are in a position to connect all the facts. Yes, it's true: I want to solve this, and I want to stop it, if I can. If that's an obsession, then at least it's a constructive one." He waited again—they would be back in Sheridan soon, even though Hiram had been driving so slowly, to prolong their discussion, that trucks had been roaring by them almost incessantly. Finally he said, "Did you see what happened to Evelyn last night?"

"We should be in a dingy green room with a glaring white light," Regan said somewhat irritably. "Yes. I saw something that might have happened—in some alternate universe, anyway."

"Was she assaulted by a person?"

"That seemed to happen, yes." It was a relief to be saying it out loud, after all.

"So tell me. What did he look like?"

Regan sighed. "I don't know. I was seeing it all from his perspective. In fact, I can't say with absolute certainty what he was wearing. From the feel of it, it was pants, maybe a sweater, no coat or jacket. I have no idea about colors."

"But no physical description of the man himself."

"I don't think he was fat. And he was about six inches taller than Evelyn, and Evelyn is about my height, so that would make him maybe five ten, five eleven—average height, no more than that."

"But you couldn't say, blond, dark, blue eyes, brown eyes..."

"He wasn't thinking about what he looked like. Evelyn was afraid of him, but not enough to run."

"He confronted her?"

"He spoke to her, that's all."

"He spoke? Then you'd recognize his voice."

Regan shook her head. "This has happened to me before. I have a vague idea what his voice sounds like to him. I probably wouldn't recognize it if I heard it from the outside, heard him speaking in real life. We never know what our own voices sound like to other people."

Hiram chuckled ruefully. "That's for certain. Every time I hear a recording of one of my lectures...but I won't get off the point. What about an accent?"

Regan thought, running over obvious examples mentally. Southern, Brit-ish, European..."No, none at all. American. He talked just like here. Except... he seemed educated. His word choice was somewhat formal. But he didn't say much, that I could judge by."

"What did he say?"

"He asked about someone who worked in the warehouse—he knew a name, a last name, anyway." After a moment, she realized that she knew a bit more. "He didn't have a clue who he was talking about. He'd overheard the name mentioned. He'd been waiting there a while. It was just a ruse, because Evelyn had seen him."

Hiram made a perplexed sound. "I wonder why he'd take such a risk. It's too bad the parking lot doesn't have security cameras."

"He knew there weren't cameras, he'd checked," Regan said with certainty. "It's not like they're invisible, after all."

There was a pause then, as Hiram took the exit off I-195 for Sheridan center. They passed the Standish Mills complex, many windows lighted—the mills also were a twenty-four hour operation. At the traffic light at the end of the ramp, Hiram finally said, "All right. We know he was waiting in the lot, and we know he only targeted Evelyn because she was unlucky enough to leave the building alone. What did he want? Why was he there? What did he do to her, Regan?" After a pause, he added, "I know you don't want to talk about it. But you'll feel better. Take my word as a clinician. Get it out into the open."

"All right, all *right*. Stop it before you have to bill me." Irritation made it easier to talk. "He...he let her think he was walking toward the warehouse. He turned around and ran after her and grabbed her from behind. She never knew he was coming until she felt it. It was very fast. He grabbed her with his hand over her mouth and he, he..." she broke off, suddenly overcome with the memory of the sensations she'd experienced in Evelyn's living room.

"It can't be worse than those cases in Gardner. Evelyn's alive and relatively unscathed. Get some distance, Regan, it's over, it's in the past."

"It's just that I felt it, I *tasted* it." Regan shuddered. "It was such a shock, it was so real, and I couldn't break the connection, I couldn't get away from it. I don't usually get pulled completely into the experience like that. It happens, but...I tapped into something powerful here. I'm way out of my league, Hiram. I've never felt anything like this."

"You're scared, and you're reacting to your fear," Hiram said calmly. "That's absolutely understandable. But your fear is misdirected. This happened to some-one else. You're safe, Regan."

"Are you really sure of that?" Regan said softly. Before Hiram could respond, she said, "He drank her blood, Hiram. Gulps of it, like you'd drink from a water fountain. That's what makes that horrible-looking injury. He opens the vein right up and drinks from it."

"Opens the vein—with his teeth?"

"No...I don't know! I don't think so, but I was fighting so hard to break away from the vision by then, I may have missed part of it. I didn't feel anything like a bite. I don't know how he makes the wound, and I can't even imagine how he makes it stop. Not a drop spilled—and these people should all be dead. They should have been dead in minutes!"

This time it was Hiram who was silent, frowning as he considered what she had said. "At least he's not murdering them," he said finally.

"We don't know that, do we? Only the survivors make a report."

"True, but I do know," Hiram broke off as he turned into the parking lot of Hong Kong Delhi, a restaurant down the road from Borrowed and Blue, "that none of the police departments I've been talking to have mentioned any deaths with injuries like the ones we've seen. I've asked them specifically about that. And they do take it seriously—cops don't like unsolvable homicides."

"Why are we stopping here?"

"I'm buying you a drink—and I could use one, myself."

He and Regan had met here several times for follow-up meetings after interviews, although never before under this much duress. Hong Kong Delhi had the advantage of booths all along three of the dining room walls, making it a cozy venue for confidential meetings, as long as your taste in Asian cuisine wasn't too highbrow. The drinks, however, were potent and excellent. Normally Regan would have met several people she knew if she stopped in on a Friday night, but tonight, although a couple of regular customers said hello, all her closest friends were up in Taunton. By the time she was nursing her second Mai-Tai, the dim lighting, generic pop music and inconsequential buzz of conversation was restoring a sense of normality. She had told Hiram about the first vision she'd had while reading Evelyn's injury, the vivid street scene.

"The smells sound very authentic," Hiram commented.

"I get smell impressions a lot, but this was extreme. It was like I was right there."

"Can you pinpoint the timing?"

She frowned, stirring the plastic-impaled cherry and pineapple around in her glass. "Not to the year, and vintage clothing isn't my specialty. But I'd say...after 1880 and before 1895. Later than that and I think there'd have been cars."

"Hmm. And you thought the location looked familiar."

"Yeah, and I just can't nail it down. It was too big to be Sheridan, but I'm almost sure it was someplace I've seen—in recent times, I mean. It would have to be someplace that had a lot of mills or factories in the eighteen hundreds."

"Well, that's almost everyplace in New England."

"I know, but...Lowell, maybe? Or New Bedford?" She shook her head. "This is going to drive me nuts. The worst thing is, this feeling of familiarity might not even be mine. I might just be picking up on the fact that it's so familiar to him. That's how I felt about the farm in Nebraska I saw when I read the figurine. Like I'd lived there all my life."

"But there's a difference, or you wouldn't be talking about it."

"There is a difference, yes."

"Are you sure that the street scene is even connected with the man from last night?"

She shook her head. "There's that, too. But the street scene must have something to do with the injury. That's what I was reading. What other connection could there be?" She took a swig of her drink. "And if there is a connection—what the hell does it mean? Why would I have such a vivid impression from a hundred and twenty years ago, when I'm trying to read an event that happened just last night? It doesn't make any sense at all."

Hiram took a sip of his own drink and was silent, evidently deep in thought. Regan, who was getting a bit of a buzz on, leaned back and eyed him skeptically.

"You know...you haven't expressed the slightest bit of surprise at any of this. Are you just playing the detached, calm professional, or have you known more all along than you're telling me?"

He blinked and looked slightly affronted. "Neither one. I'm not surprised. This is exactly what I've been expecting. I was sure that if we could somehow break past the memory blocks, this is what we'd find."

"You were expecting—" Regan glanced over her shoulder and lowered her voice. "Blood drinking? You were expecting a vampire? That's what we're talking about, isn't it?"

"In clinical terms, that's exactly what we're talking about. It's consistent with the injuries. It's consistent with the reported symptoms."

"It's not consistent with reality. Hiram, for god's sake."

"There are ample cases in the literature to support this hypothesis. We needn't be talking about anything supernatural."

"But the—Hiram, there's more going on here than Renfield's Syndrome! You don't open someone's jugular vein and send them home with a band-aid."

"I admit, there are still some very mysterious elements to the situation. But I'm confident that we'll find the explanations—if we can find the perpetrator. I think your street scene might be a clue."

"In what way?"

"There's obviously a strong emotional and mental attachment to that place and time. There might be a way to trace that. It would have to qualify as an obsession so deep it would almost be dissociative. That's *Dracula's* time period, after all, people do readily associate that era with vampires."

"And with Jack the Ripper and Sherlock Holmes..."

"Not in America so much. But there were true vampire cases here in America at that period of time, as well."

Regan sagged in her seat, thinking. "I don't know. It's possible, but I've picked up on dreams and delusions in other people. This just didn't have that feeling. It was too...multi-dimensional, and multi-sensual. Even memories usually aren't as complete and vivid as this."

"Then what would your theory be?"

Regan hesitated, then shrugged helplessly. "I have no idea."

"You said in the car that you felt you'd tapped into something powerful. If you've made an especially strong connection, for whatever reason, it would follow that all aspects of it would be heightened—wouldn't it? Comparisons to your typical readings might not apply."

"I...I suppose...but, Hiram, there's a lot here that's damned hard to rationalize away. For example: how is he managing to blank out his victims' memories so completely? So totally that hypnosis doesn't work, and I can't pick up a twinge: nothing, *tabula rasa!* I've run into false memories plenty of times. I've *never* seen memory *loss* this total."

"It's not unusual for people to blank out the memory of a traumatic event. That's elementary crisis psychology."

"Sixteen totally different individuals, with absolutely no memory whatsoever? And that's not considering all the people we're guessing have never reported at all—if they're not dead. Besides, this isn't just memory loss. All the impressions have been erased, as well. It's like he just wiped a whole block of time clean, as though it never even happened."

Hiram did not appear concerned by her arguments. "Again. There are some very unusual aspects to this case. But I'm sure they can be explained."

Regan picked up her glass and took a large gulp of Mai-Tai. "You can just see the book advance now, can't you?" she mumbled into the glass.

"That's not fair. Don't equate me with that journalist in Gardner. I'm not interested in exploiting you or these victims. If I write something—"

"Ah-ha."

"...*if* I write something, it will be for a peer-reviewed journal first, and only when we have solid, verified information."

"Right." Regan drained the glass and then pulled the cherry and pineapple off the swizzle stick and ate them, moodily.

"Perhaps you'd like something solid to buffer all that alcohol?" Hiram's voice was just a bit sardonic. "I know you didn't get any dinner before I picked you up."

For a moment, it was tempting, but at the thought of meat, Regan was reminded again of the taste of blood in her mouth, and her throat closed. She swallowed the fruit, with an effort. "Thanks, I had lunch late, and I don't have much appetite. We better get going, I need to open at ten tomorrow."

Hiram signaled their server for the check. While they waited, he said casually, "By the way—you said when I called you that you had somewhere else to be tonight. I'm afraid that I'd just gotten off the phone with the Stockards and I wasn't very receptive. I'm sorry if I made you miss something important."

"Oh..." Regan sighed. "I don't think it was that important. It probably wouldn't have been the best environment, anyway." As Hiram looked at her quizzically, she realized that two strong drinks were making her unnecessarily obscure. "I had a pass to a club date. I know the band. But Veronica—my best friend—was hoping that I could meet her latest romantic interest. Well—she's interested, anyway."

"And a club isn't a good environment for that?"

Regan smiled ruefully. "She wants me to check him out...you know. Before things get any more serious, if that's even likely. Jonathan Vaughn. I have to admit, he doesn't seem like her type. But I haven't met him yet, so maybe I'll be surprised."

Hiram signed the credit card slip and replaced his card in his wallet. "I gather that your friend Veronica has a colorful past, when it comes to romance."

"Oh my god, you have no idea. I mean, I love her dearly, but...I can't complain now, though, I was the one who convinced her to run background checks. I guess I was thinking more of criminal record and credit checks."

Hiram chuckled. "My god, dating has gotten tough. Why would he not be her type?"

"I don't know, he just sounds...boring. He supposed to be a writer, he's renting that old place way out on River Road, by the dairy farm. Nothing out there but mosquitoes and deer, and you can smell manure all summer long. I sure can't imagine Veronica moving in with him out there."

"Is he new in town?"

"Yeah. I don't know when he actually got here, but I started hearing about him from my customers about a month ago. Veronica just met him a couple of weeks ago, though—on April Fool's Day, believe it or not."

Hiram smiled. "That used to be my wedding anniversary."

"Get out."

"No, it seemed very amusing to us when we were twenty-one. Given how things turned out, we should have held out for Friday the thirteenth."

"I'm very sorry," Regan said, embarrassed.

"Ancient history."

When they were back in Hiram's car, for the short trip to Borrowed and Blue, Hiram commented, "So, there's a new person in town, who's living alone in an isolated location, is vague about his livelihood, and whom you've never met?"

"What are you driving at? People move in and out of a town like this constantly, and I never meet most of them."

"Of course, people move in and out of any town constantly, this is a mobile society. But almost all of them have jobs and references, or are going to school—people move for good reasons."

Regan turned to stare at him. "Are you actually insinuating that there's something sinister about Jonathan Vaughn just because he's new in town and hasn't made his personal life a public affair?"

"Don't get defensive. I'm not insinuating anything, I'm just noting the facts for reference."

"Well, just for reference, I'm sure that hundreds of people much more suspicious than Mr. Vaughn moved into Bristol County *before* last November. Let's not rush to make convenient scapegoats, Hiram."

"I'm doing nothing of the kind. You're certainly protective of a man you have yet to even meet, Regan. Didn't you just say that you advised your friends to have their new acquaintances investigated? I'm hearing a certain inconsistency here."

They had reached the store's parking lot. Regan sagged back against the seat. "You're right, I'm sorry. I'm a little sensitive about people being unfairly targeted. I know what it feels like." Hiram didn't respond to this, and she went on, "It's just that I haven't heard anything negative about Jonathan Vaughn, and that's weird in itself. When the new vice principal was hired at Adams Elementary, I heard that he smoked too much, his wife looked frumpy, and his car was too expensive—and that was before school even started. When the police department hired that new officer from Providence, two customers mentioned something to me about how he'd just gone through a messy divorce and he transferred up here because there had been something fishy going on in his precinct. But everyone who's met Jonathan Vaughn says he's the nicest, most charming, most polite man they've ever run into."

"There are serial killers who—"

"Yeah, I know, I know. They say the same thing about pedophiles. It's gotten to be pretty sad, hasn't it, when niceness is a sinister quality?"

"Well, maybe when you do meet him, you'll find that he's just as boring as he seems." Hiram had pulled around to the back of the store, right next to Regan's battered blue Honda Civic. "You're not going back into the store now, are you?"

"No, I'm going right home. Thank you for the drinks."

Hiram looked thoughtfully around the small space, which had a peeling painted stockade fence running along two sides. "Maybe you should park your car in front from now on."

"There's a security light back here. There's not that much parking in front, especially now with Lake Sheridan taking up half the room."

"But this area can't be seen from the street."

Regan looked blearily around the tiny graveled yard, which up to this moment had always seemed familiar and safe. He had a point.

"I'll think about it," she said, suddenly resenting him. If Borrowed and Blue wasn't a secure haven for her, then what was?

Chapter 4

Regan got to the store unusually early the next morning. She had slept very badly and finally decided she may as well get up and accomplish something constructive. By 9:30, the store was vacuumed and dusted, the front door glass washed, and any gaps on the shelves restocked or rearranged. She had hoped for a busy Saturday, but the results exceeded all her reasonable expectations. It was the first really warm day they'd had that spring, brilliantly sunny, balmy and blue-skied. After three solid days of rain during the week, no one was going to stay inside in weather like this. By mid-afternoon, Regan was starting to wonder why she had ever put the jingling copper bells on the door, she was getting so tired of hearing them. All the new flower bowls sold, and a partial set of Wedgwood china that she had thought she would have to take a loss on, she'd had it for so long. Knick knacks and statuettes, candleholders and pot-pourri jars, souvenir postcards and a Shaker rocking chair, there was no pattern to the purchases. Regan's only regret was that she was so tired. Old-time regulars who greeted her as they came in got only a flat response, and her sleep deprivation headache blossomed into a throbbing pain behind her eyebrows. The phone kept ringing, and the UPS delivery finally arrived at 2:30, with a surly driver who had to carry box after box around customers in the narrow aisles to the little storage area next to the office. Regan had no sympathy for him, as she had offered to go unlock the back door, but he didn't want to move his truck.

Shortly after the UPS driver left, there were a few minutes when the store was empty. Regan took advantage of the break to restock the display of Yankee Candles, wrinkling her nose at the clashing combination of pungent scents, which wasn't helping her headache. The bells jingled, and Regan straightened up, flexing her back. The click of high boot heels on the worn linoleum tile floor telegraphed who had come in before Regan turned to look. "Hello, Veronica," she called. "So how did the big club party go? Was Theo a smash?" Veronica stopped at the end of the aisle, and Regan had to wince when she turned and looked at her friend. "Oh, my god, I thought I was hung over. Are you just rolling out?" That would be relative in Veronica's case—she didn't set foot outside without forty-five minutes of careful hair arrangement and makeup application. Today, however, her face looked wan and strained underneath the delicate cosmetics.

"Hello, Regan." Veronica's voice quavered slightly. "I just wanted to ask—have you seen Jonathan today?" Her expression was so mournful that Regan felt a note of alarm.

"I don't think so," she said carefully. "Unless he came in and left without introducing himself, I'd have to say no. I don't know what he looks like, you know."

"Has any of our friends called you since last night, Karen or anybody?"

"No..." she trailed off as Veronica released a sigh, closing her eyes in a look of relief. "What's...going on?"

"Do you think we could talk?"

Regan glanced helplessly at the door. "Well, it's...it's been very busy today, Ver. Could it wait until after I close up?"

"I don't know. I think it's important. I need to talk to you before anyone else does."

Regan slowly crumpled up the empty candle box she was holding, digesting this statement. "Okay...let's step into my office. You'll have to wait for me if anyone comes in." Veronica nodded miserably and followed her. Regan waved her friend to a straight-backed wooden chair that she kept for visitors and vendors, and plumped herself onto the squeaking 1950s office chair that she used as a desk chair. It had a cracked brown vinyl seat and a solid steel base that weighed about thirty pounds, but castors that would still roll the length of the store with one good push. Regan shoved back now so she had a clear view of the front door. "All right, shoot—quick, before the bells ring."

Veronica had taken a wad of tissues from the Gucci bag, which was never a good sign. "I'm afraid I've done something really stupid."

"And that would be...?"

Veronica blew her nose. "I...I...well, I told Jonathan about those things. The ones you and Dr. Clauson are looking into."

Regan's mouth fell open. "You *what?*" Veronica bowed her head. "Veronica, you swore, you *swore* you wouldn't talk about that. You *promised!* Now the investigation is compromised!"

"I'm sorry! When I woke up and remembered what I'd said, I knew I had to come and tell you right away. I don't know why I did it."

"So, when did this happen?"

"Last night, at the club."

"The *club?*" When Veronica had said, "I told Jonathan," Regan had hoped she was referring to a one-on-one conversation in some private setting. "You mean in the middle of three hundred people?" Veronica nodded, dabbing at her eyes. "I hope the music was loud enough to keep anyone else from hearing."

"Well...the band wasn't playing. They were on break."

Never had the store's door bells seemed so silent. With a terrible sense of premonition, Regan said carefully, "Just exactly how many people were listening in to this conversation?"

Veronica sniffed. "Theo...most of our friends...some other people...it was a big table, I didn't know everyone there." Regan leaned back in her chair, pressing her clasped hands to her mouth for a moment. "Regan, I don't why I did it, I swear! I'm not a blabbermouth, I've never gossiped about you, *ever*. I know what a horrible time you had before you moved back here. I don't know what got into me!"

Regan sighed heavily. "Just how did you happen to get onto this subject? I thought you wanted me to read Jonathan for you. Surely you didn't want him to know about my being psychic—now he's going to be on his guard. Unless he volunteers, you're shit out of luck."

"He already knew about it. I guess someone here in town must have told him. I think it was Derek. Derek handles rentals in his dad's office now."

Regan's shoulders sagged. "Oh. I guess I should have realized that would probably happen."

"All I told Jonathan was that you might be coming to the club later on, and you were my best friend, and you wanted to meet him. 'Oh, she's the one who's supposed to be a clairvoyant, isn't she?' he said. And I just kind of laughed it off, because you're right, I didn't want him to think I was trying to trick him into anything. So he let it go, and it got later and later, and every now and then he'd say something about, where could your friend be. And someone else would say, yeah, where's Regan, it's a shame she's missing this. And somehow it just kept coming up, and Jonathan seemed so interested—"

"And you were drinking *so* much..."

"Oh, god, Regan, I don't know why I got so drunk!"

"Was it an open bar?"

"It was a cash bar. But somehow there was always a drink in my hand, and..." she flushed. "I was so sick before we left to go home."

"You're lucky that's all you were. Ver, you know you can't drink that way with your medications."

"I'm sure I'm okay with the meds," Veronica said evasively.

Regan decided to let that pass for the moment. "So...I'm guessing that finally, the umpteenth time someone asked why I wasn't there, you told them."

"I didn't mean to say so much about it. But people were so curious...Jonathan was, especially. He kept asking questions, and talking about how he'd heard about things like that, and other people joined in, and everyone was telling stories, and then we'd come back to what you were doing...I never had so many people act so fascinated by what I was talking about." Regan couldn't help feeling a pang of sympathy. Veronica tended to be the butt of dumb blonde jokes, and those were the least cruel of the jibes she heard.

"I guess you were right yesterday. People are intrigued by the whole topic."

"By the time I realized how much I'd said, it was way too late." She looked down at the floor. "That's when I got sick."

"Well...it's done. Hiram's sure not going to be very happy about this," Regan said resignedly. "Just last night I told him it was only a matter of time before some TV crew came sniffing around." Thinking about last night, the full impact of what Veronica had just said hit home. If the investigation was now common knowledge, and there was a perpetrator of some kind behind it, then now... "Oh, *fuck*," she whispered.

"Regan, I don't think...no one there acted like they thought you were weird or evil or anything. I don't think you have to worry—"

"It's not that, Ver." She got up and walked to the office door, peered out into the empty store, came back and sat down again. "Veronica, it's not just the investigation being compromised. I told Hiram last night I was done with it. I'm not doing any more interviews. But I've already been working on this case for a month. What if these incidents have some perpetrator behind them?"

"Perpetrator? You mean...like a person, a criminal?"

"Exactly."

Veronica looked slightly green. "But you never said...I mean, I thought this was just...like ghosts or UFO's, something paranormal."

"We learned a little bit more last night," Regan said heavily, "which is why I've quit."

Veronica looked horrified. "God, Regan...I never thought—but, really, there weren't that many people listening last night. I don't think any of them could have a connection to, to any criminals...what are the odds, really?"

"Well, let's see. After the party last night, the pool of people who potentially know about this includes Jonathan, all of our friends, The Akins-Klein Biotechnology Corporation, Theo's band and the New England Patriots."

"Oh, they weren't all—"

"And," Regan went on over Veronica's words, "if each one of them tells five people, and those people all tell five people, and *those* people all tell five people... what are the odds, really?" The front door bells jingled. "You can wait here for me, if you want," Regan said. She got up and walked briskly to the front counter, hoping that by the time the customer made a purchase, her hands would have stopped shaking so much. Whether she was shaking primarily from fear or anger, she didn't try to analyze.

Two more customers came in while the first was still browsing, and it was twenty-five minutes before Regan had a chance to go back to the office where Veronica was waiting, legs crossed with her foot laced behind her calf. Her arms were tightly folded over her chest, fingers of one hand pressed against her chin, and her eyes looked a bit redder than they had been. Regan sat down on the office chair and looked at Veronica helplessly.

"It's not your fault, Ver," she sighed. "I never should have told you. What's that saying, two people can keep a secret if one of them is dead?" Even as she said it, Regan felt a cold knot clench in the pit of her stomach. *And that just might happen yet...*

"You should have been able to trust me," Veronica whispered. "I'll never forgive myself if something happens to you."

"It won't. Don't even say it. I'm just curious, though—who was buying you all those drinks? Was it Jonathan?"

"I don't know. People were buying rounds--even I bought one."

"It does sound just a little bit like he got you drunk and then manipulated you into answering his questions."

Veronica straightened up sharply. "Oh, no, it was nothing like that! Jonathan wouldn't do that."

"But it does sound like it. I'm just not sure I like this guy, that's all."

Veronica bristled. "It's not his fault that I screwed up. Anyway, I think Derek bought me some of the drinks."

Regan snorted. "Okay, that's plausible. Poor Derek. But tell me, Ver, after all that time at the club last night, do you know anything more about Jonathan than you did before? Where is he from, what's his book about, where did he go to college, how old he is? Anything?"

"We didn't talk about things like that. It was party talk."

"Yeah, right..." The door bells jingled again, and Regan saw that five people were coming inside. "Look, Ver, it's probably going to get busy, this morning it was a zoo in here. I'll call you later, okay?"

"Okay..." Veronica got up, dabbing delicately under her eyes with the tissue in case her eyeliner had run.

"Thanks for coming in and telling me, though. At least now I'm forewarned if there is any fallout."

Regan's prediction was accurate—the rest of the afternoon was busy enough to blunt her apprehension about Veronica's indiscretion at the club. At 7:00 p.m. there were still browsers in the store, and Regan turned the CLOSED sign over and pulled down the shade on the front door, but let the customers tarry. She was rewarded with another $22.98 in sales by the time they finally departed at 7:18 and she could lock the door and turn out the lights.

She sank down in the rolling office chair, which had never felt so comfortable. Her feet, despite the Nike cross-trainers that she wore out of sheer practicality, were aching, and she still had the last vestiges of a headache after three extra-strength acetaminophen. She leaned back, closing her eyes, and sighed. *What a day,* she thought. *Should I call Hiram and tell him about Veronica spilling the beans?* The prospect was significantly less appealing than gum surgery. *No, he'll be calling me soon enough, I'll wait until then.*

After a moment, she roused herself. She needed to cash out and get a deposit ready to drop off, at the very least. She didn't open until noon on Sunday, so she could clean and restock and straighten up tomorrow morning, but it wouldn't do to leave this much money in the store overnight, even in the safe. For the next half hour, she busied herself with tabulating receipts and banding bills. She had just locked the cash drawer into the safe and was straightening up the desk top, when she was startled by a sound that she had been a slave to all day: the door bells jingled as someone opened the front door, then closed it.

Regan suddenly felt cold. *What the hell...?* She had locked the door—hadn't she? She was sure she had locked it. She did it without even thinking. But it had been so busy, and she'd let those last browsers stay late... There was no sound from out front, and she couldn't see the door or the main aisle from where she sat. "Hello?" she called. "I'm sorry, we close at seven. Can I help you?" She reached for the cordless, but the base unit was empty. She'd been letting calls go to voice mail, and the cordless was still up on the front counter. *Shit.* Well, there was no use hiding. She'd have to leave the office to get to the back exit, it was beside the candle display. She rolled the chair back and peered out the office door down the main aisle. There was a figure silhouetted against the backlit shade of the door, but she couldn't make out any detail. She could feel her heart beating hard, and her mouth was dry. But then the mystery visitor spoke.

"Oh, there you are. I'm sorry if I scared you. My name is Jonathan Vaughn. Are you Regan Calloway?" The shadowy figure walked easily toward the office door, his steps nearly silent on the thin carpet.

After all the time she'd spent hearing about, and talking about, this man, Regan felt as though she was meeting a celebrity. "Mr. Vaughn! Yes, I'm Regan Calloway. This is...this is quite a surprise." Jonathan reached the doorway and paused just outside it, in the wedge of light that splayed from the open door. *So this is him,* Regan thought as she took in his appearance. *I was right, he isn't Veronica's type.* Veronica liked men who were taller than she was in her heels, broad-shouldered and athletic. Jonathan was compact, lean and limber, more like a gymnast than a sports star. He had thick dark hair and eyebrows in a pale, strong-boned face that was agreeably interesting rather than handsome. His clothing, generic dark slacks and a sweater, was far more understated than the usual style that attracted Veronica's eye. After a couple of seconds Regan realized that she had been staring at him rather obviously, but then, he had been returning the favor. His dark eyes were studying her with an intensity that would have been disquieting if he hadn't had such a pleasant and disarming smile. Clearing her throat self-consciously, Regan said, "It's nice to meet you at last, Mr. Vaughn. I've heard so much about you." Her tone was a little arch.

"Likewise on both counts—as I believe you heard this afternoon," he said in a tone that matched hers. "But please, it's just Jonathan, you're making me feel old."

"Sorry." He certainly didn't look old—she would have estimated his age as five to seven years less than her own. His demeanor made him seem older.

"I'm afraid I made a mistake about your closing time. I thought it was eight. I saw your office light was on back here, and I tried the door. I guess I should have knocked first."

Why do I not believe him? The store hours were posted on the front door, but it was getting dark outside now. "I was sure that I locked it. I better be more careful."

"Yes, you should be," he said seriously. "You must be brave, to work all alone in a place like this."

What does he mean, a place like this? Regan suddenly felt annoyed. "I've never felt that I needed to be brave. This is a quiet town, I grew up here. The only problem I've ever had is an occasional shoplifter. Are you planning Borrowed and Blue's first holdup in thirty-five years, or are you just trying to make me nervous?"

He looked, for a moment, genuinely perturbed. "Of course not! I'm sorry, I certainly didn't mean to offend you."

The suspicion that she had overreacted made Regan even more irritable. "Well—why don't you sit down, since you're here." *I'm not afraid of you, for god's sake!* she thought, fuming. She indicated the straight-backed chair, and he stepped into the room and sat down, with a lithe grace not common in men. Regan wondered what kind of physical training he'd had—either dance or martial arts came to mind. As he sat, for a moment she thought he had a smile that was almost a smirk, but it instantly disappeared. *No, I don't like you,* she thought. She was also acutely conscious of the plump zippered bank deposit folder sitting on the desk, but moving it now would only draw attention to it. She tried to put all thoughts of it from her mind. "So...what can I do for you, Jonathan? Since you've taken the trouble to stop by after hours and let yourself in, I'm assuming you've got something important on your mind."

He smiled, although his eyes were serious. "I think it's important, yes. Veronica relayed to me that you were quite upset this afternoon to hear that you had been a general topic of conversation at the club party last night. I've come to apologize for my part in that. I should have known better."

"I see. Was this a spontaneous impulse on your part or did Veronica send you over here?" The thought that someone else knew Jonathan would be coming to the store made her feel safer, somehow. She was still a bit unnerved that he had just walked inside.

"She *suggested* that I stop by and talk to you, yes," Jonathan said wryly.

"I can just imagine. No problem, Jonathan—apology accepted. I'm certainly used to being talked about, and I'd be a bald-faced liar if I said I never gossiped, either. That's half the fun of running a store like this. You can just imagine the rumors I've heard about you, for instance."

His smile broadened, but he refused to be baited. "I certainly can. I hope that publishers are as interested in my book as everyone in Sheridan seems to be."

"So you don't have an advance yet?"

"No, I have the luxury of being able to wing it—although not indefinitely." His expression was teasing, as if he was just waiting for her to ask, like everyone else, what he was writing about.

"I wish you the best of luck shopping it around, then," Regan said after a moment. "I hope no one will have to leave town when it comes out."

He laughed. "Oh, my, just what kind of book am I suspected of writing here? Aside from me, who do you think would have to leave town?"

"Oh, I don't know. Me? The Standishes? The entire school board?"

His smile became almost sly. "I can promise you that I am not writing about you. On all other speculations, I'll plead the fifth. Everyone will just have to wait and see."

Okay, you win that one, Regan thought sourly. "I hope you don't think I'm insufferably egotistical, suggesting that you'd be writing about me. But it does sound like you were awfully curious about me last night. Who told you that I was...what was it you called me, a clairvoyant?"

"Derek Wilson. The rental agent who handled the house listing. He said that if I was a writer, I'd probably want to meet you."

"Derek is too kind." Regan's tone conveyed the opposite opinion. She saw Jonathan's brow crease, and before he could speak again, she said, "But I'm glad that you came in tonight, Jonathan. I've been rather anxious for a chance to talk to you in private."

"Really? What about?"

"About Veronica."

He raised his eyebrows knowingly. "Let me guess. You want to know what my intentions are. I gathered that from her."

"She's also wondering what your intentions are." Regan hesitated, then took in a deep breath. "I think you know why she wanted me to come and meet you at the club last night."

His expression had become wary, although his voice was still light. "She didn't say it in so many words, but I did figure out for myself what was going on."

"I wasn't all that comfortable with the idea, but I could understand why Veronica was asking me. Veronica is a person..." Regan hesitated, wanting to choose her words carefully, in case Jonathan was the type of man who would repeat their conversation to her friend. "...who doesn't tolerate ambiguity well. She needs clear messages, yes or no. If you don't want to be involved with her, you need to say so. Otherwise, she's going to assume...well, that the attraction is mutual. I'm not asking you to tell me, Jonathan. I'm saying that you need to tell her. She feels that she's getting mixed signals from you."

He nodded, and was silent for a moment, looking at her. "You're certainly honest and to the point."

"I try to be. I've been told I sometimes carry it too far."

"You realize," he said cautiously, "that people often think they want honesty, but are devastated to actually hear it."

"But ultimately it's much kinder. Letting someone down gently isn't the same thing as leaving them in limbo. Veronica deserves to know what she's getting into. The last thing she needs is another...learning experience. If you follow me."

"I do," he said after a moment. "She has told me a few things about her past experiences. I'm very sorry that she's had such a hard time."

"She doesn't need pity, Jonathan. She just needs some clarity. But a little openness and sharing is never a bad thing. I wouldn't mind getting some of that from you, myself."

He straightened up a little. "What do you mean by that?"

"It means that I've been wondering just who you are and what you do. Okay, I can understand keeping your book project confidential. But no one seems to know the simplest things about you—where you're from, where you went to school, whether you're single, separated, or divorced—anything like that. Why all the secrets?"

He hesitated, then raised his hands in a gesture of confusion. For some reason, Regan found it unconvincing. "I don't have any secrets. No one's asked me these questions. What do you think I could have to hide?"

"Of course people haven't been interrogating you. That would be rude," Regan said, as if stating the obvious. "Usually when someone is new, they volunteer information in conversations. That's the normal way of building trust."

He shrugged. "I've never been one to talk about myself. I wouldn't want to bore everyone to death. I'm really a very uninteresting person."

Regan almost snorted. "Jonathan. Whenever I hear someone say that, I know that they're probably the least boring person in the room."

He leaned forward towards her. "Are you sure you're asking all these things on Veronica's behalf? I think you're the one who really wants to know."

Regan suddenly felt furious. *What a cocksure little jerk!* "A lot of people in town are curious about you, me included. But if you're serious about Veronica, you should tell her these things. She shouldn't have to get it from me."

"If you're so interested, and so suspicious, then perhaps...you'd like to do that reading, after all." There was something almost baiting in his voice.

Regan drew back from him. "No. I wouldn't. I don't like being challenged to pick people's brains, and I don't like being treated as a form of entertainment. I had a craw full of being expected to magically guess every detail about people I was introduced to. I'd ask someone, 'how are you,' and they'd say, 'you're the psychic, you tell me.' It's not *funny!*" Her voice had risen, because he was suddenly grinning.

"I can see how that would get tiresome. But so does being suspected of hiding something just because I don't walk around prattling about my life. Even if I did, how would you know I wasn't lying? I'm a writer."

"Exactly. I've had some bad experiences with writers."

"Oh?"

"Yes, I've found that they generally have no qualms whatsoever about leading someone on if they think they can get a profitable story out of it."

"Is that what you think I'm doing?"

"I'm just saying that's been my experience."

There was a moment's silence as they looked at each other. Then Jonathan laughed ruefully. "Well. I'm getting the very strong impression that I'll be wasting my time asking you for any more details about the stories being bandied about last night."

Regan slowly folded her arms and nodded. "And now we get to the real reason that you came in—without Veronica. I figured as much."

"Well, really. Can you blame me for being fascinated by what I heard? And don't I get any credit for coming right to the source, instead of slithering around town trying to pick up hearsay from other people? And, no—" he held up one hand. "Before you say it, I was not plying Veronica with drinks last night to loosen her tongue and get her to answer questions. Yes, she told me about that."

"It did sound like it, you know," Regan said a bit defensively, "and it's not as if that kind of thing never happens."

"She didn't talk about you and your...cases nearly as much as she seems to believe she did. There was a general conversation going on and it rambled all over the place. There weren't many details at all about this investigation you've been doing."

Regan sighed, partly from relief. "That's because there aren't many details to tell. And the investigation has been closed. We've tried, we've dead-ended, I told Hiram I'm tired of it and I won't do any more."

"With no resolution at all?" Regan shook her head. "That's a shame. To just give up when you've invested so much time into it."

"I should never have let myself be talked into it in the first place."

"Even after reading all those people—you were doing psychic readings on them? You still didn't learn anything about what could be causing their symptoms?"

Regan gave him a long, hard look. "I really don't wish to discuss it further."

He shook his head. "You must have been burned very badly at some point. I wish I could have a serious talk with whoever did this to you."

"I wish you could, too," Regan said sarcastically. "It would be a novelty to have someone stand up for me for a change."

He made a small tsking sound. "Regan. We've just met and you already seem to have a dismal opinion of me. What can I do to fix this? Answer your questions? Fine, go ahead. Ask me whatever you like."

"I'm not going to sit here and play Twenty Questions with you. Like you said, you could make up anything you want. How would I know the difference?"

"Show you my driver's license?"

Regan looked away from him, feeling her cheeks redden slightly. "Oh, this is silly."

"Not sterling enough proof? All right..." In the silence that followed, Regan finally looked back at him, and saw that he was extending his hand toward her, as if for a handshake, relaxed and open. "I noticed that you avoided shaking hands with me when I came in. And Veronica told me why. Go on, Regan. See for yourself. I have nothing to hide from you. No blocking you off. I'm wide open. Go on."

She stared at his hand, her mouth suddenly dry. "Are you just making fun of me?"

"No. What were you going to do last night, if you'd been there? Offer to rub my shoulders? Pretend to read my palm? Squeeze in between me and someone else like it was an accident? Try to pick up something comprehensible over all the conversation and music, while wondering what I was thinking of you?"

Regan looked down, feeling her face reddening even more, to her annoyance. "You sound like you've had some experience with this sort of thing."

"I'm not making fun of you." Now his voice was low and earnest. "I'm simply pointing out that all the disadvantages you were prepared to work against last night are no longer in your way. It's fairly obvious that you don't trust people easily, Regan, and maybe you have good reasons for that. This is something that you do trust. I'm offering it freely. Go ahead."

Regan started to extend her hand, then paused. Her heart was beating hard. "You're sure...you want this."

"Oh, I'm *very* sure." His eyes were watching her avidly.

So he wants to know what it's all about, Regan thought. *All right, fine. We'll see what we get. Maybe I can pull the title of his book up and really impress him.* She rolled the office chair forward a few inches so she was in easy reach of his extended hand, rubbing both her own hands together briskly. "Okay, but remember, you asked for this," she said, and she grasped his hand with her own. She felt his fingers pressing against her skin, and registered that his hand was dry and oddly cool to the touch. Then, without any warning, a violent shock went through her from fingertips to feet, and she was paralyzed by the coldest horror she had ever felt. Although her eyes were open, she was blind to everything in the room around her. To her inner vision, usually subtle and shifting, it was as though a curtain had been brutally pulled down from a window to admit blazing sunlight. One after another, she saw the people she had interviewed, and then others, all from the perspective of an unseen attacker. She experienced each one approached and caught from behind before they even realized anyone was near, each one struggling blindly, mouth muffled, each one *drunk* from, his or her struggles suddenly stopping with limp muscles and unconscious mind. Regan could feel each of their bodies and taste their blood in her mouth, as vividly as she'd felt and tasted Evelyn's the night before. She tried to recoil, but she didn't seem able to move. *Back, let me go back* she thought desperately, and she did—back in time. Images and sounds flickered past like a fast cut film montage, people, places, costumes and buildings changing in a dizzying blur. Then she was looking at the street she had seen last night, but it was dark, lit by gaslight and moonlight. Three young men, almost boys, were facing her, one of them saying, *give it over, then.* All three of them rushed at her and she was wrestling with them, beating off their hands, wanting only to get away, until a tearing pain in her abdomen made her fall to her knees. She heard herself crying out, and she heard another voice along with her own, and realized that these impressions were going both ways. Jonathan was seeing and feeling what she was. Regan had shared impressions with a subject before, but only rarely, and never with such intensity as this. She tried to pull her hand free, but she couldn't.

It was Jonathan who wrenched his hand out of her own then, with some difficulty. He had to grip her wrist with his other hand to pull free. Finally released, Regan slowly became aware once more of the small office, the chair she was sitting in, the lamp on the desk—it seemed that she had been trapped in a nightmare for hours. She stared down at the red marks on her hand left by Jonathan's fingers, trying to comprehend what she had just seen. She drew in a long ragged breath and looked up into Jonathan's eyes. He appeared somewhat stunned, and he was bent forward a little in his chair, a hand pressed to his stomach as though he was in pain. But when he saw her looking at him, his expression hardened, and he straightened up.

"That...was quite...amazing," he said.

His voice had a hollow sound through her shock, and it was very familiar to her. It was the voice she had heard last night. She stared at him, thinking that he wasn't tall at all, just...*average height*...and then reality, and adrenaline, kicked in. Without another conscious thought she said, "Oh, *fuck*," and was on her feet and running for the door, as fast as she had ever run in her life. But he was much faster. She didn't even make it past the threshold of the office. He caught her in a sort of hug that pinned her arms to her sides, and both of them fell onto the aisle carpet just outside the doorway. She struggled against his arms and kicked hard at his legs as they fell, but within a second or two after they were on the floor, she was flat on her back and he was holding her wrists in one hand and pinning her legs down with one of his own, as he lay stretched alongside her. He seemed to be exerting almost no effort at all, but Regan felt as if she was pinned down by steel girders. This alone was terrifying. There was no rational way to explain his strength. "Let me go, let me go, I won't tell anyone, I swear, let me go..." she babbled, panicked, and then he released her wrists and pushed himself up so he could look down at her face.

"Regan, don't," he said urgently. "I'm not going to kill you, if that's what you think, I've never killed anyone, look, I'll show you—" and he pressed his open hands to the sides of her face. She was immediately overwhelmed by a torrent of impressions—thoughts and emotions and images so rapid and intense that she cried out in protest.

"Stop it, stop it, it's too much, I can't take that much in at once." He removed his hands, leaving her gasping for breath. If he had meant to prove that he wasn't a killer, it had been pointless; the tide of impressions defied her ability to interpret them. She couldn't even pick out individual thoughts or memories, it was simply an incoherent mass of psychic noise. She felt stunned, as though she had been subjected to a deafening blast of sound.

"I'm sorry," he said softly. "What else can I do to convince you?"

He hitched himself up a bit further and pressed the back of his hand against one side of her face. Thinking he was going to try again to flood her consciousness with impressions, Regan twisted her face away from him, realizing too late that she was doing exactly what he wanted her to do. Before she could react, he bent down and pressed his open mouth against the bare skin of her neck. She flinched back, but he was still pinning her down so tightly, it was impossible for her to move far. His mouth was cool and wet, and she shuddered as she felt his tongue searching her skin. Even then, it was only when the pressure tightened and there was a brief, sharp pain and an unpleasant sensation like rotted cloth tearing, that she understood exactly was he was doing. She was too shocked to do anything except whisper, "oh, shit..." For a few seconds she was afraid to move. He made a sigh in the back of his throat, but there was no sensation from his drinking at all except the soft pressure of his mouth. Regan put her hands against his shoulders, wanting to push him away, but all her muscles were going loose, buzzing and tingling like a foot getting numb, and they wouldn't obey her will. After perhaps thirty seconds, which felt like a very long time, Regan was getting queasy and she was starting to feel dizzy and breathless. Then he stirred, and there was an icy, pinching sensation where his mouth was. She could feel his tongue licking her skin for a few moments, and she winced, because it hurt. Then he sat up, licking his lips pensively. Regan stared at the blurry shelf that was directly in her line of vision, feeling sensation returning to her arms and legs, and trying to grasp what had just happened.

"And now you know everything," he said. His voice was quiet and very calm, almost blissful. He seemed in no hurry to leave, but collected himself comfortably on the floor, arms resting on one upraised knee. It seemed that he wanted to continue their conversation.

After a minute or so, Regan recovered enough to urgently wish not to be lying flat on on her back while he was so close. She had to roll on her side and push herself up with her arms to sit up, and waves of vertigo washed over her when she did. "Not too fast, you'll faint," he said. She drew in deep, slow breaths and her sense of equilibrium gradually returned. She pulled her legs under her and found a stable sitting position. At the place on her neck where he had drunk, an aching, tingling pain was awakening, as though anesthetic was wearing off. She reached up and touched it, gingerly, and felt a puckered lump on the skin, hot and damp. *Oh, great, now I'm going to have one of those ugly things,* she thought. She looked up at him, and saw that he was watching her with an expression of mild concern.

"That's what you came in here for," she said finally, her voice wavering. "You wanted to see what I would pick up from you. If I would spot you for the one who's been doing all these things."

"That was part of it. Although I must admit, I could never have imagined just how intense your readings are. Is that typical of what you do?"

"Oh my god, no. They're never like that. Last night was—" she broke off. "You knew I was lying about not having any details."

"I certainly suspected. I thought there must be some reason that you suddenly stopped these investigations, and Veronica told me that you mentioned fearing a perpetrator. She was quite upset that she might have put you in danger. I've had to swear never to mention the subject again, except to you, of course."

Regan shook her head helplessly. "I would never have identified you."

"Now I know that," he said, and she remembered that he'd seen her vision and knew that she'd been reading his point of view. "But you can imagine how concerned I was when I heard why you had quit. And it was only a matter of time before we met, and you kept your promise to Veronica and contrived to touch me. I feel very fortunate now that it didn't happen in the middle of a crowd of people."

Imagining what that would have been like, Regan closed her eyes for a moment. "No shit." But something had occurred to her, and she looked back up at Jonathan, her brows creasing. "Wait a minute, though. Why do I remember everything?"

"Would you rather forget it all?"

She recoiled. "No!"

"It's too late to do it now, anyway. I didn't blank your memory because I didn't want to. And even if I'd wanted to, it wouldn't really have helped. You know too much, and it covers too long a period of time. There's no finesse to what I do—it's like cracking someone over the head with a board. You'd wake up with a few hours missing, and the minute you looked in the mirror, you'd know what must have happened. And it would only be a matter of time before you happened to touch me, or someone else, or something else, that would blow my cover and fill your memory back in. So, what would have been the point?"

"But—you said you didn't want to?"

"No. I didn't."

"But, wh—" she stopped, for some reason unable to simply ask, "why?" Instead she said, "aren't you afraid that I'll report this to the police?"

He smiled. "Will you?"

"Well, I...I *should*."

"But *will* you? What kind of a report will you make?"

Regan ran her tongue over her dry lips, thinking, *Officer, I'd like to report that I've been attacked by a*—Jonathan was watching her closely.

"I'll tell you what," he said easily. He got up, walked to the front counter, returned with the cordless phone, and handed it to her. Regan sat looking at it stupidly. "Go ahead and call the police. Nine one one. Say you're alone in your store and you've just been assaulted, and it's the same perpetrator who's been committing assaults all over the area. The one you've been investigating with your psychic powers." She looked up at him sharply. "All right, don't say that. But you can say you need medical attention, and you can tell them everything that happened. You can even give them my name."

"Won't you—don't you care?"

"I haven't put any roots down yet. I can blow town like that." He snapped his fingers. "And you needn't worry about reprisals. You'd never see me again. That isn't what I've been planning to do, but I can do it. They won't catch me."

She let her hand drop to her knee. "Then what's the point of my reporting it?"

"Wouldn't it be the right thing to do?"

She stared down at the phone. *Of course it's the right thing, what would Hiram say if he knew I...*

"Maybe you're thinking that I'm just testing you. I've cut the phone lines, and the minute you try to dial, I'll pounce on you and—"

"I hadn't thought of that, no, thank you very much!" Her voice had risen from a mixture of anger and fear. He reached over and punched the Talk button on the cordless, and the dial tone blared between them. Against that sound, Regan could hear an imaginary male voice, after she'd hung up from her call: *Ah, it's just that nut case psychic again, now she thinks she's been attacked. Go check it out, willya? Or she'll be calling all night.* Slowly, she pushed the phone's Off button and let her hand and the phone sink to the carpet.

"What can it be," Jonathan said softly, "that scares you more than I do?"

Stung, Regan straightened her back and glared at him defiantly. "What makes you think I'm scared of you?" She half expected him to jeer at her, but he only smiled.

"Of course you're not scared of me. Look what a nice talk we're having. I left your memory intact, and you're not going to report me to the police. That sounds like a great start to me."

She stared at him incredulously. "A great start to *what?*" Without thinking, she touched the painful lump on her neck again, and suddenly she burst out, "This is all some kind of a *joke*, isn't it? This can't be real!"

"Who would be playing a joke on you, Regan?"

"Oh, *fuck* you!" She threw the phone at him. He caught it deftly in mid air. His smile was gone.

"It's no joke, Regan. There are times I've wished otherwise. But no one is playing a joke on you." He set the phone down gently on the carpet. "I'm not trying to manipulate you, or coerce you, or intimidate you...any of the things you might be thinking. I don't want to *hurt* you."

She stared at him, confused by the dissonance between his attitude and her sense of outrage. "Oh, no," she burst out bitterly, "you only—let's see, knocked me to the floor, pinned me down, and, and—excuse me, drank my blood! You *drank my blood!*" Before she could think or stop herself, she slapped his face, as hard as she could. The crack of her hand against his cheek rang in the air. He pulled back, blinking, although he hadn't flinched away from the blow, and his cheek didn't redden as a normal person's would have if struck so hard.

"Well," he said matter-of-factly, "You read my mind, secrets and all. You were going to sneak up on me and read me unawares, in fact."

"There's no comparison," Regan said angrily, but even as she spoke she felt a qualm of guilt. He was right—her moral ground might be higher than his, but not by much. "Why do you *do* that? What the fuck *are* you?"

"What do you think?" he said softly.

"Don't play with me!"

"I'm not. I'm asking you what you think. That's the only answer you'll believe."

"I wouldn't have asked you if I already..." but she broke off, realizing that she was dissembling now, even to herself.

"Oh, come on. Those were rhetorical questions if I ever heard any. If someone else had asked them, I'd say otherwise, but you?" Reckless of another slap, he leaned toward her. "Do you believe that I'm just some sort of...sociopathic rapist? Just a normal man with some serious antisocial tendencies who needs to be stopped?" He waited, as Regan stared down at the carpet. She opened her mouth to reply, desperately wanting to say *yes*...but she couldn't force the word out. It was too big a lie to say aloud. After a long silence, Jonathan said, "If that's what you believe, then call the police."

Unwillingly, Regan found herself going back to the impressions of the attacks, on Evelyn, on the others, flinching away from the tactile elements that were so overwhelming, asking herself for the first time, *I know what he did, but what was he feeling? What was he thinking?* But it was too raw and overpowering to deal with, especially now.

"Is that what you believe?" Jonathan said again.

She had to say something to defend the crumbling boundaries of her own sense of reality. "It's...it's not possible."

"Then call the police." She shook her head. The boundaries were falling, and even worse, he seemed to understand exactly what was going on in her mind. Very quietly, he said, "Everything...you're thinking...is true." She drew in a long ragged breath. When she looked back up at him, he met her eyes unwaveringly, and there was not the slightest hint of mockery or teasing in his expression.

"I don't understand this," she said.

"It's all in here." He reached out to touch her temple. She pulled back so hard she almost lost her balance, and he withdrew his hand. "I held nothing back."

Regan covered her face with her hands for a moment. "You could have," she said bitterly. "I wouldn't have minded." She let her hands fall into her lap. "I just don't know what to do."

"Why don't you sleep on it?" His voice was so low it was almost a murmur. Then he stood up. "I should let you finish out your day and go home. After all, you've got a full work shift ahead of you tomorrow." He reached down. After looking at his hand for a minute, Regan took hold of it and allowed him to help her to her feet. This time, there were no impressions from his touch—he must have been blocking them off, the way people normally did if they knew about her abilities. She swayed and had to grab hold of the shelf unit next to her for a moment, but after some deep breaths she felt able to walk. "Don't forget about your deposit," Jonathan said, and she realized that he'd noticed the folder on the desk the moment he walked in. He started to leave, but when he was almost at the door, Regan was struck by something.

"Jonathan," she said. He paused, turning back to her. "I did lock that door, didn't I?"

He smiled. "Yes, as a matter of fact. You did."

Chapter 5

The next morning, Regan awoke after a solid ten hours of dreamless sleep, the longest and deepest sleep she had experienced in weeks. She lay in bed for a time, looking up at the smooth ceiling above her, which was covered by complex overlapping patterns of soot from the candles and incense she was fond of burning. There was a faint smell of cooking bacon from the apartment below hers. The injury on her neck was sore to the touch, but felt dry and tightly sealed. She thought about what had happened last night. What surprised her was how calm she felt now. It was as though a tremendous burden had been lifted from her mind. The mystery was solved, and all her anxiety about what could be causing the incidents, how dangerous it might be, and whether she would suffer consequences from meddling in it was gone. The unknown had stopped in and introduced itself, and she had been inducted into the club.

I'm still pissed off at him for what he did. But even that sense of indignation was fading before her pure curiosity at the mystery of who and what he was. Over and over in her mind she went back to the impressions she'd collected, both in her own readings and the ones Jonathan had fed to her when he touched her face. She picked out details and went over sequential events and tried to home in on elements like feeling and thought and sound that existed in the background of the stronger visual and tactile signals. But the core answers she was seeking continued to elude her. What was Jonathan, really? That he was *something* preternatural, she had some evidence for. But all the social and psychological and fictional baggage that had accrued around the word "vampire"—what was true and what was not? Did even he know? How could she tell the difference between something that was true and something he sincerely, but wrongly, believed about himself? And most of all, why had he shown her so much and simply allowed her to walk away? He trusted her to know everything about him and not to expose him, and she didn't have a clue about his motive. *Now I'm ready to play Twenty Questions,* she thought defiantly. *I'm just going to have to talk to him.* She would have to go out to his house—she didn't have his phone number. *Maybe Veronica will give it to me,* she thought, smiling reluctantly at the irony of this notion. Then her smile faded. *I should call Veronica and let her know I met Jonathan last night. God help me if she finds out from someone else.* But she wasn't sure what she would say. An accurate summary of their encounter was obviously out of the question. She would have to think about it and come up with some plausible story.

She finally got up, and sat on the edge of the bed fighting off a moment of vertigo. *Fluids, that's what I need,* she thought, and she got up and went to her small kitchen. She drank orange juice straight out of the carton while the coffee maker brewed coffee for her breakfast and for the antique thermos. It was a little cooler than the day before but still bright and sunny. *We certainly lucked out for the holiday weekend this year,* she thought, although the light bothered her eyes a bit. She wasn't very hungry, but she knew she should eat something, and settled on toast and peanut butter.

She had to rummage in her closet to find a turtleneck sweater that would cover the injury. Most people wouldn't have any idea what it was, and she could have put a bandage on it, but if Hiram should stop in, his suspicions would be instantly aroused. Regan didn't want to have to handle that situation.

She arrived at Borrowed and Blue by 10:30, and got the vacuum out of the office. Cleaning took a bit longer than usual, as she had to pace herself. When she got to the end of the center aisle, she noticed several small cast brass pieces, an ashtray, candleholders and a little candy dish, on the side of the carpet under their shelf. She realized they must have been knocked off the shelf when she'd tried to run and Jonathan had caught her. As she knelt down to pick them up, the terror of that moment momentarily returned, and she broke into a cold sweat, her stomach queasy. But then the feeling was gone, and she gathered the items and replaced them on the shelf.

She was just putting the cash drawer into the register when the cordless buzzed. "Borrowed and Blue, yes we're open today," she answered puckishly. It was Hiram Clauson.

"Good morning, Regan."

"Oh, hello, Hiram," Regan said uneasily, her stomach feeling as though the floor had just dropped a few inches. He didn't know about Veronica and the club party yet. "Don't tell me there's been another event."

"Not that I've heard about. I knew you'd probably be very busy yesterday, and I have papers to grade, so I decided to give both of us a break. But I did wonder if we could get together tonight? I'd just like to go over some things with you, if that's possible."

Regan glanced out at the front lot. "Look, Hiram, I'm just opening, so I can't talk. But yes, if you want to stop by after I close tonight, we can go get something to eat. Make it around seven, I'll be open tomorrow and I'll need to get some work done after I lock up at six. Is that okay?"

"That works fine for me."

"Great. See you then." She clicked off the phone and went around the counter to unlock the door, feeling a deep disquiet settle into the pit of her stomach.

It turned out to be a relatively quiet afternoon, certainly by comparison with the day before. Normally Regan would have been somewhat disappointed, but today she was relieved. If she stood up too fast, she got dizzy and out of breath, and several customers asked her if she was feeling all right, because she looked so pale. She should have put a little makeup on, Regan realized, but she wore it so seldom now, she hadn't even thought of it. Her symptoms were eased somewhat by copious amounts of bottled water that she sipped all through the day. She caught herself making mistakes because she was so preoccupied. Her mind kept drifting back to the previous evening, and she found herself turning over bits of the conversation, or thinking about a detail from the two shattering psychic connections she had had with Jonathan. If she wasn't doing that, she was wondering what Hiram wanted to talk to her about, and how she could answer him. Several times customers had to repeat questions they'd just asked her. This was not a good thing, even though fortunately no one got particularly annoyed today. But there was plenty to keep her busy. When Hiram tapped on the front door at 6:50 p.m., Regan, sitting in the back office sorting the charge card receipts, jumped. She got up and went to the door. As she turned the lock, she wondered, as she had many times that day, just how Jonathan had gotten inside.

"Hello, Regan," Hiram said as he stepped into the store. He sounded tired, but not so tired that he didn't stop to peer at her closely. "You don't look well. Have you been sleeping all right?" He trailed her back to the office.

"I'm fine, Hiram. At least, I'll be fine when I can finally leave all this behind me. I told you, I'm finished with it."

"I know you said that. But there's no reason to believe these events won't continue. I won't be able to give up on this mystery until it's resolved, one way or another."

Avoiding his eyes, Regan concentrated on bundling up the receipts to put away in the safe. "Which may never happen. I said from the beginning that most of these phenomena remain unexplained. Usually they just stop, without ever giving researchers enough data to form any conclusions."

"And I agreed with you. But we've had a breakthrough. You've finally confirmed that there's a human perpetrator behind these incidents. Now our investigation can go in a new direction, a more fruitful one, I hope."

Regan locked the safe and took her jacket off its peg on the back of the office door. "I am not sure that I would agree with the word 'confirmed.' I don't think my reading qualifies as confirmation in any legal or scientific sense. And I'm not clear what you mean by a new direction. We're not the police, Hiram."

"Maybe we can talk about this over some dinner? You must be starving. Can we go to that little place down the road?"

"Sure." As she turned out the lights and they left the store, Regan had to restrain herself from heaving an audible sigh. She had told Hiram she wanted to quit, but if he was determined to continue with his investigation, she would rather know what he was doing and how much he was finding out. The best way to keep informed was to keep on working with him. But the longer she did that, the more difficult it would be to keep him from suspecting what she wasn't telling him. Hiram was an extremely perceptive man.

When they had gotten settled in a booth in Hong Kong Delhi, Regan braced herself inwardly and said, "Hiram—I've got something to tell you, and I'm afraid you're not going to be very happy about it."

He studied her over the top of his menu for a moment. "Go on."

Taking a deep breath, Regan told Hiram, as concisely as possible, about Veronica and the party conversation. Hiram listened with an expression of carefully suspended judgment. When Regan finished, he leaned back in his seat with an unhappy sigh.

"Why did you tell Veronica about the investigation in the first place, Regan? She doesn't sound like the most stable person in the world."

"She usually knows how to keep a secret," Regan said, thinking grimly of some of the secrets that Veronica had kept. "This wasn't like her, at all. Anyway, I didn't tell her confidential information like names and places, and you and I didn't have an explicit agreement not to talk about what we were doing. *You* have—you've been talking to police departments, hospital personnel, shelter managers, it must be scores of people."

"Professional people, in the course of gathering information. That's different."

"Not all of them have been sympathetic or receptive, and I'm sure they've talked to others about the psychologist who called them with this weird story—no, I'm sure they have, be honest with yourself, Hiram. And you told Evelyn the whole story, and the two people we saw before that."

"The victims have a right to know that others have had the same experience. That's often critical to any trauma victim's healing process: the feeling that he or she isn't alone, that the same thing has happened to other people."

"I'm not criticizing you, I'm just making a point. I needed someone to talk to about what was going on, a sounding board, someone besides you. Veronica's practically family, I don't think we *have* any secrets from each other. Who else was I going to confide in, my parents?"

Hiram raised his hands in a conciliatory gesture. "All right, I understand. Given the circumstances, there may not be serious repercussions. It was a big noisy party with a lot of other things going on—it wasn't like she called up a late-night radio show or talked to a reporter."

"She would never do *that*, Hiram. And she's mortified about it."

"Then let's just let it go. It does, however, add some urgency to our own priorities."

"I don't know how much more urgent we can be. We've interviewed everyone who can be interviewed for now." She took a long drink from her water glass, which was already half empty. Hiram watched her, his eyes narrowed.

"I'd like to take a different approach from this point. I'd like to contact area police departments and suggest to them that we may be dealing with a human assailant—a very clever, very skillful one with some unusual psychological quirks. If police know that reported incidents with certain elements could be more serious than they appear, they may be able to identify cases that are being disregarded now."

"And what if they do? Even if I agreed to keep on with the readings, Hiram—we weren't getting anywhere. I could read fifty more people and we'd be at the same dead end."

He hesitated for a moment. "If a new victim was agreeable to it...would you consent to another direct reading of an injury?"

"No."

"Regan..."

"Hiram, that was *horrible*. I just about threw up on the Stockards' carpet. Did you see how they all were looking at me? And I went through all that for nothing! I couldn't see the perpetrator. I couldn't see a single identifying detail. I saw nothing that we couldn't have logically inferred had happened based on what we already knew."

"There's no reason to believe that you'd react that badly every time. Maybe we can control the surroundings better, and make sure you're not tired or stressed or conflicted when the reading is scheduled. If you did more of those readings, it's possible that—"

"No." At the frustrated look on Hiram's face, Regan felt a qualm of guilt. "Hiram," she said more calmly, "You know, as well as I do, that psychic impressions aren't admissible in court. Readings like mine are helpful only if they lead to verifiable hard evidence. Even if I could identify this assailant, the police wouldn't even have grounds for questioning him without something to corroborate my claims. There are even circumstances where my involvement could be used by a defense attorney to cast doubt on the whole case. It's a very dicey situation."

Their dinners arrived, and Hiram waited until the server had put down the plates and left before he replied. "What if something entirely new comes up—a case with different details, or a victim with some memory? Or an independent witness?"

"If any of those things happen, then I might consider trying again. But not until there's something new. What's that joke about the definition of insanity, Hiram: doing the same thing over and over and expecting different results?"

He grunted and took some bites of his food. "I never cared for that stupid joke. If everyone followed that advice, no one would ever stay on a diet or persist in learning a new skill," he said, chewing sullenly.

"If you beat your head against a wall long enough, the wall will probably collapse. But right now, all I've got is a headache."

They ate in silence for a few minutes after that. Eventually Hiram said, "I didn't want to push you on Friday, because I knew you were pretty shaken up, but I was hoping that you could give me a full write-up about the readings with Evelyn Stockard. I've got all the others you gave me, and I know that initially there wasn't much variation from those subjects. But it would be very helpful if you could record everything you can recall from that second reading—given that it was so different from the ones up to that point."

Regan had to make an effort to swallow her food past the lump that was in her throat. Her hesitation, however, was not for the reason that she knew Hiram assumed. She felt a deep ambivalence about giving Hiram any information that he could use to identify the real perpetrator. She was unsure just why she felt this reluctance. If she protected Jonathan, after all, wasn't she in some way complicit in anything he did from now on? *I've never killed anyone,* Jonathan had said to her last night, and she believed him. But there were many ways to cause harm that fell short of killing. She remembered Hiram's words on Friday night: *impacting human beings and causing them pain and distress.* When did she become the kind of person who found that acceptable? But thinking about the possible implications of Hiram's continued investigation, Regan realized that she was certain of two things. She was confident that Jonathan would never blame her for whatever happened; and she knew that if he did what he said he would do last night, and disappeared forever, she would be devastated. She could not explain either of these certainties to herself, especially the second one.

"I realize that you don't want to re-live the experience you had on Friday," Hiram began, and Regan looked up at him, realizing that she had been quiet for a long time. She took a hasty gulp of tea and smiled weakly.

"No, it's all right, I was just...thinking. I had every intention of writing up your report, I just hadn't gotten to it yet. I'll do it as soon as possible, I promise. It's sort of a bad week for me, that's all."

"I just don't want you to forget too many details."

"I wouldn't worry about that," she said, clipping her words. She would have to think hard to recall as much as possible of the conversation after they had left the Stockards'. Anything she had said to Hiram would have to be in the report. Hiram had a highly trained ability to recall what was said to him.

They were almost finished with their food. In a casual tone, Hiram said, "I was just wondering if you've had a chance to meet your friend Veronica's romantic interest, as you called him. This Jonathan Vaughn fellow you were talking about."

"Uh..." *Now what do I say?* She'd always heard that staying as close to the truth as possible was the safest way to prevaricate. Keeping her voice light, she said, "Well—yes, actually. He stopped by the store yesterday."

"And is he boring?" Hiram asked, almost idly, as he poured himself some more tea. He looked up sharply as Regan, before she could stop herself, laughed out loud. "Evidently not."

"Sorry." Regan smothered her laugh with her hand. She cleared her throat and composed herself. "I feel like an idiot for having said that. No, no, he's...I misjudged him. Rather badly, in fact."

"I suspected you might be." Regan thought his inflection was just a little too innocent. "So, did you get an opportunity to check him out, like Veronica asked—or was he on alert after all that talk at the party?"

"He was alerted, all right—but he was curious about it. It wasn't a very... helpful reading." She was having some trouble thinking about last night and maintaining a natural attitude.

"Oh?"

"I've done readings that were more clear, let me put it that way. Not for lack of cooperation on his part, mind. But some people are like that. They're just hard to read."

"But you didn't pick up anything dire that you'll need to warn Veronica about, I trust."

Regan took in a deep breath. "Certainly nothing that she would take seriously," she said, with an effort. She was aware that Hiram was watching her closely and this made her uncomfortable. "I mean, Ver really wanted to know if he was a wife-beater or a dope dealer or has two ex-'s and six kids somewhere, that sort of thing. I didn't get anything like that."

"How lucky for Veronica. Was she there when you did this?"

The server cleared their plates and set down a little dish of pineapple chunks and maraschino cherries. "No," Regan said when the server had left, "He came in right about closing time, by himself."

Hiram frowned. "So you were all alone with him?"

"I am frequently alone with men, Hiram, the store is a public place."

"Well, I know, but..."

"But *what?*"

He paused, and then gave a little shrug and smiled. "You've been running the business solo for seven years, you must have good instincts."

Now who's prevaricating? Regan thought, but she started digging in her handbag for her wallet. "I'd like to think so."

Hiram sat back, studying her thoughtfully for a moment. "That's a very nice sweater. I haven't seen you wear one quite like that before."

She almost reached up and touched the collar before she stopped herself. "Oh, do you like it? I rescued it from a dollar-a-bag pile at a church thrift sale. It's genuine New Zealand lamb's wool."

"A true bargain." He took in a breath, as though there was something else he wanted to say, and then stopped.

As they were squaring up the bill and the tip, the restaurant's front door opened, letting in a gust of cold, damp air, and a group of several people came inside. Regan was busy counting ones and didn't glance up at them, so she was totally unprepared for the sound of a man's voice saying humorously, "I'm very flattered, Karen, but I think I'll wait until they've got at least one CD out before I'll talk about a book." Karen's reply was lost in laughter. Regan froze, her hand suddenly clenched around the crinkled bills.

"My god, Regan, what's the matter?" she heard Hiram say, and looked up in confusion to see him staring at her.

"The matter?"

"Are you all right? You just turned absolutely white."

"I did?" She was straining to catch more of the group's conversation, but they were moving to one of the larger tables on the far side of the dining room and she couldn't pick out individual voices. She touched her cheek, feeling some of the shock wear off. "I'm fine, I just felt...a little dizzy for a moment. I've been having these spells ever since Friday."

"Maybe you need to have that checked out," Hiram said with concern.

"I just think I need some rest." She finished sorting out her portion of the bill and put the money on the tray the server had left on the table with the check. As Hiram did the same, Regan peered around the corner of the booth at the large table. Yes, there was Veronica, whose height made her easily visible, and there was Derek, who also stood out in a crowd at 6'2". He was a perfect match for Veronica with his closely trimmed blond hair and a face that could have graced the cover of a romance novel, and he was still wearing a tailored dress shirt and tie from the realty office. There was plump Karen Tolbert, shimmering as always in brilliant colors, a ring on every finger—she was one of Regan's best customers for vintage costume jewelry. She still appeared to be on a major high from Theo's triumph at the club. With her was her fiancé Steve Hyatt, unfortunately no relation to the hotel moguls—they'd had the longest engagement of any couple Regan knew. Of the five, Derek was the odd man out, and not looking happy about it. Sitting on the other side of Veronica was Jonathan.

"Friends of yours?" Hiram said curiously, and Regan realized that he was following her gaze and was also examining the group dynamics across the room.

"Yes, they are. I'd like to go say hello, I haven't seen most of them lately." Even if that hadn't been true, she doubted that she and Hiram could have gotten out the door without someone at the table recognizing her and calling to them.

"Certainly. You can introduce me," Hiram said heartily, and Regan was confident that he guessed who some of the group were.

"I warn you, they may have heard your name from Veronica on Friday night. Be prepared for some curious questions."

"I'm sure I'm up to fielding inquiries."

They got up and walked over to the table, where the server had just left a round of drinks. As they approached, Karen spotted them first, and waved enthusiastically. "Regan! We missed you on Friday!"

"Yes, I know, I'm sorry."

"But you were there by reputation," Steve said jovially.

"So I hear. You're all going to be delighted. I'd like to introduce my co-conspirator. This is Dr. Hiram Clauson."

"Ah, the famous Dr. Clauson," Derek said.

"Hardly," Hiram said, chuckling.

"Look, have a seat, you two," Karen said. "There are two chairs right there by Jonathan, go on! Do you want anything to drink, we can call the waitress back—"

"We just had dinner, I'm stuffed. But if you'd like something, Hiram—".

"Go ahead and sit down," Hiram said, and Regan had little choice but to sit in the empty seat to the right of Jonathan, whose eyes she had been avoiding for a mixture of reasons. That seat was on a corner, so the one next to it almost put Hiram facing Jonathan—with Regan directly between them. She had noticed, from the corner of her eye, the sharp look that Hiram had given Jonathan when Karen mentioned his name, but he'd covered it very well.

"Let me just finish the introductions," Regan said. Choosing her starting point carefully, she said, "This is Karen Tolbert, whose stepbrother Theo is going to be famous any moment now..."

"Please convey my congratulations," Hiram said cheerfully.

"Thank you, I will."

"Steve Hyatt, who won't marry her..."

"Regan!" Karen sounded exasperated, but this was a running jibe between the two of them.

"I keep telling her, the dowry's just not big enough yet," Steve said.

"He means *his* dowry," Derek said.

"Derek Wilson, future real estate kingpin..."

"What do you mean, future?" Derek said.

"Oh, and he's a graduate of Yale. He wants you to know this."

"I'm impressed," Hiram said, although he looked mostly amused. Derek mumbled something into his drink.

"Veronica Standish, who I think I first met in the neonate unit, and who usually isn't this red, I don't know what's wrong with her tonight—"

"Regan, I'm going to *kill* you," Veronica burst out.

"So you keep saying! But don't fret, Hiram knows all about how you made him famous on Friday night and it's cool." Veronica looked down at the tablecloth in front of her, almost pouting. Regan took in a breath. "And this is Jonathan Vaughn, the soon to be celebrated writer."

"Pleased to meet you," Hiram said. He and Jonathan were sizing each other up obviously enough for Karen to give Regan a quizzical look. They only broke off studying each other when Steve spoke.

"Future fame, future fortune, I can't get over all the *potential* at this table," he said, raising his glass a little as if toasting their anticipated accomplishments. Only Veronica didn't echo his motion.

"And it's about time some of us started realizing some of it, too," Karen said.

"Oh, I don't know," Derek said. "Some of us have already realized plenty of potential, right, *Dr.* Clauson?"

Hiram just laughed. "I still have dreams to keep me motivated. Jonathan here doesn't look old enough to be hearing the clock ticking yet, are you, Jonathan?"

Jonathan smiled. "Some of us hear that clock ticking in the cradle. But appearances can be deceptive. I never try to guess people's ages, myself. I'll get it wrong, every time."

"So, Hiram," Karen said a little too warmly, "where is it that you teach again?"

"Bridgewater State."

"Psychology, isn't it?" Steve said.

"Yes, that's right."

"Tenure?" Derek said.

"Oh, yes. I'm not sure I'll stay in academia indefinitely, however."

Jonathan said, "You look like the type of man who daydreams about being a writer. I know that lean and hungry look."

As the others laughed, Hiram said, "Well, you never know what life is going to drop right under your nose. Many an author got started when he tripped over a fascinating subject that he'd never even realized existed."

"Wish that would happen to me," Steve said.

"Or me," Regan put in. Every time Hiram and Jonathan locked gazes, she felt like there was an invisible laser beam right in front of her nose, and she couldn't push her chair back any further without it looking odd. In her peripheral vision she could see that Veronica was watching the interplay between the two men with an expression of deep suspicion, and that made Regan even more uneasy.

"Well, you're a future business owner, you've got a lot to deal with there," Karen said.

"No kidding. I don't even have time to keep a diary."

Jonathan had turned to look at Regan in surprise. "You don't own Borrowed and Blue?"

"Oh, this is a sad story," Steve said, half smiling as he took a sip of his drink.

"You *should* own it," Derek said. "You should have applied for the loan before the rates went up so high."

"I know, Derek," Regan said tiredly. To Jonathan, she said, "I'm just the manager. The Whartons still own the business—or the children do, technically. Mrs. Wharton signed it over to them when her husband passed away. None of them live around here. But on paper, Enid Wharton is still my boss."

"I didn't know that. Would you want to buy it?"

"If I could. I broached it a couple of times and didn't get a positive response, though. I'm hoping that by the time...well, that Mrs. Wharton is unable to supervise me, her children will rather sell than have to fuss over the place. I don't think any of them are interested in carrying it on."

"How is Mrs. Wharton doing these days?" Karen asked.

"Not well, I'm afraid. She hasn't been into the store since before Christmas. In fact, I hear that she hardly gets out of the house anymore. I visited her back in March." Regan frowned at the memory—Enid Wharton's emphysema had gotten so bad, she was on oxygen, and she'd lost another toe to the diabetes.

"Maybe your opportunity will come sooner than you think." Jonathan hadn't taken his attention off of Regan, and she was beginning to fidget in her chair.

"Not to be ghoulish or anything," she said wryly. "But Derek's ready to help me with loan applications as soon as they're needed, aren't you, Derek?"

"Absolutely," Derek said staunchly. "I don't want to see any more local businesses close. It's bad for the town."

"It seems to me, Regan," Veronica said suddenly, "that you and Derek have a lot in common."

"Yeah, you both do have a certain...single-mindedness that's rather impressive," Karen said teasingly. Derek was looking extremely discomfited, but Regan just laughed.

"I think Derek and I will keep our relationship strictly professional. But now I see why you were trying to fix me up with him for the club date, Ver."

"She what?"

"I did *not!*"

The others were laughing, partly because Derek and Veronica looked as though they'd been stuck with pins. "Oh, come on, Derek, relax," Karen said, "We all went as a teeming mob to that thing."

"That's one way to put it," Steve said.

"Apparently the conversation was a lot more interesting than the faculty teas I get to go to," Hiram said. Veronica took in a sharp breath, and sat up very straight. Derek reached over and put a hand on her forearm, and she shook him off impatiently.

"I think we've all agreed, that topic's been done to death," Karen said quickly.

"Oh, don't banish the subject on my account," Hiram said pleasantly. "After all, the feline is free of the sack and on the run. I'd rather clear up any misinformation before it was repeated, than insist on a gag order."

"What misinformation do you think was given, Hiram?" Jonathan said.

"Since I wasn't there, I can only speculate."

"Look," Regan said, "*I* am not comfortable with this topic being discussed further. It was brought up inadvertently, it's been covered, and we don't need to say any more, okay?"

"Well, that's what I *said*," Karen said.

"I concede to mass opinion," Hiram said lightly. "Topic non grata, along with religion, politics, and the theme of Jonathan's book."

"I'd hardly call those equivalent categories," Jonathan said.

"Jonathan will tell us about his book when he's ready to," Veronica said tartly. "I'm sure he's tired of hearing about it."

"Not at all," Jonathan said easily. "I'm delighted that there's so much interest in my book. I believe they call that viral marketing. But I'm not going to handicap myself by satisfying all your curiosity too soon. I'm getting the most economical word of mouth promotion in history here."

"That must please your publisher," Hiram said. "Who will be bringing the book out? I'd like to watch for it."

"Oh, I'll let everyone know, Hiram. I'll probably have to let this group read the galleys, or I may be lynched."

"Don't flatter yourself, Vaughn. We're not *that* eager," Derek said. He was looking at Veronica as he spoke. She turned and gave him an angry glare, although others at the table were laughing.

"Oh, thank you, my ego needed reining in," Jonathan said.

"Well, over-confidence isn't a pretty picture," Steve said.

"And you would know, how?" Regan said, and Steve mimed a lethal stab wound to the heart. Even as she was laughing at that along with the others, Regan noticed that Veronica shifted her chair a few inches closer to Jonathan's.

"So, how are you liking Sheridan, Jonathan?" Hiram said. "I heard that you only moved in, what was it, a month ago?"

"I'm liking it very much. It's peaceful, it's safe, but it's convenient to Boston and Providence. I'm hoping to stay for a while."

"Are you from Rhode Island?" Hiram asked.

Jonathan looked at him for a moment. "Originally, yes, but I haven't lived there for a long time. What makes you think so?"

Hiram smiled. "Your accent."

"Ah, yes. Always a giveaway."

Regan licked her lips, which seemed very dry. She recalled her words to Hiram in the car on Friday night: *American. He talked just like here.*

"Where were you before here?" Karen asked curiously.

"Olympia, Washington."

"Oh, that's beautiful country out there." Steve sounded almost wistful. "Did you work for Microsoft?"

Jonathan laughed. "No, I'm not an IT person. I knew people who did, though."

Veronica stirred impatiently. "Why do you all keep on grilling poor Jonathan?"

"We're not grilling him." Karen's tone was a little offended.

"He's the new kid on the block, that's all," Steve said.

"Exactly," Jonathan said. "If I don't feel like answering a question, I'll just tell you all to go—change the subject."

"Yes, I think Jonathan can take care of himself," Regan said wryly. She noticed that as Jonathan turned back to the table after reacting to Veronica's words, he shifted position. Now he was turned away from Veronica, with his left hand resting on his knee, while his right hand was resting on the table almost in front of Regan. Regan realized that she had pulled her elbows close into her sides, automatically withdrawing for fear that she would touch Jonathan by accident and suddenly be overwhelmed by visions. He seemed to be almost inviting such a fortuitous contact. But even worse, Regan knew that both Hiram and Veronica had noticed all of this as well.

"Have you ever seen the re-enactments on Lexington Green on Patriots Day?"

Karen asked Jonathan. "Steve and I were going to go up for that tomorrow."

"No, I haven't."

"They're in the morning, of course," said Hiram. "You'd have to get up early."

Jonathan shrugged. "That's not a problem. I actually don't sleep very much, I'm one of those annoying people. Like Edison."

"There are things all day, though, a parade and everything."

"They're running the Boston Marathon tomorrow, too." Derek was keenly aware of this, since ten years earlier he had competed in the Marathon. He was still almost in good enough shape to do so again.

"Oh, Jonathan, that Lexington stuff is all so corny, really. That's for people to take their little kids to," Veronica said, curling her lip.

"Well, Veronica, you don't have to come," Karen said sharply. "Is the store open tomorrow, Regan?"

"We're having a sale. Didn't you see the ads?" Karen made a little disappointed sound. Regan didn't look to her left. "I'm afraid it's not a holiday if you're in retail."

"Our office is open, too," Derek said.

"Now lucky Hiram," said Steve, "has the whole week off, don't you?"

"With three courses worth of undergraduate papers to grade, yes."

"Jonathan? Would you like to come along?" Karen said.

Jonathan hesitated. "I probably should get some work done. I've been having far too much fun the last three days."

"Clearly you have no interest in history," Hiram said. "It seems odd, for a writer. These re-enactments are done very well. At their best, you'd almost feel that you're right in the past, or at least looking through a window to it."

"Oh, I'm sure," Jonathan said. "I wouldn't say I have no interest in history, but I'm mostly interested in what we can learn from it. I consider myself a futurist more than anything else." He turned to Regan. "You know, it's too bad you can't pack up some of your merchandize and take it on the road on holidays."

"I've been known to do that, but not on Patriots' Day. Fourth of July has some pretty big flea markets that are worth it. I have to do a lot of planning for it."

"I can imagine how much time it takes to pack all of those small items up and not have to worry about breakage. You have a lot of nice porcelain pieces."

"Which sell very well. But breakage is a major issue, yes. Moving merchandize anywhere entails a risk of loss. You have to feel there's a good chance that you'll be making enough profit to justify it."

"But..." Veronica's voice was tart with suspicion. "You've never seen Regan's store, have you, Jonathan?"

Regan felt a cold lump sink to the pit of her stomach. *Oh god, please lie, Jonathan...*

Jonathan had turned to look squarely at Veronica. "I went over there last night, after I talked to you," he said mildly. "You asked me to, remember?"

Veronica gaped at him. "But you never *said* you'd done that." She craned her neck past him to look accusingly at Regan. "You didn't tell me that you'd... you'd talked to Jonathan!"

"I haven't *seen* you, Ver, I've been working all day." Regan felt her cheeks getting hot, but she was more angry than embarrassed. "There was nothing to it, he just stopped in to talk for a few minutes. That's all! That's *all*," she repeated with significant emphasis.

"You could have called me."

"Why does Regan have to report back to you, Veronica? The store is open to the public, she can talk to anyone she wants."

"Oh, shut up, Derek," Veronica snapped. Steve and Karen exchanged looks.

"As you may recall," Jonathan said, "you thought it would be a good idea for me to apologize to Regan. So I did."

Veronica looked over at Regan again, and Regan said as casually as she could, "He did. Abjectly. It would have made a very dull report. It wasn't even worth a phone call."

Veronica looked back and forth between the two of them, her eyes narrowing. "He apologized."

"On his knees, practically."

Veronica stared at her for a few more seconds and abruptly turned away and straightened herself in her chair with a hard bounce that made the chair legs rock. "Well," she said snippily, as she picked up her glass, "as long as it was him on his knees and not you." She took a gulp of her drink, glaring at the center of the table as if it had just insulted her.

There was a beat pause as everyone got their breath back. Even Jonathan's jaw had dropped. Finally Regan forced a sour smile and said with the heaviest sarcasm that her shock allowed, "Why, Veronica, I can't *imagine* what you mean."

"Really," Karen said, much too brightly, "I think we better change the subject, before the Hong Kong Delhi gets some kind of a fine."

"Or starts selling tickets," Steve said. He was having trouble suppressing a grin.

Regan was watching Veronica with a deep sense of apprehension, wondering if she was about to make a scene. Veronica, however, appeared to be aware that she had just committed a social foul and was scowling at the tabletop. Derek leaned over and said something to her under his breath. Veronica twitched away from him, shrugging her left shoulder impatiently, although he had made no attempt to touch her again. "No, I've got my own car," she said irritably.

"I appreciate the invitation, but I'm afraid I'll have to decline," Jonathan said to Karen. "I seriously need to buckle down and get to work. As a matter of fact..." he rose from his seat, removing a slender calfskin wallet from his pocket. "I've got to get going now. There are a couple of phone calls I need to make before ten p.m., Eastern Time." He placed several bills on the table to cover his drink. "Goodnight," he said, but he gave Hiram an intent look as he did. Then he left.

"Well, I've got to open tomorrow by ten a.m., Eastern Time," Regan said briskly. "Hiram, can you give me a ride back to my car, or do you want to stay? I can walk from here."

"Don't be silly. I've got to drive all the way back to Bridgewater, and it is getting late. It was a pleasure meeting all of you."

As they got up, Regan gave Veronica a troubled look. She could see tears glittering under her friend's lowered eyelids, but her face was a tight mask. Regan desperately wanted to touch Veronica's hand or shoulder and try to divine what was going on. But she knew that not only would Veronica block any impressions, she would probably explode at the attempt. "Have fun up in Lexington tomorrow, you guys," she said to Karen and Steve. "Don't get in front of any muskets. Veronica, you should go with them." Veronica, who now had her arms tightly folded, just shrugged.

On the way up to Borrowed and Blue, Hiram said, "That was...interesting. Was your friend Veronica acting...like herself?"

"No," Regan said flatly.

"I didn't think so. Frankly, I'm rather concerned about her."

"That makes two of us. Actually, it probably makes six of us." Regan sighed.

"Has she ever..." Hiram hesitated unhappily.

"Decompensated?" Regan finished for him in a dry voice.

"Well, yes."

Regan was silent as the car pulled into the parking area, gravel crunching. "It was a long time ago. And there have been some rough times since then, mostly after a big break-up. But she's seemed so much better the last couple of years. The medications were really working for her, and she's just been on a more even keel, in general."

"Is she usually compliant with her medications?"

"Yes, she is. She hates talking about it, but I know she's absolutely faithful keeping up with her scrips. She's too afraid of being hospitalized." *Again,* she didn't add.

"Do you know what she's taking?"

Regan squirmed. "I don't think I should—"

"No, never mind, none of my business. Professional interest, that's all."

He had pulled up beside Regan's car. "I'm the last person to hand out this kind of advice...but you might want to...think carefully about pursuing any involvements that aren't completely...uncontested."

Regan sighed heavily. "I'm not pursuing *anything*, Hiram. But I can't help what pursues me."

"Yes, well...I'd be very careful about that, too. But, it's your life. I'm just speaking as a friend."

"Thank you for your concern." She got out of the car and stood watching as he turned in the lot and drove off. She unlocked her own car and got in, but she sat for some time without turning on the ignition, listening to the spring peepers chirping from a vernal pool in back of the store, and thinking.

Chapter 6

Borrowed and Blue was usually closed on Mondays, but holidays offered too much potential profit not to open. After the quiet shift she'd had on Sunday, Regan had been a little worried about the prospects for the 19th, but her judiciously placed advertisements and flyers attracted enough customers to keep the copper bells in motion most of the day. She was feeling better physically than she had on Sunday, although she still had to wear a loosely tied silk scarf. As tired as she was by late afternoon, Regan was grateful for the activity, and not simply because of the financial benefit. It was busy enough to keep her mind off the events of the weekend. When she was home she fell into long brooding spells that were difficult to pull out of, and she was playing her car radio more loudly than usual.

She had been surprised that Veronica did not call her at home on Sunday night. She had braced herself to get reamed out at length, but the only call had been from her mother, up in Vermont. Veronica was often not up before Regan left for work in the mornings, and Regan crossed her fingers and silently prayed that there wouldn't be a scene in front of customers at the store. The long silence, however, was starting to worry her by the time 7:00 p.m. approached. Derek was working and Karen and Steve were in Lexington, or Regan would have tried calling one of them to see if they'd spoken to Veronica. When she heard a tap on the door glass at 7:10 and recognized Veronica's tall slender shadow on the shade, Regan was actually relieved.

"Hello, Ver," she said as she locked the door after Veronica had come inside.

Veronica avoided meeting her eyes. "I'm sorry about last night," she said, or rather mumbled, without any preamble, not even "hello."

Regan just looked at her sadly for a few moments. "My office. Let's talk."

When they were seated in the office, Regan carefully looked Veronica over, her eyes narrowed. This was easy to do, since Veronica sat silent with head bowed, studying the darkened linoleum tiles at her feet. She was turned out even more carefully than usual, but her face seemed pale under her makeup, and her eyes were very red.

"Veronica," Regan finally said when the silence had stretched on for over a minute, "you need to tell me what's going on. I'm really getting worried. Don't treat me like an idiot."

"I'm not." There was another long silence before Veronica spoke again. "There's nothing going on." Regan didn't respond to this, but just waited patiently. Veronica drooped over her tightly clasped hands. It got so quiet, Regan could faintly hear the peepers chirping from outside. Veronica sighed. Just as Regan was about to finally speak, she said, "I totally blew it with Jonathan, didn't I." Her voice was almost inaudible, and her inflection was a statement, not a question.

"I wouldn't know, Ver. What makes you think that? Did you talk to him?"

"No..." she drew the word out into a long sigh. After another lengthy pause she said, "He's not answering his phone."

"He did say last night that he had work to do. He could have spent the day in Lexington but he turned the invitation down."

"I know." Regan waited again. Veronica finally straightened up, but only to lean back in the chair, like a rag doll that can only be propped in different directions. "Oh, it's no use. Nobody wants me. I don't know why I even try."

"You were the one who broke up with Derek," Regan said mildly.

"It wasn't going anywhere. I just got there first. That's why you didn't call me."

"That's why I didn't call you?"

"To tell me that you talked to Jonathan."

"Oh."

"You were just trying to spare my feelings. You didn't want to tell me that it was hopeless. He hates me."

"Oh, Veronica, for god's sake...that had nothing to do with it. He *doesn't* hate you. I don't think *anyone* hates you, Ver—you're not that kind of person."

"Did you see that when you read him?"

Regan hesitated unhappily. "I didn't really...get to read him that way. He knew I'm psychic and he'd figured out that you wanted me to check him out, so it made things...a little awkward."

"Was he mad?"

"He thought it was all...kind of funny, actually. But, Veronica," Regan's voice became more firm. "If he hated you, why would he have come to the store to apologize to me just because you asked him to?"

Another long silence. "I don't know." She looked at Regan dismally. "He likes you."

"Does he? He better not need a lot of attention and encouragement, because I work sixty hours a week. Veronica—I'm not looking for a relationship. And you *know* why."

Veronica only smiled, bitterly, as she shook her head. "At least your last boyfriend didn't steal nine thousand dollars from you," she said. Regan couldn't think of an answer to this, and after a moment Veronica said, "such a loser."

"You mean Terence?"

"No, me."

Regan had to restrain herself from rolling her eyes. "Oh, Veronica...you never give yourself enough credit. Look at the things you've pulled off, things I couldn't even think about doing. You planned your entire wedding, alone! Twenty six thousand dollars, two hundred guests, it was like something out of Martha Stewart, and you didn't even act stressed, at least before your mom got here."

"Right. Twenty-six thousand dollar wedding and the marriage lasted for eight months."

"You got married too young."

"I was twenty-one."

"For you—that was too young. That's a totally different issue, Ver."

Veronica's eyes were beginning to brim with tears now. "Do they all just want the money, Regan?"

"Derek sure doesn't need it."

"Oh, god, why do you keep shoving Derek at me? What's so great about Derek?"

"I'm just using him as an example. There are men who couldn't care less about your money."

"Why can't I find them, then?"

Regan leaned toward her friend. "Because you don't *look* for them, Veronica. You're always attracted to these scruffy, edgy, unconventional guys who tend not to have real jobs and seem just a little bit dangerous. Those kinds of guys... a lot of times they're just looking for a meal ticket."

"Jonathan's not scruffy and edgy."

"No...but he does fit the rest of the profile. And he isn't giving you much encouragement, Ver, so I think maybe you should just...let it go."

Veronica gave a long sigh and bowed her head, but this time she seemed to be thinking. "Maybe you're right. After last night, he's never going to speak to me again, anyway."

"He's not the one with reason to be pissed at you about last night," Regan said wryly. "And he's not going to cut you dead on the street. He's too polite. But I'd give him some time."

After another long silence, Veronica said, "Okay." She stood up, slowly, as if it took a great effort just to rise to her feet. Regan stood also, feeling a serious qualm about letting her friend leave the store.

"Veronica...are you sure that you're going to be all right?"

"I'm just tired."

"Are you sure...that you don't feel like hurting yourself?"

Veronica let her head fall back as if it was just too much to bear. "Oh, that *question*. No, Regan. I don't feel like hurting myself. I don't feel like hurting anyone else. I don't feel like committing suicide. I'm not a danger to myself or others. *Okay?*"

"Don't bite my head off. You're not acting like yourself, Veronica."

Veronica closed her eyes for a moment. "What would you know about how I'd act as myself, Regan?"

"Veronica, I've known you all your life. When you're yourself, you're happy, you're funny, you're intelligent—" she broke off as Veronica shook her head. "You *are*."

"Nobody knows who I really am when I'm myself. Nobody. I haven't *been* myself. Not for years and years now." Regan started to answer, but Veronica turned away. "I can't talk anymore. I just came by to apologize for last night. I'm going to go home and go to bed. I'm so tired."

"Well...it's still early, Ver. Are you sure you wouldn't like to rent a movie or something, we could just hang out and relax—I could use the break."

"No...I'd just fall asleep, Regan. I don't feel like any movies tonight. I'll see you later."

With a feeling of deep disquiet, Regan saw her to the door and watched as the Mazda left the parking area and disappeared down Swansea Road.

On Tuesday, Regan closed the store and went to a dealers' pre-viewing for an estate sale up in Portland. She had done so well over the long weekend, her stock was getting depleted, and she welcomed an opportunity to get out of Sheridan for a while. She tried calling Veronica before she left, and only woke her friend up from a sound sleep. Veronica groggily murmured that she was fine and hung up the phone, but other than being sleepy, she sounded normal enough, so Regan tried to put her fears from her mind.

She treated herself to lunch in a seafood restaurant on the wharf, and arranged for the items she tagged at the sale to be delivered. With several boxes of fragile pieces in her car, including a set of flawless Hummel figurines that she might resell on the collectible circuit, she drove back to Sheridan, arriving a little after sunset. Normally, after an impromptu day off, she would have called Karen or Veronica or another of their crowd and seen if they wanted to get together. But instead, Regan found herself sitting thoughtfully in the store's office for some time after she'd unloaded the boxes and placed them in the storage room. Then she locked up, got into her car, and drove out long and winding River Road.

The house that Jonathan Vaughn had rented was near the Sheridan town line, surrounded by second growth woods and just down the road from one of the last working dairy farms in Bristol County. The rambling house, its central building dating back to the early 1800s and expanded over the years with six different additions, had belonged to a thriving farm up to the 1950s. It briefly stood empty as the property was inherited by a nephew who lived down in Florida. To his lasting horror, his daughter became a hippie, and in 1966 the house was turned into a commune named Rainbow Stone Junction. The commune remained in the house until its last members finally split up in 1985. After that, different renters came and went, most of them Bohemian sorts who were happy to live in a former commune and were not too picky about the state of the building, which could most kindly be described as affordable housing. The surrounding land was peppered with meandering brooks and small bogs, and could not easily be divided into buildable lots without encroaching on wetlands and wetland buffer zones, and the town voted down costly plans to run water lines and roads into the area. Rainbow Stone house remained intact and isolated among its thickening woods, slowly crumbling under the passing seasons. Regan had been there a few times before, since a couple of her more popular crafters had lived out there. She had to admit that she cherished an affection for the old place. She knew she would be sorry when, as seemed inevitable, it was finally torn down for some more lucrative development.

Regan pulled her car into the weed-overgrown, semi-circular drive in front of the house. She saw Jonathan's nondescript compact sedan pulled up before the double doors of the barn-cum-garage. The walk to the front door was paved with heavy fired clay tiles, hand shaped and glazed in brilliant hues—the Rainbow Stone Path, she remembered it being called. The tiled walkways were all around the house and a few of them ran down into the woods, where they simply stopped dead. Some of the tiles had cracked over the years, but they had held up amazingly well. There was an elaborate bas-relief made of plaster all around the front door, with vines and flowers and fruit on each side, and a smiling sun flanked by crescent moons over the door. The barn doors still had the flaking remains of a mural featuring an arching rainbow and figures dancing in a circle with linked hands. Regan couldn't help smiling—aside from the isolation and air of neglect, it was a most unlikely venue for a vampire.

She knocked on the front door and waited. She heard no sound from inside, and after a moment she was about to knock again, when Jonathan opened the door. When he saw her, he paused for several moments, as though he was so astonished he temporarily forgot what to say to a visitor.

"Hello, Regan. What can I do for you?"

"I was wondering if you had some time to talk." He hesitated a moment, and she added, "Not about Veronica, I promise. If this is inconvenient...I know you said you had a lot of work to do."

"No, no. Come in." He stepped back from the door. "I'm a little surprised to see you here like this," he added as Regan walked past him. He sounded less surprised than intensely curious.

"What, do you think I'd be afraid to be alone with you?" Regan's tone was acerbic, but inwardly, she was surprised, herself.

"I certainly hope you wouldn't be."

Regan looked around the hallway with interest, since she hadn't been inside Rainbow Stone house for several years. It was exactly as she remembered, except for being very empty, and very clean. There were no cobwebs and no dust anywhere. The dulled and scratched hardwood floors shone in the light angling from the wide arched entranceway opposite the staircase. She touched a wall—the paint was chipped, but even it felt clean.

She followed Jonathan through the archway into the large main room of the house, the "great room," as she remembered it being called. It was too big and too central not to have its own name. The room was so empty her footsteps echoed. At the far end, in front of the fireplace, stood the immense wood burning stove that heated, more or less, this part of the house in the winter. The windows had new shades, pulled down to the sills, but nothing else covering them. There was a long heavy old kitchen table standing near the stove, almost all of its surface covered with papers, books, manila folders, a large metal strongbox with a hinge lid, and various desk clutter like pens and paper clips. But it wasn't so much the expensive laptop computer at the near end of the table, as what she saw on its screen that stopped her in her tracks in astonishment.

"You have an Internet connection."

Jonathan, who had been getting an oak dining room chair for her from one side of the room, paused and looked puzzled. "Naturally. Everyone these days has to be on the 'Net. You're deaf, dumb and blind without it." He set down the chair, near the tall floor lamp that illuminated the room. "The chief nuisance out here," he went on, "is that I can't get broadband this far out from town. Dial-up is so slow. But Verizon promises I'll be able to get DSL in a few months. It's not as though I do much downloading."

Regan sat down in the chair with a thump. "What do you use it for?" she said, after a moment.

"Oh, financial management, research, keeping my hand in things, mostly. It's not easy to keep up with current events. The veracity of the news media hasn't improved much since I was young, but now there's so much more of it." He sat down in the wooden chair by the table, which didn't match the one he'd brought over for Regan. "I do a lot of web surfing, I'm something of an addict. It's wonderful to have so much information available online now. With all my moving, I've had to abandon enough books to fill the New York Public Library." He paused and looked at her with amusement. "You have the most...betrayed look on your face. Did you think I'd be using quill pens and sealing wax?"

"Well, no, not for your writing, but..." She felt her cheeks reddening. "I didn't know *what* to expect. How would I? Since Saturday night, I've had to rip up and re-evaluate half the beliefs I based my whole worldview on. Do you have any idea what that's like?"

His smile had faded. "Of course I do," he said quietly. "I went through exactly the same thing myself."

Regan's shoulders sagged. "That's why I've come out here, as insane as it probably is. I can't stand it anymore. You have got to answer some of these questions, you owe me that. That...psychic tsunami you hit me with didn't help at all. I've been tying myself into mental knots obsessing over it. I've tried to take apart that mass of impressions and all I get is bits and scraps, with no continuity and no context. And I can hardly believe that what I am seeing clearly is real." She paused, all her frustration from the last three days reawakened. "Fuck. I can hardly believe the things I've seen and felt with my five waking senses. Half the time I think I'm losing my mind, and the other half I think I must be the target of the most ingenious hoax in history."

He smiled, but his eyes were troubled. "It's all right, Regan, don't stress so much over this. I do understand, and I have no objections to answering some questions. But let me urge you to trust your own senses, *all* of them. You don't have to convince me how difficult this is to accept. It's true, I live with this every day, and I've probably forgotten how bizarre it must seem to you." He spread his hands helplessly. "I'm not centuries old. I'm just as much a child of the modern world as you are—just a little earlier, that's all. I wasn't even very religious. I was studying engineering in university, I had absolute faith that science was going to solve all the world's problems. Nothing could have prepared me for this."

Regan leaned back in the old chair, which creaked in complaint. "All right. I'll take your word for it that I can believe my senses. But you just hit the central question, Jonathan. What, *exactly*, do you mean by 'this?'"

He paused for a moment. "Oh. You want a word."

"I think I've pretty much got the word. The word is vampire, isn't that right?"

"With some conditions, that's the easiest word to use. It has become an extremely...inclusive term, however, so I wouldn't just toss it around without some explanation."

"An explanation is exactly what I need. I'm not so stupid that I don't know the difference between fact and fiction. I've read some of the fiction, and I've seen the same movies everyone else has."

"So have I," he said wryly.

"And I've read a couple of serious books about vampire folklore—"

"Which ones?"

"Uh...well, the one by Paul Barber, of course, and then there's this doorstop by that religions scholar, I think his name is Milton?"

"Melton. Those aren't bad, I could recommend some more serious academic titles if you're interested."

"Fine, I'd like to hear them. But in the meantime, that's the limit of my previous education. That's all I know—books and movies. I've already figured out that there are some major disparities between fiction and reality. People have seen you during the daytime, I know you don't go up in flames in the sunlight." She stopped when he laughed.

"That is the silliest thing. That whole idea comes entirely from the movies, you know. All nocturnal creatures are light sensitive, but—"

"I do remember that from Milton, uh, Melton. Don't laugh at me."

He sobered. "I'm sorry. No, really. Go on."

"I know you have a reflection, I noticed that at Hong Kong Delhi on Sunday. Is anything in the literature factual?"

He was smiling, although more thoughtfully now. "In the fiction, not very much. Oh, there are little pieces here and there that seem to get it right—by accident, really. But most of the fiction, and even more the films, say much more about the people who create and read and watch them than they do about vampires. Folklore contains more truth, but you have to sift through it carefully." He sighed. "And god knows, I've certainly done that."

"But why? Didn't you..." Regan looked around the empty room, realization dawning on her. "You didn't have anyone to explain things to you?"

He shook his head. "No. I had no mentor or guide, no one handed down any teachings to me, ancient or otherwise. There's no rulebook, no instruction manual—not even a set of basic parameters or some useful tips. I woke up like this, and ever since then, I've been on my own."

"You're saying that you're the only one? There are no other vampires besides you?" Regan could hardly imagine how unspeakably lonely such uniqueness would be.

"Oh, no. There are most certainly others. I'd been surviving for some years on my own before I happened to encounter any of them, but I know at least seven others in New England. There may well be more that I don't know about. There's not a lot of interaction among us. I don't mean that we're hostile to each other, but we give one another a lot of space. That's not a formal agreement, it's just a matter of respect, and practicality. But that whole idea of a vast underground society or vampire counterculture, with a ruling class and enforcers and laws, is just...well, it's just a popular fictional convention at the moment. I wish it were true—well, sometimes I do. At other times I'm thankful it's not."

Regan was silent a moment. Every answer he gave only sparked another dozen questions. "You said that you woke up," she asked finally. "Are you saying that you were...dead?"

He shook his head with a wry half smile. "You know, I still feel like that is the number one question that nobody could ever answer, 'yes.' All I can say is that before I awoke, doctors and undertakers and my family presumed I was dead enough to bury. Obviously, there was something drastically different between my state and true death. Whatever animates me now isn't life as I understood it. I have no idea what it really is."

"You said you were *buried?*" He nodded. "And you'd never met another vampire, so you just woke up and climbed out of your grave for no reason at all? I'm sorry, but I feel like I'm missing a critical detail here."

He looked a bit flustered. "I'm afraid I'm not explaining this very well." He got up and walked across the room slowly. "The folklore stories tend to imply a kind of infection—if you're killed by a vampire, you return as one, in some cases. All the fiction has adopted that as a hard rule. You get bitten or drink the vampire's blood and you catch vampirism, like catching the 'flu, and you always know how you caught it. Well, it doesn't really work that way. But at the same time, I can't say that...exposure, of some kind, isn't part of it. I had... an experience, as a young man. I was visited by *something.*"

"You mean, it wasn't something like you?"

"I can't be sure about that, because I strongly suspect that my memory of what really happened was altered. What I remember is something that seemed to come to me as I lay in bed at night. I wasn't dreaming, but I didn't seem to be fully awake, either—I couldn't move or speak during these visitations. It would lay stretched on top of me, and it had weight, and warmth, and when it left, I was cold and couldn't catch my breath." He paused for a moment, his eyes haunted. "I was never afraid of it. But I grew very weak, and almost died, and then the visitations stopped. When I recovered my family wouldn't tell me what had happened. There were vague allusions to something having been done, something almost magical, that saved my life." He sighed heavily. "I think I really didn't want to know any more than that. I believed the visitor was...someone I'd known."

"Someone who had died?" Looking at his face, Regan guessed, "Someone you were in love with."

His eyes had a distant expression. "Yes. I was..." he swallowed, then said in a stronger voice, "I was very young, and somewhat melodramatic, and, well...you do stupid things when you're young." He was quiet a moment, then added, "Some years later I read some newspaper accounts that purported to explain what had happened to my visitor. But by then I had no way to confirm their accuracy."

Regan sat silently, fingers pressed to her mouth, a scrap of vision suddenly finding context in her mind: a grief-struck young man, sitting by a grave, in the snow, drinking from a nearly empty bottle. *Did you call up something, or did you just catch pneumonia from sitting out in the cold and damp?* After a moment she prompted Jonathan, "but you recovered."

"I recovered, although I was never quite the same as before—sadder but wiser, that's what my sister called me. I went off to university, a bit late, and tried to get on with my life." He came back to his chair and sat. "Let me try to explain my understanding of what makes us this way. It's got something critical to do both with things that happen while we're alive, and with the way we die. It's not logical, it's more..." he paused, apparently searching for the right word.

"Spiritual?"

"Not in the church-going sense. There's a very old tradition—from long before Christianity—about a right order to the universe, and everything that's a part of it, even death in its proper place. When death violates that right order—I'm talking about those deaths that make you shudder to hear about, those deaths that you feel are an offense to justice and nature—those are the ones that seem to be connected to this state. Those, and suicides, of course."

"Suicide?" She was struggling to connect what he was saying, because there still seemed to be a major missing piece. "But you didn't commit suicide, did you?"

He smiled grimly. "I think my parents may have worried about that, with some reason, but I don't believe I would ever have done it. No, when I recovered from my illness, I felt that I had been given a second chance at life. I threw myself into my studies, I did volunteer work, I had great plans. Unfortunately..." he trailed off. Regan suddenly saw again the narrow dark street, rough paving stones underfoot, three menacing young men just ahead, *give it up, then...* she pressed her hand to her abdomen, flinching. "Yes," Jonathan said dryly, snapping her awareness back to the room around her, "I knew you were going to ask about that eventually."

She swallowed, her mouth dry. "You were murdered," she whispered.

"Quite horribly. Of course," he gave a short humorless laugh, "I admit my opinion is biased."

After a pause, Regan said in a hushed voice, "What happened?"

He licked his lips before he spoke. "One night...it was in the early fall...I was walking from the home of a friend back to my quarters near the university, in Providence. I took an unfamiliar route, near the waterfront, because it was late and I was in a hurry. These three young men..." he stopped, and swallowed. "...confronted me and demanded money. I only had a few dollars with me, but I gave it to them. They accused me of insulting them. I imagine they assumed I was rich, because of the way I was dressed. They all attacked me at once, trying to pull my clothes open and search me for money or valuables. I almost broke away from them and ran, but one of them had one of those knives that fisherman used for gutting fish, the ones with a half serrated blade—I saw it in his hand for a moment. Then he...he cut me open from my ribs to the base of my belly in one stroke. The knife was so sharp, it was instantaneous. When I clutched at the wound with my hands, I felt my own entrails."

Regan, hand to her mouth, could not repress a sound of revulsion.

"I don't think he meant to do it, I think he was trying to cut my clothes open, but it was such a free-for-all. All three of them ran when they saw what had happened. I lay on the street in a pool of my own blood, for what seemed like an endlessly long time. I think someone found me, just before the end. But I've never been sure." He shook his head. "I was twenty-four years old."

Regan sat silent, caught in the horror of that scene. After a pause, she asked, "You said this was Providence? Is that where you're from?"

"Well, I was born in South Kingston. There are still some families living there who are related to me. I moved to Providence to go to Brown."

"And this happened in the 1890s?"

"That's right."

"So you were born..."

He hesitated a moment, then said, "1872."

She pulled in a shaking breath. "But that would make you..."

He raised his hands, stopping her. "I can count, thanks."

"Oh, yes, now I remember—you don't want to feel old."

"It's bad enough without putting a number on it."

"So...you're immortal?"

He shrugged. "Who knows? I can be destroyed, I know that. I've seen it happen to others. But I don't age, I don't get sick, I heal from nearly all injuries... I may have a lifespan, I don't know. But immortality is an abstract concept. Unaging and resilient is not the same thing."

"Maybe not literally, but for all practical purposes..." Regan tried to imagine what it would be like, never to have to worry about catching a cold, let alone developing cancer. "Have you met vampires older than you?"

"One or two. They don't know, either. And to make things more complicated, we have numerous differences, some of them profound. So even though we share information, none of us has all the answers, and what we've learned, through trial and error, doesn't apply to all of us."

"It sounds very confusing."

"It is."

Regan pondered the information he'd given her so far for a few moments. "What happened when you woke up?"

"Well, it was seven days later—"

"Seven days! Is that typical?"

In response he only gave her a small smile and a shrug. "There seems to be quite a bit of variation. In my case..." he paused, lost in memory for a moment. "My casket was opened. I've never known whether that had something to do with my awakening or not. You have to understand," he went on, seeing Regan about to ask another question, "that back then, records weren't kept as meticulously as now, and burials could be handled by families without much interference. Obviously, I hadn't been in any position to know what was being done concerning my own burial, and I never had an opportunity to come back and find out later on. All I know is that I awoke in a coffin that was resting on the ground by an open grave, and nobody else was there. I honestly don't know if I had been disinterred for some reason, or if the funeral had been delayed because my murder was being investigated. Usually, interments took place much more quickly than that."

"What did you do? Did anyone see you?"

"No, which was extremely fortunate. I was very confused at first. I remembered clearly how I had died, but since I was now fully awake and functional, I thought that everyone had made some terrible mistake and I'd barely escaped being buried alive. It wasn't long before I realized the truth. But my first impulse when I woke up was to get away from anything familiar. Some instinct told me that allowing anyone who knew of my death to see me would be calamitous. So I left Rhode Island, and I've never been back."

"How did you...realize the truth? Did something happen, or—" she broke off, because he had looked away from her, his expression suddenly wary.

"I think I'll save that part of the story for a later time." His tone of voice didn't invite her to press further.

I've touched a nerve, Regan thought. *I'll bet that's buried in that mass of impressions, though.* Maybe, now that she had some more information to use as anchors, she could pull it out. She decided to try some less personal questions. There was at least one explanation she was especially eager to hear. "How did you get into the store on Saturday night?"

He blinked in surprise, then looked relieved at the switch in direction. "Oh, that. I can open locks."

"You mean, pick them?"

"No, just open them." Seeing her blank expression, he said, "Like this, watch." He pulled the strongbox on the table closer, and snapped shut the lid. There was a small metal key in the keyhole, and he turned it and removed the key. He rested the ball of his thumb against the keyhole. After a second, Regan heard a soft click, and Jonathan opened the box. All Regan could do was gape.

Finally she managed to say, "And that works on doors?" Instead of answering, he beckoned her to follow him out into the hallway. The front door also had a key in the lock, which he turned and removed. Then he locked the keyed deadbolt above the doorknob and handed the key to Regan. He pressed his palm against the lock and immediately Regan heard it click. Then he put his hand on the deadbolt. There was a longer pause this time, then with a loud thunk Regan heard the deadbolt shoot back. Just to add a theatrical finish, Jonathan opened the door. Regan stared at the head of the deadbolt, flush with the edge of the door. "Holy...*shit,*" she said finally. "What else does that work on?"

"Nothing else," Jonathan said, as he shut the door and they returned to the great room. "Just locks."

"*Any* locks? What about alarm systems? What about car locks?"

"Car locks, yes. Alarm systems—only sometimes. It does have its limitations. And don't ask me to explain it. I can't. I can't bend spoons or anything, it's not a generalized skill. It's a gift—someone I know would say it's a joke that's been played on me, actually."

"Can all vampires do this?"

"I never asked them."

"Wow..." Regan stood staring incredulously at the strongbox on the table. "Think of the career you could have as cat burglar."

She'd been joking, but for a moment he looked sheepish, then broke into a laugh. "All right, I'll confess. For about the first thirty years after I left Rhode Island, that's exactly what I did. That's how I acquired the assets I live on now." At the look on Regan's face, he said, "Well, what would you have done? I walked away from my own grave with the clothes I was laid out in—and that's all. My family didn't bury me with so much as a watch fob. I couldn't even use my own name—I was legally dead. I discovered this little talent, and I applied it as resourcefully as possible. I wasn't sorry when I could give up my life of crime and live honestly off my investments, but I'm not making any apologies for it, either."

He sounded a little defensive, and Regan raised her hands in a conciliatory gesture. "Who am I to judge? I just wonder why you bother with keys at all."

"At least two very good reasons. If I don't want the whole world to know about this, I better carry keys and use them whenever someone else is looking. And other people need keys—attorneys, service people, friends."

"Is there anything that would prevent you from being able to do this?" She was thinking of the implications for the store, if there were people who could break in this easily. But Jonathan just leaned back against the edge of the table, his smile somewhat sly.

"If there was, I wouldn't tell."

"In Greece," she responded in the same tone, "they'd probably stuff the locks with garlic."

"Then they'd have very smelly locks. I'd still get in."

Regan gave up for the time being. "There's one more thing I really would like you to explain."

His smile faded. "From the look on your face, I think I better brace myself."

"It's not a personal question." She hesitated, and took a deep breath. "Exactly how do you do...this." She pointed at the spot, still covered with a scarf, where he had drunk on Saturday. "I've looked at this experience from both sides, mine and yours—which isn't easy—and I can't analyze what you're doing, and how you do it. It's..." she looked down, hating to admit it. "It's really creeping me out." Even as she said the words, she shivered, as hard as she tried to suppress it.

"I can see that." He frowned, rubbing his chin thoughtfully with a forefinger.

"Jonathan—I *need* you to answer this."

"I intend to. I'm just trying to think of the best way to explain it." After a few moments he dropped his hand with a gesture that indicated he was at a loss. "I don't know how to put it into words, at least not without..." he looked up at her, slightly apologetic. "I'll have to demonstrate it."

She stepped back from him, her heartbeat suddenly rapid. "Uh—no. I think I've had all the demonstrations of that I can handle."

"You misunderstand me," he said quietly. "I'm not going to drink, I just want to show you what I do. All I need is your arm."

"My arm?" Two of the cases that Hiram had collected had had wounds on their arms, she remembered now, and several others had been injured in other locations.

"I won't open a vein, I promise. You'll be fine."

"Well..."

"You said you wanted to know. I honestly can't think of any other way." She looked at him steadily, and he said, "Trust me."

She looked down, swallowing hard. "All right." She straightened her shoulders and stepped forward, extending her right hand. He grasped her wrist and pushed the sleeve of her jersey up to the elbow. He paused for a moment, studying the surface of her inner arm intently, tipping it slightly one way, then the other. She wondered what he was seeing.

"This will hurt just a bit." Very quickly he cupped his free hand around her forearm and pressed his thumb against the skin a few inches above her wrist.

The pressure was very light and only the ball of his thumb, not the nail, was in contact. Suddenly, Regan felt a quick pain, like a poke from a toothpick, exactly where his thumb was touching. At the same time there was an unpleasant sensation, as though there was a tear in her skin that had just popped apart. Immediately dark blood welled from under Jonathan's thumb and ran down either side of Regan's forearm.

"Oh, *fuck*," she said before she could think, and she tried to jerk her arm away. Jonathan was holding her wrist so tightly, however, that she couldn't break free, and she felt bones grind under the pressure.

"Don't move," he said sharply. "I have to close it." Even as he said that, she felt, under his thumb, the ice cold, pinched-nerve sensation that she remembered vividly from Saturday night. He let go then, and Regan stumbled back away from him, clutching at her arm with her other hand. She looked down at the spot he'd touched, rubbing away the remaining blood, and saw a small puckered injury, so tightly closed that it didn't look new. "There shouldn't be a bruise, because I didn't drink from it." Something about his calm voice made Regan look up at him sharply, and as she'd suspected, he was licking her blood off his fingers and hand—he'd caught most of it. Suddenly aware that she was feeling shaky, Regan decided to sit back down.

"I'm still confused," she said finally. "I thought you did that with your mouth."

"I usually do. It's neater that way, none of the blood is spilled. I don't believe in wasting it. But I don't have to use my mouth. All I need is physical contact."

"But I still don't...it's like the locks, then? You're just manipulating matter somehow?"

"Something like that. Look—have you ever heard of that phenomenon called psychic surgery?"

"Yes...but psychic surgery is hokum. It's all been debunked, it's fakery."

"Not...exactly. Back in the 1970s when Arigo and some of the other psychic surgeons were getting into the news for a while, I traveled to the Philippines to visit some of the practitioners and see for myself what was going on. I was wondering if some of them might be vampires."

"No...they weren't, were they?"

"They weren't. And I admit I spotted a lot of fakery. But there was some genuine psychic surgery being performed."

"And that was like what you do?"

"In some ways—the main similarity is that they could open up bodies and close the wounds again, in a matter of seconds, often using only their hands. Hypnotists here have been able to duplicate this with very suggestible subjects, so the debunkers really have no excuse for being so dogmatic."

Regan stared down at the wound on her arm. "And all vampires do this?"

"All that I've met."

"So all those fangs in the books and movies..."

"...are very impressive and intimidating. But they'd be impossible to drink with—they'd just get in the way. And the damage they'd do—we'd leave trails of corpses everywhere we went. You couldn't drink without killing. And I've never been able to figure out how those retractable fangs could really work. It's a mystery to me why the fiction-writers all seem to love them so much. For god's sake, in the final analysis, we don't even need teeth."

Regan laughed weakly. "I guess not, at least not for..." She couldn't finish the thought. She pulled her sleeve back down, because she was feeling colder than a few minutes earlier. She wanted to ask Jonathan how he'd learned that he could open people's veins just by touching them, but she suspected this would come too close to the question of how he discovered his new state of being. "You were drinking alcohol at the Hong Kong Delhi the other night, weren't you?"

"Yes. I can eat and drink anything I want, if that what's you're asking." He looked amused for a moment. "Folklore vampires would eat you out of house and home. They were worse than teenage boys."

"I guess I remember that from the books. They had a lot of sex, too, as I recall."

"There hasn't been much opportunity lately, but I don't have any problems with that, either." He had that annoying sly smile again.

"I only mentioned it for the record, that's all," Regan said, feeling irritated.

"Of course you did." But after a moment his face sobered, and he came back around the table and sat down in his chair. "Rather than go through every detail, I can give you a quick summation. Our existence...is basically a counterfeit of life. Whatever the living do, we can do...except for one thing. We can't have children, because we can't create life. All we have is an imitation of it—a very close imitation, but counterfeit nonetheless. So any questions you have...apply that rule to them, and you'll probably draw the right conclusion."

There was a long silence. Finally Regan said, "Aren't there some folklore traditions about vampires fathering children?"

"There are. But if that was ever possible, it no longer is. At least as far as I know."

"You can do things that living people can't, Jonathan."

He nodded once. "That's true. But far less than you might think. Mostly we survive through our wits and common sense, not any special talents. And most of our abilities—not all, but most—are just enhancements of what the living can do."

"You're stronger."

"The same bones and muscles that you have, and I use them the same way."

"What about your senses?"

"There's some enhancement—but they're the same five senses I always had. Just as I said, they're counterfeit. I can't psychically read people, for example, like you." He paused a moment. "I will admit, however, that I have seen some other vampires do some...truly amazing things."

"This comes under the aegis of those profound differences you referred to?" He nodded, his expression distant. "Such as what?"

Jonathan blinked, and then smiled wryly. "If I told you, you wouldn't believe me. But you may see for yourself some day."

Regan stared at him for a moment, wondering if he was teasing or serious. "*God*, you know how to be tantalizing. What are we talking about here—shapeshifting, werewolves, magic?"

He laughed. "All I can say about werewolves is that I've never actually met one. But magic is another story. Just remember that it's like vampires—or for that matter, psychic powers. The reality isn't what you see in the movies. But that's as far as I'm going on that matter. Some things *shouldn't* be believed until you've seen the proof yourself." As frustrating as his evasion was, Regan had to admit that she agreed with him on that point, at least in theory. She had some personal evidence for the consequences of unexamined beliefs.

Regan had a lot to think about by now, and she realized that she was starting to feel exhausted, the way she felt when she'd been doing readings and had taken in all the information she could absorb. "I've monopolized a lot of your time."

"Time is something I have in great amounts. But you need to be at the store in the morning, don't you?" She nodded. "You certainly work long hours."

"I enjoy it." She gazed again around the large shadowy room, remembering what it had looked like the last time she'd visited. A row of plywood and trestle tables had run along each long wall, covered with plastic sheeting and pottery in every stage of construction, and the stove had had a kiln sitting next to it. "Is this really all the furniture you have? You know, I can help you get some nice stuff, if you want."

Jonathan looked around the room appraisingly, as though its emptiness hadn't struck him before. "Well, I have a bed." At her glance he added, "yes, I sleep in a bed. I got out of a coffin once, and that was the last one I ever want to be in. I have some more chairs and lamps, and there's a table in the kitchen. I don't need much, and sometimes I have to leave places very fast, so I tend to live simply."

Regan got up and stretched, and Jonathan rose also, to see her to the door. "I knew people who lived here, a few years ago. How on earth did you find this place? The realtor?"

"No, actually, I lived here once before, back in the 1960s."

Regan turned to stare at him. "Get *out!* You lived in a hippie commune?"

He laughed. "Why not? It was informal, it was isolated and private, people came and went all the time, no one asked any questions...it was quite a remarkable time."

"Did you have long hair and grow your beard?"

"Of course I did. I had to blend in. Don't look at me like that, it was fun."

Regan shook her head, but her amusement was at her own naiveté. "I was thinking when I got here that all this faded Age of Aquarius art colony décor was completely out of character for a vampire. But you love this house."

"Yes, I do. Would you expect me to be a Goth? God, I loathe wallowing in funereal gloom. There's nothing romantic about dying. I should know."

"Are you going to be the one who finally fixes this place up, then? It would be a shame if some developer like Ron Wilson bulldozed it and put in condos."

"I don't know." Jonathan looked around the room pensively. "I have resources, but not millions. Right now, I can't be sure that I'll be staying here that long."

"Could I have your phone number?"

"Of course. My god, you're the last person in town who doesn't have it."

"Yes," Regan kept her voice carefully casual. "I could have asked Veronica for it, but after Sunday night, I wasn't too sure how she'd react."

At her words Jonathan stopped rummaging in the strongbox on the table and let his head fall back with a heavy sigh. "Oh, lord—that is a problem." He gave Regan a pained look. "She was with a whole group of people—the same ones we were having drinks with on Sunday—and I was giving the number out to everyone. I had no idea she would put the kind of significance on it that she did. Nobody else did," he added, almost under his breath.

"But...you returned her calls."

"Certainly I returned her calls, I had no reason to be rude to her. At first our conversations were quite banal, to say the least. It's only been the last week or so..." he broke off with an exasperated groan. "I have not done one single thing to unfairly encourage her," he said fervently, as if he expected Regan to disbelieve him on principle.

"I know. I'm not sure what advice to give you. I guess she's tried to call you a few times since Sunday."

His brow creased in puzzlement. "No. If I'm online, calls go into voice mail. No one has called at all." Regan was silent, thinking over the implications of this, and not liking them. "I'll confess that I've been a bit concerned about her state of mind."

"Me, too." After a moment, she said, "Look. If anything starts to blow up, I'll get in touch with you. Do you have an e-mail address?"

"I have seven of them." He went back to flipping through the strong box and pulled out a card. "Take this one," he said, handing it to her. "If I'm online, this one pops up an alert for new messages. My phone number is on there, too, but I don't have a cell phone yet. Can we trade?"

She had already found one of the store's business cards in her handbag, and she wrote her personal e-mail address and her home phone number on the back. "I can't *afford* a cell phone, but if that changes, I'll let you know."

"I may be calling you in a day or so," he said as he accepted the card. "I've got some things I want to ask you about, too—but not just yet."

Chapter 7

Patriot's Day week tended to be quiet—school was out, it was past the holiday shopping season, and early for graduation and wedding gifts. But summer orders were coming in, and Regan kept herself busy cleaning, re-organizing shelves, cataloging new merchandise, and updating Borrowed and Blue's website. Every spring, she longed to find a new location for the store, one that would have more floor space, more parking, and more atmosphere than the aging one-story building with its shingled roof and damp basement whose floor sprung puddles in heavy rains. The ancient linoleum floor tiles were darkened with age and chipping at the corners in high traffic areas, and the carpet runners in the aisles were threadbare in spots. But Mrs. Wharton would have to approve any relocation, and she was not in a condition to make such decisions now.

Regan didn't try to call Jonathan; she had too much to think about from their conversation on Tuesday night. On Wednesday evening, she turned the ringer off on her home phone and lit candles around her living room. For several hours she did deep meditations in an effort to extract more details from what she was now calling "the barbed wire ball" of Jonathan's memory impressions. While she recovered a number of extended and vivid scenarios, it was difficult to determine their significance or context. She did learn quite a bit about how to steal money from almost anyone, anywhere around the turn of the century. While this was interesting, and occasionally funny, it told her little that she really wanted to know. Memories of the hippie commune were colorful, but fractured. One thing that did appear clearly in them almost startled her out of her meditative state when she realized what she was sensing. He had, apparently, met one of the other vampires he'd mentioned at Rainbow Stone Junction: a petite, dark-haired woman with a certain edginess that reminded Regan of Veronica. *How many vampires were hiding out in communes during the 1960s, anyway?* Regan thought, by that time a bit punchy from meditating for so long. There was something very significant about this woman, but Regan couldn't get a clear feeling for just what it was. She and Jonathan seemed to have gotten along rather well. Regan thought she might recognize the woman's face if she met her, but she couldn't home in on a name—at least, nothing other than a hippie name that she was sure was a nickname. She finally gave up on the meditations, feeling frustrated, disoriented, and on the verge of a headache, and went to soak her head in the shower.

She tried to call Veronica a few times to see how she was doing, but only got her answering machine or cell phone voice mail. On Thursday morning, Regan called Karen to see if she'd heard from Veronica, but Karen, who assistant-managed a busy hair and nail salon up at the mall, was putting in extra hours during the holiday week and had not seen Veronica. Regan called Derek, who was brusque with her because he hated to take personal calls at the office. He said that he thought Veronica was home with a cold, but he was sure she would be fine. Hiram had left a message on Regan's home answering machine on Tuesday night, but when she tried to call him back, she only got his office voice mail. She wondered what he wanted to talk about.

Regan had been brooding about all this too much on Thursday afternoon, and was feeling gloomy. At 6:00 p.m., there had not been a customer for an hour, and she was sitting at the office computer catching up on e-mail. When she heard the door bells jingle, she left the office to go to the front counter. To Regan's mild surprise, it was Veronica, tricked out head to toe in expensively pre-faded denim with tasteful rhinestone accents, an outfit she'd bought in a Newbury Street boutique two months earlier. Regan recalled kidding her at the time that all she needed was the cowboy boots and she'd be ready for the Grand Old Opry. Then, Veronica's response had been to laugh and try four different shops looking for the boots. Today, Veronica did not appear likely to laugh about anything, although she didn't look like she was recovering from a cold. Her makeup was less precise than usual, and her eyes were red, but hard and over-bright. As Regan came up the aisle, she noticed that Veronica was peering over the tops of shelves and into the corners of the store with quick, abrupt movements, as though she thought someone was hiding out of her range of vision. "Hello, Veronica. You look nice today."

Veronica started and turned sharply on her heel to pin Regan with an un-blinking glare. "You don't have to waste your time trying to flatter me, Regan, I know what you think of my over-priced designer frou-frou. Isn't that what you called my wardrobe?"

Regan felt several mental warning klaxons trigger, and she caught her breath. *Not even a hello...this isn't good.* "Maybe once when I was in a really bad mood," she said, trying to keep her tone light, "and I wasn't talking about your *whole* wardro—

"I stopped by on Tuesday, but you weren't here," Veronica interrupted her. "Why wasn't the store open? Isn't that what we're all hearing about morning noon and night, how hard you work and how the store is *always* open and you never have time to do anything, not even come to a once in a lifetime club date that Karen got you a pass for especially and I especially asked you to come to as a favor to me?" She stopped only because she'd run out of breath.

Regan was suppressing a sense of panic. "I went to a pre-sale on Tuesday."

"Well, good for you. I suppose Jonathan went with you?"

"*What?* Veronica, for god's sake! Why the hell would you think that?"

"I know you've been seeing him. Do you think I'm stupid? I saw the way he was acting around you at Hong Kong Delhi on Sunday, he was two inches from crawling all over you, and he couldn't get far enough away from me. Why didn't you tell me that you'd seen him on Saturday night?"

"I *told* you, there was nothing to t—"

"You knew how important it was to me, you knew how much I needed to know what you found out. You just didn't want me to know that you were grabbing him right out from under my nose, did you?"

"That's ridicu—"

"I'm not the only one who thinks it's strange that he goes to meet you and neither of you says anything to me about it and suddenly the two of you just drop off the face of the earth! What do you think I am, an idiot, a dumb blonde, I can't put two and two together and figure it out?"

"Veronica, you're building this up out of nothing! There is nothing going on." She only got a complete sentence out because Veronica had begun pacing up and down the main aisle of the store, stalking on her high heels as though on stilts.

"There's something going on, I know it. He doesn't answer his phone. He doesn't return his messages. There's something going on. There's something going on."

"He's working, Veronica. Maybe that's what writers do. I'm not a writer, I wouldn't know. *I* tried to call you yesterday, three times."

"What are you doing, checking up on me? Trying to make sure where I am so I won't catch the two of you screwing me over? Or maybe just screwing, is that it?"

"Veronica, that's *enough*," Regan had raised her voice, without meaning to. "If you're going to talk trash in the store, then get out."

Veronica stood giving her a hard, angry stare for a few seconds, then suddenly turned and began pacing up and down the center aisle again, muttering to herself. "Talk trash in the store...talk trash in the store...I wasn't talking trash, that's just the truth..."

"I wasn't checking up on you, Ver, I was checking *on* you. I was worried about you." Regan had to raise her voice to speak over Veronica's mutterings, which continued.

"Talk trash in the store...talk trash in the store..." She stopped dead and rounded on Regan so suddenly that, even though she was standing six feet away, Regan involuntarily took a step back. "I saw you," she said in an almost triumphant tone.

"What do you mean?"

"On Tuesday night. I saw you—" Veronica stalked forward until she was standing so close to Regan she was almost touching her, glaring down at her. "I saw you in your car, turning back onto Swansea from River Road! I *saw* you. Now explain *that*."

Caught, Regan couldn't think of an excuse that wouldn't sound patently false even to someone in Veronica's state of mind. "I can't remember! River Road is miles long, and it's none of your business anyway."

"River Road is the middle of nowhere and there's nothing on it but fucking cows, fucking woods and Jonathan's house. So which one were you visiting at nine fucking thirty at night?" The cordless phone was by the cash register, Regan recalled—she turned to go around the counter and Veronica shrieked, *"Answer me!"* and grabbed a fistful of Regan's hair.

"Veronica, damn it, let go!" Regan shoved back at Veronica and managed to thump her solar plexus with an elbow, hard enough to surprise her into letting go of Regan's hair. Regan spun around and put several feet of space between them as fast as she could. "If you don't stop this, I'm calling the police, Ver."

Veronica was trying to catch her breath. "What, are you afraid of me, Regan? Go ahead and call the police! Go ahead! Call them! It won't be the first time."

It wouldn't be, and Mrs. Wharton had been furious about the store getting bad publicity, as she called it, from the resulting news item in the local paper, whose editor had a police scanner. "Is that what you want, Ver? Handcuffs and the whole bit, that's what you really want?" Her scalp was stinging: Veronica's long nails had drawn blood.

"Oh, is that how you'll get me out of the way, you and Jonathan? Have me arrested so I can't bother you anymore? I don't care! Answer me, Regan! What were you doing on River Road on Tuesday night? You were with Jonathan, weren't you? Weren't you?"

"Yes, I was. Are you happy, Ver? I went out there to talk to him. Make anything you like of it, I can't stop you. You'll believe what you want, anyway." She had the cordless in her hand, and waited, her knees shaking. There were two things that could happen now, she knew from experience: either Veronica would lunge at her in a fury, or...

Veronica's face twisted, her shoulders sagged and she let out a sob, her hands dropping limply to her sides. As pained as she was to see this, Regan also let out a sigh of relief. "Such a loser...such a loser..." Veronica was saying, or that's what Regan thought she was saying. It was difficult to understand her. Veronica put a hand over her eyes so tightly it looked like she would hurt herself.

"Veronica...you need to just...calm...down. Remember what we talked about on Monday?"

"Monday?" Veronica looked up blankly, her face glistening. "I don't remember talking to you on Monday."

"You came in to talk about what happened Sunday, at Hong Kong Delhi..."

Veronica was staring at her blankly. Tears were still running down her cheeks, but her expression was hardening. "Monday? I haven't talked to you since...what did we say?"

Against her better judgment, Regan said, "I just said that maybe you should...cool off a bit, you know. I said that if a guy is trying not to encourage you, it might—"

"What do you mean? Is that what you two decided to tell me?"

"No, that's what *I'm* telling yo—"

"You're a fucking liar, Regan! I never talked to you on Monday! You're making this up, you're making it all up! You were out there talking to Jonathan about me on Tuesday, weren't you? You told him everything about me, all the shit you promised you'd never tell, and now he doesn't want anything to do with me!"

"Veron-"

"Who the fuck are you to give me advice? What do you know about guys, you fucking little workaholic? Everyone thinks you're so great, my father thinks you're so wonderful, running a whole business, this crappy little dump, it's nothing but your way of pretending you're not a loser! You're so fucking superior because you think I'm a stupid rich bitch who's never had a job—but you're the one who doesn't have a life, so you have to steal mine! I've had relationships with more guys than you've even met and you're telling me what to do? Stay the fuck away from my men!" She snapped her purse handle up on her shoulder and wheeled toward the door. "I'm going out there. Nobody blows me off. Nobody!"

The bells clattered furiously as the door almost hit the wall, which took considerable force to do. Regan stood by the counter, clutching the cordless so hard her knuckles were white. After a moment she said, "Jesus fucking Christ." She heard gravel spraying across the parking area as the Mazda spun in a wheelie and then its engine gunned and roared out of the lot and down the road. Regan closed her eyes involuntarily—Veronica clearly had not bothered to look before she pulled out. It was another second or two before Regan broke out of her shocked immobility. Then she went over and locked the front door and ran back to the office. She rummaged helplessly in her handbag and then turned it over and dumped it out onto the desk, ignoring the coins and pens and Chapsticks that promptly rolled off onto the floor. She found the card with Jonathan's phone number and dialed it, her fingers shaking. One ring...two... three...four...then some clicks, and a generic mechanical voice: "please leave a message at the tone." Jonathan must be online. "Jonathan," she said, her voice quavering, "Veronica just left here and she's on her way out to your place. She's really in some kind of state. You might want to just leave the house. She can be—" it seemed so unfair to call Veronica violent. *She'd never hurt anyone, not really...* "unpredictable, when she's like this. Call the police if you need to." She clicked off the phone and stood looking down at it, numbly trying to think of something else she could do. *Should I call the police?* But she didn't want to send the police to Jonathan's house without warning him first. She had no idea what trouble that could cause for him, no matter what Veronica was doing. After a moment, she remembered what he'd said about his e-mail's new message alert. She sat down at her computer, opened her own e-mail window, and sent a message to Jonathan's e-mail address, containing basically the same words she had just left on voice mail. All this took time to do, and each key click seemed to eat up whole seconds. *How long would it take Veronica to get out there?* On Tuesday night, it had taken Regan about fifteen minutes. But the way Veronica was driving... *and that's if she gets there at all.* In the past twenty-five years, there had been six fatal accidents on River Road. It had some very treacherous bends.

The cordless phone buzzed, and Regan reached for it so fast, she swept the rest of her handbag contents off the desk. "Borrowed and Blue," she said breathlessly, then, her voice dropping, "Oh. Hiram. Yes, I got your message. We've been playing telephone tag."

"I'm sorry, Regan. I went out of town for a couple of days. I needed to get away."

"I know the feeling."

"Is everything all right? You sound upset."

"No, no, everything's fine. Look, Hiram, I've got customers in the store, I can't talk."

"I understand. I just picked up your message from my voice mail, and I wondered if you'd be free to get together tonight? I've got some information I really think you should know."

"Uh...I'm sorry, I can't tonight, Hiram, something has come up, it's pretty urgent." She jerked around at a tapping on the front door glass. "Look, I've got to go, I'll get back to you later." She hung up without waiting for his reply and hurried out into the store, expecting to see a police officer or worse standing on the step. But it was only a customer, peering through the glass with her hand shading her eyes. Regan unlocked the door.

"Are you open? It's not seven yet."

Regan glanced at the clock over the cash register—it was 6:35 p.m. "Yes, come in, I'm sorry. I was just...in the bathroom." She hadn't turned over the CLOSED sign when she locked the door. As the customer came inside, another car pulled into the parking area. Regan tried to compose herself. She went back to the office and got the cordless and shut the office door, so the customers wouldn't wonder why her handbag had been emptied all over the floor. *I can't just go running out there,* she thought desperately. *I at least have to lock up the cash drawer and shut things down for the night. Jonathan must be able to handle someone like Veronica, she's not my responsibility—and neither is he. It's not like she's a mad ax murderer, for god's sake...*she jumped as one of the customers spoke to her.

"Are you okay?"

Regan forced a smile. "I'm fine. What can I help you with?"

The customer was holding a plastic grocery bag, and she opened it and removed a heavy tarnished brass tray with an elaborate pattern of embossed grape vines and pinecones around the broad border. "I was wondering if you had a pair of candleholders that might go with this? I've been to a couple of places already."

Regan stood staring blankly at the tray, thinking, *my god, that thing is ghastly.* After a moment she realized that the customer was waiting, her eyes plaintive, and gave herself a mental shake. "I might have something you'd like. Come on back here." She led the customer down the aisle to the storeroom, where she had some brassware she hadn't put out on the shelves yet.

It turned into one of those days with a flurry of last minute business, and it was 7:12 before Regan was able to lock the door, turn over the sign, draw down the shade, and close out the cash register and credit card terminal. The cordless phone had been mercifully silent—if it had rung, Regan thought she probably would have screamed. As it was, she had gotten several odd looks from customers. She locked up the cash drawer and receipts, and was on her knees in the office gathering up the contents of her handbag and stuffing them back into the bag when the cordless buzzed. Regan felt her stomach drop to her ankles. She stumbled to her feet and knocked the phone across the desk reaching for it.

"Hello?"

"Regan...?" Jonathan's voice sounded distracted, but very calm, as though he'd just been awakened from a deep sleep. "I wonder if you could come out to the house? I need your help with something."

She didn't waste time asking questions. "I'm on my way."

Regan didn't want to risk attracting attention by speeding, but she almost missed the third dangerous bend on River Road herself. As she pulled up to the house, one of her questions was immediately answered—Veronica's Mazda was parked directly in front of the entrance, askew, as though she'd pulled off the road and slammed on the brakes just before the car went through the front door. *Well, that's certainly obvious—anyone who drives by will see it.* The sporty little car was as conspicuous and incongruous in front of the old house as a man sitting on the beach in a tuxedo. Leaving her own car behind the Mazda, Regan went to the front door. As she was about to knock, she thought for a second that she glimpsed something light colored over in the woods south of the house, on the very edge of her vision. She jerked around, her mouth open to call Veronica's name, but nothing was there. She started violently as Jonathan pulled the front door open. "Come in," he said.

"What's going on?" Regan followed him into the hallway. It seemed ominously still in the house.

"I got your messages, but not soon enough. She was already here."

Regan hurried past him into the great room, but stopped in the archway in confusion. The room was empty. "Did she leave?" she asked blankly, even though a terrible suspicion was already forming in her mind. She turned and looked at Jonathan, who was standing at the foot of the stairs.

"When you said she was in a state," he said quietly, "you were making a severe understatement."

"Where is she?" Regan whispered. It was the look on his face that frightened her more than anything else. Regan had only seen that look on the faces of people who had very bad news to convey and hated themselves and her for the fact that they were the ones who had to tell it. When Jonathan looked down without answering, Regan put a hand over her mouth, cold with horror. "Oh, my god. What have you done?"

He looked up sharply. "She'll be all right. But..."

Then Regan knew. "Oh my *god!* Jonathan, how *could* you?"

"I don't know!" He almost shouted, and she took a step back. "I didn't mean for it to happen," he went on more calmly. "But she was just...she was completely out of control. I had to physically restrain her—and she's taller than I am, it wasn't easy to do without hurting her. Then...well, things just got out of hand. She was..."

"Are you blaming her? For what you did?"

"No, I am not. It was so unexpected, and she wouldn't...wouldn't let go of me. First she was trying to hurt me, and then...I just couldn't stop myself."

"Oh, don't give me that bullshit! Of course you could have!"

His shoulders stiffened a little and he looked away from her. "Well, I didn't. And it's done now, so arguing about it is pointless."

Regan took a deep breath, trying to regain her composure, which she knew she was going to need. "All right. So, where is she?"

He gestured toward the staircase. Dry-mouthed, Regan followed Jonathan silently up the unlighted stairs to the second floor. She had to keep her hand on the wall to guide her way in the almost complete darkness—Jonathan apparently could see perfectly. But there was dim light falling into the upstairs hallway from an open door. Jonathan walked quickly into the room, and stood aside so Regan could enter. It was the former master bedroom of the house, spacious and empty with only a full size box frame and mattress standing on metal feet, a small pine dresser and a wing-backed armchair, next to which stood a floor lamp with a dark red shade. Most of the room was dim and shadowed except the chair, in which sagged Veronica's limp form. Regan stopped frozen at the sight of her, one hand pressed tightly to her mouth.

"She'll be all right," Jonathan repeated earnestly. "But she'll be unconscious for some time."

Reluctantly, Regan walked slowly to the armchair and peered down at Veronica's face, which was so pale, it was almost luminous in the reddish lamp light. There were brownish streaks of makeup dried on her cheeks and her lipstick was smeared—beneath it, even Veronica's lips were almost white. Regan reached out and turned Veronica's head—yes, there it was, the ugly puckered wound, like a little mouth. The contusion around it was still reddish and darkening. Her breathing seemed shallow. Regan swallowed hard and drew back from the chair. "We need to get her to a hospital." But Jonathan took a quick step forward.

"That would be—very unwise, under the circumstances, Regan."

"Look at her, Jonathan. She could go into shock. How much did you drink? Was it more than usual?" He looked down, swallowing. "At least put a blanket over her," Regan said, reaching for the blanket on the bed, but Jonathan caught her arm.

"She can't stay here."

"But if we're not taking her to the hospital, we have to—"

"She mustn't wake up here."

Regan looked at Veronica and back at Jonathan, suddenly realizing why he was saying this. "How much did you make her forget?"

"With someone in her state, it's difficult to be sure. I pushed very hard—possibly too hard. But with luck, she won't even remember coming to the house. Where her memory will pick up, though, we won't know until she revives. And she might not be very coherent when she does. We have no idea what she might say."

Oh, god... "Then what are you saying? That we take her out and dump her in the woods somewhere?"

"Of course not! But...that's why I called you. What *do* we do?" As Regan sank down onto the side of the bed, he said despairingly, "I should never have let her into the house."

"Oh, screw the self-pity, Jonathan! *Should* is the most worthless word in English. Just shut up, and let me think a minute."

He complied. Regan sat, gnawing at the knuckle of her thumb and running over possible schemes in her mind. "It would be better if we could wait until later, but we can't, because she's going to be waking up. We've got to get her car out of here. Everyone knows Veronica's Mazda. Anyone that goes by the house will know she's here the second they see it. But if anybody else is seen driving it, it would look very suspicious. Veronica never lets anyone drive her car. She won't even use valet parking." She thought some more. "I think I have a plan."

Jonathan sat on the edge of the bed next to her. "What do you need me to do?"

"I'll take Veronica back to her condo in my car. You need to get her car to some isolated spot without being seen driving it. Do you think you can do that?"

"If I'm careful. I should just leave it by the side of the road?"

"Yes."

"Keys in it?"

"No. You're going to have to get the keys to me, and I'll need to know where the car is. Lock the car, too." She took a deep breath. "If anyone asks me, if someone sees me taking her back to her condo, I'll say that she called me on her cell to come pick her up, and I helped her get home. That's happened before. Go get her purse."

Jonathan returned with the purse. "This seems very risky," he said uneasily, as Regan found Veronica's cell phone and dialed the store's phone number. When the voice mail picked up, she waited several moments and terminated the call. "What are you doing?"

"Making sure my number is the last one dialed from her cell. Come on, help me get her into my car."

Jonathan carried Veronica down the stairs and, after carefully checking the road for passers by or approaching traffic, placed her on the back seat of Regan's car. Regan had decided that it wouldn't be wise to have Veronica upright but obviously unconscious in the passenger's seat. Privacy was one of the selling points of Veronica's plush townhouse unit on the east side of town. She could pull her car right into the garage, which had an automatic opener, and get Veronica inside without anyone seeing her.

"Now you understand what to do with her car?"

"Yes," he said uneasily.

"You'd better move it inside the barn until you go. I hope no one already saw it sitting out here."

"There's very little traffic at this end of the road. There's nothing past here but the dairy farm, and the road stops there."

"The police patrol this road, Jonathan. Kids come out here and have camp-fires and parties in the woods, and the dairy farm has had some problems with vandalism. In fact, it's school vacation week, the cops are probably patrolling even more. So let's move the Mazda. Wait a moment." She went over and took the garage door opener from the driver's side visor. "I'll talk to you as soon as I can."

It took her twenty minutes to drive to the condo—she was being as careful as she possibly could, obeying the speed limit to the mile, signaling every turn, keeping other cars far ahead of her. She expected Veronica to start waking up in the back seat, or a cop to pull her over, or both, at any moment. The seat beneath her was soaked with sweat by the time she pulled cautiously into the driveway of the condo and pressed the button of the garage door opener. The door groaned slowly open—glancing around, Regan saw no one, but she imagined that Veronica's neighbors were peering suspiciously from their windows, or that she would be greeted by a crowd of officers and cameras as she struggled into the house, half-dragging Veronica with her arm around Regan's shoulder.

Regan kept herself fairly fit, and the store was anything but a desk job. But as thin as Veronica was, Regan was winded and sweating by the time she got her friend to her bedroom, with its Crate and Barrel furnishings and coordi-nated drapes and bed set. She pulled Veronica's boots off, undid the painfully tight jeans and peeled them off Veronica's thin legs, and tucked Veronica into bed. Veronica stirred slightly and her lips parted. She whispered a few words but Regan couldn't make out what she said. Regan was so relieved to see these signs of life, however, that tears welled in her eyes. She went to the bathroom and washed her hands and face, and straightened her clothing, pulled askew with the effort of getting Veronica to her room. She searched carefully through the medicine cabinets and the drawers of the vanity and was not surprised by what she found. Then she returned to the bedroom and pulled a wooden chair, with a ruffled cushion on the seat, over by the bed and sat down.

Veronica sighed deeply, and her fingers curled; her lashes fluttered a few times, and she seemed to be closer to natural sleep now. After a long time, Regan slowly reached down and took Veronica's cold hand. The fingers curled around her own. Regan closed her eyes and relaxed, opening her inner senses—and immediately a flood of chaotic emotions made her reel. Shame, rage, longing, need, grief, and an unbearable emptiness overwhelmed her, making the cheerful bedroom as oppressive and smothering as a tomb. Regan dropped Veronica's hand, and had to take several deep breaths and consciously ground herself to regain at least some sense of center.

Veronica was still quiet. Regan bent down and very gently set the tips of her fingers against the injury on Veronica's neck, by now almost purplish-black. She grimaced a little at the feel of it, hard and hot and ridged to her touch. Then she closed her eyes, heart thumping, and the scene at Rainbow Stone house blurred into her mind's view, from Jonathan's perspective, which was disconcerting. She jumped at an impression of loud rapid banging, followed by something that sounded like glass cracking. *Did Veronica break into the house?* Then came a sensation of physical blows to her face, her chest...Regan would have pulled away then, but just as had happened with Evelyn, she felt locked into the memory, she had no power to move until it played out. *You've been seeing her, you lied to me about it, you let me think you cared about me and all the time you were laughing at me behind my back...*She felt herself speaking in reply—*Veronica, I hardly know you, we're just friends. Aren't friends rare enough in this empty world? When did I promise you anything else?* Veronica dissolved into a chair, sobbing helplessly, choking out almost incomprehensible accusations, *You hate me, you hate me because I'm not special, like Regan, I'm just a dumb little blonde chick, you hate me like everyone else does...*sobbing and sobbing, until Jonathan went to the kitchen and returned with a towel. He bent over Veronica to offer it to her, say-ing, *I don't hate you, Veronica, I couldn't, you're a beautiful woman, please try to pull yourself together.* Veronica stood up and threw her arms around his neck and clung, desperately, as though she was dangling in mid-air over an abyss, still weeping into his sweater. Regan, shaking, experienced Jonathan's sensations and move-ments as though they were her own, as he slowly put his arms around Veronica, at first putting hands on her shoulders with the thought of gently disengaging her embrace and pushing her away, but then stopping, because the smell of her, rich and warm and toothsome, like the smell of roasting meat, was filling his mind. He tried again, but the real obstacle was not her persistence but his own reluctance, he didn't want to push her away. *There's no need for you to be so upset, try to calm down and let's talk about this, like friends...*and her response was only to cling to him more tightly. He bent forward and breathed in the fragrance of her hair and the smell of her skin, and slid one arm around the small of her back. Very suddenly, he gripped the nape of her neck with his other hand and bent her backwards, over his arm, causing her to let go of him with a panicked gasp—*what are you doing?*—and he had already battened onto the soft skin of her neck, wet and salty with her tears. Regan, shuddering, forced herself not to break contact, even as her mouth filled with the taste of blood. She felt Veronica's hands clutching hard at handfuls of sweater, but her position made effective struggle impossible, and just as Regan remembered from her own experience, her muscles quickly lost their tension, as if from the effect of some drug. The images began to blur then, and Regan was finally able to pull her hand away and straighten up in the chair, forcing down a feeling of nausea.

Regan sat in the chair, watching Veronica sleeping, her mind going over memories of all the tumultuous years they had known each other. There was the date rape in high school that Veronica had confided to no one except Regan, and only after Regan had sworn an oath on a Bible never to tell anyone. She'd deeply regretted that oath when she heard what the secret was, but she'd never broken her word. After that Veronica's grades bottomed out and her father sent her to Concord Academy, where she recovered academically enough to finish four years at Brandeis. Regan went to Fitchburg State and got an apartment in Gardner after graduation, but she was still the friend that Veronica called when she wanted an abortion in her sophomore year. The father of the baby had beaten her senseless on several occasions. Regan had been Maid of Honor at Veronica's wedding, swallowing down all her doubts about the groom; that this one didn't hit women was the best thing that Regan could say about him. But after Regan moved back to Sheridan, her confidence and peace of mind both reduced to glass-edged shards, it was Veronica who listened to her vent and rave, never acting bored, shocked by nothing that she heard. It was Veronica who tried to encourage Regan to date, or at least get out more with their friends, even as she herself had latched onto boyfriend after boyfriend, culminating most recently with the sticky-fingered Terence who had fled to Texas with most of Veronica's bank account. But Regan doubted she had any right to offer Veronica advice on relationships. Her own relationship history over the same period of time was much duller and considerably more sparse. *Veronica was right,* Regan thought bleakly. *What do I know about men? I can't believe what I'm doing for one right now. It's bad enough that I'm an accessory after the fact by protecting Jonathan in the first place. This goes way beyond that. This is direct accomplice. If this blows up, I'll be in MCI Framingham—and that's if I'm lucky. And I'll deserve it. I'm betraying Veronica—even worse than if I had stolen Jonathan from her, much worse. How could I do this to her?* And yet the idea of coming clean and confessing, telling the police or even Hiram the truth—she couldn't even consider it. *Why? Wouldn't that be the most honest and courageous thing to do? What kind of an excuse for a human being am I?*

Her bitter reverie was interrupted when Veronica moaned, coughed a couple of times, and opened her eyes. She stared blearily at the sparkling plaster of the ceiling above her. "Where am I?" she said finally. Her voice was hoarse and whispery, and Regan had to lean forward to understand her.

"You're at home, Veronica. You're in your own bed."

"How did I...how did I get here? My neck really hurts..." she pushed a hand up from under the comforter to touch the injury, and flinched when her long varnished fingernails poked it.

"You had a...little accident, Ver." Regan licked her lips unhappily. *Liar, liar, pants on fire...*

"Accident?"

"Do you remember calling me?"

"No..."

"Do you remember leaving my store this afternoon?"

Veronica's voice was beginning to quaver. "No...is my car wrecked?"

"You weren't in the car. I guess you got a little confused, Ver."

"Did I hurt myself?"

"I think you fell. You called me on your cell. Don't you remember?"

"No..." She stared up at the ceiling. "I feel awful."

"Do you want to go to the hospital?"

Veronica suddenly clutched at the comforter and half sat up. "No! No hospital. No hospital, I'll be all right, please, Regan..." she broke off, coughing, and her face turned grayish white. Regan rose from her chair and put her hands on Veronica's shoulders, pressing her back down on the pillows.

"Okay, no hospital. I know how you feel about them, Ver. You don't have to go. Just breathe. It's okay. No hospital." Veronica subsided, breathing heavily, as if the exertion of even trying to sit up was enough to leave her winded.

"Jonathan..." she whispered after a few moments, and Regan tensed.

"What about Jonathan?"

"He was...I was looking for him. I think...I think I was going to come to the store and ask you if you'd seen him." Her brow furrowed. "But I don't think I got there...what happened, Regan?"

"I don't know, Ver." She leaned forward, and touched Veronica's hand. "Veronica...what happened to your prescriptions?"

Veronica stared blankly at the ceiling. "Flushed them."

"Why?"

"I thought...I thought he wouldn't like me if I was all drugged up. I thought he'd like me more if I was really me, not pills."

"You mean Jonathan?"

"Anyone," she whispered.

"That's not the only flushing you've been doing, is it? You been purging again, haven't you?"

Veronica was silent. Tears began to slip from the corners of her eyes and soak into the hair at her temples. "He won't like me if I'm fat. I can't be fat."

Regan shook her head sadly. "Veronica, there hasn't been one day in your life that you've been fat."

Veronica turned her face away, silent tears running over her cheek and down to the pillow now. "It doesn't make any difference. He doesn't want me, Regan. He doesn't want me, no matter what I do. I'll never, never, never be good enough." She closed her eyes; there were no hysterical sobs now, but perhaps she simply didn't have the energy.

Regan sat quietly for a time, then she got up and went to the bathroom and wrung out a washcloth in warm water. She returned to Veronica's room and wiped her friend's face off carefully with the cloth. *I guess we won't have to talk about that little scene in the store today,* she thought. *She doesn't even remember it. Thank god no customers came in, anyway.* "Veronica," she said gently, "I don't think it's safe to leave you here alone. Do you think it's time to...to go somewhere where you can get some help, and be looked after?"

Veronica smiled faintly. "Do you think I'm going to hurt myself, Regan?"

"Are you?"

"What does it matter? Who would care?"

"I'd care."

"I can't pay for that place up in J.P. My dad's cut me off."

"Cut you off?"

"He says he's sick of paying to clean up my messes, and it's time that I grew up. I can't pay for anything, Ver. My credit cards are maxed out. My dad's going to sell the condo."

"God, Ver—you never said anything about this."

"Just happened." She turned away again. "See, Regan—nobody wants me. Nobody. Not even my father. So who cares what I do? I thought...I thought maybe I'd found a really nice guy. Just in time. God or something sent me a nice guy, and everything would finally be okay."

"Veronica...you can make it on your own. Truly. You don't need a nice guy. Nice guys are like...a dessert at the end of dinner. You're not going to starve without one. You're the one who makes your life what you want."

"Maybe that's true for you, Regan. I can't do what you do. I can't do it alone."

"But you could, Veronica. You're smart, I know you could."

Veronica closed her eyes again, as if the light was too bright and was hurting them. "But I don't want to," she whispered finally. She was silent then, and after a few minutes, Regan realized that Veronica had fallen asleep.

She sat by Veronica's bed the rest of the night, dozing in the chair off and on. At around midnight, she was startled to hear a very light tapping on the kitchen window, which looked out over the back yard of the townhouse. She got up and went to investigate, and saw Jonathan peering up from the yard below. Alarmed, she went out on the back deck and down the steps, where he met her in the shadow under the deck.

"Jonathan, what the hell are you doing here? What if you're seen?"

His mouth tightened. "I had to get the car keys to you, and let you know where I left it. And I wanted to know...how is she?"

Regan sighed heavily. "She's a mess," she said after a moment. "But I'm not sure that's your fault. She flushed all her medications, she told me—I don't know how long ago. I'm guessing about a week. Oh, god, I should have seen this coming. She said something on Saturday...and even Hiram, on Sunday, asked me if she was compliant with her medications. I can't believe I let her blow up like this."

"You had some major distractions to preoccupy you. And that *is* my fault.

You're not her keeper, Regan." Regan just shook her head. "Does she remember anything?"

"Nothing after sometime this afternoon. She doesn't remember coming to the store. But she does remember that she was looking for you. There's nothing we can do about that."

Jonathan looked up at the kitchen window above them. "I'd give anything if I could take this back."

"I know you would. I wish you could, too." He looked slightly surprised. Before he could speak, Regan said, "Why did you let her inside the house, Jonathan?"

"I wasn't going to. But she was hammering on the windows with her bare hands. She cracked one of the panes, and I was afraid she would put her hand through the glass and seriously injure herself. I thought she might calm down if she could talk to me." After a pause, he said soberly, "I had no idea about the medications, or her history, or I might have handled the situation differently."

Regan looked at him sadly, wondering how many people in Veronica's past had thought exactly the same thing, too late. Jonathan glanced away uncomfortably and fished in his pants pocket. "Here's the keys," he said, handing them to her. "The car is on Proctor Road, the unpaved part—it turns off of River about a mile before the house, and runs north through the state park."

"Did you wipe down the car before you locked it?"

"Yes, I did, just in case." He gave her a calculating look. "You seem to have done things like this before."

"I've helped Veronica out of a few difficulties, yes. But those aren't the only life experiences that have left me just a little paranoid. You better get going, before the next door neighbor hears us."

He turned and left, and Regan was startled at the way he seemed to simply melt into the darkness, without a single sound. Perhaps she hadn't needed to worry about his being seen.

She went back inside the house, wiped off the car keys and put them into Veronica's purse, and sat back down by the bed. As the eastern sky was growing light and birds were beginning to chatter and sing out back, Regan woke up from a doze with a start. Veronica was awake, staring up at the ceiling.

"You've been here all night." Her voice was stronger, but so oddly flat that her words were a monotone, without emphasis, like a computerized voice message.

"Yes, I have."

"I think maybe I should go to the hospital, Regan. I think you were right. I need to go someplace for a while."

"I'll take you."

"All right, but I don't want you to come in with me."

"Why not? Veronica—I'm not just going to drop you off at the E.R. entrance and drive away. I'm going to come in with you and make sure you get checked in and seen."

"No." Veronica turned her face away. "I don't want you there, Regan. I don't want anyone there. You can come in, but then you need to leave. Promise me."

Regan was silent for a moment. "Okay, I promise. As soon as you're checked in with the triage nurse, I'll go. Can you get dressed by yourself?"

Veronica was able to get out of bed and collect her clothes, although she was very shaky. While she was in the bathroom, Regan, listening closely to the sounds from the half-open door, went to the bedroom window and leaned her forehead wearily against the frame, barely seeing the flush of deep red and orange that was seeping under the clouds on the eastern horizon. *I should hate you, Jonathan Vaughn,* she thought. *Why don't I hate you?*

Chapter 8

Regan managed to yawn her way through Friday without needing to close the store early. She had waited at the hospital until Veronica was checked in, and after the nurse took Veronica's vital signs, Veronica was ushered into an examination room almost immediately. Regan had no idea what the nurse thought about the injury, but Veronica vaguely hinted that it was self-inflicted. Regan called Derek Wilson to give her a ride up to Proctor Road to pick up Veronica's car. Derek seemed to feel oddly guilty when he heard about Veronica's breakdown. He was one of those friends who Regan couldn't get away with touching surreptitiously, so she could only speculate on why he was taking it so personally. Perhaps he blamed himself for their break-up, or thought that he should have realized how serious Veronica's mental state was. In the mid-afternoon, Regan received a terse call from a social worker at the hospital, telling her that Veronica Standish had requested that Regan be notified that she was being transferred to a facility near Haverhill.

Regan called Jonathan just to let him know where Veronica was. On Friday night, she went home, collapsed, and went to bed early, sleeping for a solid ten hours. She awoke on Saturday morning feeling rested for the first time in days—but her mind was active, turning over thoughts and questions and refusing to quiet itself. She thought about what she'd said to Veronica on Thursday night, about relationships and not needing a nice guy. *When did I convince myself of that platitude? Do I even believe it?* It seemed that now, she could think of little else but Jonathan Vaughn. *At my age, this is embarrassing—especially given what a shit he's been.* Her superficial self-recriminations had no effect. Over and over she caught herself thinking about things that Jonathan had said, or mystifying details from the barbed wire ball, or unanswered questions about how he spent his days and supported himself. He was like a loose tooth that she couldn't stop poking and wiggling with her tongue no matter how hard she tried.

By the end of the weekend, daffodils were blooming on sunny banks, and the forsythia had come out everywhere in messy tangled eruptions of bright yellow, like fireworks frozen in mid-burst. Business was slow. It was good yard work weather, with mild temperatures and a break in April's almost unceasing rainfall. With less to keep her occupied, Regan felt uncharacteristically spring-feverish and fidgety having to spend all day in the store. But to her surprise, Jonathan came in on Saturday afternoon. When the bells jingled and he walked through the door, Regan felt a bit of a chill, since she had just been reflecting on the fact that it was exactly one week since their eventful first meeting here after hours. She hadn't seen him since the whispered conversation underneath Veronica's deck.

"I thought I would come in and check it out," he said cheerfully after he greeted her. "I didn't get a fair look at it the last time." There were two other customers in the store, a middle aged woman and a sadly overweight young mother in sweat pants and sweat shirt, with a whining four year old in tow. Regan watched as both of the women kept glancing at Jonathan as he meandered up and down the aisles, apparently oblivious to them. His clothes were as casual as always. Like his car, they seemed calculated to attract little attention and provide few details to stay in anyone's memory. Today he was wearing dark blue slacks and a gray sweater, and generic black-rimmed sunglasses that he could have bought off a rack in any CVS store. But someone who looked like Jonathan would have had trouble dressing down to full invisibility. It wasn't his face but his body that caught the eye—or rather the way he moved in it, lithe and controlled. It took a while before Regan realized that she herself was keeping her eyes on him a bit too much.

She watched with amusement as he struck up a conversation with the middle-aged customer, who was lingering, undecided, over a selection of pressed glass water goblets and plates—she'd been looking for a "small" wedding gift for a friend's niece, she had told Regan when she came in. The customer's somewhat tight expression softened into a smile under Jonathan's attention and she kept tugging at her cardigan sweater as though she thought it wasn't hanging correctly on her plump shoulders. With smooth subtleness, Jonathan persuaded her to choose the most expensive pieces on the shelf, and as Regan wrapped them carefully in tissue paper, found a gift box, and ran the customer's credit card, he offered some wrapping suggestions. As the customer left, smiling, the sweat suit-clad mother poked her head around the end of an aisle and asked Jonathan his opinion on whether she should buy a brass wall-hanging candleholder or a terra cotta plant pot. She all but simpered as Jonathan gave her his full attention, and left the store with neither the candleholder nor the plant pot, but an art nouveau cast bronze statuette that cost more than both put together.

"My god," Regan said when she and Jonathan were alone. "Would you be interested in going partners, by any chance?"

He grinned for a second. "I couldn't do this all day. I am in awe of your stamina. But this is a very nice place. I can see how much work you put into it, and not just during business hours."

"Of course, there are pros and cons to that. I work long hours, just barely make a living, and it has been said, by some, that I don't have much of a life. The store is open six days a week. I come here, I go home, I get on the computer looking for sales and reading trade e-mail lists, I go to bed, I get up, I come here."

"There are no other employees?"

"Can't afford it. I wish there was some trustworthy person who loved old stuff and small businesses enough to want to volunteer—even ten hours a week. But I haven't found one. Plenty of inquiries about whether I'm hiring, but—these days, no one can afford to volunteer."

Jonathan looked around the store speculatively. "Have you thought about branching out into mail-order or online auctions?"

"I've thought a lot, about both. But those involve a whole different business paradigm. I'm afraid the owner is not interested in taking a risk on that kind of expansion." He nodded, not asking her for more details. She decided to change the subject, as it was making her irritable. "So, you've managed to pry yourself away from your book for a little while?"

"Just taking a break, yes. I've been thinking about what you said the other night, about buying that old house and restoring it. I haven't made any decisions yet, but the more I consider it, the more attractive the prospect seems. I want to wait and see whether my life here settles down a bit more, before I make that kind of commitment, but...I was struck by your comment about it being torn down for condos. That would be a shame."

"I don't know if you *could* put condos on that piece of property, but I know what the housing market is like in this state right now, and I don't think the family wants to hang on to that old place forever. Some developer's going to go to the Planning Board with a 40B and it'll be history. Did Derek have any idea what it might go for?"

"It's just listed for rental right now. But I can ask him."

"Good, let me know, I'm curious." Keeping her tone carefully casual, Regan added, "By the way, if you're taking some time off this weekend, maybe you'd like to do something with me tonight? Or tomorrow night I close at six and won't be open on Monday."

"Do something?"

"Like go out to a movie, or whatever you feel like."

He started to smile. "Are you talking about...a date? With me?"

"Silly man. No one *dates* anymore. We'll just be, you know, hanging out."

His smile faded. "Do you really think it would be wise for us to be seen hanging out together, right after what just happened to Veronica? I'd hate for all your friends to think that her jealousy wasn't baseless, after all."

Regan suddenly felt a surge of anger, although not at Jonathan. "I'm not going to let Veronica control my life, Jonathan. You're not hands-off just because she fixated on you without your giving her the slightest encouragement. God! There are women in this town that would snap you up without a second thought, why do I always have to be the one who ends up standing out on the corner?"

He was staring at her blankly. "Calm down, Regan."

She stopped, suddenly realizing that she'd been on the verge of a rant. "I'm sorry. But people will think what they want to think, Jonathan. I'm sure none of our friends have any real illusions about you and Veronica. We've seen her go through this too many times before."

He considered a moment, examining his sunglasses in his hand. "Well. I have some things I need to do this afternoon, but I wouldn't mind taking in a movie with you tonight. Should I pick you up here or at your house? Or—"

he grinned suddenly, "this being the twenty-first century, maybe you'd like to pick me up?"

I am picking you up, Regan thought wryly. "Meet me at my house, that way I can clean up a little. We can flip a coin on whose car to take." She took one of the store's cards from its holder on the countertop and wrote her address on the back of it. "Can you find this, or do you want directions? It's really very easy, it's right on the main road."

He nodded, reading the card. "Would eight o'clock be early enough?"

"Almost too early, if we go to the Cineplex at the mall. Have you been up there yet?"

"No, I don't go to shopping malls too much. I very seldom do any shopping." Jonathan was at the door and about to pull it open, when he paused and bent down, shading his eyes and peering intently across the street, squinting painfully even though he had put his sunglasses back on.

"What is it?"

He gestured to her to come to the door. With a sense of apprehension, she joined him. "Look over there. I can't see too well in full daylight—but is there someone back in the shadows, in the trees?"

Regan peered out. "I can't make anyone out. Why? Did you think you saw someone?"

"I'm not sure. But it seemed to me that someone was standing under that large oak there, watching the store. Just as he would have seen me about to open the door, he ducked back into the shadows. There was something furtive about it."

Regan stared at the undergrowth. "Did it look like it could have been a young person, maybe a kid? Because last weekend I thought I saw one just in that spot. But he could have just been passing by. Should we go look?"

She and Jonathan stared at each other for a moment. "Let's go look," he said.

They walked across the parking area and then crossed the two lanes of Swansea Road, and went to examine the area around the oak. They had to step over a shallow, muddy ditch and then clamber a short, steep bank to level ground. Regan had never taken a good look at this side of the road, which was undeveloped and mostly an impenetrable thicket of blackberry brambles, poke plants, waist-high grass and milkweed, with dense second-growth woods behind it. But Regan was surprised, and a little alarmed, to see that a sort of beaten trail ran through the undergrowth behind the oak tree, paralleling the road for a ways and then winding off into the woods. It looked as though it was part of a network of paths made by local kids—there was a bicycle tread visible in the ground at one point. East of this woody patch, several housing developments had gone up over the past ten years, and the proximity of Adams Elementary had made them a draw for young families. The figure that Regan remembered seeing had looked older than grade school, but all sorts of people might use these paths, especially with no sidewalks along the busy road. As she was studying the trail, Jonathan pointed to the base of the oak tree. There were several small candy wrappers lying on the ground, all in one spot, and they looked quite new. Jonathan knelt down and studied the ground, but there was such a mixture of closely overlapping footprints, it was impossible to discern details about the size and type of shoe.

"Someone is spying on my store?" Regan said, hushed. "What does it mean?"

"I don't know. You haven't noticed any evidence of attempted break-ins or vandalism?"

"No. But I sure am going to look a lot more closely from now on. Maybe I better ask the cops to do some random patrols, too."

Jonathan stood up, frowning darkly. "It wouldn't hurt. But...I'm not sure the store is what interests them." He looked at the paths. "If whoever I saw took off when we came out the door, he could have been half a mile away by the time we crossed the street. Maybe he won't come back now that he's been spotted. Or maybe he'll try something else."

"What do you mean?"

"Just keep your eyes open for anything unusual."

"You're making me paranoid, Jonathan," Regan said as they walked back across the road.

"A little paranoia can be very helpful. I'll see you at eight."

The movie excursion was entertaining but not particularly intimate, as Regan and Jonathan ran into Karen and Steve as they were standing in line for their movie tickets. Karen wanted to see *Ella Enchanted*, Steve wanted to see *Kill Bill Vol. 2* and neither of them wanted to compromise, so the argument was far advanced when Karen called Regan over and dragged her into it. All four of them ended up seeing *Hellboy*, which Steve loved, Karen hated, and Regan found mildly enjoyable. Jonathan was fascinated by the special effects, but he commented to Regan afterwards, "Not exactly what I'd call a date movie."

"Oh, I don't know. It was a love story. It had a happy ending."

"More or less." In the car on the way back to Regan's apartment, he said idly, "I guess we'll see now what your friends think about our hanging out together, won't we?" Regan reflected that Karen had not seemed particularly surprised to see her and Jonathan taking in a movie.

At 10:15 Sunday morning, Regan was drinking cold coffee and studying eBay listings on her computer at home. When the phone rang, she picked it up without taking her eyes off the screen—she often got several calls on Sunday mornings before she left for the store. "Hello...oh." She cleared her throat uncomfortably. "Hello, Hiram. Sorry I cut you off like that on Thursday. I had a personal crisis going on, and I guess I was a little panicky."

"That's quite all right. Is everything okay?"

"It is now."

"Do you have a few minutes to talk?"

"Sure. You mean this is something you can discuss over the phone?"

He scoffed. "I prefer talking about anything important in person, that's all. But with classes resuming tomorrow, I don't have a lot of time, so driving down there to meet with you isn't an option."

"I'm at your disposal, go ahead. You said something on Thursday about some information I needed to know? That was right before I hung up on you."

"Yes, that's what I'm calling about. I've got some information about your friend Mr. Vaughn." Regan sat silent for a moment, suddenly feeling cold. "Regan...?"

"Yes, uh...what kind of information?"

"Well, I spoke to a Detective Colin Fellman in the Sheridan police department. He's been very helpful. You recall that one of the victims was from Sheridan—the high school student. The Sheridan police have been extremely concerned about this because of the boy's age. They haven't gotten anywhere with the case and the parents have been raising a bit of a stink about it. So Detective Fellman was more receptive to my suggestions than he might otherwise have been."

Shit... "We didn't interview that one, though." The boy's parents had been quite hostile to the suggestion.

"No, but the basic details were identical to the cases we did see."

"Hiram—you didn't tell Detective Fellman that I—"

"No, Regan, I didn't mention your name, don't worry."

"Wasn't that incident back in mid-February? How could you connect that to Jonathan Vaughn? He didn't even move here until a month later. He was out in Olympia, Washington."

"What makes you so sure?"

Regan leaned back in her chair, closing her eyes for a moment. "Hiram... I seriously, seriously, don't want to play this little Holmes-Watson guessing game. Spit it out. Please."

"Detective Fellman ran records checks on Vaughn for Massachusetts, Washington and Rhode Island. According to him, what's strange about the Washington and Massachusetts records is what's not on them. Oh, they're clean enough—not even a parking ticket. But they go back just so far and stop. Vaughn's Social Security number, for example. He was issued a new one in 1993. At that time, according to the Social Security Administration, he did give an address in Washington State, but in Seattle, not Olympia. According to his credit report, he left Washington a year ago."

"A year ago? Then where did he go?"

"We don't know yet, but he's been here since last August."

"You mean in Sheridan?"

"No, Brockton. He sublet an apartment up there—rather a nice one, actually. The lease expired in February and he packed up with no forwarding address.

The building manager said he left the apartment in pristine condition. Looked like it hadn't even been lived in, he said."

Regan recalled how clean Rainbow Stone house looked, even the walls appearing to have been scrubbed. "I'm having trouble seeing that as suspicious."

"Anyplace that might be a crime scene and is too clean is very suspicious indeed."

"Were there any incidents in Brockton?"

"Not that I know of, but that doesn't mean there weren't. Detective Fellman is checking with the P.D. up there, he'll be able to get information that I can't."

"Well..." Regan had a dreadful sense of foreboding. "What about Rhode Island? He said he lived there a long time ago."

"If he did, it wasn't under the name Vaughn. They never heard of him in Rhode Island. He hasn't mentioned a specific city or town to you, has he? Or someplace he went to school?"

"No, he hasn't. I haven't seen much of him, Hiram, I've been working."

"Ummm," Hiram said non-committally. Regan wondered if he'd been at the mall the night before. She didn't think Hiram was in Sheridan's gossip loop all the way up in Bridgewater.

"Why have you gone to all this trouble to check out Jonathan, Hiram? Are you picking on him for some reason you're not telling, or have you looked at other suspects, as well?"

"I admit, I just had this feeling about him—even before we met him at Hong Kong Delhi. I don't know why. But no, there's been at least twenty persons of interest among the various police departments I've talked to before now. They've all been cleared, one way or another—usually by process of elimination when all the different incidents were factored in. None of the men questioned so far could have committed all of them, they had alibis. But Vaughn's been completely off the radar."

"He might have alibis for all of them, if you asked him."

"He might. There's more, though, if you want to hear it."

Regan sighed. "Go ahead."

"I used a mapping program on my office computer and entered the locations of the sixteen incidents—or assaults, I should call them now—that we know. I wanted to see where they were centered. Taken all together, the sixteen of them are scattered around a point roughly between Taunton and Bridgewater. But when I split them up, and just enter the ones that occurred between November and February, they're distributed in a rough circle right around Brockton. When I enter the cases that were reported from mid-February up to now, those cases are centered approximately on Somerset."

Regan let out her held breath. "And here I thought you were going to say Sheridan, after all that build-up."

"There aren't that many cases to triangulate. But Somerset borders Sheridan, doesn't it?"

"A little piece of it does, yes." Rainbow Stone house was on the corner of Sheridan closest to Somerset.

"You didn't pick anything at all up from Vaughn when you met him, Regan?"

"Nothing like this! But what do I know, I didn't pick up that Veronica's last boyfriend was forging her signature on checks." Regan rubbed at the bridge of her nose tiredly—she was starting to get a headache. *God, am I getting to be a good liar, or what?* "Did you tell Detective Fellman about this mapping exercise?"

"I haven't yet, but I'm going to. He's my most sympathetic liaison so far, I'll let him communicate with other police departments. He'll have better credibility."

"You haven't heard of any other incidents since Evelyn Stockard, have you?"

"No, I haven't. But the victims have to contact me. I've gotten some information from police departments, but since HIPAA went into place, health care providers are so strict about confidentiality, they won't give out any information without a signed release."

"Which is not a bad thing, Hiram."

"Oh, I fully appreciate the need to protect private records from being misused. It's just a hindrance in cases like this one."

Then he hasn't got a clue about Veronica. I wonder if the hospital gave her Hiram's card? Regan thought. With a sudden qualm, she wondered if Veronica would contact Hiram after she got back from Haverhill. *She'd talk to me first...wouldn't she?* "It just doesn't make any sense, Hiram. Where was Jonathan Vaughn for a whole month? He didn't move in until March."

"He didn't sign a lease until March. He could have been in the house before that."

"What, just squatting there, no utilities, nothing?"

"The Sheridan police had two calls from the dairy farm reporting suspicious activity around the house between mid-February and mid-March. Once they saw lights, and once they saw someone moving around outside. The police checked and found no evidence that anyone had broken in or done any damage. But they did think it was strange."

"That part of town is a problem, Hiram, kids mess around up there all the time. The cops are out there a lot."

"I gathered that. It's just the way it fits into the larger picture."

Regan was silent, thinking. "Well," she said finally. "Keep me informed, all right?"

"I will. And, Regan..." he paused.

"Yes?"

"Just be careful. That's all. You're a grown woman and I can't tell you what to do. I won't argue that Jonathan Vaughn seems to be a very charming and civilized man. There may be nothing suspicious about him at all. But...be careful."

"I appreciate your concern, Hiram." Regan said after a moment. "You're a good friend."

After the call concluded, Regan sat thinking for some time, tapping her fingers on the top of the computer desk unhappily. What most troubled her was something Hiram had *not* said. *He didn't ask me to be sure and tell him if I learned anything new*, she thought uneasily. *I wonder why not.*

After some indecision, she called Jonathan and gave him a summary of the phone conversation. When she finished, he was quiet for a few moments.

"This is all very interesting," he finally said.

"Was that really you at the house in February?"

"No. I was in the area, though. I'm not denying that. Regan—you're not surprised by any of this, are you? You surely realized I had to have been here since last year."

"Of course I did. What's disturbing me is how much Hiram knows. Don't you find it disturbing?"

"I create the records with the intention of them being found. That doesn't bother me. And Derek Wilson knows I was in Brockton. I gave him the landlord's name as a reference. What does give me pause is Clauson's little map game. That's getting into uncomfortable territory."

"What if the police question you?"

"I'll cooperate. I've been questioned by the police before. I've been questioned by police, since the days when that meant you got taken out in the back alley and worked over a few times. I'm not afraid of the police."

"What if they arrest you?"

"Then I'll have to make a decision, whether to bluff it out or disappear. I can't be kept in custody, but if I break out of custody, I'll have to run. I'd prefer not to do that unless it's absolutely necessary."

Regan sighed heavily. "You know, I wasn't even sure I should tell you about all this."

"Why?"

"Because I'm wondering if Hiram told me with the expectation that I'd tell you. I don't think he trusts me anymore, Jonathan. I think that started on Sunday—I'm sure he thinks I'm hiding something to protect you."

"So you think maybe he's using you to feed information to me, in hope of trapping me somehow?"

"It sounds ridiculous, doesn't it?"

"Not if you have reason to believe that Clauson is that crafty and manipulative. I'll keep that in mind in deciding how to handle what might come up, though. One thing I've learned about cat-and-mouse games is that the loser is always the one who panics first."

Chapter 9

On Sunday evening, as Regan was locking up the store at about 7:00 p.m., she was startled to hear Jonathan's voice behind her. "You have a day off tomorrow, don't you?"

"God, don't do that! Where's your car?"

"Sorry, I didn't mean to scare you. I parked my car at that little strip of stores where the Laundromat is, about a quarter mile down the road. I wanted to see if I could catch a glimpse of your prowler—the one we saw yesterday. I walked up the trail until I could just see the oak, and waited there a while. I saw a couple of kids go through, but they didn't resemble the one I thought I saw yesterday, and they didn't linger anywhere on the way."

"You could be right—that now we've scared him away. And maybe he was never interested in the store, anyway. Do you want a ride back to your car?"

"That would be fine."

As she pulled out onto the road, Regan said, "to belatedly answer your question, the store isn't open on Mondays—but I hardly ever take a day off. Most Mondays, I go to sales or flea markets, or power-clean the store, things like that. But I might just relax tomorrow. I was open this past Monday."

"You deserve a rest. I enjoyed seeing that movie last night. Would you like to go to another one?"

"Tonight? I don't know...no, I think I feel more like staying in tonight. I've had enough of the public for a day or so."

"I can understand why you might feel the need for a little solitude. It must be very wearing to deal with customers all day, every day."

"I didn't actually say I wanted solitude," Regan said, as she pulled into the Laundromat lot beside Jonathan's car. "Why don't you come over to my place and we can just talk for a while?"

"Come to your apartment?"

"Why not? You didn't get to see it last night. You'll like it. It's got furniture." Jonathan smiled, but seemed to be pondering something. After a moment, when he didn't answer, Regan said, "If you think you'll be bored, we can rent a DVD or something."

"Oh, no, I wasn't thinking that. I'd be happy to see the inside of your place. Should I just follow you over there?"

"Follow away."

When they got to the house, Jonathan pulled his small car up behind Regan's. She unlocked the door into the back stairs that led directly up to her third-floor apartment. The paint was worn off the middles of the wooden treads and the stairs creaked at each step, while the stairwell as a whole echoed the noise. "You can see why I never worry about anyone sneaking up on me, although coming in late can be problematical."

"The other two floors are occupied?"

"Yes, and the landlady's on the first floor, so I have to behave myself. I'm the only resident in the whole house who's under sixty." They reached the top, and Regan shook out her door key and unlocked the door. "Welcome to my home," she said, and then mischievously quoted *Dracula*. "Enter freely and of your own will."

"Oh, stop that." Jonathan followed her inside and looked around, amazed. "Very nice. Very...eclectic."

"Decoration by thrift shop, a combination of what I couldn't sell and couldn't bear to sell. But have a seat, make yourself comfortable."

"If you don't mind, I think I'll circulate once or twice first."

"Go right ahead. Would you like some wine, or something to eat?"

"I'd like some wine, yes. But you haven't had any dinner, have you?"

"Oh, I'm not hungry." She went into the kitchen, and took a bottle of wine out of the refrigerator. "I hope you don't mind inexpensive wine." Jonathan had come to the doorway and was looking around at the white metal cabinets and chipped Formica counters. There was a 1950s kitchen table with chrome tube legs in the center of the room, with two matching chairs, the vinyl seats re-covered. Hanging on hooks on the wall above the counter and below the cabinets was a row of kitchen implements dating from the 1910s to present day—whisks, ladles, wooden and steel spoons, knives of all shapes and sizes, turners, a set of polished copper measuring spoons. The vinyl floor was worn through in places, revealing green and black linoleum squares underneath.

"It does seem a bit worse for wear," he commented as he accepted the glass of wine.

"But it's got a working fireplace, and the price is right." Regan went into the living room and struck a match to light candles on the mantel and then on the low table. Jonathan walked around the room, looking at the row of small sculptures on the mantel, the books and curios in two tall glass-fronted bookcases, and the pictures on the walls.

"Is there any significance to these little knick-knacks that you collect?"

Regan could understand why he asked, as there was no obvious theme to them at all. They ranged from kitsch to hand made sculpture, cute to avant-garde, plastic to bronze, human, animal or still-life. The only similarity among them was their small size. "They have their own significance."

He looked puzzled for a moment, then his expression cleared. "They all have a story."

"Exactly. That's why I keep them. These are the ones that I picked up, and immediately felt some strong feeling, or a vivid portrait of a person, or sometimes an entire tale, start to finish. Too bad I'm no writer, I could have a whole volume of short stories by now. This one, for instance..." she reached up and took a little plastic figurine of Walt Disney's Cinderella from the top of the nearer bookcase.

"This belonged to a little girl who was being treated for leukemia. Someone gave it to her while she was in the hospital. It was her favorite movie. She slept with this figurine under her pillow." Regan stroked the figurine's plastic gown with one finger. "She died."

"That seems very sad."

Regan sighed and replaced the figurine. "They're not all sad. But the sad ones are the hardest ones to sell. Sometimes I feel like...like I'm meant to remember these things, because everyone else has forgotten."

"That sounds like a heavy burden to take on."

"Is it? Is memory a burden, Jonathan, or a gift? What are we without our memories and our stories, after all?" She gave him a sudden sly look. "Are you *really* writing a book?"

He smiled, but straightened his shoulders. "I most certainly am. I started it about thirty-five years ago, but—"

Regan laughed. "Don't rush into anything."

"No, but I am hoping to get it finished now. And I really have published some magazine articles. I didn't just make all that up."

They sat at either end of the long couch, which had a slipcover with several layers of hand made quilts and afghans on top of that. The cushions were thick and pillowy. Regan kicked off her shoes and sat cross-legged against one arm of the couch, facing Jonathan who settled at the other end with one foot tucked underneath him, as flexibly as a yoga teacher. Regan was sorry to see him sitting still, she was so fascinated by the way he moved. "I was wondering just what you were thinking about, when I invited you back here. I wasn't sure you were going to answer."

He smiled down at his wine. "I was thinking what it might mean, when a lady invites a gentleman to come up to her place."

"Well...what would you like it to mean?" He hesitated, and she said, "I don't want to put you on the spot. I don't know what sort of invitation you would find welcome. I guess that's part of what I'd like to figure out."

He abruptly took a gulp of wine. "If I didn't want to be here, I wouldn't be."

"I'm glad to hear it. I don't need any favors."

"No, you seem very independent."

Regan laughed, a little bitterly. "And does that put you off?"

"On the contrary. I admire it." His expression became serious. "But don't disdain favors. Everyone needs them sometimes. I definitely owe you a couple of them."

"Careful. I'll remember that."

"You should."

Regan cleared her throat, not having intended the conversation to turn so solemn. "I've been wondering how you ended up out in Washington."

He shrugged. "Why not? I've lived all over the United States. When you don't age, you can only stay in one place for so long, even if you don't have to cut cables and run for some other reason, which has happened to me several times, as well."

"With all that stealing you did, I can just imagine."

He laughed. "There was that, and there were one or two other sticky legal situations in which I decided I'd better disappear before I risked exposure. I generally go underground for a few months, sometimes longer, before I emerge someplace else with a new identity. Documenting the new identity usually takes some time and planning, and sometimes traveling, if I want to plant hard copy."

"Plant hard copy? What, you mean sneak into records offices and put documents into their file drawers?"

"That's exactly what I mean. There are two reasons to open a lock, you know, and only one of them is to take things out."

"Do you fake your own death?"

"Rarely necessary, since a missing person is presumed dead after seven years. I never left any loose ends that would bog down that process."

"That must be hard to do, though," Regan said pensively. "Don't you have to cut all your ties and leave everything behind?"

"That's the hardest part, yes. That's a major reason I tend not to form close relationships. It does get very lonely." He took a sip of wine, as Regan thought about what he'd just said. "You know," he went on, "I've been answering a lot of questions. Do I get to ask you any?"

Regan drew back a bit, not even aware she was doing so. "Sure. That's only fair."

He was watching her skeptically. "You're so guarded, Regan. The minute I asked that, you looked like I'd pulled out a weapon. I don't want to offend you. But from my point of view, you're the mysterious one."

"Oh, that's crap. Compared to you, I'm dull, boring and average. In fact, compared to Veronica, I'm dull, boring and average."

"Don't I recall your saying something about people who claim they're boring, when I tried to do that?"

"Well," she snorted. "And look what *you* turned out to be."

"Well...just look what you turned out to be. I shook your hand and my life passed before my eyes."

Regan laughed weakly. "All right, touché. So what is it that you want to ask?"

He studied her thoughtfully for a moment. "Tell me...why you dislike writers so much." Regan pulled in a long breath. "I have a feeling this isn't a standalone question. Why did you retire from doing psychic readings? That's what Veronica told me. Why did you leave Gardner? What's made you so bitter at such a young age? Why do you live for your work?"

Regan sat quite still, a fist pressed tightly to her mouth. Finally she said, "People have been talking."

"Just a bit. Nothing I would call malicious...I do have a rather strong suspicion, however, that Derek Wilson has been trying to rouse my interest in you, before I get too interested in Veronica." He took another sip of wine and added, "It worked, by the way." He paused, watching Regan closely. "Tell me your story. I've told you mine."

There was a long pause, as Regan worked her toes into the quilt and Jonathan watched her expectantly. Finally Regan reached over and set her wine glass down on the table. "Why did I leave Gardner and retire from doing psychic work. Okay. I'll answer that. It's a long story, so make yourself comfortable." She hitched herself a bit straighter against the arm of the couch and sighed deeply before she began, without any further preamble. "I'd had something of a reputation, a following, even, since college. I didn't do fortune-telling or run séances—I've never seen a ghost, and I don't try to predict the future. But I could find things, like lost pets or valuables, and I could read people by touching them. So, by word of mouth, people would come to me every now and then to help them out. I never thought of it as being that big of a deal. I usually kept my abilities quiet, because people didn't always react positively to them. Either they'd be spooked or they'd make fun of me. Everyone knew that I avoided casually shaking hands or hugging people, and I only did readings on what you'd call a referral basis." She paused a moment, looking hopefully at Jonathan to see if he had any questions that would allow her to prolong the introduction.

"Have you had this ability all your life?"

"Yes, but I didn't really start using it for anything practical until my teens. That's when it really focused. Before that I was just kind of a daydreamy kid."

He nodded. "I've heard other psychics say something similar. But please go on."

She sighed heavily. "I got my degree in business management, in 1992, and I got a job right after that as assistant manager for an office supply store in Gardner, so I more or less settled down up there. My supervisors liked me, and after four years, it looked like I might be in line for the manager's position. That's the most exciting thing that was going on in my life—normally, the Montachusett region is even duller than down here.

"In the fall of 1996, life around Gardner suddenly stopped being dull, for anyone. A five-year-old girl disappeared in one of the neighboring towns. There was a massive search. This was before the Amber Alert system was implemented, but there was extensive coverage in the local news media. Well, three days later, that little girl's body was found. She had been...molested, and, uh...mutilated." Regan swallowed hard. "A week later, another girl, this one seven, was abducted from a school bus stop on a country road in a different town. Her mother usually met her at the bus stop, but she'd been delayed fifteen minutes, and when she got to the intersection, the little girl was gone. This girl was found two days later, same...method. So now, it looked like there was a serial killer-rapist targeting little girls. You can imagine the panic that was setting in. The FBI had come in, and there were profilers working, and curfews, and twenty-four hour police patrols. Parents escorted their children door to door, or they were supposed to. But you know how it goes. You've got two parents working three jobs, the kids have to go to school, and people just can't believe it would happen to them. Ten days after the second victim was found, there were no leads, no suspects, and... a third victim was abducted."

"Good god."

"In situations like this, law enforcement spends huge amounts of time sifting through tips from the public, including a lot of calls from people who style themselves psychics, or who say they talked to a psychic. Generally speaking, the psychic tips get tossed right in the trash can. The officers and agents have enough on their hands following up on the straight calls. I knew this, so even though a couple of my friends suggested it, I had no intention of trying to get involved. But law enforcement officers are human. When they've got something like this on their hands, they get desperate. So, one day I got a call."

"How did they know to call you?"

"It wasn't entirely official. There was a new officer on the Gardner force who knew me from Fitchburg State. He'd graduated a couple of years ahead of me, criminal justice, and he'd gone to the police academy and been hired in Gardner. Gardner was involved because some possible suspects had been from Gardner and were questioned there, and anyway, every police force in north Worcester County was involved in the case by then. So this officer, his name was Brendan Elliott, called me and asked if I'd come in and do some readings on some of the personal effects belonging to the first two victims. I agreed to do it, and when I got to the interview room at the Gardner station, there were detectives from several different towns, and two FBI agents there. They had some items on the table, clothing mostly, and I just sat down and took things one at a time and tried to see what I could get." Regan was silent for a moment. "It was *horrible*."

"You experienced the crime from the victims' point of view."

"Every...detail. This guy was *sick*. You can't even imagine. Full fledged sexual sadist. I won't even tell you what he did. But it was the pain and fear he got off on. And he stretched it out as long as he could. But that wasn't the worst of it. The worst of it was that I didn't really learn much that could help the case. I relived all that suffering, and I didn't even get a name, because I didn't learn anything the victims didn't know, and he didn't tell them his name. I did get a very thorough description. I could have picked this guy out in the stands at Gillette Stadium. I could tell the police what every square inch of him looked like." Regan's lip curled. "I could provide a detailed sketch of his little...dungeon, too. And they took it all down. I had descriptions of vehicles, two different ones. But no name, no license plate, no idea where the victims had been held while they were being tortured, because the victims themselves didn't know. I didn't have a description of the location exteriors, because he taped the victims' eyes with duct tape until he got them inside.

"Anyway, the officers all thanked me politely, I went home and threw up for two days, and on the third day, they found the body of the third victim." Jonathan let out a breath that was almost a hiss.

"The investigating team wanted me to come back and try again. Even though I hadn't been very helpful, as far as I was concerned, they were impressed at the amount of forensic detail I pulled up that was known only to the pathologist and detectives at that time. And, they'd thrown me some curve balls, put in a couple of items that had nothing to do with the victims, and I'd identified those immediately. So my credibility with them was pretty high." She sighed. "I was having nightmares every night, but I wanted them to catch this scumbag, so I went in to do a session with the third victim's effects. When I went in, besides the law enforcement personnel, there was a forensic psychiatrist and a couple of reporters. They were videotaping the session, and the atmosphere was very tense. I decided that I would push myself as hard as I could, try to see things from the perp's point of view, not just the victim's. I'd asked for anything they'd allow me to touch. I worked on it for an hour, and I went through every moment that child had suffered, but I didn't get any closer to an identification of the perp. Finally, the FBI agent who was heading up the team asked me if I thought I would be able to touch the child's body. I said I thought I could do that, if I didn't have to look at her face. So we got into cars and drove over to Heywood hospital, and trooped down to the morgue, and, uh..." Regan drew in a long shuddering breath. "They pulled this poor little cherub out of the fridge, and I...gave it a try." She was quiet for a moment. "Have you ever held the hand of a dead child?" she said softly.

"Yes, I have. My little brother."

Regan swallowed. "That's the last thing I remember."

"What happened?"

"I woke up, some time later, in Heywood's inpatient psychiatric unit, not in restraints, fortunately, the medications were enough, but...my official diagnosis was situation-induced brief psychotic disorder, or what you'd call a psychotic break."

"Oh, god."

"And it was all on videotape. I've never been able to watch it."

After a pause, Jonathan said, "Then they didn't catch the killer?"

"Oh, there's more to this story. They kept me in Heywood for ten days, mostly because they had to detox me off the medications once the shrink decided I was going to be okay without them. During that time, all kinds of excitement was going on in the big wide world. One of the reporters who'd been present did a whole write-up about the investigation so far, including a vivid description of my breakdown. Then, on day seven of my little vacation, a fourth victim was abducted. Officer Elliott, I was told, sat and watched the videotape of my breakdown, which wasn't that long, for more than four hours, picking it apart word by word, and piecing together things that I said until he thought he had a description of the perp's location. It did not conform to the profiles that had been developed by the FBI based on the available forensic evidence. But he called together the team and they triangulated the abduction locations with known structures that fitted Officer Elliott's profile, pinpointed a spot, and took an unmarked car to have a look, on the remote chance that something would pan out."

"Was the killer there?"

"Yes, he was, and very soon so were helicopters and S.W.A.T. teams and hostage negotiators, and to make a long day sound short, the perp ended the police standoff by shooting himself, and the fourth victim was recovered alive. Officer Elliott was a hero. I, on the other hand, was that nut case psychic."

"Oh, surely—"

"With the perp dead, and no trial to worry about, the news media were free to publish all the information about the case and investigation that they wished. The law enforcement people were lionized; I was made out as a well-meaning but pathetic and delusional amateur. The Boston *Globe* was the kindest—they made me sound almost like a fifth victim. Other papers were more harsh. The Lowell *Sun* pretty much implied that I was an attention-seeking con artist. A psychologist named Curt Parker managed to get quoted in a number of the stories, debunking psychics in general and using my breakdown as evidence that self-proclaimed psychics, as he put it, are all just mentally ill. He cherry-picked details to prove that all the information I'd given police were things that I could have made up or inferred, and suggested that it was just coincidence that Officer Elliott found clues in what I said during my breakdown. Pretty soon all the media were taking that slant. Before I wised up to this, I was interviewed by a number of reporters, and they all edited their quotes or video to make me look completely loony. Six months later one of them churned out a book about the case, and he went even further. He devoted a whole chapter to me and my background, and it wasn't very flattering. He used lots of quotes from Dr. Parker."

Jonathan shook his head in bemusement. "I haven't heard any such negative opinions of you here."

"Well, nobody ever went broke underestimating the attention span of the general public. These uproars never last very long. Once I was run out of town up in Gardner, everything sort of died down."

"What do you mean, run out of town?"

Regan picked up her wine glass and drained half of it before she answered. "Thanks to my ten-day stint in the hospital and all the publicity around that, I was fired by the office supply store. I collected unemployment while I started a job search, but my prospects in the Gardner area weren't too good. After all the news articles came out, I started to get prank mail, things about how I was doing the devil's work and the Bible said witchcraft and mediumship was an abomination, and that sort of thing. It was postmarked within Massachusetts, but otherwise it was all anonymous. Mostly I ignored it. But then I started to get prank phone calls, much the same sort of thing. I changed my number to an unlisted one, but I would still get an occasional hang-up call. Then, one day..." she paused for a moment. "I found my pet cat out in the back yard. He'd been shot to death with a pellet gun."

"Oh, my god."

Regan sighed heavily. "Mind you, I never could be sure that what happened to Sammy had anything to do with the letters and phone calls, or the publicity around the murder case. I didn't live in the greatest neighborhood, and it might just have been stupid, sick kids. But the police suggested that I might want to change residences...and so did my landlady. I lived in a house like this one, and the neighbors were spooked. I could understand it. What if this happened to their pets next, or to their children. I'd have been thinking the same thing. So the landlady broke the lease, and returned my deposit, and I moved back down here. Karen Tolbert, actually, told me that Mrs. Wharton was looking for someone to manage the store. I drove down and interviewed with her, and the rest is history."

"I'm very sorry. I mean about all your troubles, not that you got the job with the store. That's terrible about your cat. It's just so senseless."

"Yeah," Regan said, sighing. "I was sad about Sammy, but I think the worst thing was, I felt that I'd failed him, that he'd suffered because I was weird and different, and it was his bad luck to belong to me. Anyway, I've never owned another pet. And there's no lease on this place, just a tenancy at will agreement. In case I have to move again, it will simplify things." She took another long swig of wine and forced a smile. "So now you know."

"I'm sorry I asked."

"No, no, you were quite right. There's hardly been an equal exchange of information. I picked your brains, in more ways than one, but I refused to tell you any of my secrets. Not fair at all." She turned her empty glass upside-down and then got up from the couch. "Would you like a refill?"

"Thank you," Jonathan said, handing her his glass. Regan noticed that his eyes followed her as she walked out to the kitchen and got the bottle of wine from the refrigerator. "Is that why you're still single?" Jonathan asked when she returned with their glasses.

"Lord, I don't think anyone has one reason for being single. What do you mean?"

"I just wondered if perhaps you were afraid that anyone involved with you would suffer because of you. Or that your children would."

Regan frowned thoughtfully as she sat back down. "I guess I do think that, maybe. At least sometimes." She smiled grimly. "But that's not the main reason, no. It's not me who's resistant to relationships. Let's face it. How many men do you think are anxious to get intimate with someone who does what I do? I actually had a boyfriend break up with me by telling me that he couldn't sleep with me because he was afraid I'd be able to see all the nasty things he did as a little kid, and tell everyone about it. He was right, I might have seen those things, but it really hurt that he assumed I'd gossip about them. I have a lot of contact with people without picking up things about them, especially things they want to hide. But people seem to have trouble trusting you, when they think they can't fool you." She drank some wine and ran a finger around the rim of the glass pensively. "So here I am, living a life of involuntary celibacy, while everyone just thinks I'm a strong independent woman and probably a dyke. You say you don't have close relationships because you know you'll have to leave. I don't have them because no one wants to get near me. Life's a bitch, isn't it."

Jonathan smiled down at his glass. "Oh, I don't know...have you ever had an intimate relationship?" His voice was studiedly casual.

"Oh, sure, when I was young and reckless and my heart hadn't been broken too many times yet. I guess I did as many stupid things as anyone else, and was luckier than most. But ever since Gardner...I suppose I've been paying the price of infamy. It's been pretty quiet. I dated Steve for a while, when I first moved back here, but we just didn't mesh. And the store took up so much of my time—as much as I wanted it to, which obviously was a lot."

They were both silent for a few minutes after that. Regan found herself looking at the stretch of quilt between her own feet, and where Jonathan sat, and it seemed that the air between them was too thin, making it difficult to breathe. Her heart was racing, and she had no idea why. She realized that Jonathan, also, was studying the middle of the couch as though it held him fascinated.

Finally he said, "Well, I think that you already know everything about me that I'd want to hide."

Regan took a slow sip of wine, looking at him thoughtfully. "And I still don't know why."

"Given how much you were learning about me, whether I liked it or not, I really only had two options. I could have just left—or I could try to win your trust, by revealing everything to you without any conditions, and see what happened." His voice suddenly had a harder edge. "I get tired of holding everyone at a distance, all the time. Sometimes it seems that all I do is lie. There's not any point to existence without friends, peers, partners—people who trust you, and who you can rely on. I've come to believe that more and more as the years go by. For a long time I've been very cautious, and I've gotten sick of it."

"I can relate to that. I wonder if you've really shown me all your secrets, though. Who knows, there might still be things you're hiding, and don't even realize it."

"There's one way to find out. I'd be willing to risk it."

"What would you be risking, exactly?"

He broke his gaze to look down for a moment. "There have been people...

who were unpleasantly surprised when they got as close to me as they thought they wanted to. It's rather discouraging to see revulsion in a would-be partner's eyes, just because..." he trailed off.

"Because of what?" Regan was more curious than deterred. "Did these partners know that you're a vampire?" He shook his head. "Well, then," Regan said, and he only smiled faintly and shrugged.

There was another silence, and now Regan was beginning to feel her fingers trembling. "With everything I know about you, I still have trouble imagining that I would ever feel revulsion."

"No? But then, you're sitting way over there."

Regan deliberately got up, set down her glass, stepped over and sat on the edge of the couch, so close to Jonathan that their knees interlaced like fingers. He drew back a little, out of surprise. "Now I'm over here," Regan said, taking his wine glass out of his hand. She put her hands against his chest and moved them slowly along the curves of muscle and bone she could feel under the soft sweater he wore, then down his abdomen. He hitched back a bit so he could sit up straight, and Regan moved closer, sliding her leg between his thigh and the couch. "No revulsion yet," she said. He bent forward and kissed her, and they kissed for a long time, unhurriedly exploring with lips and tongues, as Jonathan wound the fingers of one hand in Regan's hair. They finally broke off for a moment.

"Still no revulsion," Regan said, reaching back to pull the scrunchie off her ponytail and let her hair fall loose.

"All right. I'm sorry I said that."

"I forgive you for your insecurities." Regan moved so that she was straddling Jonathan's lap, cupped his jaw with her hands and kissed him again. "I'm sure I have plenty of them, too."

"Where?" He sounded like he was trying not to laugh. He was getting bolder now, running his hands over her denim-clad hips, then sliding them under her sweater to touch her bare skin. They kissed for even longer, and broke off more reluctantly. Regan felt as though every inch of her skin was both cold and hot, and she was shaking, but definitely not with fear.

"Shall we move off the couch? It's comfy, but a little cramped." He swallowed hard, but didn't answer, and she wondered what was behind his ambivalence. "Okay, I'll be perfectly blunt," she said lightly. "Do you want to have sex with me, Jonathan? If you say no now, you'll only get one more chance. Okay, maybe two."

He smiled, but still hesitated. "I do...but...it's been quite a long time."

"Are you saying that you're out of practice? Then I confess: me, too. I'll make every allowance."

He almost laughed. "No, it's not that."

She waited patiently, then got up. "Well, I'm not going to do all the work here, and I'm not going to try to coerce you into anything. Come along, if you decide that's what you want."

She walked into the front bedroom, without turning on the light, and picked up a box of matches from the top of the bureau. She was almost finished lighting the candles on the dresser and nightstand when she turned and saw Jonathan in the doorway, leaning one forearm against the jamb, his hand rubbing his brow as though he were tired. "I am a perfect fool," he said.

She blew out the match. "Does that mean you're staying or going?"

"Staying."

"In that case, you're a little overdressed."

She pulled her own sweater off and tossed it on the small armchair by the dresser, and was reaching to unfasten her bra when he stepped up behind her. "Let me," he said, and she stood motionless as he unhooked her bra and slipped it off, letting it drop to the floor. Regan closed her eyes as Jonathan bent over her, cupping her breasts in his hands as he half-kissed, half-nuzzled her shoulder. After a minute or so he straightened and stepped back to pull off his own sweater. Regan, with a small sigh of regret for the pause, pulled back the antique handmade quilt she used for a bedspread, sending throw pillows flying. She shucked off the remainder of her clothing and sat on the bed to watch Jonathan as he did the same, a bit more methodically. The view of him undraped completely lived up to the imaginings that had teased her as she watched him walk around the store.

He came over and half reclined on the bed. She bent down and kissed him deeply, and they shifted and stretched out to achieve the maximum amount of skin contact, legs intertwining, hands sliding easily anywhere within reach. When they broke off the kiss, Jonathan asked, "won't you be cold?"

"Check out the radiators. This room tends to be too hot, at worst." She leaned over and started teasing Jonathan's nipples with her tongue and he fell back on the bed, sighing. Regan realized that his skin was cool to the touch, even where a living man would have been warm under any circumstances, but once she became used to that, she disregarded it. She could see how it might seem off-putting to a partner who didn't know the reason for it. But abruptly, Regan pulled back, and half sat up, blinking. "Oh. This is what you meant."

He slowly pushed himself up on his elbows. Regan ran a finger down the knotted white scar that ran jaggedly across his lower abdomen from the ribs on his left side almost to the pelvic bone on the right. She hadn't seen it when he undressed because the candlelight was so dim. She closed her eyes, catching her breath, seeing in her mind's eye the flash of the vicious serrated knife. Jonathan reached out and put his hand over hers.

"Don't..."

"I can't be in bed with you and not feel it, Jonathan. It's all right. I'm not going to jump up and get dressed." She slowly ran the flat of her hand along the scar, until the novelty was exhausted and she could allow the images to recede from her immediate awareness. "I'm not hurting, am I?"

"No," he said softly. "Each of us bears the scar of our last wound."

"It's impressive. But you'll have to do better than that to scare me away." She trailed her fingers down the middle of his belly. "Oh," she said in a tone of regret, "now look what I've done. What a spoilsport. I better fix this," and her hand continued down past the scar, curling affectionately around what had been a healthy erection until she'd thrown such a damper on things. Jonathan spoke one syllable and fell back onto the pillows. "I'm not hurting, am I?" she asked innocently.

"No," he said, muffled.

"Well, that's good," Regan said, fingers busy, "because I haven't had one of these to play with in ages, and I'll be crushed if you take it away."

He gasped once before he could say, "Don't worry."

For quite a while, they relished the experience of unrestricted contact with naked skin, basking in the pleasure of teasing and caressing, trading the active role back and forth. Eventually they both came to the point at which all this gentle excitement, however pleasant, was not enough. At the shift in mood, however, Regan felt a qualm. Jonathan sensed it and paused. "What is it?"

She cupped his face with her hands and kissed him, wanting earnestly to avoid hurting his feelings. "I've run into one of my insecurities. It's just been so long...let me be on top, it's easier that way."

He looked relieved. "Anything you want, I'm not fussy at all," and even as he spoke they were shifting in one motion, so that he was lying flat and she was straddling him. "I'm all yours."

She reached down and deftly tucked him into her, and slid backwards slowly, her teeth set because she half expected it to hurt. It didn't, but the sensation was so poignantly intense that she dug her fingers into Jonathan's chest, where she was bracing herself, without realizing it. He was caressing her thighs almost absently with both his hands and didn't even seem to notice her pinching fingers. It was a few moments before he managed to say, "you do that amazingly well for someone who's out of practice."

"Oh, well, it's like riding a bicycle, you know—" he started laughing. "I mean, you don't forget."

"I understand." He could reach farther than she would have thought.

"I can't—ouch—I can't laugh while I'm doing this."

"Then make me stop laughing. Ah...*that's* good..."

It went on for too short a time, as always. Regan found that she had almost forgotten what it felt like to climax with a partner, especially one whose own climax echoed through her body as intensely as Jonathan's did, a minute or so later. After that, she stretched out on top of him and he wrapped his arms around her like a child hugging a teddy bear. She was soaked with sweat, enough that she did feel a bit cold, but not enough to be worth moving. For some time nothing was said, as they simply drank in the consolation of physical closeness. Finally Regan sighed deeply. "Well. That was certainly...revivifying."

Jonathan chuckled. "Did you need reviving?"

"More than I could possibly have imagined. There's only one problem, though."

"And what's that?"

"Now I *am* hungry."

He laughed. "I'd better buy you dinner. Although that seems a bit backwards, doesn't it?"

"Not necessarily, not at all. But I don't feel like getting up and getting dressed, anyway. I won't starve." She was starting to feel fidgety, though, and apparently so was he. After a moment they were kissing again.

"Can you do this more than once in the same night?" Regan said hopefully.

"Oh, yes."

"You're probably going to wear me out."

They shifted position and kissed again, longer and more energetically. "Oh, I don't think so," Jonathan said when they broke off. "I don't think so at all."

Chapter 10

Regan slept in late on Monday. Jonathan had not stayed overnight, since they agreed that attracting the disapproving attention of the neighbors was probably unwise. The landlady, Mrs. Ferreira, tended a Holy Virgin shrine in the flower patch on the side of the house, and the front yard sported Republican campaign signs in election season. Although it would have been nice not to have woken up alone, Regan still spent the morning drifting around the apartment in a dreamy post-coital bliss she hadn't been able to indulge in for some years. Not even the fact that she was sore enough to be slightly uncomfortable diminished her mood. She'd toughen up soon enough.

By 2:00 p.m., she was feeling more energized, and was trying to decide whether she felt like going up to the mall. It was dark, gloomy, and raining, which made it a good shopping day. She was paging through the mass of Sunday circulars, looking for the new Target ad, when the phone rang. She had a cordless like the store phone, and she had to dig it out from underneath a pile of newspaper.

"Hello...Jonathan. What's the matter?" The tone of his voice as he said her name had been eloquent.

"Would you be able to come out here, as soon as possible? I need you to see something, and I may need your help."

"Well..." This sounded urgent. "I *can* do that. What's going on?"

"I'm not sure I should say more over the phone."

Now what the heck does that mean? "I'll be there in about half an hour, if that's okay."

"I appreciate it."

When she arrived at Rainbow Stone house, she noticed nothing out of the ordinary. She assumed that Jonathan must have put his car into the barn, and a passer-by would have seen no signs that anyone was home. But Jonathan opened the door almost immediately when she knocked.

"I'll have to give you a key. Come on in."

She followed him into the great room, almost afraid to look around. The last time she had been summoned out here for an emergency, she'd ended up helping to move a body, in a manner of speaking, at least. But there was no one else in the room, unconscious or otherwise. Instead, Jonathan went to the long cluttered work table and picked up a small box, which he handed to her.

"Do you know what these are?"

There were several small items, made of plastic, which had been hand-painted with model airplane enamel in a sort of camouflage pattern. They were connected in pairs with a short flexible cable, and they were all slightly damp. Regan turned them over in the box, thinking that they appeared very familiar—and then she realized what they were.

"Cameras? These are webcams! And these must be battery packs, with some sort of wireless node. Jonathan—what are these for?"

"I found them."

She stared at him blankly. "Found them *where?*" Then, recalling her apparent stalker, "At the store?"

"No, here. Outside, in the woods. They were hidden rather well. They're spy-cams, technically, they're weather-resistant."

She stared down at the box, aghast. "But how did you know to look for them? Did you just spot one by accident, or has something happened?"

He shook his head. "After what we saw at your store on Saturday, I couldn't shake the feeling that someone else was around the house somewhere, and that I was being watched. For several days now I've been looking around outside for any evidence, like footprints or those candy wrappers we found. Foolishly, it was just last night that it occurred to me to start looking *up.* The catch with surveillance cameras, of course, is that unlike microphones, they have to be in sight, at least the lens. If you can't see them, they can't see you. I actually found these rather easily, once I took my nose off the ground, because they have an LED." He pointed to one of the tiny red lights.

"Should we even be standing here talking near them?" Regan asked cautiously.

"Oh, their batteries are dead. These don't seem to have an audio component, anyway. Since they were sitting in the trees outside, they wouldn't have picked up much except bird chirps."

"Are these all?"

"I have no idea. These are all I found. There might be one trained on your store, too. We may take a look later on."

"Oh my god...that's what you meant when you said the prowler might try something else. Why didn't I think of that?"

"What normal person would? But we have a serious problem here. We don't know how long these have been in place, what they've recorded, who has been watching, what their motives are and where the information has gone."

Regan thought about this for a moment, and suddenly her mind went back to events that had taken place here the previous Thursday night. "Oh, *shit.* If those were here last week, when Veronica—"

"My thoughts exactly." He took the box back and put it on the table. "I was wondering if Hiram Clauson could have anything to do with this."

"Hiram? Oh, I don't know, Jonathan—it just doesn't seem like his style. I know he seems fixated on solving these cases, but he's always struck me as being very principled—to a fault, even."

"You were afraid he might be using you to manipulate me, remember?"

"He is a psychologist."

"Horrors," Jonathan said dryly.

"I mean that he knows how to use coercive verbal tactics. I can't see him climbing up in trees to plant cameras, from an ethical or a practical standpoint. For one thing, I doubt anything on these cameras would be admissible in court. Hiram would care about that."

"I wasn't suggesting that Hiram Clauson was directly responsible. I have very little doubt that our candy-eating friend from the store rigged these cameras. My question is whether Clauson may have hired him to do it, or be employing a private detective who's doing so."

Regan picked up the box of components and rattled it a little, brooding. "I just don't know. I don't think licensed detectives would hire minors, and I'm sure Hiram wouldn't. And anyway, look at this stuff, Jonathan. These are cheapie home brew parts. You can buy this stuff on eBay, or trade it around on newsgroups. You'd expect a professional to have access to something more sophisticated."

"That's a good point." He looked thoughtfully at the box. "Could you try reading these?"

Regan frowned dubiously. "I can try...electrical devices are tough. The electrical current tends to scramble the impressions. And these are new, they haven't been handled much. Not only that, their owner intended them to be secret. That means he'll have been blocking while he handled them. But let's see..." She set down the box and picked up each device, loosely turning and rolling it in her hand as she cleared her mind and allowed impressions to come in. The first two pairs brought nothing but a fuzzy jumble of images, like a radio station heard through heavy static. With the third one, she suddenly had an image of a boy, small and skinny, about ten years old, his brown hair overgrown and shaggy and his face dirty, wearing a stained t-shirt and shorts, saying *this is way cool, can I have this...*She blinked, feeling that she knew this child but couldn't remember from where. And why was she getting an impression of him from this camera?

"Anything?" Jonathan had been watching her intently.

"Nothing that helps us." She replaced the spy-cam in the box. "So, what are we going to do? We can't report this to the police, we don't know what this person knows. How are we going to find out who's doing this?

"I have an idea about that, actually."

"Which is?"

"I looked up some information on these devices. They don't just sit and run indefinitely, like the security cameras in a convenience store. They go through their batteries very fast, so whoever is monitoring them either put them up within the last twelve hours, or has been changing their batteries regularly. They also have a limited broadcast range. These are recording, until their memory is full, but their purpose is to broadcast the images somewhere else—a laptop, like that one, most likely. We're in the middle of the woods. There's nowhere with power around here where our stalker could be set up and watching continuously, and

I haven't noticed any mysterious panel vans parked down the road."

"There could be a kind of base unit somewhere, maybe with a laptop computer and wireless receiver..."

"There could be, but that also would only run a few hours on a battery pack."

"Are you absolutely certain there's nothing hidden inside the house, and plugged into AC current?"

"I've been over every inch of both buildings since I found these—looking for audio bugs as well as more of this camera equipment. You've seen how clean the house is—and it's almost entirely empty. I didn't find any evidence that anyone's been inside the house, or the barn, at all—except for one thing. I think someone may have been inside the cellar."

"A perfect place to hide a receiver, and audio bugs."

"I all but scoured it, especially the beams and joists. I didn't find a thing. But I'm sure the bulkhead doors had been opened, and there was a little fresh dirt on the steps. Fortunately, the door from the cellar into the kitchen is bolted on this side. No one can get into the house that way. I've bolted the cellar bulkhead from the inside, now."

"Have you been at this all day?"

"Yes, obviously. If I can't guarantee the house is safe, I'll have to leave—immediately."

Regan sighed. "You were saying, about your idea."

"Counter-surveillance. I think this stalker will be back. He has to be around here somewhere to monitor the camera images. He has to replace the camera batteries, and there's little point in doing that if he's not going to be monitoring them for a while. I've already moved my car about a quarter mile down the road, toward the dairy farm, and parked it in a little cut, out of sight. I think you should do the same, and walk back. We'll shut everything down in the house, lock the doors, and take to the woods."

"Jonathan—it's raining. Do you really think our stalker will be coming out to check his cameras in the rain?"

"I'm guessing he checks every day. Besides, it's that much safer for him—he won't expect anyone to be outside in this weather. He'll probably be less cautious than usual."

"What makes you think that he'll be back in the middle of the afternoon?"

"Well, for one thing, I downloaded the images from the cameras—"

"You did?"

"Yes, of course," Jonathan said a bit impatiently. "There's nothing to it, you just plug the damned things into a USB port. I wanted to see what the pictures contained—they'd be the ones recorded first when the cameras were last turned on. There's nothing but pictures of the house, but it's daylight—looks like mid-afternoon, from the shadows. Judging from the amount that the trees are leafed out in the pictures, the cameras were reset yesterday or the day before, at the earliest. The cameras don't register much in dim light. If these have been planted by the person both of us saw at your store, then he might come up here after he gets out of school."

"If he doesn't cut school to do this," Regan said doubtfully. "Okay, I'll go hide my car."

Half an hour later, Regan was huddled somewhat uncomfortably out in the woods to the east of the house, watching a clear space about ten feet away. Jonathan was convinced that the stalker was coming from this direction, using a network of trails through the woods between here and town. The trails were kept open by hikers, animals, people doing illegal hunting, and kids, but they didn't continue on the other side of the house, where the dairy farm's property began. The terrain there was boggier, heavy with brush and poison ivy, and all but impassable. "I think he either walks all the way, or leaves his transportation somewhere out of sight and walks through the woods so he won't be seen from the road," Jonathan had hypothesized. "He probably checks the front of the house for cars or people, or any other signs of activity. If he doesn't see anything, he'll reset his cameras and settle down."

"So what, exactly, am I supposed to do if you're right and he comes slithering along this path?"

"Nothing—just wait and watch. My guess is that he'll panic when he realizes his cameras are gone. He marked the trees they were in—very subtly, but in a way he could recognize even in the dark. He'll know the cameras have been found, right away. While that shock is still sinking in, you step out and confront him."

"Are you kidding me? What if he's armed? Kids carry Uzis these days, for god's sake."

"Kids in Sheridan?"

"Well..."

"Remember what he did when we spotted him at your store? No, I think he'll just bolt—back the way he came. And that will be his big mistake, because I'll be waiting down the trail for him. It doesn't matter to me whether he's armed or not. I'll be ready for him, because I'll already have seen him, on his way in."

"But Jonathan—if he's got some idea of being a vampire slayer, he might have something that could hurt you, couldn't he?"

"Oh, you mean, like wooden stakes or holy water?"

Regan flushed. "Don't make me feel stupid. You did say you could be destroyed."

Jonathan said somewhat dryly, "If he's carrying, say, a grenade launcher filled with white phosphorus, then I'm in a lot of trouble. But it would take considerably more to destroy me than a poke with a piece of wood. And I don't have any problems with the folklore deterrents like garlic or crucifixes. That's just three hundred year-old wishful thinking."

"If he'll pass you first, why not grab him then, when he'll be completely taken by surprise?"

"Because I want to make sure it is our stalker. I want to make sure he's checked the cameras, or tried to."

Swallowing hard, Regan asked, "Then what are you going to do with him?"

Jonathan looked at her for a moment. "That depends on a number of things," he said finally, "but I do want to talk to him first."

But this is just a kid we're talking about... Regan thought unhappily. "What if there's more than one of them?"

"In that case..." Jonathan hesitated. "In that case, we have a much more complicated problem here than I'm assuming. I think this person is acting alone. I could be wrong. But we'll find out."

"Great..."

The trees were only beginning to leaf out, and the woods were brighter and less claustrophobic than they would be in high summer. But they grew dimmer and more shadowy as the afternoon crept on, the air taking on a misty look. Rain fell steadily, sometimes a light drizzle, sometimes pattering on the new leaves and the open ground. Regan was thankful for the Burberry raincoat she'd picked up at a yard sale for five dollars. Its tan color provided some protective camouflage, as well, although by now her hair had been soaked for hours. She had no idea how long she had been sitting there, screened on three sides by mountain laurel and sassafras bushes, when she was suddenly snapped to alertness. At first she wasn't sure what had caught her attention, for she hadn't heard a sound. Then she realized that she could *feel* footsteps, in the springy ground beneath her. As she crouched, heart racing, a blue jay suddenly took off from a nearby branch, giving its piercing cries signaling an invader. At that, the footsteps stopped, and Regan distinctly heard a soft sibilant word—"Shit..."

There was a very long pause. Regan wondered if the blue jay's warning alone might make the approaching person turn back. But then she saw someone walking cautiously and almost soundlessly along the trail in front of her. It was a teenage boy, shorter and thinner than average, wearing a stained windbreaker over a baggy T-shirt, oversize khaki shorts, and a baseball cap pulled down low to keep the rain off his face. His unkempt brown hair was pulled back into a ponytail, and he was carrying a large brown satchel on a shoulder strap, which could easily have held a laptop computer and quite a bit else. He carried it as if it were heavy. The boy looked familiar to Regan, but she couldn't positively identify him in the dim light, through the branches of the bushes. Almost not breathing, she watched him as he walked on down the trail to a point past the first camera post, where he could reconnoiter the front of the house. Once again, there was such a long pause that she wondered if he was really coming back. Just as she was about to try to stretch a little, to relieve incipient cramps, she saw the teenager come back up the trail and turn aside to check on the camera.

Regan watched as the teenager frantically felt around on the wet trunk of the tree, and she half stood up. He glanced rapidly around him, and she heard him say "shit" again, then he hoisted the shoulder bag and trotted back to the trail, breathing heavily. She stood up fully, ducked around the bushes and started marching toward the trail, trying to look and sound like an authoritative adult, and shouted as loudly as she could, "Hey, you! What are you doing? Come here, we need to talk!" Her own words sounded inane to her, but they were the best she could come up with for a "confrontation." Leaning casually against a tree with a heavily sardonic "Looking for something?" would get high points for style, but Regan doubted she could pull it off. But Jonathan's prediction about the teenager's reaction was, if anything, underestimated. The teenager, his voice about an octave higher, squawked, "Fuck!" and pelted down the trail as hard as he could, the satchel slamming against his side. Regan was glad that Jonathan hadn't expected her to tackle the boy, because she would have been mown down. No more than a second or two after the boy had vanished over the little rise to the east, she heard a blood-curdling scream, and she started running, too.

She topped the rise and saw Jonathan grappling with the teenager who was struggling violently and yelping repeatedly at the top of his lungs, "No! No! Lemme go! I didn't do anything! Leggo!" Jonathan finally twisted one of the teenager's arms up behind his back, eliciting a sharp cry of real pain, and then the teenager stopped struggling and stood frozen, gasping for breath.

"That's better," Jonathan said as Regan, almost skidding on the muddy path, ran down to where they stood. "Now no more fighting to get away, or I might have to break something. Understand?" When there was no reply, he jerked the teenager's arm up again, not very hard, and there was another yelp. *"Understand?"*

"Yes! Yes..."

"Good. Now come with us. And don't try to break and run. I *will* catch you and you will not be happy about it when I do. Now walk." He turned the teenager to face back up the trail, let go of his arm and shoulder, and give him a hard shove in the middle of his back. He gestured at Regan to pick up the teenager's satchel, which was a few feet away as though it had gone flying when Jonathan grabbed its owner. Regan spotted the teenager's hat on the ground and scooped that up as well. She knew who the boy was, now—once Jonathan let go of him and turned him around, recognition finally kicked in. *God*, she thought, as she climbed up the slope after Jonathan and his prisoner, *what are we going to do now?*

The boy kept his head down and seemed to be choking back tears as the three of them walked to the house and through the back yard in single file. He made no attempt to escape. Jonathan remained close behind him, motioning to Regan to step forward and unlock the door into the back hallway. He put a hand on one of the teenager's shoulders and guided him, none too gently, straight down the hall and through the archway into the great room, where he pulled one of the heavy wooden chairs out into the middle of the floor with his free hand and pushed the teenager down onto it with a thump. He walked around in front of the chair and studied the teenager, arms folded. Their prisoner slumped, head down, hands gripping the edges of the seat. But before Jonathan could speak again, Regan put down the satchel and walked around to stand next to him.

"Wait a moment," she said to Jonathan, then leaned forward and chucked the teenager's chin so he looked up at her, startled. "Sean. What the fuck do you think you're doing?"

"You know this boy?" Jonathan said, as Sean fidgeted, looking rapidly between the two of them.

"Sean Neeson. I've known him since he was at Adams Elementary. He used to come in after school looking for odd little curios. His mother brings me stuff that she wants me to buy from her sometimes. She's..." Regan broke off with a sigh, not wanting to stand there and talk about Sean's mother in front of him. That his home life was nightmarish, everyone in town knew. DSS had had an open case on his mother for years. Regan knew, thanks to gossipy customers, that Sharon Neeson would leave Sean alone at home for several days running and go on benders in Fall River. She drank every day at the best of times. The neighbors gave Sean meals rather than see him put back in foster care—he had a reputation for being self-contained and trouble-free, if somewhat introverted. "Sean's one of my oldest customers."

Jonathan took the box of cameras off the long table and held it out to Sean. "I think you were looking for these, Sean?" Sean looked at the box, looked down, and hunched his shoulders. "Is this all there are?" No answer. "Sean. I think you owe me an explanation. You've been spying on me—and on Regan. What have we done to deserve that kind of disrespect?" Still no answer, but Sean swallowed hard. Jonathan waited a moment, then said, "Who's paying you?"

That got a reaction. "What? Paying me? What do you mean?"

"Just what it sounds like. Who's paying you to spy on us? I can't believe you're doing this on your own. You'd never be able to rig cameras like this."

"Why wouldn't I? You think I'm stupid? It's a no-brainer, rigging cameras, you just—" then he broke off, realizing that he'd been tricked. "Fuck you. I never did anything to hurt you! What are you going to do to me?"

"Why the cameras? Why were you watching Regan's store? What are you after, Sean?" Sean stared at the floor, and Jonathan lowered his voice. "Sean," he said very quietly, "what are you going to *make* me do?"

At that, Sean jerked his head up to stare at Jonathan, and there was real fear in his eyes. "What are you saying, that you'd kill me, just for this? I haven't done anything!"

Jonathan looked surprised for a moment, then his expression darkened. "Kill you? What in god's name makes you think your life is danger, Sean? I think you're being a little melodramatic. I just want to know what the story is with these cameras."

Sean took in a breath and hesitated a moment, then his face grew even paler and he stiffened his shoulders. "I know what you are!" he suddenly blurted out. "I saw what you did to that other lady! I know what's been going on, I know you two are working together—" and again he broke off, as though his mouth had gotten loose and betrayed him before he could force it shut.

Jonathan and Regan exchanged bleak looks. There didn't seem any point in playing dumb at this stage. If nothing else, Sean now had direct experience of how strong and fast Jonathan was. The only way to find out how much information he had was to take him seriously. Jonathan straightened up and studied Sean for a moment. "All right," he said deliberately, "What am I, and just exactly what is going on?"

A drop of sweat trickled down over Sean's temple. "You're...you're..."

"Go ahead. Spit it out. What am I, Sean? Let's hear you say it."

Sean swallowed so hard it was audible. "You're a vampire," he whispered. "Not like the movies. I know that shit is all made up. You're for real."

The silence in the room was so heavy, Regan was afraid to breathe. "What makes you think so?" Jonathan said very quietly.

Sean bent his head down, squeezing his eyes shut for a moment. "This is all so fucked," he whispered. Jonathan waited, and Sean said, "There's this kid in my class. He was out for a couple of days, and when he came back, he acted kind of weird. Everyone was saying that he'd gone out in the woods and tried to commit suicide, cut himself. I saw his arm during gym class. The whole inside of his elbow was all black with this big cut in the middle, right where the vein is. It looked like he should have bled to death. He didn't want people to see it and he was pissed that I did. I asked him if he did it to himself and he said no and to fuck off. Then I heard this story that the same thing had happened to a lot more people, and some doctor was investigating it and wanted to talk to the kid, and his 'rents wouldn't let him." He stopped.

After a pause, Jonathan said, "Go on."

Sean hadn't raised his head. He heaved a sigh. "So I really wanted to find out more about these other people. My mom's been dating this guy who works in the E.R. at a hospital in Fall River. One night when he was at the house, I asked him about it. He said oh, yeah, if anyone comes in with this certain kind of injury, they're supposed to give them this doctor's card so they can call. He said he'd get me one of the cards. Then he said the doctor was working with someone here in Sheridan, Regan Calloway. My mom went, Sean, you know her, she runs that store you like. And I said, why is she investigating stuff with this doctor, and my mom went, don't you know, she's this psychic. So I said, I never heard that before, and my mom went, look it up. So I did, all that stuff up in Gardner with that pervert who killed the little kids. They made you sound like a fruitcake, but I read all that and thought man, she's really for real."

"Thank you," Regan said. "So you started watching my store."

"Sometimes, yeah. And then..." he hesitated again. "Then some kids in school were talking about the old hippie house had been rented out by this guy, and he was living out there all alone and he was supposed to be writing this book. It just seemed weird. No one's ever lived out here all alone. So I'm putting it all together, and then..." his voice dropped to a whisper. "I saw you."

"You saw me?" Jonathan said. "You saw me doing what?"

"Just walking down the street. But I was with some kids and someone went look, that's him, the guy from the hippie house. And I looked, and I just...knew. I just knew there was something...I can't explain what it was. I just knew."

"So you started watching Jonathan," Regan said.

"Yeah," Sean said, and swallowed hard again.

"When?" Jonathan said.

"About...two weeks ago."

"And the cameras?" The quietness of Jonathan's voice was unnerving Regan—she could only imagine the effect it was having on Sean.

"I got them from a kid in school, he's really a geek. I couldn't be out here very much, and it took so long to get here, so I thought I'd rig these cameras and maybe I'd see some more."

"When did you put them up?"

"About a week ago. But I was out here last week, when...when that lady came out here. The crazy lady." He looked up then, but at Regan, not Jonathan. "That's when I knew you were in on it. When you came out and helped dump her body."

"You think we killed someone?" Regan said, appalled.

"I *saw* it. But I knew you'd have to know, about him being a vampire, I mean. You're psychic, you'd know right away. You'd be the only one. That's why you were helping him. After that I was really sure."

"Then why didn't you report it to the police?" Jonathan asked. "You thought you saw a murder and you didn't report it?" Sean stared at him, his throat working, and then looked down. "Did you tell the kid in school why you wanted the cameras?" Sean shook his head. "Why not?" Sean shrugged. "He wasn't curious, he didn't ask any questions?"

"No one gives a shit what I do. He couldn't care less."

"Have you told anyone about any of this, Sean?"

"No."

"That's hard to believe."

After a pause, Regan said, "Were you too scared to tell anyone, is that it?"

The reaction was surprising. Sean jerked his head up, his expression suddenly urgent and earnest. "No! It wasn't that! I wasn't scared, I was—" and he suddenly shut down again.

"What were you planning to do with the pictures on the cameras?" Jonathan's voice was harder. "Supposing you did collect any photos that were...evidential. What did you want them for? Were you going to give them to the police?"

"No!"

"Send them to Dr. Clauson? Post them online?"

"Nothing like that, I swear to god!"

"Blackmail us?"

Sean's face flushed. "Not...I mean, blackmail isn't the right word...I just...
I had to be able to prove it."

"To whom? I'm running out of patience, Sean."

"To you! I had to be able to prove to you that I really knew! If I didn't do
that, you'd never—" he stopped.

"I'd never what?" When Sean didn't answer, Jonathan said, "I'm getting very
tired of having to pry answers out of you. Let me take a guess. You've decided
you were the only person who had it all figured out. And just like Blade, or Buffy,
you were going to save the town from the forces of evil, is that it?"

Sean gaped. "No, that's *not* it! I'm not into any of that slayer shit! I'm on
your side, I swear!"

"You think I killed somebody and you're on my side."

"Hey, look," Sean said desperately, "You must have had some good reason,
right? That lady was nuts, she almost drove her car right through the front
door! Then she was running up and down hammering on the windows, fuck,
she scared *me!* Maybe you couldn't help what you did, I get that. I don't think
you're evil, I don't think you're running around killing people every night like
Lestat or something, that's not it at all!"

"No," Jonathan said, with heavy clipped emphasis, "if I were like Lestat—you
would be dead. And that just might happen." Regan caught her breath, even
though she was almost certain Jonathan didn't mean it. Sean, lacking her insight, grew paler.

"You can't kill me," he stammered. "You can't do that."

Jonathan walked to the end of the long table and leaned against it, crossing his legs. "Of course I can. Who knows you're here? No one. You've been
keeping all this to yourself, haven't told a soul...why couldn't I kill you? What's
stopping me?"

"But it's not *fair!* And besides, I, I lied! I have told people! There's people
would look for me—and there's the pictures, on my hard drive! If anything
happens to me, someone will check my computer!"

"I'll bet you have it password protected. How will anyone get in?"

"It's not that hard—they do it all the time on *CSI!*"

Jonathan straightened up and walked over to stand in front of Sean's chair. "I
think you're lying now. I don't think you have any incriminating pictures. It was
much too dark last Thursday night for that. You may have seen, but you didn't
get pictures. And besides..." he paused, as Sean stared at him, lips trembling.
"We can get your computer, before anyone even knows you're missing. Regan
knows where you live, and I have quite a knack with locks."

Sean stared back at him, and suddenly jumped to his feet and bolted for
the archway—or took one step in that direction. It was all he could manage

before Jonathan grabbed both his shoulders, yanked him back, and slammed him back into the chair so hard the chair rocked back on two legs and clomped down again. "Please, just listen to me, please," Sean was saying, "You don't get it, please, you just don't get it..."

"I'm not even going to ask you what I don't get, Sean. I'm sick of this little game. But I'll give you one more chance." He looked at Regan.

Regan sucked in a deep breath. "I don't know, Jonathan. He's going to be blocking me." Jonathan gave her an exasperated but pleading look. "Okay. I'll give it a try."

"What are you going to do?" Sean said shrilly, as Regan stepped over to him.

"Sean, just—just relax. This won't hurt." She reached out to touch his temples, but he reeled back as though he thought she was holding poisoned needles in both hands.

"Stop it—"

He could only pull back so far, and she made contact, focused—and hit a solid wall. His fear, and something else, was shutting her out completely. The fear was all she could feel. She withdrew her hands and stepped back.

"No use. He's completely blocked." She looked at Jonathan and immediately she realized what he was going to do, and had to brace herself. Jonathan stepped forward, and without any warning, slapped Sean's face, not once but forward and backhand twice, so hard that Sean was knocked into a daze. A little blood trickled from one of his nostrils, and he sagged sideways and almost slipped off the chair. Jonathan took his shoulders and shoved him back upright.

"Try it now."

She did, touching Sean's temples which now felt uncomfortably cold and clammy under her fingers. He moaned in protest, but the images immediately began to flow through her mind, as if he finally couldn't hold them back any longer and let them go with a sense of both relief and despair. She saw Sharon Neeson's face, a distorted mask, ugly with senseless rage, *the school called again about you, you fucking little bastard, you're just like your old man, he slacked off too, never was worth a pile of shit and you're gonna be just him, where the hell did you go today if you weren't in school? You wanna go to a foster home again, you stupid little shit?* Regan winced and pushed past this dismal memory—*why, Sean, why?*—and then she had it. No wonder he didn't want to say anything. That's why he wanted the photographs. So he could come to them and say, *see I know all about it, I'm one of you, I belong, you have to accept me now.* She saw him sitting in front of his computer, which was old and cranky, poring through websites late at night, piles of paperback books in messy stacks on his desk and on a splintered pine bookcase and on the floor. Most of the books had parts of their lurid covers torn off, as though he was trying to disguise them, or just found the covers offensive. She saw him impatiently but persistently following link after link after link online, rarely asking a question because that would be too self-revealing. She saw him seeking for *the truth,* convinced that if he didn't belong anywhere at school and didn't belong to his drunken mother or absentee father, then there must be somewhere that he did belong. And now he thought he'd found it.

With a deep sigh, Regan pulled back and straightened up, feeling suddenly very tired. "Okay. I get it now. He's never told a soul." Jonathan looked at her quizzically, but she saw the tension in his posture relax. Once again Regan felt bemused and humbled at the trust he placed in her. Sean had opened his eyes, and on his face was an expression of mingled defeat and betrayal. *He probably feels like he's been raped,* Regan thought unhappily, *and in a way, he has been.* She disliked reading people without their knowledge—she had never before read someone who was actively resisting. She looked at Sean sadly. "You want me to tell him? Or do you want to? It's better if you do."

Sean leaned forward, his elbows on his knees, covering his face with his hands. "This is all so fucked," he said again. "I wasn't ready to talk to you yet. I never meant it to go down like this."

"You never would have been ready, Sean," Regan said. "You weren't going to be in control of the situation. There's no way that could have happened."

Sean dropped his hands from his face. Still bent over his knees, he suddenly looked older, and the shrill panic of a few minutes ago was replaced with a dull acceptance. He looked up at Jonathan, meeting his eyes. "I just wanted...to be part of all this. I don't mean...I wasn't going to ask to be turned or something stupid like that. I didn't think I could just walk in and ask. But I wanted to...I wanted to get to know you. Find out what it's really about. Just have a chance." He looked at both of them, his brown eyes wounded and pleading. "I just wanted to prove that I'd be worth it. If I found out all about you, and documented it, and everything, without you guys ever catching on, then I'd prove that I deserved for you to listen to me, at least...take me seriously, or..." he dropped his head.

Jonathan was studying Sean soberly. Without a trace of mockery in his voice, he said, "Isn't there...a word, on all those websites and messageboards—yes, believe it or not, I read them—for what you've been acting like, Sean? Something like, 'wannabee?'"

Sean sighed. "I guess."

"And suppose there was a possibility that we would, in a sense, accept you into the tribe—why would we do that now? You've stalked us, spied on us and planted hidden cameras to record us. How can we ever trust you?"

After a moment, Sean said dully, "I guess you can't. I guess I really fucked up."

Jonathan looked at Regan and shrugged. "So what do we do?"

She sensed that the mood in the room had changed, although she wasn't quite sure how. "What are the options?"

"There's no possible way to blank his memory at this point, so I guess we have three," Jonathan said, looking down at Sean speculatively. Sean was sitting hunched over with his hands clasped so tightly between his knees that his knuckles were white. "I could disappear. We could kill Sean." Sean heaved a sudden sigh, almost a sob, but otherwise didn't react. "Or...he'll just have to join the team."

"I don't like the first two."

"I don't, either."

"But I'm not sure I want someone on the team who thinks we killed someone and still wants to join."

"Oh, I don't know." Jonathan walked over to Sean's chair and stood looking down at him with an odd smile. "It's rather touching that he's willing to forgive us anything, don't you think?" He looked at Regan. "Can we trust him?"

Regan thought about what she'd just read from Sean. "Yes. I think we can."

Sean had raised his head finally and was staring at Jonathan. "Are you going to turn me?" He looked terrified at the idea.

"No, Sean. It's not nearly that simple. The prospect of all the explanations ahead of us is just a bit daunting, I admit. But you already know that. That's in your favor." He stepped back from Sean's chair. "Can you keep secrets?"

Sean was staring at him incredulously. "Yes," he almost gasped.

"Do you trust us?"

Sean looked from Jonathan to Regan in confusion, as if he didn't understand the question. Finally he said, "Yes."

"Can you stand up?"

"Uh..." He could, although he had to try twice. He stood unsteadily, looking inquiringly at Jonathan, then at Regan, than back at Jonathan, seeming half panicked and half just embarrassed. It probably didn't reassure him that Regan, strongly suspecting what Jonathan was working up to, couldn't meet his eyes.

After what seemed like an interminably long time, Jonathan walked unhurriedly over and moved the chair aside so he could stand behind Sean. "Stand still. There's something I'm going to show you. Pay very close attention. You may find this a little unpleasant. Are you ready?"

Sean opened his mouth but no sound came out. Finally he managed to say, "Okay." Then he gasped as Jonathan, who was about five inches taller than he, reached around with one hand, cupped his jaw and pulled his head back, holding his shoulder with the other hand. From pure reflex, Sean reached up to clutch at Jonathan's hands, and Jonathan said, "No, hold still. Drop your hands to your sides." Sean complied, squeezing his eyes shut, and Jonathan locked his mouth onto Sean's neck. Sean's back stiffened, and then he let out a short cry, as much startled as hurt. He took in two gasping breaths, like a beached fish, and then the anesthetic-like effect of Jonathan's drinking took hold and his body sagged back against Jonathan, who deftly caught him with one arm around his chest. Sean made a soft sound between a moan and a whimper, and after that, he didn't move for about half a minute, when his knees buckled. A moment later, Jonathan took his mouth away from the wound on Sean's neck, and carefully let him down to the floor.

"I thought you weren't going to blank his memory," Regan said anxiously. Her fingernails had left dents in the palms of her hands, but she had forced herself to watch.

"I didn't. He just fainted. He'll wake up in a minute." Indeed, Sean's eyelids were already fluttering, although his face was pasty white.

"I better get him a glass of water," Regan said, and she went to the kitchen. Standing at the sink filling a glass with cold well water, Regan suddenly felt a wave of vertigo hit her, and she had to sit down in one of the kitchen chairs for a moment. Sean, the little boy who used to stop by the store and hunt through the shelves for curious knick knacks, the unhappy DSS lifer who was so desperate to change his fortunes that he would spy on two people he believed had murdered someone, was now...what? *Good god, what have we done now?*

Chapter 11

The first week of May was marked by several unseasonably hot days, and in some sheltered spots, tulips and small iris burst into early bloom. Regan devoted Monday the 10th to an especially vigorous spring cleaning at the store, but this year, she had some help. Sean had asked her for a job, and when she explained that she couldn't afford to pay him, he'd offered to come in for free. So he was working in the store with her after school and on weekends, and she, feeling that a high school junior at least needed pocket money, slipped him an allowance of sorts under the table. Sometimes he simply sat in the office and did his homework, which she earnestly encouraged. His home environment was far from conducive to study, and his grades could be better, although he was very bright, and wasn't failing anything. The state MCAS exams for juniors were coming up, also, and Sean was sweating over study guides handed out in his classes. Regan was grateful that she'd been well out of public school before those horrors came along.

This afternoon, however, Sean had been working very hard, scrubbing down every shelf, after it was emptied of merchandize, with detergent, wiping it with clear water and then drying it with a towel. Each shelf unit was moved so that the tired linoleum floor beneath it could be vacuumed, washed with detergent, given a coat of finish and buffed. It wasn't possible to move all the shelving out of the store and do the whole floor at once, so it had to be done in sections. Over the weekend, they had cleaned the ceiling and washed the walls, working their way down. It was amazing how much grime was emitted by the little building's old furnace. They were sitting on the front steps taking a break at around 6:00, discussing a shelf rearrangement for the new summer stock that was arriving now every day, and an increase in Sean's responsibilities. On the former topic, Regan had to admit that Sean had some refreshing and useful ideas, and he was winning her over with his insistence that the store would do better if it had more to appeal to high school age customers. On the second point, Regan had been dragging her heels, reluctant to give Sean the tasks of opening or closing, or access to the safe, at least so soon. As store manager and sole employee, she had carte blanche to make decisions, but she knew that Mrs. Wharton wouldn't approve of a teenager running the store.

"You know, if I closed up for you, you could leave early some days. I don't know how you stand to work so much."

"I know, Sean. I just think you should have a little more experience here before I leave you all alone for more than a lunch break."

"I know how to cash out. I can drop off the deposit envelope. I can lock the door. I can put the cash drawer in the safe. I can turn out the lights. What's the big deal?"

"You're awfully young, is the big deal, Sean. It would be different if I owned the business, but I don't."

"I just turned seventeen, for god's sake. Macdonald's would trust me. Wal*Mart would trust me. The fucking U.S. Marine Corps would trust me. They'd trust me with a gun."

"I do trust you, Sean. That's not the point." Regan could tell that she was going to lose this one. She couldn't possibly match Sean's energy, since he had been wetting his whistle of cleaning dust all afternoon with Mountain Dew and was now well into his second two-liter bottle. He probably wasn't going to sleep for a week, let alone give up on an argument.

"You could have Sundays off. That's only six hours."

"Well...I'll think about it."

"But if—"

"I said I'll think about it. Not all day Sunday. But maybe I'll let you close up some nights. There are some auctions coming up and it would be very helpful if I could go to the pre-viewings without having to close the store early."

"Sweet." He took a long swig of soda. "Could I go to an auction with you sometime? I'd like to see how they work."

"Well, you can't go if you're covering the store for me. We'll see." *Sean coming along to an auction? Could be fun.*

They got up and went back inside. They needed to replace the merchandize on the last row of shelves and vacuum the aisle carpets. As Regan was shaking out the vacuum cleaner's tangled cord, she heard the thump of a car door. She looked up and saw Sean staring down the center aisle toward the parking area.

"Whoa," he said quietly, "I see dead people."

"What? Oh my god. Veronica's back." She put down the vacuum cleaner, and frowned at Sean. "I explained all that to you, Sean, didn't you believe me?"

"Yeah, of course I believed you. But that lady looked seriously dead, let me tell you."

Veronica, as she walked up the steps and stood in the open doorway, now looked almost ethereal, Regan thought. Two weeks in the private hospital had left her thinner than ever, and her pale skin was stretched over the bones of her face. She wasn't wearing any make-up, Regan realized when she got closer, and her natural hair color had grown out about a quarter-inch at the roots. As Regan approached, unsure whether to give her friend a hug, Veronica crossed her arms tightly against her chest. Evidently a hug was not in order.

"Veronica, it's good to see you. How long have you been home?"

"Hello, Regan. I got out of the hospital on Friday. That was all I could pay for." She smiled tautly. "Who's this?" She nodded at Sean, who was frankly staring at her.

"Oh, this is Sean, Sean Neeson. He's helping me out in the store."

"Hi, Sean."

Sean raised a hand in her direction. "'Sup."

Veronica turned back to Regan with the same tight, forced smile. "Well. I was hoping to get a moment to talk to you, but if this is a bad time..."

"Oh, hey, I can go take a break," Sean said helpfully.

"You just had a break," Regan said over her shoulder. "You can start the vacuuming. Come on," she said to Veronica, "I put the lawn table up, let's sit out here, if you just have a few minutes." Veronica followed her back down the front steps and around to the side of the building, where there were planting boxes that Regan put flowers in for the summer and a round cast resin table with matching chairs that looked like wrought iron, a special at Home Depot a couple of years ago. It was a heartbreakingly perfect spring day, sunny and 70 degrees. The vacuum cleaner whined resentfully inside the store.

"I thought you said you couldn't afford to hire anyone," Veronica said as they sat. "Is business picking up?"

"Well, Sean's not really a paid employee, strictly speaking. He just likes coming in to help out."

"Working on his Eagle Scout badge in business management?"

Regan sighed. "I'm glad to see that you're your old self again, Ver. Nope, no scouting badge, unless he's not telling me something." She looked at Veronica dubiously. "So, how are things going? The night you left, you told me that your dad wasn't being too helpful."

"You put things so nicely, Regan. Well, let's see. He's canceled my health insurance. He's stopped paying for any of my credit cards. And the condo sold yesterday. I'm supposed to be out by the fifteenth."

"Jesus, Veronica. What are you going to do?"

"Well, I'm going to be out by the fifteenth. There's not a lot of choice there."

"Can Derek help you find something?"

"Not when I don't have any income. But don't worry, Regan. I remembered what you said to me, about my life being what I make it. I think everything will work out just fine."

"Do you need help packing or anything?"

"What's the point in packing if I'm not going to be taking it with me?" She started laughing. "Unless you want to buy it all, Regan. You could sell it in the store." She threw her head back, laughing as though she couldn't stop. As Regan watched with concern, she got control of herself and quieted.

Regan, against her better judgment, said hesitantly, "I suppose...I suppose I could put you up at my place for a while, Veronica. You'll be on the couch, because the second bedroom is full of overflow from the store. But you're welcome to stay..."

"Oh, *thank* you, Regan. You're *such* a good friend. But I'm sure that would be *very* inconvenient for you. And it wouldn't solve anything, anyway. I can't spend my life being a mooch and a sponger. Or that's what I've been told, anyway."

"Are you going to get a job?"

"Where? Wal*Mart?"

"Well, I don't know...you have a bachelor's degree."

"And no work experience. My dad says he'll give me a job in the mill. Entry level, no special treatment, I can work my way up the ladder just like everyone else. Of course, you can't actually live on what my dad pays his entry level workers, but I guess that would be my problem."

"Are you going to do that?"

Veronica smiled down at the ornate molded tabletop. "No, I'm making some other plans. My dad said I didn't have to take his offer. I'll be all right, don't worry about me, Regan."

"It's hard not to, Ver."

"I know, and it's not fair. I've spent my whole life making everyone worry about me, and I guess it's time for me to grow up and make some serious decisions. And I'm doing that."

There's something not right about this... "I wish you'd tell me more about what you've got in mind, Ver. Maybe I could help, as a friend, really. What are friends good for, if not to help out when things get tough?"

"Oh, Regan, you've picked me up off the ground so many times...but it's okay. Really. I had a lot of talks with my therapist up in Haverhill, and that changed some things for me. And I'm leaving Sheridan, so I won't be where you can help me, anyway."

"Leaving Sheridan? Where are you going?

"I don't know yet. But I can't stay here now. It's over for me. Sheridan is, I mean. But that's okay."

"Do you ever hear from your mother?"

Veronica shrugged. "Christmas and birthday."

"Maybe you could go out there."

"It's a thought. I don't know what her husband would think." Veronica picked up her purse and stood up. "But I have to get going now, Regan. I just wanted to stop by and see you."

As they walked back to the parking area, Regan said, "You could probably get some bucks for that car. Trade down to something inexpensive—"

"Like a Honda Civic, maybe?"

"Don't knock it. You could clear a few thousand, get an apartment, you'd have a place to stay until you started working..."

"You're so practical, Regan. I've always envied that about you. But you're forgetting the credit cards. I'd have to file for bankruptcy and sell the car anyway." Regan had no response for that. Veronica got into the car and then hesitated as she reached for the key. She turned to look up at Regan. "I've been very lucky to have you as a friend, Regan. I just want you to know that." She started the car and immediately backed away from the store, as Regan stepped back quickly for fear that her toes would be run over. The Mazda peeled out of the parking area in a spray of gravel.

Regan walked slowly up the steps and into the store. Sean had finished vacuuming and was on one knee by the empty shelf, setting items carefully in place. "There's something going on with her," he said as Regan walked in. "I don't know what it is, but she looked weird."

"I know." Regan leaned her hip against the counter and frowned down at the bright new plastic mat by the door. "Her father must have taken Tough Love classes. He's really turning the screws on her. He's cut her right off."

"Who's her father?"

"Jerry Standish, owner of the Standish Mills."

"Shit. That guy has balls made out of rock salt. I'd rather be dead than have to work for him."

"Yeah. Me, too." She felt a deep chill settling into the pit of her stomach, and abruptly, she picked up the cordless and dialed Veronica's cell phone number. The phone buzzed and clicked, and then she heard a recorded voice, "We're sorry, the wireless number you have called is not in service..." She hung up. *She wouldn't, would she?* Veronica had never actually attempted suicide, not even pills. *She can hardly bear to wax her eyebrows, let alone do anything lethal to herself...* "Sean...if you thought someone you knew was going to hurt themselves...what would you do?"

"You mean like, off themselves?"

"Yeah."

He sat back, tossing a small pewter picture frame from one hand to the other as his brow creased. "Well...we got some speaker in at the school talking about that last year. Good Samaritans, or someone like that. They said that you should try and let somebody know, and that people committing suicide really want to be stopped. I don't know, though." He went back to stocking the shelf. "I always kind of thought, if someone wanted to do that, it was their own business, and maybe they had a good reason for it. Who am I to tell someone else whether they should live or die? I don't know what it's like to be them."

"But...things are hardly ever as hopeless as suicidal people think, Sean. That's the problem, they can't see any other solution. That doesn't mean other solutions don't exist."

"Yeah, well," he shrugged. "Is that what you think about your friend who was just here? So call someone. What else can you do?"

"Okay..." She took the cordless and went into the office, closing the door behind her. She sat at the desk and flipped through the rolodex. She had Jerry Standish's numbers, although she'd had very few reasons to speak to him. But with Veronica lurching from one crisis to another, it had seemed prudent to have her next of kin's numbers on hand. By 6:30 p.m. on a Monday, most people would be home, but Regan knew that Jerry Standish's work hours rivaled her own. Mr. Balls of Rock Salt might be a taskmaster and a union buster, but he worked harder than any of his employees. He'd never remarried after Veronica's mother left twenty years ago, so Regan imagined he didn't have much else to do.

If he had either hobbies or social life, Regan had never heard about them.

She dialed the mill's main number and punched in Jerry Standish's office extension when the voice mail recording prompted it. The phone picked up on the first ring.

"Standish."

"Hello, Mr. Standish—"

"Who is this?"

"My name is Regan Calloway, I'm a friend of Veronica's—of your daughter's."

There was a pause. "Yes?"

"I run a store up by—"

"I know who you are, Ms. Calloway. How can I help you?"

Regan could feel herself sweating. "Mr. Standish, Veronica was just here at the store to see me, and frankly, I'm very concerned about her. The way she was talking makes me suspect...well, I'm afraid that she might be going to do something to hurt herself. Or worse."

"Did she say that?"

"Not in so many words, no. But I have a very bad feeling. I've never heard her talk quite like this before."

Another pause. "You're that...psychic, aren't you?"

"Well, some people call me that, but this has nothing to do with that, Mr. Standish."

"Did my daughter ask you to call me with this story?"

"No! Mr. Standish, if Veronica knew I was talking with you, she'd probably kill *me*."

"Hm." He cleared his throat. "I appreciate your concern. But I believe you've known Veronica for a very long time. So you know that she is melodramatic and histrionic. You also know that follow-through is not her strong suit."

"I agree, but—"

"Now I'm sure that she's painted a very grim picture for you. She's not at all happy about the ultimatum I've given her recently. But I wouldn't let my own daughter starve on the street, Ms. Calloway. I've offered her a good job. With benefits. There are no strings attached. If she wants to work somewhere else, she has my blessings. But she needs to learn how life works, Ms. Calloway. Where would you be if you hadn't learned that?"

"You make a good point. Just the same, the way she was talking..."

"Do you have training as a psychotherapist?"

"Well, no, but—"

"Veronica has been getting all the professional help she needs. If they believed she was at risk, I'm sure they'd have communicated that to me."

Regan sighed. "I hope so, Mr. Standish."

"For what they charge, I hope so, too. This will be good for Veronica, no matter how upset she is about it now. Is that all?"

"Yes. Thank you for your time." The line clicked off.

Regan sat at the desk for a few minutes, then got up and went out into the store, where Sean was nearly finished with the first side of the shelf.

"Who'd you call?"

"Her father."

He turned and stared. "No shit! You called old man Standish, just like that?"

"Who else? He's Veronica's only next of kin. I've got his direct extension."

"So, what did he say?"

Regan sat down on the carpet next to Sean, broodily regarding the neatly arranged items. "He thanked me for my concern."

"That's it?"

"He says she's melodramatic and histrionic, and it will be good for her to learn how life works." She sighed. "I don't know. Maybe he's right."

"He sounds like an asshole."

"Yeah. That, too."

Chapter 12

After she and Sean finished with the last shelf and locked up the store, Regan gave Sean a ride back home. Sharon Neeson appeared to grudgingly approve her son's new interest. At least, she had said to Regan, "you must be a saint to put up with him, that's all I can say. As long as he doesn't miss any more school." Things were a bit more tolerable at home, Sean reported, but he didn't say much more than that. After she dropped Sean off, she drove to the townhouse complex. There was no sign of life in Veronica's condo. The windows were dark and the curtains were open. Regan walked down the driveway and stood on tiptoe to look into the garage door window. The garage was empty. The next door neighbor startled her by calling from the front yard, "Hi, can I help you?"

"I'm a friend of Veronica's, I was just trying to see if she was home."

"Haven't seen her. She's moving, you know."

"Yes, I know." Regan wasn't sure whether the empty townhouse was worrisome or not. But where else would Veronica be? She cruised up and down the main streets of the center of town for twenty minutes, looking for the little Mazda parked somewhere, but she didn't spot it. But Veronica could have gone to the mall, or to Boston, or almost anywhere.

Regan drove out River Road, her emotions tangled. As she approached Rainbow Stone house, she slowed her car, looking carefully for any sign that Veronica might have come out to talk to Jonathan. But there was no silver car visible in front of the house or on the side of the road, and with some apprehension she pulled into the front drive. She did have a key, now, but she wondered if she should just let herself in. After a hesitation, she did, and walked into the great room, where Jonathan was sitting at his computer. He looked up and smiled, but at her expression, his smile faded.

"What's the matter?"

She went over to the table and sank down in one of the wooden chairs. "Jonathan, have you heard from Veronica this weekend?"

"No. She's back?"

"Since Friday, evidently. I had no idea. She stopped by the store today, and... I don't know." Regan described the conversations she'd had with Veronica and with Jerry Standish, and Veronica's present MIA status. Jonathan leaned back with folded arms, frowning darkly as he listened.

"I can understand why you're concerned. Not only how she was acting, but according to you, she wouldn't let you touch her."

"I know. But she's always been able to block me if she wanted to, anyway."

Jonathan shook his head. "I hope your fears are groundless. But, Regan, remember when you said, rather forcefully, that you weren't going to let Veronica run your life? You talked with her father. You tried calling her, and you went to her house just now. What more can you do?"

"I don't know. I just wonder if we've been as discreet as we should have been, the last two weeks. Maybe we shouldn't have met at my house quite so often. It's been pretty obvious that your car has been there most of the evening, several times."

"But never the whole night."

"I know...but if Veronica heard about it..."

"How would she? Does she often socialize with your neighbors?"

"Word gets around. And it's not that hard to tell when two people are having a fling, anyway. Sean hasn't had any trouble figuring it out."

"Sean is in a unique position to do so. There are a lot of things he knows that no one else does, or could."

"That's true, I guess." She sighed, and then got up. "I'm sorry I bothered you with this, Jonathan. I'm not in a great mood tonight, I think I'll go home."

"Are you sure that's where you're going?" Jonathan looked at her skeptically. "Tell me that you're not going to spend the night driving around looking for Veronica."

Regan stopped, her back to him, and her shoulders slumped. She turned back slowly. "I guess that would be pretty stupid."

"If she doesn't want to be found, she won't be. You could drive in circles until the sun rises."

"You're right."

He pushed aside papers and found his own cordless phone and offered it to her. "Call the police and tell them why you're worried, and give them her license plate number. They'll be doing patrols all night long. That's their job. If they see Veronica's car, they'll check it out."

Regan felt chagrined that she hadn't thought of this. "Good idea," she said, and she took the phone and called the police and did as he suggested. The dispatcher took down the information without apparent concern.

"Thank you ma'am. I'll make sure the officer on duty is aware." Regan clicked off the phone, her sense of helplessness unabated.

Jonathan got up from his chair and walked around to stand behind Regan, massaging her shoulders. "You *are* tense. And you smell like dust."

"Oh, that feels good...yes, I was cleaning the store all day today. Sean helped, after school." She closed her eyes. "Mmmm...my knees are about to fold."

"Then sit down. Unless you want to go upstairs."

She thought about it, but anxiety was still making her stomach knot. "I just...I just can't tonight, Jonathan." She broke away from him and sat back down in the chair.

"I understand. There's something else I need more than that tonight, anyway." He had moved to stand behind her chair, and he smoothed her hair back away from her face and shoulders, in long caressing moves.

Regan swallowed. "I thought you were going up to the dairy farm for that."

"I can't do that all the time. And besides, sometimes I need more than animal blood, Regan. I explained about that."

"Yes, I know, that's what you said."

"You're not afraid, are you?"

"Of *course* I'm not afraid." She felt more irritated by the question than she would have been normally.

"I won't take much, I promise. You won't feel any lasting effects."

"I know."

"But if you really have a serious objection..." he paused, drawing back from the chair a little.

She closed her eyes. "No, no, I don't mind, I'm just...tired. And I hate the sensation. Not the beginning so much, the ending."

"I'm sorry. I'll make it quick."

"And do it someplace that won't show."

Without hesitating, he raised her left arm, pushing her sleeve up, and then pressed his mouth against the skin in the crook of her elbow. She winced at the familiar jab of pain and the odd feeling of being pulled open. After ten or fifteen seconds followed the ice cold pinched nerve sensation that closed the wound. He relaxed the pressure and she felt him cleaning the remaining blood from her skin with the tip of his tongue. As he sat back on his haunches, licking his lips, she opened her eyes, and stared unseeing at the cluttered table in front of her. She felt a little dizzy and the wound he'd made was starting to tingle and sting, but otherwise she was experiencing no ill effects. "What are you thinking?" he said softly.

"I'm thinking...that something terrible is going to happen. I can feel it." Something about what he did opened her senses in a way that wasn't usual with her, and she had a chilling sense of premonition that she couldn't explain.

"To Veronica?"

"No. To me."

This seemed to disturb him. He tugged her sleeve down neatly and went back to sit in his own chair, where he could face her. "What sort of thing?"

"I don't know," she whispered.

"You must be used to these kinds of premonitions, aren't you?"

"Premonitions? No. I'm not a fortune-teller, Jonathan. I don't see the future. I read concrete facts about the past and the present. The future's not real."

"But there are probabilities. What we do in the present holds the seeds of the future."

"Yes, that's true..." The feeling was passing now, and she looked down at the papers and manila folders on the tabletop, and the glowing screen of the laptop computer, with its generic Microsoft Windows wallpaper. The banality of the ordinary world was beginning to reclaim its usual precedence. "Never mind,

Jonathan. I'm having anxiety attacks. I probably need lorazepam."

"Don't start down that slippery slope." He was smiling a little, but he still looked troubled.

"Not too likely, with no health insurance. Of course, you can get a hit of lorazepam just by going to the emergency room and complaining that you feel panicky." She was quiet for a moment. "I wonder if you should have told Sean all those things you did."

"He was curious. I didn't mind. Why? Does he seem to be reacting badly, or are you starting to have second thoughts about trusting him?"

"It's not that. I just wonder if it's safe for him to know. He's only seventeen. I hate to think that he's going to end up involved in...in whatever happens."

"He wanted it. Desperately."

"Maybe I'm showing my old age, Jonathan, but I think sometimes adults owe it to young people to protect them from the things they want that badly."

"Adults can try. But all too often, such efforts end up backfiring. Remember your Shakespeare."

They talked for a while longer, as Regan asked Jonathan about his plans to restore the old farmhouse. He had still not gotten a definite answer about a selling price, and there was a possibility that the owner would carve a lot for the house out of the surrounding property and sell the buildings with a smaller piece of land. That would involve some legal gerrymandering and slow down the transaction. But, Jonathan said, this was all being negotiated. Despite Regan's fatigue, her emotions calmed enough that they ended up in the bedroom after all, where the damp night breeze blew through the open windows, and they could hear the trill of peepers and frogs from the nearby ponds and bogs. The sex was more relaxing than exciting, but sometimes that was more than enough. Regan almost fell asleep, lying close and intertwined with Jonathan's body, but stirred herself finally. She needed to be at the store in the morning.

On the way home, Regan couldn't resist the impulse to cruise up and down the empty streets of the town center once more, and then she drove again to Veronica's condo. The garage was still empty, and the curtains in the bedroom were open, just as they'd been earlier. Every window was dark, but that would be expected this late. The open curtains made Regan sure that Veronica could not be there. Veronica never left curtains open even a crack after dark, just as she was unable to sleep unless every closet door, drawer, and cabinet was tightly closed. It was as though she feared she might see something looking at her through the cracks. Regan finally went home, and checked her answering machine and the store's voice mail system. There were no messages.

There were still no messages in the morning, and Veronica's home phone didn't answer. Regan opened the store and, until customers arrived, sat in the office checking tracking numbers for shipments and opening two boxes that had arrived the day before while she and Sean cleaned. Her left elbow was sore from the injury Jonathan had left the night before, which was one of the disadvantages of using that spot, and she kept fidgeting with her sleeve. She was unpacking and checking in ceramic items from a crafter up in Stowe, Vermont, when the cordless buzzed, and she picked it up automatically. "Borrowed and Blue."

"Regan...? It's Karen." At the sound of her voice, quavery and thin, Regan was instantly on alert, her heart pounding.

"Karen, what is it?"

"It's...h-have you heard? About Veronica?"

For a moment, Regan felt as though she couldn't breathe, and the light around her was too bright, blindingly bright. She closed her eyes. "No, I haven't heard anything. What's happened?"

"She...she's dead, Regan. She—" Karen broke off with a deep sigh. "She killed herself."

For a few moments, Regan couldn't speak. She felt as though a red hot wire had stabbed through her body from her heart to the bottom of her stomach. "When did this happen? And how?"

"Last night, they think. She took all her pills, and others, they're not sure what, and where she got them."

"Where was she?"

"In her..." Karen gulped back a sob. "In her condo. The new owners found her when they came in with the realtor." There was a pause as Karen evidently was trying to control her voice enough to continue speaking. "She—she had left a note on the table."

"What did it say?"

"Something about...being out by the fifteenth. Oh, Regan, I didn't even know about the condo being sold! Jerry Standish has closed the mills today, did you know that? He closed the whole plant and sent everyone home." Regan sat, holding the phone, staring at the cheerful glazed ceramic bowls lined up on the desk in front of her. *Where did those come from?* She heard Karen's voice, "...Regan?"

"I'm here." She cleared her throat, realizing that she needed to pull herself back to the present. "That's...that's terrible news, Karen. I'm so sorry for her parents. Are there any arrangements yet?"

"I don't think so. Veronica's mother is flying in from Phoenix. I think there's some kind of problem with the autopsy."

"Autopsy?" Of course, Jerry Standish would want an autopsy. He'd want to know exactly what pills Veronica took, how many, where she got them, and who he could file a wrongful death lawsuit against. He was that kind of man.

"Her mother doesn't want one, I think. But I don't really understand."

"Well, thanks, Karen. I really appreciate your calling me. I'd hate to have seen it in the newspaper."

She clicked off the phone, and sat looking at it in her hand. *Well, it's over,* she thought. *No more all-night support sessions...no more trips to the E.R. at two a.m...no more listening to her obsess for hours about her new boyfriend, who you think is an asshole...* She should be crying, but no tears came. *I'll probably break down just in time to humiliate myself in front of Sean,* she thought. But though she was shocked, she wasn't truly surprised. And though she mourned for Veronica's throwing away her life, she couldn't feel grief. All Regan could feel was fear: cold, stomach-knotting, leg-shaking fear. Of what she was so afraid, she didn't have the slightest clue.

She was startled from her immobility by a car screeching to a halt out on the road. After a moment she called Jonathan to let him know what had happened.

Chapter 13

Somehow she got through the day without breaking down. The cordless kept ringing, other mutual friends asking Regan if she knew, or passing on more information, or asking Regan if she had any. Jonathan offered to come to the store and keep her company, but Regan wasn't sure this was a good idea. She told Jonathan what was happening in the aftermath of the discovery of Veronica's body. He seemed oddly disquieted by the information.

"Why is her mother blocking the autopsy, do you know?"

"I'm not sure, Jonathan. Apparently she belongs to a religious denomination out in Phoenix that doesn't believe in them. Autopsies, or cremation, all that sort of thing. Something to do with a belief that the body has to be whole for the Day of Judgment."

"Does she also object to embalming?"

"I have no idea. Why?"

"It just seems strange, in this day and age, that's all."

"As long as her father is trying to have an autopsy performed, they'll probably hold off on embalming, especially if he wants evidence about the drugs Veronica took. It's only required under certain conditions."

Jonathan was silent for a moment. "Is there some suspicion that this wasn't a suicide?"

"If there is, no one's said anything to me." Regan wondered why Jonathan was so concerned. But he didn't pursue the topic further.

Sean had heard the news in school. Regan wondered how the story had spread there so fast, but the one-day closing of the Standish Mills had shaken the town to its foundations. "I'm sorry about your friend," he said when he came in. "That's really harsh."

Jerry Standish had enough pull to keep the suicide aspect out of the news. There was a bland and flattering obituary in the local paper and in the Fall River *Herald* that said only, "died suddenly." In lieu of flowers, donations in Veronica's name could be sent to the Home for Little Wanderers in Boston. Regan could see the hand of Veronica's mother in that one. But there was nowhere to send flowers, in any event. The days passed with no visiting hours, memorial service or funeral being announced. The obituary named a local funeral home, Burgos and Sons, but said only that "arrangements were incomplete." On Friday, Ellen Hayes stopped into the store to pick up a piece in her heirloom china pattern that Regan had found in a job lot sale. "It's disgraceful, the way that family is letting this drag on," Ellen said as Regan was wrapping the china. "They can't even put that poor woman into the ground without a big fight." Ellen had been a close friend of the former Anita Standish and had kept in touch with her after the divorce.

"What is the fight about?" Regan asked Ellen.

"Everything they can find. He wants an autopsy, she doesn't. He wants to sue, she doesn't. He wants cremation, she doesn't. It's a wonder they stayed married long enough to produce a child in the first place. And meanwhile, their daughter sits in the funeral home cooler, without even the dignity of a casket. He doesn't want to pay for an expensive one, she does."

"Good god." Regan had known that the Standishes had fought bitterly and gone through an ugly divorce when Veronica was in junior high school, but Veronica had never talked about the details. If this final battle characterized her parents' whole relationship, Regan thought that it explained a lot about Veronica's own stormy life.

On Friday evening, Jonathan unexpectedly let himself into the store after Regan and Sean had closed for the night and were finishing up with the receipts and deposit. "I need to talk to you both," he said without even saying hello.

"Well, come on in," Regan said, disturbed by his grim expression. She locked the door behind him and the three of them went back to the office. Jonathan seemed tense and restless. Regan had never seen him quite this distracted.

"We may have a very serious problem on our hands. Extremely serious. And I honestly am not sure how to handle it."

"What, for god's sake?"

"I think Veronica is waking up."

Sean and Regan stared blankly at him for a moment, unable to connect this astonishing statement with reality. It clicked with Regan first.

"Oh, my god. Oh my *god*. She committed suicide!"

Sean said, "You mean...you mean she's turned? But she's crazy!" Suddenly catching himself, he looked in chagrin at Regan. "I mean, I know she was a good friend of yours, but—"

"She was crazy. I know. Jonathan, why didn't you know about this before?"

"I suspected that it might happen, but I was hoping that it wouldn't. I didn't have much contact with her. I only drank the one time. It's true, it wasn't a long period of time after that before she died. But I was expecting that there would be an autopsy and an embalming. That should have stopped her from changing, at least an autopsy would have. There's certainly no question about cremation. But now none of those things has happened, and it's been more than three full days."

"You told me that you woke up after seven days."

"I also said there was a lot of variation. I've heard anything from twenty-four hours to a week. But all that is moot now. I'm sure she's waking up. I can *feel* her."

"Have you ever caused anyone to change before?"

He shook his head slowly. "Not unless it happened long after I'd lost contact with the individual, and we never crossed paths again. I've never changed someone on purpose."

Regan sank down into the office chair, feeling somewhat numb. "So...what do we do?"

"We actually have three options. One, we both leave town tonight and disappear, because if Veronica is immediately seen or caught, she could say anything, and life could get very sticky for us."

"Except that Veronica never remembered or knew anything about you being a vampire, Jonathan. God, she won't even know that she's one, will she?"

"She may not, at first. But we have no idea what will be in her mind when she first awakens. We don't know what was in her mind when she chose to commit suicide."

"So what's option number two?"

"Stay, and be prepared for whatever spin control is necessary when all hell breaks loose."

"And door number three?" Sean said.

"Intervene somehow. Either stop her from awakening at all, or be there when she does, and at least keep her from roaming about on her own."

"Stop her from awakening?" Regan's imagination shrank from the possibilities that came to mind. "How would we do that?"

Jonathan hesitated. "It isn't easy. The only completely certain method I know of is burning. Dismemberment might work, but that means removing all the viscera and severing the spine multiple times, not just cutting off the arms and legs—"

"Oh, fuck, you gotta be *kidding*." Sean looked green. "What would we have to do to stop her, if she's already awake?"

"I would be extremely reluctant to take such action. The necessary procedures are the same, but there's no time when we're so unconscious or inanimate that we don't fight back. It's very violent and very ugly, and not easy by any means to do. And I'm not sure that I have the right to destroy another vampire, unless she has proven so irrational and so vicious that reforming her is clearly impossible."

"If you're already feeling her waking up," Regan said uneasily, "isn't it too late to prevent it, anyway?"

"I'm afraid that may be the case."

Sean and Regan looked dismally at each other. "Well, what do we do?" Regan said again. "She's in a refrigerated drawer at the funeral home, as far as I know. There's no way we can get in there. There's someone there twenty-four hours a day, and they have a security system. And even if we could get in, attempting to interfere with human remains is a serious crime. We might just as well walk down to the police station and make a full confession, as get caught trying to break into a funeral home. How do you propose pulling this off?"

Jonathan was silent for a moment. "I don't know. Short of causing some mishap at the funeral home..."

"What, you mean like set it on fire? Oh, great, let's add arson to our resumes."

"If the power failed, they might have to move the bodies that are there."

Sean said, "I think they've got generator back-up, though. I mean, if there's some kind of disaster, they want to keep all the bodies on ice. Places like that have generators, they must have." As the other two looked at him, he said, "Okay, I don't *know* that. But it makes sense, and anyway, how could *we* cut the power to the funeral home? And wouldn't that just bring a whole crew of utility trucks with fifty million watt spotlights, repairing it? Hello, let's attract the whole town's attention here."

"He's right. Besides," Regan said, "if they move Veronica to another funeral home, or a hospital morgue, we're no better off than we are now."

Jonathan frowned down at the floor, thinking. "Without more time to plan this out, I see just one other option. We'll simply have to wait outside the funeral home for her to emerge, and hope that she manages to get out without anyone seeing her."

"Is that *likely?*"

"I know that when I awakened, the only thought in my mind was not to be seen. It was instinctive. I don't think it was just coincidence that I happened to wake up in that brief span of time when no one was nearby. I had been half-awake for some time, but I didn't feel impelled to move until I was alone."

Sean and Regan looked at each other. Sean's raised eyebrow communicated, *this is nuts.* Regan said, "Can she get out of those refrigerator drawers by herself? Don't they have latches, even locks?"

"I don't know. But that won't stop her."

Sean was suddenly struck by something. "Will she be running around naked?" That question, too, was relegated to the unknown column. It depended on where the tug-of-war between Jerry Standish and his ex-wife was at the moment. If Anita had prevailed, Veronica might have been dressed for burial, but if an autopsy was expected, she probably had not been.

"You're not going, anyway," Regan said.

"What do you mean? You're going to need all the help you can get."

"You're not going. The last thing on god's green earth that you need, Sean, is to get arrested for suspicious activity outside a funeral home. I don't want you involved in this."

"Uh, news flash. I *am* involved in this."

"Not this part of it, you're not. Veronica isn't your problem, and she's not going to be. You've got plenty to worry about without that. I'll take you home, if you want."

"Forget it, I've got my bike," Sean said sullenly.

Regan looked at Jonathan. "Okay. When do you want to go over there? It's close to sunset now."

"I think we have one or two more hours, but not more than that."

"All right, then—" Regan stopped abruptly as there was a firm knocking on the front door of the store. "Who the hell is that?" she whispered. "Sean, go take a look."

Sean sprinted back from the front door. "It's a cop! What do we do?"

"Let him in," Regan said, hastening to the front door. When she opened it, she saw a tall man in a simple gray suit, his dark hair conservatively cut. Beyond him she could see a police cruiser parked in front of the steps.

"Hello, ma'am," he said, holding up an identification badge. "I'm Detective Fellman, from Sheridan P.D. I'm looking for Jonathan Vaughn, would he be here?"

It was pointless to lie with Jonathan's car sitting right out in the parking area next to the cruiser. "Yes, he is. Is there a problem?"

"Can I speak to him, please?"

Regan looked behind her, suddenly panicked. Before she could answer, Jonathan came up the main aisle to the front door.

"How can I help you, Detective?"

"I'm sorry to interrupt, Mr. Vaughn. I went to your house, but you weren't there, and I thought that Ms. Calloway might have some idea where to find you. I wonder if you could come down to the station and just answer a few questions."

"About what?"

"We'll explain all that at the station, Mr. Vaughn."

Regan felt an icy chill over her entire body. What did this mean? Had Veronica already woken up? Had she said something to someone before she died? Jonathan glanced at her quickly, and she saw the same apprehension in his eyes.

"Am I under arrest?"

"No, sir. But if you're willing to cooperate, we may be able to clear some things up."

"Does it have to be right now? I'm afraid there's something very important that I need to take care of."

"Yes, we need you to come in now, if you can."

Jonathan hesitated. "All right. Shall I follow you in my car?"

"We'll take you, sir. We'll see to it that you get back to your own vehicle."

"Just give me a minute," Jonathan said tensely. He walked a few steps back down the main aisle, away from the door, and Regan followed him. "I think you'd better go on ahead, to that...rendezvous we were just discussing. Stay safe, above all else. I'll join you as soon as I can."

"But...but Jonathan, what if—"

Glancing back at the door, Jonathan said quickly, "She won't know. She won't know what she is or why she feels the way she does. She'll be confused and disoriented. Remember the last words she said to you? She'll trust you. I won't leave you to handle this alone, I promise." At the look on her face, Jonathan put a bracing hand on her shoulder. "I *promise.*" He quickly went out the door and accompanied Detective Fellman to the waiting police cruiser.

Regan stood bleakly at the door watching the cruiser pull into the road. *But...where will I take her? What do I tell her? What if she doesn't want to see me, or you? What if she just runs? And what do we do if you're arrested?*

Sean had come up to stand next to her. "Guess I'm going, huh?" His voice didn't have a trace of satisfaction in it—he sounded frightened.

"Come on. Let's lock up and go."

Chapter 14

Burgos and Sons Funeral Home had a very convenient location. It was right next door to the largest and oldest cemetery in Sheridan. There were no other buildings within a mile of the funeral home, and the surrounding land was thickly wooded, the cemetery stretching off into hilly ground to the west. This seclusion allowed Burgos and Sons to operate one of the few crematoriums in the area. When she and Sean arrived, Regan drove on past the attractively landscaped building to scout out the situation, and immediately saw something alarming. There was a wake going on that evening. The parking lot of the trim white clapboarded building was filled with cars, and there were lights in the front windows and people going in and out the door. Regan hadn't even thought to check the funeral home's website for its schedule of services. This had all happened too fast, and she had been too flustered.

"What do we do?" Sean whispered. Regan had pulled over, a hundred yards down the road, and was thinking. The whole evening had become so surreal that it suddenly didn't seem to matter what they did. It occurred to her that the most outlandish course of action might end up being the best they could try.

"Let's go pay our respects."

"Are you nuts? We're crashing a funeral?"

"It's a wake. You go in, you sign the guest book, you express your condolences to the next of kin...anyway," she said as she pulled into the parking lot, "whoever it is, I'll bet they visited my store at least once."

"How do you know it's a wake?"

"They don't have funerals at night. And there's no hearse out front. We're not doing anything disrespectful, Sean, for goodness sake."

"Is there going to be a body in there?" he whispered as they went up the steps.

"Shhh."

They walked into the front hallway of the funeral home, which was thickly carpeted and tastefully wallpapered, with subdued track lighting. There were closed doors on either side, and an open door ahead on the right with a murmur of voices drifting from it. Regan, with Sean reluctantly following, walked through the open doorway into a low-ceilinged double room. In a larger area to the left, there was a low stage that had doorways on either side. In the center of this was the casket, in which the deceased was reposing, eyes firmly closed, white hair coiffed, cheeks rouged, nose pointing straight up despite the quilted satin pillow. Her deeply wrinkled hands were folded on the midsection of her flowered dress. There were flowers behind and in front of the casket, but fewer than Regan had sometimes seen at a wake, and the living contingent of the room was not numerous. Like many very elderly people, this one appeared to have survived most of her friends and relations. The door by which Regan and Sean had just entered led into an anteroom, and directly across from the door was a table with a large floral arrangement, some photographs, and a guest book with a pale blue moiré cover. Regan went over to look at it.

"Oh my god," she said softly to Sean, "It is one of my customers! I didn't even know she was ill." She picked up the pen and signed the book. Sean stood close behind her, fists in his pockets and his shoulders hunched, casting sidelong looks at the casket.

"Is she really real?" he whispered to Regan.

"Yes, she's really real. Haven't you ever been to a wake, Sean?"

"I've never been inside a funeral home before, for anything."

"I'm just going to go offer my condolences. Look around a little and see if you notice any of the staff, and where they come from, okay?"

She went into the front room, where a few family members—children and grandchildren, she guessed, no one of the deceased's generation—had a receiving line. Both rooms were amply furnished with chairs, benches, and discreetly placed boxes of tissues, but the bereaved appeared to be handling their grief well. Regan expressed her sympathies, eliciting polite thanks, and after she had finished with the line, she walked past the casket, in order to check out the doorways on either side of the platform. All that was visible through them were plain white walls and carpeted floors, a more utilitarian carpet than in the public rooms of the facility. But these doors must lead to the private areas of the funeral home, because there was no other way for the casket to be wheeled in.

She went back to the anteroom, where she motioned to Sean to sit with her on a pair of curve-back chairs with heavily upholstered seats. "Do we just sit here and wait?" he whispered.

"For a few minutes, anyway. We can't hang around outside until people have left. Visiting hours are six-thirty to eight-thirty, according to that little sign on the table. It's getting close to eight-thirty now."

"One thing for sure, no one is acting like anything weird is going on downstairs. If one of their, uh, clients was getting up and walking off, you'd think there'd be some excitement." Regan could only shrug. "What do you think the police want to talk to Jonathan about?" Sean said after a short silence.

"I don't know."

"I thought one thing was kind of funny. How come that cop was so sure that you'd know where to find Jonathan?"

"Oh, small town...I guess gossip gets around. But maybe—" she broke off as Sean gripped her upper arm, so tightly that it hurt.

"Oh fuck..." he said under his breath, "oh fuck oh fuck..."

Following his line of vision, Regan almost said the same thing. Standing on the side of the larger room near the casket was Veronica. She must have come out of the door from the back hallway. How she had managed to avoid being seen by any of the funeral home staff, Regan couldn't guess. Anita must have prevailed, at least for this round: Veronica was wearing a simple, modest dress of pale blue that matched her eyes. Her hair fell around her shoulders in curls, which was not how she usually wore it. Her face was heavily and carefully made up, disguising the waxen pallor of her skin. She simply stood there, looking around the room, and the most incredible thing of all was that no one paid any attention to her. One or two people glanced at her briefly, but obviously assumed she was another visitor. Had the lights been brighter, they might have noticed some of the peculiarities in her appearance, but the visitors at the wake had other things to think about.

"They don't recognize her," Regan whispered to Sean. "No one here knows who she is."

"Oh my *god*, what do we *do?*"

"Don't panic, for god's sake. We've got to get her out of here. If the funeral director or any of the staff see her, it's all over."

"How are we—oh my god. She's coming over here."

It was not apparent that Veronica had seen or recognized them. Her expression had an odd blankness to it, and she threaded her way through the few visitors still remaining, moving behind them as much as possible. She bumped into one or two people but walked on, paying no attention to their murmured apologies. As she approached the door to the entrance hall, she slowed down and hesitated, and Regan stood up.

"Veronica," she said softly.

For a moment Veronica didn't move or react. Then, she slowly turned her head and looked at Regan. Her face did not change, but after a moment she said, "Regan." Regan felt an icy finger run down her spine. It was as though a ventriloquist had somehow made Veronica's mouth move while imitating her voice.

"Yes, it's me, Veronica. I'm here to help you. Let's leave before anyone else sees you." Veronica just stared at her with the same blank expression. Regan braced herself and reached out and took Veronica's hand. She couldn't repress a shudder. The hand was cold, not just room temperature, but refrigerator cold, and clammy with condensation. There was just one other time when Regan had held a hand this cold, and that was the last memory on earth she wanted to recall. The limp, unresisting fingers did not clasp hers in return. But neither did Veronica attempt to pull away. No psychic impressions came from this hand, but Regan was consciously closing herself to any input. She nodded to Sean. "Check the hall."

Sean, who had been staring at Veronica in fascinated horror—fortunately unnoticed by any of the visitors—ducked over to the door and looked out. "It's clear," he hissed, like the point man of a commando squad checking for snipers. Regan hastily pulled Veronica out into the hall and in a few moments they were all safely outside, unseen by any of the funeral home staff. Veronica was beginning to show a little more animation as Regan led her to the car. As though on auto-pilot, she mechanically got into the passenger's seat as soon as Regan opened the door. Sean squawked, "*Fuck* that! I'm not riding in there with her."

"No, you're not. You have to stay here and wait for Jonathan, or he's not going to know what's happened."

"Oh, *shit*."

"We've got to get out of here before anyone discovers she's missing, or sees her." Regan closed the passenger's door and hurried around the car, digging in her pocket for her keys as Sean trotted after her.

"But where are you *going* with her?"

Regan got into the driver's seat and started the car. "Jonathan's. I can't think where else to take her. It's isolated, it's off on a lonely road, and I can't take her to the store or my place, it's too likely that she'll be seen. You and Jonathan come on out there as fast as you can, when he gets here, got that?"

"But what if she...what if you...are you sure that—"

"I don't have any choice." Regan glanced quickly at the steps of the funeral home as several visitors emerged. "Try not to act suspicious, Sean, for god's sake." It was almost 8:30. Without stopping for more discussion, she backed her car out of its space and pulled onto the road. Veronica, not wearing a safety belt, rocked forward and then slammed back into the seat with the car's motion, like a jointed doll. Her eyes stared straight ahead at the road.

It only took about twenty minutes to get to Rainbow Stone house, even by back ways that avoided street lights, traffic and settled areas. Regan could feel every inch of her skin crawling. Jonathan didn't affect her like this. Never had she so viscerally understood the horror of the truly uncanny, that thing that defies the laws of Nature and logic. She had to use every ounce of self-control not to slam on the brakes and flee the car, with the same blind instinct for self-preservation that she would have felt if the car burst into flames. She pulled into the front drive of the house and got out of the car so fast that she stumbled. There were no outside lights on and no moon that night, so it was very dark.

Regan went around to the passenger's side, but before she reached it, the door opened and Veronica stepped out. She was shoeless, Regan noticed for the first time, wearing old-fashioned hose that were slipping down her legs like sagging knee socks. Of course, the funeral home wouldn't dress the deceased in pantyhose, what would be the point? But Veronica was now acting much more normally. She got out of the car, stretched several times, and even yawned. She looked around and pursed her lips in a puzzled expression. "Where are we?" Her voice now had a more natural inflection, although still a bit flat. But Regan observed these changes with some alarm. It was a relief to see Veronica acting less like the walking corpse that she was, but she might be more difficult to handle.

"We're at a house, out on River Road."

Veronica looked up at the façade of the house. It was barely visible to Regan, but Veronica appeared to be studying it carefully. "River Road..." she said thoughtfully. "This is Jonathan's house?"

"Yes."

"I've never been here." She took a step forward. "Is he here?"

"No, but he'll be here soon. Let's go inside, we can wait for him."

Veronica turned and looked at Regan steadily for a few moments. In the dark, Regan could not read her expression. "I don't think I want to do that."

Regan fought down a stifling sense of panic. "Veronica, a lot has happened in the last few days. There's a lot that you may not understand right now. Jonathan can explain everything to you."

"He can? Why?"

"Because he's..." Regan fumbled, not sure what to say, most especially standing out in the pitch dark in front of the house. Suddenly, Veronica's complete lack of memory about what had happened to her here and what Jonathan was had become a problem. To make things worse, some of Veronica's more difficult personality traits appeared to be reviving as her flesh warmed, such as her impatience and her impulsiveness.

"I don't want to be here," Veronica abruptly pronounced, and she turned and walked rapidly around the drive and out into the road, taking a direction not toward town but west, toward the dairy farm.

Oh, shit. Regan started after her, stopped, went back to the car and pulled a hazard flashlight out of the glove compartment, and ran after Veronica.

She caught up with her friend, but Veronica would not slow her pace or stop. Regan grasped her arm once and was instantly shaken off with force. She realized that Veronica was now almost as strong as Jonathan. "Veronica, wait. Please wait. You really have to understand some things before you just go striding off like this."

Veronica stopped dead and swung around to face Regan, so unexpectedly that Regan almost ran into her before she could stop, as well. "Such as *what* things?" Her voice now had an angry energy to it that made Regan recoil.

They had come about a half mile down the road, and Regan realized that they were quite close to the dairy farm. The woods ended up ahead, and the landscape opened up into fields where the cows were put out to graze. The lights of the main barns and farm house could be seen shining in the distance. Only a few feet ahead a grassy cut-in off the main road led to a small outbuilding among the trees where equipment could be stored, although it was empty now and one side of the doors was slightly ajar. Regan indicated the cut-in with her flashlight. "Veronica—let's go in there and talk. We shouldn't just be standing in the middle of the road like this." Again there was a steady stare, and then Veronica tossed her hair back and walked briskly off the road to the outbuilding.

They went inside the windowless structure and Regan pulled the door closed. She turned on the "lantern" side of the emergency light and set it on a crate by the door. It needed new batteries, and the light was dim and yellowish.

"Now just what is it that we have to talk about?"

"Veronica..." Regan hesitated unhappily. "Do you remember what happened to you just before tonight? Do you remember how you got here?"

Veronica blinked, and she looked down, her brow creasing. "How I got here? I was in your car."

"Before that."

"There was...a room full of people...like a party or something..."

"And before that? Where were you when you woke up? Before the party?" Regan sensed that there were dangers in this line of questioning, but she didn't know how else to keep Veronica from continuing to walk straight on for the rest of the night—just as she imagined Jonathan must have done when he first awoke. Regan certainly couldn't stop her by physical force.

Veronica was still, searching her memory. "I was...I was in this stupid drawer. Why was I in a *drawer?* I had to get out all by myself."

"You were in a morgue, Veronica. That was a cold room in the funeral home."

"A morgue? A funeral home?" She paused a moment. "They thought I was *dead?*"

"Do you remember taking those pills, Veronica?" Veronica's face became very still. "You remember, you wrote a note to the new owners of your condo, saying that you were out by the fifteenth as promised. And you took all your pills, and lay down on the bed. Do you remember that?"

Veronica swallowed, slowly. "I...I remember thinking...that this would solve everything. My father has a life insurance policy that would pay all my debts. Everything would be settled and no one would have to be responsible for me anymore. It would even pay for the...the...funeral..." her voice dropped to a whisper on the last words. She looked down at herself. "I'm...I'm dressed for the funeral! I don't have any *shoes!* God, I've got—I've got about ten pounds of makeup on my face!" She rubbed at her face with both hands, smearing the pale pink lipstick across her cheeks and chin. "Those *assholes!* They thought I was dead! I completely fucked it up and they thought I was dead! My father will sue their asses off!"

"No, he won't, Ver. Your father can't ever know about this."

"What are you *talking* about? They thought I was *dead!*"

"You *are* dead, Veronica!" Regan hadn't meant to shout, but Veronica's agitation was infectious. Veronica stood rigid, staring at her.

"You're crazy."

"Look at yourself. How could the EMT's, the doctors, the funeral director, make a mistake like that? You've changed, Veronica, you're not a normal human now."

"You're crazy. Dead people don't get up and walk around."

"I can't explain this to you, Ver. But there's a lot you need to know now, and only Jonathan can help you. You've got to come back to the house with me. *Please.*"

Veronica paced back and forth across the hard-packed dirt floor of the room, shaking her head. "Jonathan, Jonathan, Jonathan, you keep going back to that. That's all you can think about, isn't it, Jonathan, he's god almighty, he knows everything, he'll solve all my problems. Well, fuck that!" Her voice had risen. "I know exactly what was going on, Regan. Derek told me."

"Derek? What did Derek tell you about Jonathan?"

"You were *fucking* him! You and Jonathan, screwing like bunnies, every night, while I was in the hospital! You probably didn't even wait until I was out of the E.R.! You were probably fucking him that same night!"

"I didn't! Veronica, it's not—"

"Don't you dare stand there and say it's not true! I know all about it! Everyone knows! Derek told me what a fool I made out of myself, how everyone was laughing at me, because I threw myself at Jonathan and chased him like some pathetic little groupie, and all along, you and he were just laughing at me!"

"We *weren't!* Veronica, I haven't heard *anyone* say they were laughing at you, for anything."

"Well, why would they tell *you?* Derek wants me back, god knows why. He cared enough to be honest. He cared enough to tell me the truth. He told me how stupid I'd been, to think that Jonathan gave a shit about me, when he couldn't wait to stab me in the back."

"How can you believe Derek, if you know he was just trying to get you back?"

"I can believe him more than you, can't I? You were my best friend, Regan... my best friend. How could you do this to me?" Veronica's mouth twisted, as if she was holding back sobs. "I wrote it all up," she went on, more quietly. "I wrote it all up, everything you and Jonathan did, and I mailed it to my father. Before I took the pills. I told my father what a shit Jonathan was, and everything that happened before he dumped me for you. So he's going to have to face the consequences. And so will you."

That's what the police wanted...oh god... "What did you say in this letter? What's the point of just trying to make trouble for Jonathan?"

"You see? That's all you care about. You don't give a shit about me, Regan."

"Ver, how can you say that? Why would I be here trying to help you if I didn't care?"

"Because you're doing it for him! You're trying to shut me up to protect him, you lied to me, Regan, you never cared! You were glad I was dead, everyone was glad!"

"I *wasn't* glad, Veronica—"

"You just wanted me out of the way! *That's why you didn't try to stop me, Regan!*" Veronica's voice cracked, she screamed the last words so loudly. Then she swung her arm across her body, moving so fast that Regan had no time to react, and struck Regan a backhand blow across the face. She struck with such force that Regan was spun completely around and stumbled into the wall behind her, and the rough wood scraped skin off her cheek. Stunned, Regan struggled not to fall, and Veronica grabbed one of her wrists and wrenched Regan into the middle of the room, then swung her into the opposite wall. Regan struck a heavy support beam and pain lanced down her entire back. She thought she must have broken something. She could hardly breathe, but she saw Veronica reaching for her again and ducked away as hard as she could. Veronica's hand slammed into the wall where Regan had been and she let out an incoherent cry of rage. She jumped after Regan, clutching handfuls of Regan's sweater in her fists, and shoved Regan backward to the east wall of the room. She slammed Regan back against the heavy boards again and again to punctuate her half sobbed words. "You backstabbing bitch! You let me die! You wanted to get rid of me!"

But with this, her burst of rage seemed to wear itself out. She held Regan against the wall for a few moments, her grip slowly loosening. Regan could see tears shining on Veronica's face. She herself was shaking so hard, that she knew she would fall when Veronica let go of her sweater. Her whole body hurt and her ears were ringing, and she could feel something trickling down her cheek, which was throbbing and stinging painfully. "Veronica," she whispered, "please stop. I never wanted you to be hurt, I swear. Let's go back to the house."

Veronica didn't quite let go of Regan, but she let her slide down the wall to a sitting position, dropping to her knees as well. "Regan," she said softly, "I don't know...I don't know what's wrong with me..."

"I know. It's not your fault, Ver—"

"Something's wrong with me, Regan..." she reached out and rubbed her forefinger up over Regan's wet cheek. She drew her finger away dark with blood. Regan watched with a numb sense of inevitability as Veronica put her finger to her mouth and sucked the blood off with an expression of concentrated attention. When her finger was clean, she sat still, licking at her lips like a cat, her eyes staring into the distance.

Regan, trying to move slowly enough to avoid attracting Veronica's attention, hitched back awkwardly toward the door. *It's just a foot away, maybe if I can get out and latch the doors shut...*

Veronica slowly looked down at her in the dying emergency light's beams. "I'm so...*thirsty,*" she said softly. They stared at each other, as Regan drew in a long ragged breath. Then Veronica pounced on her.

Regan flailed wildly in an effort to block Veronica's arms, or kick her, but she couldn't even connect with anything solid. Veronica was too fast. In a second or two, Regan was pinned flat to the floor, Veronica's hand over her mouth so tightly she was almost smothered. Veronica brutally twisted Regan's head sideways, her knees digging into Regan's ribs to hold her still. She bent down and locked her mouth onto Regan's neck and dug in with her teeth for a moment, but to hold, not to bite. Suddenly there was a sickening, tearing pain that ran from Regan's neck down to her shoulder, and Regan felt a spray of wet warmth soak her hair, her sweater and her face. Veronica stretched out until she was almost lying flat on top of Regan, drinking down gulp after gulp of blood without stopping. Regan put her hands against Veronica's upper arms, but her muscles were already going loose and she couldn't even exert pressure to try and push Veronica away. After several minutes, the room spun with vertigo and Regan could see bursts of white light all around her, like flash bulbs in the dimness. The ground underneath her was wet, the back of her sweater was saturated, and she gasped for breath, because she was suffocating, she couldn't breathe, even though Veronica's hand was no longer covering her mouth. There was a tight squeezing sensation in her chest. "Veronica," she whispered, or thought she did, "please stop." But even if Veronica had heard and complied, Regan knew it was already too late. She couldn't feel her arms or legs, but opening her eyes, she saw her hand slide off Veronica's shoulder and slap limply onto the dirt floor. Regan closed her eyes, or it became too dark to see. *Jonathan,* came her last despairing thought, *Jonathan, you promised me.*

Chapter 15

At the same time that Regan and Sean were leaving Borrowed and Blue for the funeral home, Detective Fellman and Jonathan arrived at the Sheridan police station, a thick-walled brownstone building off Main that had been built in the 1930s. The dispatcher, sitting behind a double wall of bullet-resistant Plexiglas, buzzed the two men into the back hallway, where Detective Fellman ushered Jonathan into a small interrogation room near the end of the hall. There was a heavy metal table, which was bolted to the floor, and several steel frame chairs with padded seats and backs. "Have a seat, Mr. Vaughn," Detective Fellman said, and Jonathan sat, slowly, in the chair nearest the door. Detective Fellman sat down in the chair at the end of the table, where a yellow legal pad sat on top of a manila folder, and took a pen from his jacket pocket. "Relax, Mr. Vaughn. You seem very tense."

"Not about talking with you. I'm afraid you have very bad timing."

Detective Fellman smiled faintly. "Since you seem to be in a hurry, I'll get right to the point. Are you aware that there have been some unusual cases of apparent assault in southeastern Massachusetts over the past six months?"

"Unusual cases? Apparent assault? Perhaps you could be a bit more descriptive."

"There have been seventeen of them reported so far."

Noting the number, Jonathan was immediately wary. "That seems like a lot."

"It does."

"I haven't seen anything in the news about that many unusual assaults. I've just noticed the usual ones."

"These haven't been covered by the news. In fact, if it wasn't for the efforts of some private citizens, we wouldn't be aware that there was a connection, or even that the assaults were being committed." As Jonathan frowned darkly, Detective Fellman went on, "The victims don't remember much about what happened."

"Then...why would *I* be aware of these assaults?" Jonathan waited a moment. "That's obviously a rhetorical question under the circumstances, isn't it?"

Detective Fellman made a note on the legal pad. He had very small handwriting. "When did you move to Massachusetts, Mr. Vaughn?"

"Last summer. It took me a couple of weeks to find a suitable apartment."

"Where had you been living before that?"

"The West Coast. I tend to move around quite a bit."

"What do you do to earn a living?" Detective Fellman was idly drawing a little chain of circles along the top of the legal pad, and almost looked bored, but Jonathan was not fooled. He doubted that any move he made or fluctuation in his voice was going unmarked.

"I'm a freelance writer. But I also have some investments. They pay most of the bills."

Detective Fellman made another note. "Have you been published?"

"A few articles here and there. I write under pseudonyms, though."

Detective Fellman opened the manila folder and checked, or pretended to check, a page of notes that topped the papers inside. "When you came to Massachusetts, you got an apartment in Brockton?"

"That's right. I had a six-month lease."

"And you moved to Sheridan in March?"

"Yes."

"There was a one-month gap between the time you moved out of Brockton and the date you signed the lease here in Sheridan. Where were you staying?"

"Hotels. It took a while to find a rental I could afford that met my needs."

"You don't have any friends or family in this area?"

"None that could put me up for a month."

"What were your specific needs, Mr. Vaughn? The property you've rented isn't exactly prime real estate."

Jonathan hesitated. "I didn't want another apartment. The place in Brockton tended to be noisy. I was looking for someplace peaceful, low traffic, secluded... not necessarily as isolated as the one I found. The realtor suggested it. And I couldn't beat the price. My income frees me to follow my muse, it doesn't make me Bill Gates."

"And you're writing a book now?" Detective Fellman made a note.

"That's right. It's the biggest project I've worked on so far."

"You must have gotten an advance."

"No, I'm writing on spec. It's a controversial topic, so I prefer not to discuss it."

Detective Fellman nodded soberly. "I can understand that. Is there any particular reason you moved to southeast Massachusetts to write this book?"

"Definitely. I need to do a lot of local research for it here. There's just so much you can find on the Internet."

"Oh, I'm aware of that." Detective Fellman checked the manila folder again. "Why did you change your social security number, Mr. Vaughn?"

"I was a victim of identity theft. It was a mess, and it cost me several thousand dollars before I got everything straightened out. Even at that, I got off cheap compared to some. As you can imagine, that experience has made me pretty cautious about protecting my privacy."

"I'm sure it would." He opened the folder, but this time paged through the contents and removed a Polaroid photograph. He slid it across the table to Jonathan. "Have you ever seen anything like this, Mr. Vaughn?"

Jonathan picked it up. It was a close-up shot of the injury on one of the assault victims. There was nothing in the picture that gave any clues to the victim's gender, let alone identity. Jonathan was desperate to know who the seventeenth victim might be, but there was no possible way to ask. "My god," he said quietly. "No, I've never seen anything even remotely like this, but it looks ghastly. What is it?" Instead of answering, Detective Fellman removed nine more photos, some of them digital, and lined them up on the table. Each one showed a very similar injury, some of them newer and some of them more healed. "I take it these are the unusual assaults you mentioned?" Jonathan pushed the Polaroid back across the table and Detective Fellman replaced the photos carefully in the folder.

"Yes, that's correct. All the victims have an injury like this."

"Were they sexually assaulted?"

Detective Fellman looked at Jonathan for a moment. "That would be confidential information, I'm sorry."

"Didn't you say the victims don't remember what happened?"

"They don't remember much. We're still investigating."

"Have any of these assaults been fatal?"

"Not so far." Detective Fellman leaned back in his chair, watching Jonathan. "Mr. Vaughn...you seem to be a solitary type, don't you?"

"Most writers are."

"No roommate in Brockton, no housemate here, no neighbors at all, you're self-employed...what do you do to relax?"

"Oh, I go to the movies sometimes. I went to a club date a couple of weeks ago with some people. I have friends, Detective."

"No girlfriend?" He raised an eyebrow. "Or boyfriend?"

"I've been between relationships for a while," Jonathan said dryly.

"I'm not judgmental."

"I'm not offended. I know why you're asking. No, I probably could not give you an alibi for any of these mysterious assaults, no matter when they took place. Maybe one or two, but I work alone, I eat alone, and I sleep alone, and in between all that excitement I take long walks and think deep thoughts. So if I really had to prove that I couldn't have assaulted someone on a given day, chances are I'm S.O.O.L."

Detective Fellman smiled down at the table. "I appreciate your honesty."

"Are we done here? I don't know what else I can tell you."

"No, not quite. There is something else." Detective Fellman was thoughtfully silent for moment, idly toying with his pen. "You may have heard that a Sheridan woman named Veronica Standish was found in her home, deceased, this past Tuesday."

"Yes, that *was* in the news."

"Is that all you've heard, what was in the papers?"

Again Jonathan hesitated, finding himself on the slippery footing between untellable truth and risky fibs. But Detective Fellman had just seen him at Borrowed and Blue talking with Regan and Sean, and obviously had known enough to ask Regan about Jonathan's whereabouts. "I know a number of people who are friends of Miss Standish, so, no. I heard that she committed suicide. It's a terrible tragedy."

"Suicide always is. Yesterday her father, Jerry Standish, received a letter that had been mailed on Monday, before Miss Standish's death."

"An anonymous letter?"

"It was from Veronica Standish."

Jonathan hesitated. "I see. And why does this concern me?"

"The letter allegedly contains some rather serious claims concerning your behavior toward Miss Standish."

"My behavior?" Jonathan stared blankly at Detective Fellman, who only looked back at him impassively. "I can't imagine what Miss Standish could have written about me. We never even went out on a...date, if you will. In fact, I scarcely spent any time alone with her at all, under any circumstances. May I see the letter?"

"Since it's a private communication to Mr. Standish, that would be up to him."

"Have you seen this letter?"

"I haven't seen it yet, no. Mr. Standish filed a complaint against you, through his attorney. As it stands right now, there's nothing we can charge you with based on the information he's willing to give us. I just wanted to know how you'd like to respond."

"I can't make any response without knowing more details. Just what am I supposed to have done?"

"The gist of the complaint is that Miss Standish claims a sexual relationship with you that got pretty rough. Apparently, she also accuses you of heartlessly dumping her for someone else."

"I *never* had a sexual relationship with Veronica Standish, so I couldn't have dumped her, even if that were a crime, which it is not. And I don't like rough sex, period."

"Jerry Standish claims that he has emergency room records from April twenty-third describing some actual injuries suffered by Miss Standish."

"What kind of injuries? Did you see these records?"

"He didn't give any details, and no, I didn't."

Jonathan paused to frame his next words carefully. "Detective Fellman... rumor has it that Miss Standish checked herself into a mental health facility on April twenty-third. She committed suicide three days after she was released. Isn't it possible that her letter might not be entirely factual? And given that she committed suicide two weeks later, isn't it possible that she injured herself on April twenty-third?"

"Anything's possible. Posthumous communications are always a problem. Usually they need some independent verification to be considered valid evidence. But that can depend on a number of things."

"Of course," Jonathan said darkly.

"Just for the record, where were you on the night of April twenty-second?"

"Home. Alone. Working. Sleeping."

"Is there anyone who can verify that?"

Jonathan raised his hands helplessly. "There might be some date and time stamps on my computer files."

"You didn't make or receive any phone calls on your home phone?"

Jonathan felt a warning twinge—Regan had taken Veronica to the emergency room, so connecting her to himself and that night was dangerous. On the other hand, the police could check his phone records if they wanted to, and lying would look even more suspicious. "I spoke very briefly to Ms. Calloway. But that doesn't cover much of the evening."

Detective Fellman just nodded, making a note. "Do you know where you were the night of February seventeenth, 2004?"

"Oh, lord, *I* can't remember. I'd just left Brockton, I was in some hotel somewhere. I was in a whole string of them, they all blur together."

"Could you check your records on that?"

"I could, but chances are I was alone all night."

"But there might be a desk clerk, someone who'd remember you."

"There might be. I'll get back to you."

"I'd appreciate it," Detective Fellman said, writing.

Jonathan remembered quite well what he had done on the evening of February seventeenth, but he didn't think there was anyone who could verify his whereabouts the rest of the night. It might be worth trying to find out. "Am I under arrest?"

"Not at this time."

"May I go, then?"

"Yes, I think we're done for now."

As Jonathan got up to leave, he said, "I think I'll get in touch with Jerry Standish and see if he's willing to have a talk. Maybe we can settle all this reasonably."

"That's your prerogative. I'm sure this is a very difficult time for his family."

"I wouldn't want his grief to be made even more bitter by a suspicion that Miss Standish was driven to suicide because I mistreated her. She was a troubled young woman."

Detective Fellman pressed the buzzer to open the interrogation room door. "I wish you the best of luck with that, Mr. Vaughn. I hope you can clear things up. Would you like a ride back to your car?"

"Yes, I would. I'm afraid that I'm already running very late."

Chapter 16

It was no more than a twenty minute drive from Borrowed and Blue to Burgos and Sons, but Jonathan didn't make it that far. On a lonely bend in the road, before the funeral home was in sight, Sean stepped out of a small copse of trees and waved frantically at Jonathan, just as the car was passing him. Jonathan braked so hard that the car skidded ten feet on loose gravel, but Sean was running around to the passenger's side before the vehicle had even stopped.

"Don't go any further! Don't go to the funeral home!" he said breathlessly, clambering into the car. "Turn around, you don't want to be seen there."

"Why?" Jonathan was turning the car even as he spoke. "Where's Regan?"

"I'll tell you, but just go! Just go!" Before they had gone more than fifty feet down the main road back to town, Sean waved his arm at a tiny side road to the left. "There—turn off! Turn off! There's going to be cop cars, they'll see us!" As Jonathan peeled around the turn, Sean fell back against the seat, heaving a sigh. "Oh, *god*. We are in such deep shit."

"More than you can possibly imagine," Jonathan said grimly. "Tell me what's happened. Where's Regan? Why will there be cop cars? Where are we going?"

"Go to your house. Regan's got Veronica with her."

"You mean she woke up?"

"Woke up! Jesus, she came walking right through the middle of this funeral! Or wake, or whatever the fuck it is."

"What? You mean she was seen?" Jonathan said, aghast.

"Well, yeah—but no one knew who she was. But the funeral home is going to figure out she's gone, and they'll call the cops—and all I could think was, you were going to drive right into it."

"Well, thank you for heading me off. Can you tell me exactly what happened? What do you mean about a wake? Not for Veronica."

"No, some old lady." Sean rattled off a rapid account of what had occurred at the funeral home. "It was all so fast," he finished. "I mean, we walk in, boom, we're out. And nobody even noticed us."

"But people did see you. And Regan signed the guest book?"

"She said she knew the dead lady. And I guess it would have looked kind of suspicious, if we'd just walked in and hung around."

Jonathan shook his head. "I wish you hadn't gone inside."

"Me too, but what could I do? I was just following orders."

The road stopped at a T intersection. "I don't even know where we are, Sean. Which way?"

"Left, go left. It comes out on River Road. Careful, you're going to run us right off the road!" Jonathan had turned so sharply that the car's tires spun in soft ground at the shoulder and the car fishtailed wildly.

"This is taking us by a very roundabout route, and we can't waste any time. I'm desperately afraid that I made a serious miscalculation, sending Regan and you to intercept Veronica."

"That makes two of us! But she sure wasn't putting up much of a fight—Veronica, I mean. She was practically a zombie—fuck, I've never been so creeped out in my life."

"That may partly be the refrigeration. She won't stay that way for long."

"What do you think she'll do? Will she hurt Regan? Jesus, Jonathan..."

"I know! I was assuming that Veronica would still regard Regan as her best friend—that she'd automatically turn to her for help, since that seems to be the pattern of their entire relationship. But Veronica did not die with good feelings toward anyone, it seems—and especially not me and Regan."

"You mean, maybe Veronica was a little pissed off that Regan was boffing you? Wow, I guess your genius grant's in the mail."

"I didn't think she would even know about it. She'd been in a hospital for two weeks."

"Yeah, well, she's female, right? So what's the first thing she's going to do when she gets sprung? Pick up the phone and find out what she's missed. And even my mom knows that you and Regan are an item. You think all Regan's friends don't know?"

"All right! So I'm a dolt. I didn't think it was anyone else's business. Regan was right, we should have been more careful."

"What did the cops want to talk to you about, anyway? I guess you didn't get arrested."

"Not yet, at least." Jonathan turned the car onto River Road. "Let's focus on one crisis at a time."

They turned into the drive of the house, and Jonathan pulled up behind the Civic and stopped as Sean tumbled out of the passenger's door. "Well, they made it here, anyway," Sean said.

"But why are there no lights on in the house?" Jonathan said uncertainly. He walked over to the Civic and peered through the window.

"Looks normal to me," Sean said, looking in from the other side. "She took the keys."

Jonathan straightened up and stood listening for a moment. There was a breeze hissing through the trees, blowing from the east. After a moment, he shook his head uncomfortably. He went to the front door and unlocked it. He and Sean went inside. The house was completely dark, silent and still. "Regan...?" Jonathan called out. Sean followed him into the great room, which was dimly illuminated by the ghostly light of the screensaver on Jonathan's computer. Jonathan turned on the two floor lamps, as Sean flinched in the sudden brightness. They looked around bleakly.

"God, this is awful," Sean said. "We're going to find a body or something, I know it."

"Be quiet."

They searched the house, room by empty, echoing room, calling Regan's name every few minutes. No sound came to their ears except their own voices and footsteps. The last place they looked was the basement, but it was as empty and undisturbed as the rest.

"Where could they have gone?" Sean said when they came back up into the kitchen.

"I don't think they came into the house at all. I'd smell them, even if they came in and left immediately."

"But why not? Why wouldn't they come in?"

"I suspect that Veronica bolted, and Regan went after her."

"So...maybe Regan's out there, trying to find her, or get her to come back," Sean said hopefully.

"I had a feeling that Veronica might not be cooperative. It wasn't a prominent trait of hers when she was alive."

"If she was mad at Regan, maybe she just said, fuck off, and walked. But we've still got to find her, right?" Jonathan was silent. "Which way do you think she'd go?"

"I don't know. She might try to avoid the town, or she might be attracted to it, because of..." he trailed off.

"Because she'll be hungry."

"Yes."

"But you said—she wouldn't know she's a vampire."

"But she will find out eventually. It's a state that tends to impress itself upon one rather forcefully. She won't need to be taught. Her instincts will kick in on their own."

Sean swallowed uncomfortably. "I guess we better...we better start looking outside, right?" Jonathan didn't answer, but he went through the house and out the back door, as Sean trailed him closely. "Wish you had some flashlights," Sean said uneasily as he stumbled over the rough ground of the neglected back yard. "I know you don't need them, but—"

"Flashlights would only help her, by making our presence obvious. She could avoid the light easily enough."

They reached the side of the yard. The night air smelled sweet with opening leaves and distant flowers, and there was a trilling sound all around them from the night singers of the woods and ponds. Jonathan stood still at the edge of the trees, his face raised to the sky as though he was sniffing the air, as well as listening. Then he sighed unhappily. "I wish there wasn't such a stiff breeze."

They hiked up the wooded slope, following the path that joined the network of trails that Sean had used himself when he was watching the house. Sean knew the trails well and had followed them in the dark, but he still stumbled a few times over roots or stones. As they paused at the top of the rise near the house, looking down the slope in the direction of town, Sean looked behind them and suddenly stiffened. "Jonathan," he said, almost not daring to whisper out loud, "Jonathan, look. What's that?"

They both turned to look, and saw a light-clad figure walking slowly along the trail below them. Jonathan immediately stepped back into the shadows of the trees. "Sean," he said, very quietly, "don't move. Don't move at all."

Sean, his eyes locked on the approaching figure, whispered, "if I don't move, she won't see me?"

"She's already seen you. She can smell you, too. Be quiet." He withdrew even further off the trail, without making a sound.

Sean waited, almost not breathing, as the figure walked—walked, effortlessly, not climbed, despite the steepness of the slope—toward him. In the darkness, he could just see the blur of Veronica's pale hair floating behind her in the breeze, her white face and legs, the pale blue dress. She was wearing something dark over the dress—some kind of scarf or sweater. A mosquito whined in Sean's ear, but he didn't move. The figure paused, swaying, about ten feet away.

"I know you..." It was Veronica's voice, but unlike her usual tone—it was low, seductive, almost sleepy. "You're that cute little thing that Regan hired. She was starting quite a collection of men, wasn't she?" Veronica walked several steps closer. She leaned forward and sniffed into the breeze that blew past Sean. "Umm. Are you up here all by yourself? You smell..." she paused, sniffing again. "Afraid. You smell scared to death. Well, you should be."

She took one more step and then something went by Sean so fast that he only caught a blur of it, like an owl crossing through a car's headlights late at night. Sean saw Veronica suddenly knocked off her feet, and then Jonathan was holding her, in a solid bear hug from behind, pinning her arms to her sides and lifting her feet off the ground. She kicked wildly, arching her back and twisting, but she couldn't break his grip, and after a few minutes she threw her head back and let out a scream of such inhuman rage and such volume that Sean put his hands over his ears and cringed at the sound of it. The struggle went on for at least another minute, until Jonathan finally relaxed his grip enough to allow Veronica to bend forward at the waist, trying to pull forward and away from him. Then he pivoted to the side, and cracked Veronica's outstretched head against the trunk of a pine tree. Veronica went limp, although her hands still clenched and unclenched spasmodically.

"Oh my god, you killed her!"

"Not even close." Jonathan hoisted Veronica over his shoulder like a sack of fertilizer and strode down the hill toward the house. "Come on. We only have a few minutes." He was walking so fast that Sean had to run to keep up.

"What are we going to do with her?"

"First we'll have to restrain her, obviously."

"But how? You guys can open locks by thinking about it."

"We're taking her down to the basement—you remember that coil of chain that's down there? You saw it, didn't you?"

"Yeah, I saw it—with the hooks on the end?"

"We're going to need that." They were already at the back door of the house. Sean opened the door, and pulled it shut after Jonathan maneuvered Veronica's body inside. "Lock it. And go ahead and open the basement door. Quick." Veronica made a lurching movement, like a fish flopping, and Jonathan had to clutch at her. Sean ran through the back hall and great room, and into the kitchen to unbolt and open the basement door.

By the time they reached the basement, Veronica was pushing with her hands against Jonathan's back and moaning. "Pull that chest up against the support beam there, and get the chain," Jonathan said. Sean moved with the stumbling haste of panic. When the old wooden chest was in place, Jonathan dumped Veronica down onto it, propped up against the beam, as Sean, panting, half dragged the heavy chain in from the adjoining room. Taking the chain as though it were light clothesline, Jonathan bound Veronica to the beam, so tightly that the links dug into her flesh, and finally fastened it by hitching the hook at the end into one of the links. There was no lock or latch that Veronica could undo with her preternatural talent for escape. As both Sean and Jonathan drew back a little and regarded their prisoner, Sean for the first time got a good look at Veronica in the dim light of the basement overhead fixture. Even with the chains wrapped around her, it was obvious that she was almost entirely covered, from neck to knees, with blood, soaking the light blue dress. The lower part of her face and her throat were bloody as well, although the blood was drying and rubbed off in patches.

"Jonathan," Sean said in a shaking whisper, "whose blood is that? She's got blood all over her. Whose blood is that?" Jonathan didn't answer, just stood, watching Veronica slowly return to consciousness. "Where's Regan?" Sean's voice was quavering. There was a long silence. "Oh, my god..."

"Sean. I think you should go upstairs." Jonathan's voice was very quiet.

"Fuck that! I want to know what's happened to Regan."

"We already know what's happened to Regan."

"But...but...no..."

"Either go upstairs or sit down."

Veronica raised her head and gave it a shake, grimacing as though in residual pain from the blow. She realized that she was bound then, and began twisting against the chains, emitting incoherent grunts and sounds. Her struggles escalated to something like convulsions as she screamed in helpless rage, her bare heels kicking sprays of dirt from the hard-packed earth floor. The chains withstood her without so much as clinking, and her seated position prevented her from exerting all her possible strength. She subsided slowly, as though exhausted, and then began all over again. Three times she fought, never looking at or acknowledging the presence of her captors only a few feet away. It was almost half an hour before she finally relaxed for a longer space of time, and glared balefully at Jonathan.

"You can't keep me here forever, you fuck."

"Yes, I can."

"Let me go!"

"Where's Regan? What did you do with her?"

Veronica stared at him, and quite unexpectedly, spat at him. "Are you missing your girlfriend? You cocksucking piece of shit! Are you missing that skanky little slut?"

"What have you done with Regan?"

"You'll never find her! Never! They'll dig up her bones some day, when you're nothing but dust! You'll never have her, Jonathan—you were mine!" She started twisting against the chains again. "Let me go! Let me go!"

"Never."

Veronica became quiet for a moment. "I'll get loose. I'll get loose and you know what the first thing is I'll do? I'll come after this little one here, Regan's little toy—what's the matter, little boy, are you scared of me? Don't even try to hide, I'll find you. Oh, he's so cute, Jonathan. Are you fucking his cute little ass? Better kiss it goodbye while you've got the chance. You can't keep me prisoner forever."

Jonathan stepped forward, deliberately propped one foot on the edge of the chest, next to Veronica's legs, and leaned forward until his face was inches from hers. "Maybe I won't even try," he said, very softly. "Maybe I'll just walk upstairs, set fire to the house, walk out and never come back. This house would make quite an impressive inferno, don't you think? A few gallons of gasoline and I don't imagine it would take twenty minutes for the whole building to be fully involved. And every flaming beam of it would end up right on top of you."

Veronica stared back at him, and now there was real fear in her eyes. "They'll catch you. You wouldn't get away with arson."

He straightened up, unhurriedly. "I have done, several times. Come on, Sean. We don't have anything more to talk to her about." He started for the stairs, but then saw that Sean had half stood and sat back down because his knees were shaking so hard. He reached over and hauled Sean to his feet. "Go upstairs."

As the two of them went up the stairs, Veronica howled, "Go ahead! Go ahead and do it, you rotten fuck! Go ahead and burn me! It won't bring Regan back! She'll never come back! I fixed that! You'll never have Regan back, never!" Her feet drummed impotently on the floor. Jonathan closed the basement door and bolted it, shutting off the sound of Veronica's struggles, although her keening voice could be heard dimly through the heavy floors.

Jonathan walked into the great room and sat down at the long table, staring unseeing at the computer screen. Sean crossed the room unsteadily and sat down on the edge of one of the other chairs. After a long silence, he said, "You wouldn't really do it, would you? Burn down the whole house?"

"Not tonight," Jonathan said finally.

Some minutes later, Sean said hesitantly, "maybe...maybe she was lying, you know? I mean, maybe she just wanted to hurt you...how do we know that was Regan's...you know..."

Jonathan kept on staring blankly through the computer. "No. As soon as I got my arms around Veronica, I knew what she'd done. I knew by the smell."

Sean sat with trembling lip for a moment, and suddenly he took in several heavy breaths. "I'm...I'm gonna be sick," he said, and ran to the kitchen to vomit into the sink.

Listening to the racking sounds from the kitchen, Jonathan looked at the chair Sean had left empty. Almost in a whisper, he said, "I envy you."

Chapter 17

At around 2:00 a.m., Jonathan finally stirred in his chair, and looked at Sean with an almost apologetic expression. "You've been very patient." Sean had returned to his seat, with white face and empty stomach, and had not moved since then.

"I guess I'm kind of in shock."

"I should take you home."

Sean shook his head. "Nah...whatever needs to be done, I want to help. If I went home, I'd just go crazy." Abruptly he yawned, but his yawn was choked off as the dim sound of Veronica's voice started again from beneath them, as it had been doing at intervals all night. Sean couldn't make out her words through the floor, for which he was grateful, but Jonathan could, and his lips tightened. Seeing this, Sean said, "Don't listen to her. She's lying, I know she is."

"How are you so sure?"

"Because she doesn't know shit, that's why. And what she thinks she knows, is probably all wrong, just like I was wrong about a lot of what I thought. How could she keep Regan from coming back?"

"I told you how, remember?"

"But Veronica wasn't there when you did. And can you see her doing that?"

"There was," Jonathan said grimly, "a hell of a lot of blood on her, Sean."

"So what did she use? She wasn't carrying a chain saw or anything. It's not that easy to...to..." he swallowed hard. "...to do what you said."

"With her strength, she could have—" Jonathan broke off. "She wouldn't have needed any tools. And she came from the direction of the farm. There are probably tools available there."

"But she still wouldn't have known to do it. I think we should try and find Regan. At least then we'll know. Besides, we don't want anyone else to find her first, do we?"

"No, that's true." Jonathan rubbed his hands over his face tiredly. "We won't get any useful information out of Veronica. And we can't leave her down there in the basement. I'm still not prepared to destroy her permanently."

"Why the fuck *not?* Jonathan, not only did she kill Regan, she's after *my* ass! She's officially dead, I say we waste her."

"You might think twice about that if you'd ever seen it done, Sean."

"And I might not! The way I feel right now, the more she suffers, the better."

"Well...you may be able to revel in it yet. But not right away." He stood up. "Right now, we have to move her. There's a strong likelihood that this house may be searched—if not, the police will probably be out here asking questions at the very least."

"Looking for Regan?"

"Possibly, but initially they'll be looking for Veronica. The funeral home will discover that she's missing eventually." He started toward the doorway into the hall. "You'd better come along, Sean—I'd rather not leave you in here alone."

They went out the back door of the house and into the barn via its side entrance. Sean watched uneasily as Jonathan rummaged around at a long dusty workbench along the back wall. He found an ash wood handle that might have fitted an axe or mattock and sawed a piece about six inches long from it. Then he wrapped one end of the short piece of wood with duct tape, and around the taped end he tightly wrapped and knotted a length of nylon rope, leaving two yard-long trailing strands. He picked up the longer piece of the handle and the roll of tape, then handed Sean a hammer and a grimy plastic container filled with heavy framing nails. "Come on, Sean—you should enjoy this."

Jonathan walked back to the house, through the great room and down to the cellar as Sean trotted behind him. They went down the stairs and Jonathan flicked on the light. Veronica was just as they'd left her, but there were rents and tears in the blood-soaked dress now from her struggles against the chains, and in places the rough iron links had rubbed her skin away, leaving raw bleeding flesh behind. She blinked in the sudden light.

"Jonathan." Her voice was hoarse. "Have you gotten tired of listening to me? Are you going to set me loose?"

Jonathan silently set down the duct tape and the short cord-wrapped piece of wood. Veronica's eyes followed those items uneasily. As Jonathan grasped the longer piece of wood two handedly and stepped forward, she shrieked, "It's over, Jonathan! You'll be destroyed for this! My father will—" Her voice cut off as Jonathan swung the handle like a baseball bat and cracked the side of her head so that her face snapped sideways. She went limp. Jonathan dropped the handle and picked up the short piece of wood. He pulled Veronica's head upright by her hair, forced the wood into her mouth and almost all the way down her throat, and then tied it around her head with the ends of the nylon rope. He then duct taped the rope to her face, sealing her nose and mouth tightly.

Sean, who had been watching this, flinching, blurted out, "but she won't be able to breathe, will she?"

"She doesn't need to breathe. If she can't get any air into her lungs, she'll be able to make much less noise. You'd be amazed how much noise it's possible to make even with a gag, if the person can still draw in air." He continued working rapidly as he spoke, unhooking and unwinding the chain and pulling Veronica off the chest onto the floor. He folded her body into a tight fetal position, hands behind her back, and wound the chain around her, binding her ankles and legs, then her wrists, chaining her wrists and ankles together behind her, and then wrapping the chain around her body, so tightly that Sean could hear little popping sounds that might be a joint dislocating or a small bone breaking. He had to stop watching. When the chain was all used up, Jonathan hooked the end of it into a link, as before. Then he opened the wooden trunk that Veronica had been sitting on, stuffed her body into it, and slammed it shut. "Give me the hammer and nails."

Despite how tightly Veronica had been bound, by the time Jonathan finished nailing the lid of the chest shut, there were small thumps coming from inside. Sean wondered what Veronica could still move in order to strike the inside of the chest. "So, now what?" He was inwardly thanking whatever powers may be that his lurching stomach was completely empty.

"We've got to get this chest a good distance from the house. Anyone looking for a missing cadaver would be extremely interested in a box like this one."

"Are we going to bury it?"

"No. Digging a hole large enough to accommodate this trunk would displace too much dirt. Searchers would find it easily. We've got to hide it in some way that won't leave obvious traces."

"How can we do that?"

"I know a spot back in the woods where it won't be seen unless someone gets very close—and we can move the chest, too, if necessary. I'm hoping—" he broke off as he took hold of one handle of the chest, and then, with a guttural grunt, heaved it onto his shoulder. His voice a bit strained, he went on, "that we can avert suspicion before a thorough search of the house and grounds takes place. Open the bulkhead doors, Sean."

Jonathan put the chest into a tiny natural cave in a granite outcropping in the woods, about a quarter mile behind the house. There were no paths leading to the outcropping and the underbrush was so heavy, Sean couldn't follow Jonathan all the way. Jonathan pushed a heavy boulder so that it almost concealed the cave mouth, and then carefully covered the marks he'd made and arranged dead leaves and debris to disguise the fact that anything had been altered. "Let's hope for a hard rain," he said as they headed back toward the house.

They looked for Regan until full daylight. There was no way to be certain where Veronica had been coming from when they first saw her. But it seemed reasonable to assume that she had headed west from Regan's car, and most likely had been walking along the road. The wind had died down, and Jonathan was using his sense of smell, as much as anything else, pausing and testing the air as they walked slowly down the road toward the farm.

"You know, I don't think they could have gone that far," Sean said. "Regan didn't leave the funeral home until almost eight-thirty. We got to the house before it was even nine-thirty. And it wasn't even an hour after that when we saw Veronica."

"Yes, but she could move fast if she wanted to. Two hours, from our perspective, is a very long time."

"I don't think she'd go that close to the farm, though. They've got dogs and stuff up there."

"You're probably right about that."

The woods to the south of the road, like those east of Rainbow Stone house, were criss-crossed by a network of trails dating back to the days of the commune. Some two hundred yards west of the house a narrow dirt road cut off into the trees on that side. Jonathan paused there, examining the ground and sniffing the air, but he shook his head. The entrance to the cut-in was thick with new grass, undisturbed and covered with cobwebs on which dew glittered. No one had walked that way tonight.

About a half mile down the road, close enough to the dairy farm for even Sean to catch an occasional whiff of manure on the breeze, Jonathan stopped in the road. He was looking at another narrow cut-in from the main road into the woods on the north. This one appeared to be used from time to time—there was less grass growing in it, and there were heavy tire tracks that appeared to have been made not long ago. By now the sky was light and Sean could see quite a bit in the pre-dawn twilight. He followed Jonathan's gaze and saw the small outbuilding, set among the trees. Despite the cheerful bird song all around them, Sean felt his knees go weak. "Do you think...?" he said, his voice shaking. Jonathan abruptly started toward the outbuilding, walking fast, not bothering to examine the ground at the mouth of the drive. The door to the building was tightly closed and hooked with a rusted iron staple dropped into the loop of a hasp. As Sean caught up with him, Jonathan removed the staple and tossed it away, pulling the door open wide. The musty cool air inside gusted out over them, and Sean fell back, gagging. Even he could smell the stench of wet dirt and blood.

Jonathan peered around inside the room and then stepped inside. Sean could not see anything in the dark interior, but he saw Jonathan, in the light from the door, looking around the small building carefully, scanning the walls, the rafters and the floor. Then he moved to one side and knelt down. Sean stepped just inside the door and looked around himself—the room appeared to be completely empty, except for a few small open crates. On one of these, by the door, was a yellow hazard flashlight. "Hey, this is Regan's. I've seen it in her car, I'm sure of it." He picked it up and flicked the button. "Battery's dead." He looked down at Jonathan, who was sitting with his hand resting on his knee, frowning at the floor. "What is it?"

"It's blood, but..." he was silent for a minute, evidently studying the damp patch on the floor which Sean could barely even see. "You might be right, Sean. Maybe Veronica was just taunting me about fixing it so Regan couldn't come back." He stood up.

"But there's so much blood."

"She *opened* an artery. That's why."

"On purpose?"

"Possibly not. We may never know." He looked around the room again, helplessly.

"Did she bury Regan in here?"

"The floor's too hard. We'd be able to tell. But Veronica didn't have any dirt on her. I don't think she buried Regan anywhere. It would have been obvious if she'd been digging, even with some kind of tool." He left the outbuilding, re-latching the door after Sean followed him.

"Shouldn't we do something about the floor in there, dig it out or cover it up?"

"I might come back tomorrow night. We're out of time, Sean. They're already well into milking over at the farm. No amount of blood could be as suspicious as our being seen here. We'd better get back before the sun comes up, and hope no cars go by on the road."

When they got back to the house, Jonathan decided to take the risk of their being seen and roll Regan's car into the barn where it would be out of view. Should there be a search and it was discovered, they would have to deal with the repercussions then, but for the time being, no better solution suggested itself.

Later in the morning, Jonathan convinced Sean that it would not help matters if his mother reported him missing to the police or DSS. He drove Sean to the store, where Sean had left his mountain bike locked up in back. Sean stared at the CLOSED sign on the front door with regret. "God, I wish she'd given me a set of keys. I know she wouldn't want this place to stay closed, with no one knowing where she is."

"How would you explain where Regan was and why you were there alone? And what would you do about school? It would just draw more suspicion."

"I know."

Late that afternoon, Jonathan was working at his computer, and not liking what he was learning. He had cleaned up as much as possible and burned the clothes he'd worn the night before, which had gotten a lot of blood on them from Veronica. He had been expecting the knock on the front door for some time when it finally came. He waited five seconds, got up and went to the door and opened it.

"Detective Fellman. What can I do for you today?"

"I'm sorry to bother you again so soon, Mr. Vaughn. I wonder if you had a moment? This isn't related to the discussion we had last night."

Jonathan, with a show of irritation, ushered Detective Fellman into the great room and offered him a seat. "I'm in the middle of a chapter, so I hope this won't take long."

"I hope so, too. Mr. Vaughn, do you have any knowledge of the present whereabouts of Regan Calloway?"

"Not at this moment, no. What's the problem? Has something happened to her?"

"That's what we're trying to determine. She didn't open the store today, and she's not at home. We can't locate her vehicle, and she didn't mention to anyone that she was going away. Mrs. Wharton, her employer, is quite upset that the store is closed without any explanation."

"I haven't seen Ms. Calloway since I left the store with you last night. She didn't mention anything about going away to me."

"Did she mention what her plans were for the rest of the evening?"

"She was going to stop by a wake for one of her long-time customers. I was planning to go with her until you intervened. I believe the wake was at Burgos and Sons."

"Apparently she did go to the wake, because she signed the guest book. But no one has seen her since."

Jonathan shrugged as nonchalantly as he could. "It isn't unusual for her to take a day off and go to an estate sale or auction. Why are the police so concerned? She's not even considered missing until she's been gone for seventy-two hours, isn't that the rule?"

Detective Fellman hesitated. "This information hasn't been made public yet, but the reason for the concern is that there's been a problem at the funeral home since last night."

"Oh?"

"Yes. Unfortunately, one of the deceased that was in the custody of the funeral home...is missing."

Jonathan affected a blank stare. "Are you serious? The funeral home has lost one of its clients? How is that possible?"

"We're still investigating that, Mr. Vaughn."

"Did this deceased disappear during the wake last night?"

"There's quite a large window of time during which the loss could have taken place. But last night's wake was the only period of that time when the funeral home was open to the public."

"And you're questioning everyone who attended, I presume."

"Eventually we will. But Ms. Calloway is of particular interest."

"Why?"

"I'm afraid I can't answer that, Mr. Vaughn. But if you should happen to hear from her, please have her give me a call right away." Detective Fellman extracted a business card from a plastic folder in his pocket and handed it to Jonathan.

"I'll do that, Detective."

On Monday morning, Jonathan called the main office of the Standish Mills and asked to speak to Jerry Standish. He was transferred to the mill owner's secretary, to whom he repeated his request.

"Who shall I say is calling?"

"My name is Jonathan Vaughn."

After a pause of some thirty seconds, the secretary came back on the line. "Mr. Standish asks that you direct all inquiries to his attorney."

"Fine. May I have his attorney's name and phone number? I'll call him immediately."

"That would be Theodore Green." She gave him the number. Mr. Green had an office right in the center of downtown Sheridan, not far from the main entrance to the mill complex.

Jonathan called Theodore Green's office. His secretary answered the phone.

"I'm sorry, Mr. Green is on another call right now. Can I have him get back to you?"

"Certainly," Jonathan said, and gave his number.

"Can I tell Mr. Green what you're calling about?"

"When he hears my name, I'm sure he'll know. I'm calling about Mr. Jerry Standish."

Within two minutes, Jonathan's phone rang, and he answered it without a sense of surprise.

"Mr. Vaughn? Ted Green. What can I do for you?"

Jonathan smiled grimly. He had little doubt that it had been Jerry Standish on the other line with Mr. Green. He'd probably called as soon as his secretary reported that Jonathan would be contacting the attorney's office immediately. "Mr. Standish's office asked me to go through you, Mr. Green. I've been speaking with Detective Fellman of the Sheridan police department, and I was hoping to arrange a meeting with Mr. Standish—man to man, as it were. I'd very much like to speak with him, and it sounds like he may have some questions for me."

There was a silence on the line. "I'll have to see if I can arrange that, Mr. Vaughn. You understand this is a very difficult time for Mr. Standish."

"I understand that completely."

"Will you be bringing your own counsel?"

"I wasn't planning to. Do I need to?"

"That's entirely up to you. Hold on just a moment." Jonathan waited patiently, as the automated phone system hummed light classical music into his ear. "Mr. Vaughn? Would you be free this afternoon?"

"I'll make myself free, at Mr. Standish's convenience."

"We'll call you back if I can arrange a time."

At 3:00, Jonathan was ushered into a conference room in Ted Green's small but well-appointed office suite. Already seated at the glistening mahogany table was Jerry Standish, wearing a black suit over a dark gray shirt and tie. A tall beefy man with a salt and pepper crew cut, ruddy skin and a rather large nose, Jerry Standish looked like a college football star who'd kept himself in fairly good shape. Although there was nothing even remotely feminine about him, Jonathan could see a family resemblance to his daughter—mostly in his chin, and the shape of his mouth. Ted Green, wearing a hand-tailored suit that might have been air-brushed onto his body, shook Jonathan's hand at the door. "Hello, Mr. Vaughn. I'm Ted Green, Mr. Standish's counsel."

"Pleased to meet you, counselor."

"Have you met Jerry Standish?" The mill owner returned Jonathan's polite greeting with a tight-lipped nod. When all three were seated, Ted Green said, "Mr. Standish has agreed to this meeting reluctantly. You are of course aware that he recently suffered a family tragedy."

"Yes, I am. And I'm very sorry for your loss, Mr. Standish."

"Thank you." Jerry Standish's tone of voice was more appropriate to a sharp retort than an expression of gratitude.

"This discussion is all off the record. Mr. Vaughn, you said on the phone that you hoped to clear some things up."

"Yes, thank you. Mr. Standish, I've been informed by the police that you swore out a complaint against me. I admit to being somewhat confused. What do you think I did to Ve—to your daughter?"

Jerry Standish fixed Jonathan with a hard stare. "Didn't the police tell you about the letter?"

"They told me *about* the letter, and that's all. Apparently you wouldn't let them see it."

"I told them what they needed to know about it."

"You didn't tell them enough to have me charged with anything." He paused, meeting Jerry Standish's unfriendly gaze. "May I see this letter?"

"No, you may not."

"In that case, it's going to be very difficult for me to respond to any of these so-called allegations. I hardly knew your daughter. I never even went out with her."

Jerry Standish's face reddened. "Are you calling my daughter a liar, Vaughn?"

"I'm not accusing anyone of lying outright—but there may be a question of exaggeration, or misinterpretation. Forgive me, but I learned very quickly, Mr. Standish, that Veronica was..." he paused significantly, "melodramatic and histrionic, to use another's words." He saw that Regan's report of her conversation with Jerry Standish had been accurate—the mill owner's face flushed even darker, although with anger, not chagrin.

"Don't you throw around a lot of psychobabble bullshit about Veronica, you son of a bitch," he said, raising his voice, as Ted Green motioned to him to calm down.

"I'd like to know just what allegations have been made against me. Are there any criminal charges, or are you simply accusing me of being a scoundrel? I'm sure that I haven't stolen large amounts of money from her, and that I never beat her, like two of her former boyfriends allegedly did."

"How do you know that?" Ted Green said.

"I don't. Veronica told me those things. Perhaps her accounts were not accurate." Jonathan leaned back and looked directly at Jerry Standish. "Mr. Standish, I'm not stupid. Let's speak directly. Are you suggesting that you think I'm to blame for Veronica killing herself? Are you hoping to find some way to have me charged with negligent homicide? Or are you simply hoping to trick me into saying something that you can use as grounds for a wrongful death lawsuit?"

"Now, let's not jump ahead of ourselves—" Ted Green began, but Jonathan cut him off.

"On the contrary, let's jump. I have no intention of walking into a legal booby-trap. Do you have actual evidence that I did anything to hurt Veronica, Mr. Standish? Or are you just trying to sooth your own guilty conscience by attacking me?"

Jerry Standish stood up, and so did Ted Green, hastily. "Mr. Standish, Mr. Vaughn," Ted Green said.

"You're going to make me spell it out, you bastard? Fine. You were screwing my daughter. You promised her a pack of flowery lies and then you ditched her for her best friend, and let the whole town know about it. That's the humiliation that drove her over the edge. If I'd known that was going on, I'd never have—" he stopped abruptly, and sat down.

"Is that what she wrote to you?" Jonathan said. He leaned across the table toward Jerry Standish. "Well, Mr. Standish—it's just not true. Veronica may have wished that. She may have felt rejected and concocted a fantasy about that. But I would never have initiated a sexual relationship with a woman as unstable as Veronica. I'm not that reckless."

Ted Green said, "Veronica not only stated that you and she had an intimate relationship, Mr. Vaughn, she went into considerable detail about the particulars, including dates and times. Among other things, she said that you liked it pretty rough. And to back that up, she did have some kind of injuries, according to the nurses who treated her at the emergency room on April twenty-third."

Jonathan hesitated a moment, then caught himself. "I wouldn't have the slightest idea what you're talking about. But you're forcing me to remind you that Veronica admitted herself to a psychiatric facility that same day. She may have harmed herself. Surely you're aware of that."

"How do you happen to know about Veronica's admission to a psychiatric hospital?"

"I was told about it by the person who assisted Veronica that night. She thought Veronica would want me to know."

"You mean, a medical professional at the hospital?"

"Of course not. Veronica's oldest friend."

"And who would that be, Mr. Vaughn?"

Jonathan straightened up and folded his arms. "I'm under no obligation to give you her name. Surely Mr. Standish knows who his daughter's friends are."

"It's no secret who you've been spending your time with, Vaughn," Jerry Standish said.

"Then why ask?"

"Veronica made it damned obvious that the two of you couldn't give a shit about how badly you both hurt her. What girl wouldn't fall apart when her fiancé runs off with her best friend?"

"Fiancé...oh, for god's sake. Mr. Standish, if you had paid attention to the phone call this friend of Veronica's made to you on Monday, Veronica might still be alive."

Jerry Standish burst out, "Who do you think you are, to tell me—" but Ted Green cut him off.

"Wait a minute. What phone call are you talking about?" Jerry Standish glowered down at the table. "What phone call?" Ted Green repeated.

"Veronica's friend called Mr. Standish last Monday afternoon to report her very serious concerns about Veronica's state of mind."

"But you just have her word for this."

"Her assistant was present for the phone call. And I'm sure that if litigation were to become an issue, we could arrange to obtain her phone records. She used her business phone."

Ted Green motioned to Jerry Standish and they put their heads together. They spoke in sub-whispers, although Jonathan was able to hear every word they said. He sat back in the leather executive chair, waiting for them to finish their discussion.

"Jerry...if they can prove that they attempted to inform you in advance of Veronica's state of mind, then legally, they're covered. In fact, they could counter-sue you on grounds of mental distress for disregarding that warning."

"That's ridiculous."

"It probably wouldn't hold up, but it could get ugly. I don't think you really want to expose your family to that kind of publicity."

"But they're responsible for Veronica's suicide. They—"

"It's hearsay, Jerry, and Veronica's medical records will work against us. I said that from the beginning." They straightened up, Jerry Standish still scowling. "Just what is it that you're after, Mr. Vaughn?"

"I'd like to see that letter."

"No," Jerry Standish said.

"Then I'd like Mr. Standish to withdraw his complaint. As it is, it only makes him look foolish. I fail to see what you gain from it, Mr. Standish, unless you're prepared to give the police a lot more information."

"Meaning that you'd also have that information," Ted Green said.

"I have a legal right to see any complaints filed against me, as you know."

Ted Green glanced at his client, who was glaring at the tabletop with folded arms. "We'll discuss it."

Jonathan looked at Jerry Standish for a few moments and then sighed. "I guess we've accomplished all that we can, in that case." He rose to his feet, and so did Ted Green. Jerry Standish remained exactly as he was. "Thank you for your time, Mr. Standish. I'm sorry you don't believe me."

Before he got into his car in the tiny parking area by the trim red brick office building, Jonathan glanced up at the narrow window of the conference room. Jerry Standish was standing there watching him. When he saw Jonathan looking up, he stepped back out of sight.

By the time Jonathan got back to Rainbow Stone house, Sean was waiting there, having ridden his bike straight from school. He was sitting on the front stoop reading a paperback book with such intense concentration that he started when Jonathan's car pulled into the drive. "Has anything happened?" he asked as they went inside the house. "Where have you been?"

"I had a visit from Detective Fellman on Saturday afternoon asking about Regan. Mostly, I've been staying right here at the house. There's been plenty to do here, cleaning up."

"Did you try looking more for Regan?"

"I have, but I haven't found anything. It's..." he paused, troubled. "It's rather mystifying. I did clean up in the outbuilding, as much as possible. No one seemed to have been there, but the dairy farm does appear to use that building, from time to time. I don't want to risk being seen around it." They went into the great room, where Sean dumped his school knapsack on the floor and collapsed onto a chair. "Has anyone talked to you about last Friday? You worked for Regan, and you probably were seen at the funeral home."

"I haven't heard a thing. I don't know if anyone knew my name, though. Wouldn't the cops have to have my mom's permission to talk to me?"

"I don't know if they would, just to ask a few questions. How did things go with your mother when you got home Saturday? Wasn't she concerned that you were out all night?"

"She didn't have a clue. She'd been out all night, too. She didn't get home until Saturday afternoon." Sean pulled a can of Mountain Dew out of his knapsack, popped the top, and drank about half of it without stopping. "Word's getting around about Veronica's body disappearing from the funeral home," he said, and then belched. "Even the kids in school were talking about it today."

"Detective Fellman admitted that the funeral home had lost a client. But he wouldn't tell me who. I think they suspect Regan of having something to do with it."

"Because she's disappeared, too? You got to admit, it looks kind of fishy. I knew she shouldn't have signed that stupid book at the wake."

"It would look suspicious anyway. You asked where I'd been—I just got back from a meeting with Jerry Standish and his attorney." Sean choked on a swallow of Mountain Dew.

"What? Old man Standish and a lawyer? What happened?"

"Oh, I was the one who requested the meeting." He told Sean about the complaint and his unsatisfactory meeting at Ted Green's office. "So, you see—now they've got this letter saying that I betrayed Veronica with her best friend, and they know who that is. And now Veronica's body and the best friend are both missing."

"Jesus. Jonathan, if they find Regan's car in your garage, you're fucked. They'll think you killed her."

"I'm open to suggestions, Sean. We can't do anything with the car unless we hot-wire the ignition, and then we could be seen trying to move it. I'm sure there's an alert out for the license plate." Sean shrugged helplessly. "Anyway, there's more."

"More?"

"Come over here and look at my computer." Sean came around and hunched down next to Jonathan's chair, so he could read the laptop's screen. "This is a piece of software that allows you to do records searches and background checks on almost anyone."

"Oh, yeah, I've seen those CD's—"

"I had this one customized, it's almost as good as the ones professional detectives use. It's got a function that alerts you if someone else is trying to access your records." He clicked on a screen.

"Whoa. Look at that. Who's checking you out, the cops?"

"That is. But not these. These are all someone else."

"But who? Old man Standish?"

"I ran a lookup on the IP number for the user who was doing these searches." Jonathan clicked up another screen. Sean gaped.

"Who would be checking you out at Bridgewater State College?"

Jonathan leaned back, folding his arms. "Someone...I obviously have not been taking seriously enough."

"That Dr. Clauson, the one Regan was working with when she was investigating all those people? What can they find out about you on the Internet?"

"Not much. They'll eventually suspect that some of my background is fabricated—but some of it will check out. I put a bit more effort into my identity changes than hacking data bases."

"Yeah, but this is post-nine-eleven. They're going to think you're a terrorist."

"Or in the Witness Protection Program. It doesn't matter. My financial assets are untraceable. If I'm arrested, I'll just disappear. I've done it six times so far. I can't be kept in custody for very long."

"Oh, right, the lock thing. Then what does matter?"

"What does matter is...I can't allow my real nature to be discovered. And that's a serious danger if they find Veronica."

Sean straightened up, frowning. "So...is it time to find a nice hot incinerator and throw her in it, yet? We can't just leave her nailed into that box, Jonathan. Remember what you said back at the store, about not destroying another vampire unless they were vicious and irrational? I think vicious and irrational is what we've got here."

Jonathan was silent for a moment. "I don't want to just give up on her like that."

"She's crazy, Jonathan. She's not going to change. She shouldn't be here, she didn't want to be here, she committed suicide! Maybe that's why everything is so screwed up, because she's meant to be dead."

"Her being here violates the right order of things, you mean?"

"Well...yeah. Doesn't it?"

Jonathan shook his head slowly. "But it's my fault. None of this would have happened if I hadn't...I lost control, and I should have known better. If I hadn't touched her, she'd probably be alive now."

"Jonathan, I met the lady. She was out there. From what Regan told me, she killed herself because her dad was putting the screws on her to get a job, and maybe because she was jealous about you and Regan. She didn't even remember what you did that time, so how could this be your fault? None of the other people committed suicide, did they?"

"I haven't heard that they did. But I knew how fragile she was. I knew that."

Sean stared at Jonathan. "You feel guilty! After everything she's done, after what she did to Regan—"

"And I'm responsible for that, too! And destroying Veronica to clean up my mess just seems like...we're not very numerous, Sean. She's one of my kind now, and that's not something I can completely control. I owe her something, just for that."

"Oh, yeah, and putting her in that box is your way of showing loyalty to vampire kind? She's really going to be understanding of that, I'm telling you. I've had nightmares every night since—"

"It's the only way to protect her from herself."

"What about your loyalty to Regan?" Sean said hotly. "If you gave a shit about her, you'd make sure the bitch who killed her was—"

Jonathan stood up, slamming his chair back so hard that it crashed to the floor behind him, and he had one hand on Sean's throat and had pulled him almost off his feet before the chair had finished falling. "Don't. You. Ever. Speak like that to me." His voice was not loud, but every word had an edge like a freshly honed razor. For a long frozen moment, neither one of them moved or spoke. Jonathan could hear Sean's heart hammering, but Sean only stared back at him, as though waiting to be released or murdered. After a long minute, Jonathan's grip relaxed and Sean staggered back away from him.

"I'm sorry," he whispered, rubbing at his throat with one hand.

Jonathan looked away from him. "Maybe you should go home, Sean."

Sean backed away, following the edge of the table with a shaking hand, until he reached his chair, and sat. "I'm not going home. Like it or not, I'm the only friend you've got left." After a moment, he said, very cautiously, "About... about Regan, Jonathan...I wanted to ask you..."

"What?"

"Well...have you felt anything? Like you said you did with Veronica, have you felt her...waking up?"

After a moment, Jonathan slowly shook his head. "And I've tried. But there's just...nothing."

"You said you didn't wake up for seven days. It's only been three."

"I know."

They were silent for a while after that. Then Sean said, "You know, if you think old man Standish and that guy from the college are doing background checks on you...what if they've hired a private detective, or are doing surveillance, just like I did? Old man Standish could afford the good stuff, night vision technology, the works, if he wanted to. And we're dead meat if anyone has pictures from Friday night."

Jonathan considered. "The isolation of this house would make surveillance a challenge."

"Tell me about it. I can look, if you want. I'll come out every day—"

"After school."

"This is more important."

"Regan wouldn't want you to cut school for this, Sean, and neither do I."

"All right, after school. I can get some electronics that will pick up wireless signals, to see if anything's broadcasting out. It won't detect anything that's just recording, but I can do visual sweeps, check for cameras, bugs, stuff like that."

Jonathan stared gloomily at his computer screen. "That would be helpful," he said finally. "But your being out here that much could look very suspicious, Sean. If this whole situation comes to the worst case outcome, you might end up with criminal charges. You're seventeen, you could be charged as an adult. If there are cameras, and you find them—you'll be on them."

"If there were cameras on Friday, I'm already on them. I'll risk it."

"You say that too fast and too glibly, Sean. I know you'll hate me for this, but you're very young. You haven't been in serious legal trouble. It's no fun."

"I don't think any of this is fun. I'm doing it for Regan." Jonathan looked up at Sean, a little surprised, but Sean didn't look back at him. "Anyway," he went on, forcing a grin, "What's the prob? You're coaching me for the MCAS, Mr. Writer."

"Which you should find some time to prep for, mind you."

"I will." Meeting Jonathan's skeptical look, he said, "Oh, was that too fast and glib?"

"Much too much. You know, Sean, I wouldn't let you go on with this if I didn't know perfectly well that I couldn't stop you, and you'll be in more danger hanging around the edges than where I can see you. I can be gone without a trace in an hour. You'll still have to live here."

Sean looked down at the floor between his knees for a few moments. Then he sighed and looked up at Jonathan, and his face was so serious, for a moment he looked much older than seventeen. "I'm not some pesty little kid," he said quietly. "If you really don't want me to help anymore, I'll respect that. I mean it." There was a pause, and then he said, "Is that what you're saying?"

"Not just yet," Jonathan said finally.

Chapter 18

Sean went outside and searched for signs of cameras or other surveillance equipment until dark, when Jonathan insisted that he come in and work on homework. Tuesday afternoon, and Wednesday, they repeated the same routine. Late at night, Jonathan went out and searched the woods for some sign of what had happened to Regan. He relied on smell a good deal of the time, knowing that bodies had lain undiscovered on bare ground for decades in terrain just like this in Massachusetts, often within sight of major highways or well-used hiking trails. But he found no trace, and remained perplexed as to where Veronica could have hidden her friend's body so completely.

On Wednesday, Sean arrived at the house a little later than usual. "There's something going on at Regan's store."

"I'm sure they're searching it for any clues as to what happened to her. Store employees have been found murdered in their establishments before."

"Oh, yeah, they did that—a couple of times. But I went over there today, and there was a car parked out front—one of those Lexus Infinitis, and it had Georgia plates."

"Georgia?"

"There was some guy, looked about forty years old, suit and tie, bald on top, he had keys to the place. He was inside looking around. He was pretty unhappy. I went up to the door and he told me the store was closed and to get lost. Then I told him who I was and that I was working for Regan. So he asked me if I knew where she was and I said no. I said, who are you, and he said his name was Bill Wharton. Says it's his mother's store."

"Well, you knew Regan didn't own the store."

"Yeah, I knew she said that. This Wharton guy says his mother's in the hospital. He seemed really upset with Regan. He sure didn't seem worried about what's happened to her, anyway."

Jonathan frowned. "I don't like the sound of this. Maybe I'll see if I can find out what's going on."

"I told him about the cleaning job we did last week, and all he said was, that's good. He was kind of a jerk." Sean sat brooding for a few moments, and then took his electronic kit out of his backpack. "Guess I'll go sweep."

Sean discovered no signs of surveillance equipment in his daily searches, and there were no further indications of Internet sleuthing into Jonathan's background. "But they've found what was there to find," Jonathan said, after Sean had finished his search on Wednesday. "I wouldn't be surprised if Hiram Clauson is doing leg work, trying to get hard copy documentation. That, he can be craftier about."

"That's still not going to prove anything. It's not against the law to change your identity."

"Not per se, no. But he's watching me, and that's a problem. I'm sure that he wants to connect me with all those incidents he was investigating. And I'm also sure that he assumes I have something to do with Regan being missing. What Jerry Standish's real motives are, I'm not as certain. He may be more interested in finding some way he can blame me for Veronica's death, and let his own conscience off the hook."

"What are we going to do? I mean, it's not like you can call up the cops and complain that this guy is stalking you."

"Not the police, no..." Jonathan turned to look at his computer thoughtfully. "But Clauson is using his office computer to do all this research, based on the IP numbers I checked. I wonder what the Bridgewater State administration would think about college resources being used for such a purpose?"

Sean shrugged. "It's not like he's collecting kiddy porn or something."

"These days, there's quite a bit of concern about privacy rights and what-not—certainly in liberal venues like academia. Let's see if we can throw some distractions at Dr. Clauson." He began clicking rapidly through the Bridgewater State website, looking for the contact information he needed, and Sean, after watching him for a moment, pulled some homework out of his backpack.

At around 10:00 p.m., as he did each night, Jonathan gave Sean and his bike a ride home. Sharon Neeson seemed unconcerned about her son's daily trips out to Rainbow Stone house, so at least there was one person in Sheridan who thought Jonathan was a valuable member of the community. On the way through town, Sean said, "You know what's making me really nervous, Jonathan? Regan's car. What are you going to do if the police come to your place with a search warrant? Regan's been gone for five days now. She's officially a missing person. It's been in the papers and everything."

"I know. I've seen it."

"I hate to say this, but usually when a woman disappears, everyone thinks the boyfriend did it. Have the police even talked to you?"

"I've talked to the police every day this week."

"You never told me that!"

"I called them, I didn't wait for them to contact me. I thought it would look better if I appeared concerned and just as mystified as everyone else."

"What do they say?"

"Mrs. Wharton, who owns the store, reported Regan missing on Monday. The neighbors don't know where she is. No one is sure whether she came home on Friday night or not. The landlady let the police look through Regan's apartment. Apparently, they didn't find anything there that offered any clues, but there was a printout for an estate sale on Saturday in the printer."

"I remember her talking about that, but she wasn't going to go."

"The police don't know that, though, and it makes me look better, because

I mentioned to Detective Fellman that Regan would go to estate sales. So I understand that lead was checked out, fruitlessly of course. Mrs. Wharton let the police search the store. That didn't help them, either. Regan's parents have been notified, and now they're calling the police every day, I've been told. But since there's no evidence of foul play aside from the fact that she's missing, no one is talking about criminal charges. The police haven't asked to search my house. But you're right—they probably will."

They rode in silence for a couple of minutes. "You're hoping she'll come back, and that will solve all this, aren't you?"

Jonathan didn't answer for a moment. "I don't know how much hope I have for that, by this time."

"You're still not feeling anything?"

"Nothing. Nothing at all."

"You know, we can swap the plates on the car, even paint it. Then we can take it up to the mall and just leave it in the parking lot. They'll figure out it's Regan's car, but at least it won't be in your barn."

"Mall parking lots have security cameras."

"Then we'll find somewhere that doesn't! Come on, Jonathan. Doesn't that lock thing you do work on car ignitions?"

"It does, to unlock them. I can't magically start the engine. But that's easy enough to accomplish." Jonathan sighed heavily. "I suppose we better do something like that, and soon." They pulled up in front of the peeling three-decker house where Sean and his mother lived.

"I'll bring some cans of Rustoleum with me tomorrow, and I can get some old plates. Later," Sean said, as he got out of the car.

But the following afternoon, Sean brought his bike skidding to a halt in front of the house and hammered on the door, gasping for breath, he'd been pedaling so hard. Jonathan jerked the door open in alarm, and Sean stumbled into the house, his arms flailing as he struggled to get his backpack off so he could pull something out of the top of it.

"Sean, for god's sake, what's happened?"

"Look at this."

Sean thrust a copy of the Fall River *Herald* at Jonathan, folded to an inner page. Jonathan took the paper and read the headline aloud, "Standish Mills owner accused of body snatching: former wife files lawsuit for $1.4M. Oh, my *god*."

"Just when you thought things couldn't get any weirder, right?"

"I *never* think that things can't get any weirder." He walked toward the great room, scanning the article, as Sean followed. There was an old, rather glamorous photograph of Veronica accompanying the piece.

"Basically, she thinks old man Standish paid off the funeral director so he could get his autopsy done. But look what she's saying: she's accusing him of having something to do with Regan being missing. That should take some of the heat off you, right?"

"I don't know." Jonathan folded the paper. "And it gives Jerry Standish even more reason to prove that someone else is guilty. He's not a man I covet as an enemy." He looked at Sean. "Did you bring the paint and plates?"

"Yeah, I did, and masking tape. You want me to start that right away, or go out and look for bugs first?"

"Start the painting. Regan's parents are going to be coming down on Saturday. They may insist that the police initiate a much broader search. We should get the car moved tomorrow night."

As they drove back to Sean's house that night, Jonathan eyed his paint-stained clothes. "You should probably burn all of those, Sean. You don't want the paint on the car traced back to you. Where did you buy the paint?"

"Actually, I, uh...I lifted it. From school."

"Sean. Shame on you."

Sean grinned. "Look who's talking. I'll get rid of my clothes. But I don't think anyone's going to worry too much about my clothes, with this article in the paper. Now the whole world knows that Veronica's body vanished from the funeral home. You know what you said last Friday, about spin control when all hell breaks loose? I think it just broke."

The following afternoon, Jonathan made his daily call to the Sheridan police department and asked for Detective Fellman. When the detective picked up the phone, his voice had a more cautious tone than he had used on previous days.

"Mr. Vaughn. I was just about to call you."

"Is there some new development?"

"Well, there's some new information. I'd very much appreciate it if you could come down to the station."

"Now?"

"If you can make it."

"I'll be there in about twenty minutes."

When Jonathan went inside the station and told the dispatcher who he was, she asked him to wait a moment. Detective Fellman came out to the front lobby immediately. "Thank you for coming, Mr. Vaughn. We're going back to the conference room." The dispatcher buzzed them into the hallway as he spoke.

In the conference room, Jonathan paused in surprise. Sitting in chairs, with coffee cups in front of them, were two middle aged women he had never seen before. "This is Mr. Jonathan Vaughn," Detective Fellman said to them as he came into the room. "Mr. Vaughn, this is Mrs. Alice Swann and Mrs. Eleanor Thornton. They're nieces of Mrs. Letty Brownmiller."

"I'm sorry, I'm not quite sure who Mrs. Brownmiller is," Jonathan said uncertainly as he sat in one of the chairs near the door.

"Mrs. Brownmiller passed away recently, and her wake was held at Burgos and Sons Funeral Home last Friday evening."

Suddenly, the situation became much clearer to Jonathan, and he struggled not to let his apprehension show on his face. "I'm very sorry for your loss, Mrs.

Swann...Mrs. Thornton." They nodded acknowledgement, but their faces looked very serious.

"We're just waiting for one more person," Detective Fellman said. He remained standing by the door, and there was a stiff and awkward silence for several minutes. All Jonathan could derive from it was that the two nieces did not appear to be either staring at him or avoiding his eyes, as he might have expected people to do who had something damning to say about him. They seemed a bit puzzled as to why he was here, which gave all three of them something in common, he thought. He tensed a bit when Detective Fellman gestured to someone in the hallway, probably the dispatcher, and went to meet, presumably, the last participant in this conference. Jonathan's trepidation was not lessened when Detective Fellman returned, ushering into the room an agitated looking Jerry Standish. The mill owner needed a haircut, and his hair bristled on the top of his head and around his ears. He looked like he hadn't shaved today, either. When he saw Jonathan seated at the table, his face, already blotchy, reddened. However, he sat down without comment, except to grunt when Detective Fellman introduced the nieces to him. He did not offer them his condolences.

"I've asked you, Mr. Vaughn and Mr. Standish, to come in," Detective Fellman said, "because Mrs. Swann and Mrs. Thornton came to me today with some very interesting information, and I wanted you to hear it from them directly." He nodded at the two ladies. They glanced at each other self-consciously, and then Alice Swann cleared her throat.

"We live in Worcester," she began, "and so we really don't get much news from down here unless it's on the TV. But one of my daughters lives in Fall River, and she e-mailed me yesterday with something that was in the Fall River paper. Look mom, she wrote, wasn't this the lady that was at Nana Letty's wake? When I saw that photograph, I nearly fell off my chair."

"Which photograph?" Jonathan asked.

"Why the blonde girl, of course, the one they're saying was stolen from the funeral home."

Eleanor Thornton broke in, "There must be some mistake. There must be. That girl walked right through the room. She bumped into me, that's why I remember her. But I'd have remembered her, anyway. Such a beautiful girl, but she looked like a sleepwalker. I thought she must be one of Letty's husband's relations. I don't know all of his family."

Jonathan chanced a glance at Jerry Standish. The mill owner was rigidly upright in his chair, mouth gaping, staring at the two kind-looking women as though he was about to assault them. There was sweat standing out on his forehead. Detective Fellman, Jonathan noticed, was not seated and had taken a furtive step toward Jerry Standish, so that he was in reach of the mill owner's shoulder, should any sudden moves be made. "Are you absolutely positive you saw the woman in the newspaper?" Jonathan asked Alice Swann.

"As positive as I could be. I still have twenty-twenty vision."

"When she bumped into me," Eleanor Thornton said, "I turned around, and her face wasn't two inches from mine. I recognized her the second I saw the photograph." She shook her head, looking at Detective Fellman. "I don't know how this girl was declared dead, but I know I wasn't seeing a ghost. She bumped me so hard, I almost stumbled. There must be a mistake."

"What happened to her? Did you see where she went?" Jonathan asked.

"Of course. I was watching her, because she seemed so unsteady on her feet, I was afraid she might be going to fall. She went out with the other girl, the one that now they're saying is missing. The one who ran the store that Aunt Letty liked so much, what is her name?"

"Regan Calloway."

"That's right, she signed the guest book. I thought it was so sweet of her to come. She spoke to us in the receiving line, and then she must have been waiting for the blonde girl, because she took her hand and helped her out of the room. There was a boy with them, too. He seemed very shy, he didn't speak to anyone."

"Did you see where she came from? The blonde girl, I mean?" Jonathan asked.

"No," Alice Swann said, "but I just assumed she and the other girl, Regan, had come together. Since they left together." She looked nervously at Jerry Standish, then at Detective Fellman, and spread her hands helplessly. "That's all I can tell you, I'm sorry. But we're sure that's the same girl."

"Thank you, Mrs. Swann and Mrs. Thornton," Detective Fellman said "I very much appreciate your coming all the way down here from Worcester. I'll call you if we have any more questions."

The two ladies gathered up their purses and coats and edged their way to the door, murmuring goodbyes to Jonathan, but avoiding even looking at Jerry Standish, for which Jonathan could not blame them. The mill owner was now slumped in his chair, his arms tightly folded, staring at the table. Detective Fellman directed the ladies down the hall but didn't leave the conference room doorway. When they were gone, he sat in the chair between Jonathan and Jerry Standish, keeping his eye on the mill owner as he spoke.

"After we talked with Mrs. Thornton and Mrs. Swann," Detective Fellman said, conversationally, "we called a number of other guests from the wake. Three of them, including Mrs. Swann's daughter, had seen the photograph, or were able to look it up online, and are prepared to swear in court that this is the woman they saw walking out of Letty Brownmiller's wake, on her own two feet. With Regan Calloway, who is now missing. I wonder if either of you two gentleman have anything to say that might shed some light on this mystery?"

Jerry Standish didn't move or acknowledge the question. Jonathan looked at Detective Fellman for a moment, then flung his hands apart in a gesture of helpless confusion. "I'm...thunderstruck. This is the most bizarre...not that I mean any disrespect to Veronica Standish or her family, but this is...incomprehensible.

If Regan and Veronica left the funeral home together, where are they now?"

"I was hoping that you might have some ideas about that, Mr. Vaughn," Detective Fellman said.

"I do not."

"Are you sure about that?"

"Good god, do you think I'm hiding the two of them in my house? Come and take a look, any time! Perhaps I've missed something." It was impossible to guess what Detective Fellman thought of this bluff. He just frowned, and took a different tack.

"If Regan Calloway and Veronica Standish had gone somewhere together, do you have any idea where they might have headed?"

Jonathan paused long enough to appear he was giving it some thought. "No, I'm afraid not. I just didn't know either of them well enough to speculate about that. They'd been friends since childhood."

Detective Fellman turned to look at Jerry Standish. "Mr. Standish? Any thoughts?" Jerry Standish only heaved a deep sigh, exhaling like a bull snorting. "All right, then." Detective Fellman rose from his chair. "You can both leave. Thank you for your time. We'll continue the ongoing investigations, in light of this new information. You both have my number, if you learn anything that would help us solve these cases—both of them, if they actually are separate cases."

Jonathan and Jerry Standish stood up, and Detective Fellman moved into the hallway to allow them to leave the conference room. Jerry Standish stepped around the corner of the table, and Jonathan clearly saw what he was going to do. He could easily have ducked out of the way, but he didn't want the other men to see how fast he could move, and in any event, this would tend to act in his favor. He let himself be a clear target when Jerry Standish said, not loudly, "You son of a bitch," and socked him in the cheekbone. Jonathan reeled back, not because the blow made him do so, but because it would look good. As if in slow motion, he saw Detective Fellman turning, his mouth open, reaching to grab Jerry Standish's arm as he lunged forward to hit Jonathan again. In a second, there were two other officers in the room, and it took all three of them to hold Jerry Standish back as he raged at Jonathan.

"You set this up! You're in on it, you bastard! You, Veronica, my ex-wife, that Calloway bitch—you're all in on it. You set this up to bring me down, all that bullshit about no embalming and no autopsy, you've fucked me over! You're not getting away with it! You're not getting away with it!"

"Mr. Standish, get yourself under control, or I'm placing you under arrest," Detective Fellman said, loudly enough to be heard over Jerry Standish's furious voice.

Jerry Standish slowly relaxed and stopped struggling with the officers, and they cautiously let go of him. He coughed a couple of times and straightened his suit coat and tie. In a voice that was calm but still full of anger, he said to Detective Fellman, "Don't you get it? The phone call, the suicide, the letter, and now this damn lawsuit...it's all a huge grift, a con job. Isn't that obvious? They're all in on it, all four of them. I've been set up."

"We'll investigate that, Mr. Standish."

"Mr. Standish," Jonathan said, "I've never met your ex-wife in my life."

"Shut up, you. I know what you're getting out of all this."

"Okay, that's enough," Detective Fellman said. "Are you all right, Mr. Vaughn?"

"I think so."

"Do you want to press charges?"

"God, no. I appreciate the amount of strain that Mr. Standish is under right now. Just as long as he doesn't hit me again."

"You should thank him for that," Detective Fellman said to Jerry Standish. "I'd book you, if it was left to me."

"He can suck my dick," Jerry Standish muttered. Jonathan had difficulty repressing a laugh.

"I'll ask you to watch your language in the station. Are you ready to leave? Then let's go." Detective Fellman escorted him down the hall.

After about five minutes, the detective returned to the conference room. "I apologize for that. I should have realized he might do that. Are you sure you're okay? One of the officers can take you to be checked out, if you want."

"I'm fine. I ducked back, it was only a glancing blow. Don't worry, I won't sue the police department."

"Well, thank you. Would you like an escort home?"

"I seriously doubt that Jerry Standish is going to follow me. He does seem a little paranoid, doesn't he?"

"Yes. Well. Even paranoids are sometimes right."

"Do you think that I'm really conspiring to extort one point four million dollars from Jerry Standish and shut down the biggest employer in Sheridan?"

Detective Fellman turned and gave Jonathan a steady and absolutely serious look. "Are you?"

"No."

The detective smiled strangely, as though the afternoon had reached such a level of absurdity that he couldn't do anything else. "If you come up with any more information, you have my number."

When Jonathan got back to the River Road house, Sean was there, checking the perimeter with his electronic kit. "Where'd you go?" he said as Jonathan got out of the car.

"I just had a very interesting meeting at the police station. Come inside when you're done and I'll tell you about it."

"I'm done now." They went inside, and Jonathan told Sean about the two nieces from Worcester and Jerry Standish's outburst. When he finished, Sean sat staring at him in stupefaction. "So now they think Veronica is alive, somehow, and we're all just trying to scam old man Standish?"

"I don't know what they think about Veronica being alive. They could suspect an impostor of some kind."

"Is this good or bad?"

"For us? I don't know."

Sean seemed a bit preoccupied, and he sat glumly in the chair without saying anything for a few minutes. "Have you...you know, felt anything yet? From Regan? It's been seven whole days now."

Jonathan looked away from him. "No. Not one single thing...nothing. And with Veronica, it was almost like a scream. I couldn't even think, it was so strong."

"Well, yeah, but look at what she woke up to."

"Not at first, though."

"Well..." Sean squirmed back in his chair. "Jonathan...I, uh...I heard something today...but I kind of hate to even tell you about it. I know I have to, but..." he swallowed hard.

Jonathan looked steadily at Sean. "Go ahead."

"Um...I heard this from one of the kids in school. So it might not be accurate. I didn't have any way of checking it out, that wouldn't look really susp—"

"Sean."

"This kid told me that there's an incinerator up at the dairy farm," Sean blurted out rapidly.

"An incinerator."

"He thought it was a pretty big one."

Jonathan got up from his chair and walked slowly to the middle of the room. "An incinerator. I've never seen smoke coming from the farm."

"They might only burn at night. A lot of incinerators do that." A heavy silence hung in the room. Sean finally said, "I just thought maybe you could check it out. Because not knowing is killing me, Jonathan. Anything is better than this."

"I know," Jonathan whispered. He stood motionless for a few minutes, then turned back to Sean. "I'm going to go out for a while. Do you want to stay here by yourself, or would you like me to drive you home?"

"I'm okay here. Where are you going?"

"I don't know. Out. Anywhere. When it gets dark, I'll check on Veronica. I'll check out the dairy farm later. They turn in very early up there, I know their habits. I don't know when I'll be back." He paused in the hall doorway. "If I'm not back tonight, you're welcome to stay." Sean opened his mouth to ask whether they were still going to move Regan's car tonight, but the front door opened and closed before he could speak.

Chapter 19

What awoke Regan, after a long time when she drifted in a cold, dreamy fog, was something crawling over her face. Suddenly, she opened her eyes and her body jerked, and she reached up and plucked a very large beetle off her cheekbone and flung it away. It took several attempts because the beetle clung to her finger. She heard the beetle bounce off the wall a couple of feet away. She lay blinking into the foggy grayness around her, wondering why there was a beetle on her face. *I'll really have to have a word with the landlady.*

She gradually became aware of a constant rustling all around her. She was lying on cold earth, but she didn't seem to be outdoors. It was close and enclosed, but open above her, as though there was no ceiling. One of her ears was against the floor, and she could hear water rushing, distantly, through the ground. *I'm not in my bedroom, silly girl. Where am I?* She decided to get up, and only when she started to move did she realize what an awkward position she was in. She was half on her left side, her left arm doubled beneath her, and her back against a very rough, bumpy wall that was sticking hard things into her in numerous places. Her right leg was splayed out on the floor and her left leg was half twisted up against the wall. She was like a rag doll that had been flung across the room by a child and left crumpled where it fell. Nevertheless, she didn't feel the slightest stiffness, no aches or pains or twinges. She untangled her limbs, pushed away from the wall and stood up in a single smooth movement. She spent a couple of minutes shaking and combing sowbugs, spiders and earwigs out of her clothes and hair. The fact that she was literally crawling with small creatures formerly would have bothered her much more, but now it was simply a minor annoyance. Her clothes, especially the back and shoulder of her sweater and the back of her jeans, were stiffened, as though with starch, and stuck to her skin, so she had to peel them loose. Much of her hair was stiff and matted with something, as well. *What the hell did I get into?*

She looked around in confusion. She could see, dimly, but everything appeared strange, as if it was glowing faintly with its own inner light. Slowly she adjusted to this new sensory input, and the muddled visual field resolved into a recognizable image. Stone walls, but very rough ones—large heavy field stones, piled upon each other with no concern for a close fit or a smooth surface. She was entirely surrounded by these walls, forming a roughly circular chamber no more than five feet in diameter. She went around, feeling the walls for any door or window, but there was none, and she could sense heavy, dense earth behind the stones. There was debris on the floor, old bones and trash, flattened paper and rusting beer cans. She peered upward. There was some sort of ceiling about ten feet over her head—smoother than the walls, but she couldn't see what it was made of. Suddenly Regan realized where she was. *This is a well. I must be in an old well…or a root cellar or something like that.* This part of the state had suffered from persistent droughts and over-building for the past forty years, so the ground water level had receded significantly. Otherwise she would have been in water, which would have been most unpleasant. *But how did I get here?*

The answer to that question seemed extremely important. Regan leaned her forehead against one of the cool stones and closed her eyes, trying to reconstruct what had happened. The store…Jonathan coming to the store…Veronica was waking up. She and Sean went to the funeral home…Regan shuddered suddenly, as memory flooded back to her, all at once. The nightmarish drive with Veronica next to her in the car, the walk down the road, the argument in the little outbuilding, and then…without thinking, she felt the side of her neck, and touched a ridged scar, cold and thin and knotted, the last scar she would ever bear. She swallowed hard. *Veronica…Veronica killed me. She killed me…and I've woken up.*

She remained motionless for some time, struggling to believe what she remembered. *It can't be true, can it? Veronica killed me—and threw me down a well?* With rising panic, Regan wondered how long it had been since that night. Three days? A week? A week, with the store closed, and her absence unexplained? And what had happened to Veronica? What had happened to Sean? What did the police want to talk to Jonathan about? What did Veronica say in her letter, the one she bragged she'd mailed before she committed suicide? *I've got to get out of here!*

She peered up at the ceiling above her. What was it? She found foot and hand holds in the wall easily and climbed up the ten feet so she could touch the ceiling, which turned out to be the stone cover to the well. It was a solid stone slab, much thinner than a millstone, but heavy enough. She braced herself against the wall and pushed upward. The slab moved, just a little, before one of the stones she was standing on shifted and pulled out of the wall. Regan lost her balance and dropped back down, landing lightly on her feet, dodging the wall stone that fell with her and hit the earth floor with a heavy thud. *How can I move that?* she thought for a despairing moment, but then she recalled how strong Jonathan and Veronica were. Veronica must have moved the stone, to put her in here, and then replaced it. Regan doubted that she'd had help.

She climbed up again and tested the foothold stones, before she braced herself and pushed upward on the slab. She raised the slab several times, but it was difficult to raise it far enough to clear the edge of the well. She slipped and dropped back down three times before she finally managed to lift the stone and thrust it far enough to one side for her body to wiggle through the space it left. As she lay on the ground by the edge of the well, Regan finally realized that the reality of her new state was undeniable. Whatever animated her body now, she was no longer, technically, alive. She should have been sweating and out of breath, with pounding heart, but she was aware only of a sense of enervation. She had to rest, because she had used up energy and was temporarily weak, but that was all. She had no heartbeat, no breath, no pain anywhere, no perspiration, no sensations of organic bodily needs of any kind. Except for one thing—she was very thirsty.

As that thought entered her mind, Regan's stomach contracted painfully, and she rolled over, digging her fingers into the mossy ground by the well edge. *Thirsty*...and not for water. *Drink blood, I could never do that*, a small voice in her mind protested, but that voice was an echo from her old life. The moment she actually thought about it, her mouth started watering. She'd never starved in her life. She'd never had an addiction. She'd never even had food cravings. But now she felt almost overwhelmed by the most overpowering pure desire she could ever remember experiencing. For a moment, she was almost panicked. *What am I going to do, how am I ever going to control this?* But even more urgently, *how am I going to get blood to survive?* After a few minutes, her stomach contractions subsided, and so did the urgent compulsion that had come with them. Her mind cleared, and she remembered that she was still lying on the ground, and there were things she needed to do.

She stood up, emotionally shaky, although physically, she had never felt so limber and strong. Movement was effortless. She looked around to determine just exactly where she was. She could see easily, although it was two days past the new moon and the only light came from the stars overhead. The woods around the well were about forty years old and were not very dense. A low stone wall snaked among the trees some thirty feet to the west. Turning in a full circle, Regan spotted the building where she and Veronica had had their last conversation, about a hundred yards to the south. That meant the road was just beyond. She didn't know where else to go except back to the house. She hoped her car was still there. For the first time, it occurred to her to wonder what Jonathan thought had happened to her. Did he know she would be waking up, as he'd known Veronica would?

She decided to push the stone slab back into place over the well. She wouldn't want anyone to fall into it, after all. The slab had an iron staple set into the top surface, and was much easier to move from up here than while hanging onto the wall underneath. When it dropped into place, nearly flush with the ground, and Regan stepped back from it, she saw that it was almost invisible even from a few feet away. The dark slate was discolored and thickly covered with layers of flattened dead leaves stuck to its surface, making it indistinguishable from the terrain around it, and the area around the well was thickly grown up in low brush and bushes. Veronica must have known about the well, for she could never have found it by accident. During their high school years, Veronica had spent a lot of time partying, and she knew the trails and campfire spots around Sheridan better than Regan, who had always worked after school. Some boy must have shown her the well years ago. He probably would never have guessed the use to which pretty blonde Veronica would one day put it.

Regan walked to the road, not glancing at the outbuilding as she passed it, and stood at the edge of the pavement looking up and down the open stretch of asphalt, silvery in the starlight and crisscrossed with darker lines where road crews had patched cracks. She crossed and began walking east, staying close to the south edge of the road so she could quickly duck into the trees if a car's headlights came into view around the bend up ahead.

She had only gone about a quarter of a mile when her attention was caught by an acrid smell, and she stopped to sniff. It was wood smoke, like a small campfire, piney and aromatic. She paused, listening carefully, and heard voices, and the tinny sound of recorded music. The sounds and smells were coming from quite far away, through the trees. Just ahead, to the right, was a cut-in like the one that turned off to the outbuilding, two grassy ruts, all that remained of some little unpaved road into the woods. Regan stood sniffing at the smoke and listening to the faint sounds. *Just keep walking,* said the little echoing voice in her mind. *Don't go down there. Keep walking on the road, keep going...* But she couldn't remember why. She turned off the road and followed the cut-in.

After she'd walked in some distance from the road, the ground started to slope downwards. Below her, Regan could see the tiny orange light of a small fire through the trees, and she smelled pot smoke and the yeasty aroma of beer mingled with the wood smoke. There was something else, too, a rich warm smell, very faint, underneath the rest. It didn't really smell like cooking meat, but she thought of that because it made her mouth water. Without making a conscious effort, or even realizing what she was doing, she was moving without making a sound. Not a broken twig, not a stumble, not a footfall betrayed her approach. She might have been drifting above the ground like a ghost.

She came to a pick-up truck, parked at a point where the cut-in stopped at a large boulder and the trail beyond was narrower. She veered off into the woods to the left, circling carefully around through bracken and blueberry bushes, making sure she stayed in the shadows, but gradually moving closer to the fire. Three teenaged boys were sitting around it, two about Sean's age, she guessed, while one appeared a little younger. They had a boom box on the ground next to them, thumping out a sort of techno-hip-hop music of which very little was distinguishable except the hard fast beat and a staccato patter of voices. The conversation of the boys was interrupted frequently with laughter. She settled down to watch them. She waited for some time, as the trio passed a joint back and forth and talked, but she was neither impatient nor bored. Like a cat watching birds through a window, she was completely and unflaggingly absorbed.

She had no sense of how much time was passing, but the fire died down to embers. As the clearing grew darker, Regan noticed that she could still see the boys plainly against the trees, as if they were glowing. It was as though she could see the warmth of their bodies. Two of the boys stood up, turning off and collecting the boom box. The third, however, remained sitting on a half-buried log, still nursing his can of beer and staring at the red coals of the campfire.

"You walkin', Nick?" the older of his two friends said, and Nick grunted something. "You're not going to sit out here all night, are you?"

"Nah, you go ahead."

"You sure?"

"Look, all I gotta do is cut straight the woods and my house is right over that hill," Nick said patiently. "I'll wait till the old man's asleep."

The other two glanced at each other, and Nick's friend said, "Yeah, well look, we gotta go."

"I know. No prob." He flashed them a quick grin. "Whadya think, the coyotes are gonna get me or something? Get outta here."

After a pause, the older boy shrugged *whatever* and started up the trail. The younger boy followed behind, recklessly swinging the boom box as he hiked up the slope. After a minute or so, Regan heard the pickup truck's engine start and recede up the cut-in toward the road. Eventually its sound died away entirely and there was nothing to be heard but the trilling night song of insects and pond life. Nick, left alone in the thick darkness, tossed a few more dry pieces of wood on the coals and flames leapt up, illuminating his somber face in flickering yellow light. Regan wondered what was weighing so heavily on his mind. *Maybe I'll find out.* She knew exactly how to do what she needed to. She'd realized that as she'd sat watching the boys and thinking about what to do next. The practical information had somehow been planted in her mind, like an instinct. The only question she still had was how to get hold of him. She didn't expect that he would cooperate.

The dry wood burned rapidly, and soon the campfire was again merely red coals. Regan left her vantage point and moved noiselessly around to the trail, so that she would be walking down behind Nick. He got off the log and hunkered down next to the fire, and started shoving the remaining coals into a mound with a piece of wood. Regan walked to within three feet of him and hunkered down as well, watching him. He was skinny, and had thick light colored hair that was longer than his collar, with unkempt bangs almost hanging in his eyes. But it wasn't his appearance that interested Regan. It was his *smell*. This close, it was intoxicating. It was like walking into a steakhouse after hiking all day without eating.

Nick dropped the wood he was using as a shovel and groped around for his beer can. The end of the wood that was in the coals suddenly flared up in a tongue of flame. Nick glimpsed Regan's shape from the corner of his eye and jerked around, startled to see her sitting there motionless a mere yard away from him. From his expression, he might have been kicked in the stomach.

"Fuck!" He jumped to his feet, staggered backwards, tripped over the log and landed flat on his back. He was far from sober and after hunkering down for so long, he would have been dizzy when he stood up under the most relaxing conditions. Regan was on top of him before he had completely hit the ground. She couldn't let him get away, that wouldn't be good at all. She couldn't understand why he was so panicked. He was kicking so frantically that he'd caught

his foot on the log and knocked his shoe off, and he was flailing at her with both arms. But he seemed to be moving so slowly. She had no trouble avoiding his hands. "Jesus Christ, what are you, get the fuck off me! Get off!" That was as much as he managed to say before she got a good grip on his mouth to stop him from talking. His body was heaving underneath her, and she had to dig her knees into his sides to keep him from throwing her off.

"Hold still," she said, but he didn't seem to hear her. He was clawing at her right hand, which was holding his mouth. She grabbed his wrist with her other hand and pinned his arm to the ground, and twisted his head sideways, which made him squeal. She bent down and put her mouth against his neck, feeling the hard pulse of his young heart, almost doubled with adrenaline. She locked on and *opened* and her mouth was suddenly full of warm blood, but it didn't taste like she remembered blood tasting, salty and metallic. It burned her throat with raw energy when she swallowed, and sent heat radiating out through her body. It was like drinking liquid light. Nick had flinched violently at the sensation of being *opened,* but his struggles were subsiding as his muscles turned loose and numb. Regan drank and drank, feeling warmth and life tingling through her skin and her fingers and her toes, and the taste of Nick's blood in her mouth was more quenching and sweeter than any liquid she had ever drunk when she was alive. But after a space of time something warned her that she'd taken quite enough for Nick's good. Yanked back to the present moment, Regan was momentarily alarmed, and in haste she *closed* the injury she'd made, with regret, because physically she hadn't had nearly enough. But somehow she knew that no amount of blood would ever really be enough. Nick shuddered at the unpleasant sensation of *closing,* but Regan could clearly read that he was in a state of total disbelief. He could not accept that this was really happening and thought that someone was playing some kind of prank on him. He wouldn't have to cope with the truth. While she was still touching his skin, Regan gathered her mental energy and blanked out Nick's memory and his consciousness. Nick's body gave one convulsive jerk and went limp, his mind as dark as a blackened stage. What Regan didn't expect was the impact of the memory-blanking on her own mind. She felt as though she'd fired a powerful gun without realizing there would be a violent recoil.

She sat up, feeling a bit dazed, and looked down at Nick's unconscious face. *You just assaulted a high school kid,* she said to herself sternly, but there was no emotional force to the thought at all. Nick's blood was giving her a sense of well-being that bordered on euphoria. But there was more than that. She didn't feel that Nick was something she had callously used—she felt, instead, a deep sense of gratitude toward him. She doubted that he would appreciate that, but nevertheless, it was how she felt. There was still quite a bit of blood on his neck. It seemed wrong to waste it. She bent down again and carefully licked Nick's skin clean. Then she put her hand on his forehead. Her first try at memory blanking had been a bit too much. He wouldn't even remember how he got to the woods tonight, let alone what had just happened. He was going to have a nasty injury, worse than any of the ones she had seen. Obviously she had something to learn about finesse.

She remembered now where she had been going, and all the questions that had been so urgent when she was in the well. It was time to continue back to the house without any more detours. She tugged Nick's jacket closed, folded his hands neatly on his stomach, found his shoe and put it back on his sock-clad foot. She didn't want him to get too cold. She emptied his beer can onto the dying embers of the campfire. Then she headed back up the trail toward the road.

It only took another ten minutes or so to reach Rainbow Stone house. Regan ducked through the brush and saplings on the west side of the barn, walking swiftly to reach the deep shadow of the building and get out of sight of the road. The only car parked in front of the house was Jonathan's. She pushed through the weeds to the window on the side of the barn and peered inside. There was one car there, which she realized after a moment was her own, although something looked a bit strange about it. There were lights on inside the great room, she could see from the cracks around the drawn shades. She went on around the house to the back door. It was locked. She closed her hand around the knob, feeling the cold metal against her skin, and then, *feeling* with another sense the inner mechanism, bars and tongues and tabs of steel. The lock clicked a couple of times and she opened the door and stepped inside, closing it behind her without making a noise. She walked through the back hall to the archway and paused there. The floor lamps were turned on, and Sean was sitting at the end of the long table. Jonathan was not there, and she couldn't sense anyone else in the house. It looked like Sean had been doing homework and fallen asleep; his head was resting on his forearms, and he didn't move. It occurred to her that he probably would be rather surprised to see her, and it might not be wise to just walk over and tap him on the shoulder. His feelings aside, even from this far away he had quite a delicious smell, and she wasn't sure she could trust herself if there was any kind of physical struggle. She drew back into the hallway, where she was out of sight.

"Sean," she called softly—more softly than she intended. Her voice was hoarse and whispery. She cleared her throat and tried with more force. "Sean." That came out sounding a bit more normal.

Sean twitched and then sat up suddenly, "Wha—hello? Who's calling me?" He seemed suddenly quite frightened. Regan wondered why.

"Sean," she said again, more loudly.

Sean jumped up out of the chair and backed toward the kitchen. He really was scared. She could smell it on him, and she could hear, just barely, his pounding heart and rapid breathing. "Who is that? Come out where I can see you."

"Sean, for god's sake. What's the matter with you? It's Regan."

Sean froze. "Regan...?" he whispered after a moment.

"Yes, it's me. I didn't want to startle you."

"Come out where I can see you!"

She stepped into the archway. The floor lamps did not reach this far, but there was enough shadowy illumination for him to recognize her. Sean stood, staring, his mouth open, in an almost comical expression of complete stupefaction. He opened and closed his mouth a couple of times. "Regan. Where—where have you been?"

Regan was tired of standing in shadows. She walked forward about halfway to the table, feeling a pang of hurt to see Sean draw back further as she approached. As she reached a more brightly lit part of the floor, a look of both fear and horror came into his eyes that was humbling to see. "At the bottom of a well, apparently."

"A...a well?"

"An old dry well near the dairy farm. That's where Veronica left me."

"An old dry well..." Sean repeated. Suddenly his knees buckled.

"Oh, Sean!" Regan stepped forward, aghast, as Sean collapsed to the floor, but stopped when he scrambled back from her on all fours, crabwise, his eyes frantic.

"Stay away! Don't come closer, please, Regan, just...just don't."

"Sean..." She knelt down, hurt and grief stabbing through her. "Don't be afraid of me, Sean. I'm not going to hurt you. Look..." Without rising fully, she moved across the last few feet of floor between them. Sean crouched without moving, drawing in gulping breaths like sobs. She held her hand out to him. He stared at it and shuddered, with reason—it was dark with blood stains and dirt. "Take my hand, Sean," she whispered. After a long pause, Sean sat up slowly, reached out and clasped her hand. He squeezed his eyes shut as she closed her fingers firmly around his. His dread of touching her blocked out anything she might have read from him, but she felt that dread suddenly melt into recognition.

"Oh, god." He squeezed her hand back and opened his eyes. "You're really here."

"Yes, I'm really here." Regan released his hand and shifted so she was sitting cross-legged on the floor. Despite the physical energy she still had from Nick's blood, she suddenly felt psychologically exhausted.

"We gave up hoping, Jonathan and me. We thought...he kept saying he couldn't feel you, and then it was so long..."

"How long has it been?"

"It's been seven days, Regan. This is Friday again. It's been a whole week."

"A week." She closed her eyes for a moment. "And the store's been closed."

"Yeah. And there's a problem with that..."

"Problem?"

"There's been some guy coming around...someone named Bill Wharton. He's really upset."

"Mrs. Wharton's son. Oh, god..."

"Jesus, I'm sorry, Regan. I'd have cut school and run the store for you, only, there's things you didn't show me yet, and anyway I didn't have the keys."

Regan blinked, and then she dug into her jeans pocket and brought out her keys, which had been there all along. She sat and looked at them in the palm of her hand, then tossed them onto the floor. "The things you don't think of." Her head fell back with a despairing sigh. "The next time I get murdered, I really must remember to leave the keys for you."

"I'm sorry."

"I wouldn't have wanted you to cut school, Sean. How did you and Jonathan move my car?"

"We just rolled it. But we were going to take it somewhere tonight and leave it, because we were afraid the police would be getting a search warrant for the house." He looked at her despairingly. "So much has happened this week, I don't know how to tell you about it. It's been hell. You're on the missing persons list, Jonathan keeps getting called down to the police station, old man Standish is getting sued by his ex-wife, that professor from Bridgewater State is running background checks on Jonathan—"

"Whoa, whoa, whoa. You're going to have to start at the beginning, Sean. Where is Jonathan now? His car's out front."

"I don't know. I'm kind of scared for him. We've been looking for you all week. We thought we looked everywhere. We found the, the building, where... you know, we found the blood and all that...but we couldn't...and Veronica wouldn't tell us. What she did with you."

"Wouldn't tell you? You mean you found Veronica?"

"Oh, yeah, we've got Veronica." he looked away, his face twisting a little. "Have we ever got her. When I heard your voice, I almost thought for a minute, that somehow she'd gotten loose. She's got it out for me, big time. She gets loose, I'm toast."

"Sorry to scare you."

"But she claimed she did something, to fix it so you couldn't come back."

"Fix it? What, you mean like chop me up into little pieces?"

"She wouldn't say what. She just kept screaming that Jonathan would never get you back. He didn't want to believe her, but I could tell it was getting to him. And then when he couldn't feel you waking up, like he did Veronica...He said he was trying hard but there was just nothing there. I kept on hoping, but I know he was thinking that you were really dead. Then tonight...I hope I haven't done something really stupid."

"What?"

"I heard from some asshole in school that there's...there's an incinerator up at the dairy farm. I told Jonathan about it. I had to tell him, in case...well..."

"In case Veronica burned my body, you mean? Sean, that incinerator is tiny. They couldn't burn a dead dog in it."

"Oh." Sean heaved a sigh. "Maybe he'll see that, then. He was going to go check it out. But I could tell...I could tell it really sucker punched him, when I said it. Like that explained why you didn't come back. He got up and said he was going out, and left."

"Well," Regan said after reflecting on this for a few moments, "maybe he'll be back soon."

"I hope he comes back at all." Sean fell silent and stared at Regan as if mesmerized, until she finally gave him a questioning look. He swallowed hard. "Don't take this the wrong way, but...you look horrible, Regan."

Regan reached up and touched her matted hair and then the side of her face, which she could feel now was covered with something both stiff and sticky. She got up and walked over to the nearest window and raised the shade so that she could see her reflection in the glass. When she saw the face looking back at her, she pressed both hands against her mouth in shock. Half of her face and neck, and her hands, were covered with dark dried blood, and her hair on the right side hung in blackened, snarled strings. Her sweater was soaked with blood that had dried and hardened, and her hands and face were smeared with dirt from her climb out of the well. There was dirt under all her nails, and her skin, where it wasn't stained, was livid white.

"Oh, my god. No wonder he was so scared of me."

"Who was?" Regan turned slowly and stared at Sean, her hands still covering her mouth. "Regan? Did someone *see* you? That's not good. What happened? Who saw you?"

Regan lowered her hands slowly and drew in a long sigh. She was going to have to tell sometime. "It's all right, Sean. He won't remember anything."

She watched Sean's face mutely as the implications of this sank in. "*Fuck. Did you...but how did...who *was* this?"

"His name's Nick. And don't refer to him in the past tense, he'll be fine."

"But...what happened?"

"I was walking back here, and I smelled campfire smoke. There were some kids down in the woods. I just sat down there and watched them for a while, and finally only one of them was left, by himself, and, uh..." There was a silence. Regan thought about what Nick's blood had tasted like, and what his body had felt like underneath her, and she ran her tongue over her lips. *I wish I didn't have to stop.*

"But he's going to be okay?"

She looked back up at him. "Yes."

Finally Sean said determinedly, "Well, you had to do it. If you stopped yourself from killing him, you're a lot more in control than Veronica."

Regan touched the scar on the side of her neck. "Not much to brag about, really, being more in control than that."

"Shit, this is just going to add more gasoline to the bonfire we've already got going, though. And it's so close to Jonathan's house here..."

"I know. I just...wasn't thinking. At all." She looked at him soberly. "You're lucky. If he hadn't been there, it would have been you."

Sean stared back at her, and he swallowed so hard she saw his throat move. "We've noticed people partying out there, a couple of times this week. The weather's getting nicer," he said after a moment, flustered. "How long have you been awake?"

"I don't know. A few hours, anyway. It took me a while just to get out of that fucking well."

Sean hunched his shoulders, shivering. Then he bent his head down, covering his face with his hands. "God, I'm not dreaming this, am I?" he said, his voice shaking. "Please let me not be dreaming..."

Regan went over to kneel by Sean, and took both his hands firmly in her own. She would have hugged him, but she didn't think he would welcome the gesture, as gruesome as she looked. "Sean," she said urgently, "You're not dreaming. Don't fall to pieces on me. I'm going to need your help." She gasped suddenly, as a flood of images poured into her mind from Sean's touch—Veronica writhing against chains, her face distorted with rage, howling, spitting venomous words at Sean, *are you fucking his cute little ass? Better kiss it goodbye while you can...* Regan jerked her hands away.

"What is it?" Sean said, startled, and then, realizing, "Were you reading me? Through my hands?"

Regan shook her head to clear it. "Veronica. My god. That bad?"

"Oh, god, you have *no* idea."

Regan stared at Sean, appalled. "Oh, Sean. I'm so glad you weren't hurt. We should never have gotten you into this, never."

Sean looked away from her, blinking hard, and she realized there were tears in his eyes. He wiped at his eyes quickly, clearing his throat. "Fuck, I'm glad you're back," he said, a little hoarse. "You bitch, you made me cry, you know that?"

"Well, get a grip, Sean."

"I mean in school."

"Oh, god. Then I'm *really* sorry."

"I don't think anyone noticed," he said bitterly. "We couldn't let anyone know what happened to you, anyway."

Regan settled back into her cross-legged position on the floor. "If we're going to have to wait for Jonathan, you might as well fill me in. Go back to when I left you at the funeral home, and tell me everything."

It took more than an hour for Sean to finish his story, with a certain amount of backing and filling, and many questions from Regan. When he had covered everything that he knew, Regan went into the kitchen and rinsed out her hair and washed a little at the deep three-basin sink, so she didn't look as much like, as Sean put it, "an accident victim in one of those driver's ed snuff movies." There was nothing she could do about her clothes without going back to her apartment, but Sean was a bit more relaxed with her.

"You know, there's one thing I seriously don't get," Sean said, after they were sitting in chairs at the big table.

"If there's only one thing, you're doing a lot better than me."

"Yeah, I know. But, why couldn't Jonathan feel you waking up, like he did Veronica? I don't understand that—and neither will he."

"Oh, that's an easy one."

"It is?"

"It's obvious. Only Veronica could feel me waking up, Sean. Because she was the last one—she killed me. And she hasn't been in any position to say anything about it, so you didn't know. But I'm sure she knows that I'm awake. And I'm sure she isn't very happy about it, either."

"Jesus..." Sean said after he'd thought about this for a moment. "That makes sense, I guess. You know...I think we better break this gently to Jonathan, when he gets back. He's going to freak. He's been totally wrecked ever since we found Veronica last Friday. Sometimes he's really scared me—and what he did to her..." Sean shuddered. "I've been having nightmares, every night. It's getting so I don't know what he'll do anymore."

"But you still come out here, every day."

"Hey, it's still better than home. Besides, I couldn't stand not knowing what was going on—as if any of us did know what was going on. But just sitting at home wondering about it—I'd be crazier than Veronica by now." Perhaps reminded by the topic of home, he suddenly said, "Oh, god, I forgot to tell you—Jonathan said your 'rents are coming down here tomorrow."

"My parents? Oh my god, they must be frantic. I better call them. Can I use Jonathan's phone, do you think?"

"I don't think he'd mind. I hope it's not bugged."

Regan froze, the cordless phone in her hand. "Are you kidding me?"

"He's been calling the cops every day, I don't think it is. But we've gotten seriously paranoid."

"Well, if this phone is, probably my phone is, too."

"You know, it's after midnight...never mind."

"Hello...mom? It's me...Yes, I'm okay...I know, mom...I know...well, I really can't explain right now...I just got in..." Sean got up and went into the kitchen for a can of Mountain Dew, which was one of the few things in the spotless refrigerator. There wasn't much to hear from Regan's side of the conversation. A few minutes later, he ventured back for the end of it. "...I *know*, mom. I promise I'll tell you everything, but right now I'm still doing damage control...yes...no, I don't know that yet. I haven't been home yet. I wanted to call you right away... I don't know that. I'll have to talk to him...Yes, I know. I love you, too. Don't make dad drive all the way down here. I'll come up and see you soon, okay? ...No, I will. No, don't call the police department. I'll have to talk to them anyway... yes, I probably will do that. Bye." She clicked off and looked down at the phone in her hand, sighing heavily.

"Must be nice, having folks who give a shit," Sean said. Regan looked at him sadly. "She pretty upset?"

"About me disappearing for seven days, without a call, while they file missing persons reports and every day expect that they'll have to identify my body in a morgue? Yeah, she's as upset as you'd expect. Give her twenty four hours, she'll be furious. I'll have to come up with a damn good story. But at least it will be me telling it, and not the police. I'll probably have to remind her of that, to calm her down." She put the phone down on the table. "That," she said wearily, "was the easiest conversation I'm going to have in the next few days." She looked gloomily at Sean. "Not that it's your fault, but after hearing what's been going on this past week...I'm almost sorry I'm back. I don't like any of this, and I'm really nervous about Bill Wharton being here. That can't mean anything good. I'm starting to think we should have taken option number one last Friday, and just blown town then. We've got a bigger mess on our hands right now than Fallujah."

"Right, except for less bombs. Give it a couple of days, though."

"Don't even joke about it."

"Maybe...maybe you should call the cops, that Detective Fellman. At least to let them know you're back and they can call off the search."

"Not until we've got our stories straight, Sean. I haven't even started to think about all that. I'm conspiring to extort money from Jerry Standish? I stole Veronica out of the funeral home? Jesus Christ, what have I walked into?"

"They haven't arrested Jonathan. They didn't even tell him not to leave town or anything. They just keep asking questions. And at least if you're back, they'll stop thinking that you've been murdered." He was silent for moment. "God, I hope Jonathan hasn't done anything really stupid. Where the fuck is he? He was really weird when he left here, and he doesn't even have his car."

Regan thought about this, and without realizing it, she hugged herself tightly, almost shivering. "I'm not sure whether I want him to come back or not."

Sean stared at her. "What are you *talking* about?"

She suddenly stood up. "I'm just not ready to see him, Sean. I just...I just can't."

"But why? For god's sake, Regan, I thought you two were...I mean, fuck it, he loves you, doesn't he?"

"I thought he did, when I was alive. But after everything you just told me, and what he did to Veronica...what if he's revolted by me now, what if...god, if he looks at me the way you did, or Nick did, I couldn't bear it, I just couldn't."

Sean looked flustered. "I'm sorry, Regan, I didn't mean...I never expected to see you again. And you did look pretty gross. But I got over it. You don't look revolting now. And I told you, Jonathan wouldn't even destroy Veronica, he said he owed her something just because she was a vampire now."

Regan stood silently, looking down at the floor. "I've got to go, Sean. We don't know if Jonathan will be coming back at all, or when, and I'm not just going to sit and wait for him. I only came here at all to see if my car is here."

"So, you're running, is that it? You and Jonathan are both just going to disappear, and leave me here by myself to deal with all the mess?"

Regan blinked. "Of course not. Where would I run to? I just need to go home. I need to clean up, and check my answering machine and e-mail, and get an idea of just how bad things are. I suspect it's even worse than I'm fearing."

Sean spread his hands helplessly. "So...what am I supposed to tell Jonathan?"

"Anything you want. But I wouldn't try to break it gently, Sean. Just tell him. If he still wants to see me, he knows where I live." Regan turned away from Sean's bewildered face and walked rapidly toward the archway. After a moment, Sean caught up with her and walked with her to the front door. Regan paused before she opened it. "I hope my car will start, after a week in that barn. There's probably an APB out for it, so I hope I don't get pulled over. Are you sure you don't want a ride home?"

"By this time, I think I'm just crashing here. Mom's in Fall River."

"What happened to AA? Didn't you say she met her boyfriend there?"

"Yeah, that's what she does in AA, all right, meet boyfriends. In fact, that's where she is now. She claims she's been sober, and I haven't seen her drinking around the house, anyway." He looked gloomily at the floor for a moment, then said resignedly, "Hey, she's trying. She really is. But it seems like she just switched to a different drug, you know?" Regan looked at Sean helplessly for a moment and then, on impulse, put her arms around him and hugged him. "Hey," he said, muffled, but after a moment of stiff embarrassment he suddenly put his arms around her and hugged her back, relaxing enough that it almost felt natural. Then he stepped back, his cheeks a little flushed. "Wow, feel the love in this room," he said, smiling crookedly.

"Good luck, Sean. If you end up stranded out here—I mean, if Jonathan doesn't come back—you can give me a call."

Chapter 20

Her car started up with no problems, possibly stimulated by its change in color. Regan took back roads as much as she could, and got to her apartment without being pulled over by any police. Driving presented some unexpected difficulties—she was now so light-sensitive, oncoming headlights nearly blinded her, while she could have turned her own headlights off and driven in complete comfort. She would have to ask Jonathan if he had any tricks for dealing with this problem. As she parked in her usual space in back of the building, she was aware that the neighbors would probably report her return when they realized her car was there. There wasn't much she could do about that. She didn't want to leave the car anywhere else. If anyone spotted it, it would probably be towed to a crime lab and torn apart in search of fingerprints and blood stains.

She opened the exterior door to the back stairs, with her key. The squeaking treads challenged even her new abilities for walking silently, but she put her toes on the very edges and sides of the boards and was amazed to get up both flights with only three squeaks that would have been audible to anyone inside the house. At the top landing, she hesitated, wondering what she would find inside, since Sean had told her about her apartment being searched. She unlocked the door without using the key, just out of curiosity, to see if she could open deadbolts as well as locks. When she entered the apartment and looked around, she immediately saw that someone had gone through her belongings. But there was not the complete disarray that a full-fledged search would have left, and her computer, intact, was still on her desk in the second bedroom.

The answering machine light was flashing, but she wasn't ready to deal with that yet. She peeled off every stitch of her clothes and tossed them into the fire grate. She took a long shower, grateful that there apparently was no validity to the superstitions about vampires and running water, at least if it was running from above. She lathered herself vigorously at least three times before she felt really clean. When she had dried and found fresh clothing to put on, everything seemed oddly loose, as if she had lost weight. When she worked up the courage to check her reflection in the bedroom's full-length mirror, she found that there was nothing exceptional about her appearance, now that all the dirt and gore had been washed off. She looked thinner, and she was very pale, her skin almost translucent. There were shadows under her eyes that hadn't been there before. But these changes wouldn't be too suspicious in someone who could reasonably claim to have had a stressful week.

She went into the living room and took a bottle of lamp oil off the mantel. She poured a liberal amount onto her bloody clothing in the grate and then burned the clothes to ashes. Then she sat down and pressed the "play" button on the answering machine. Someone—the police, probably—had played some of the messages, so she skipped through the new ones rapidly and then started the whole series of messages from the beginning, mostly not listening to the entire message.

"Regan...this is Enid Wharton. I just got a call about the store not being open today. Where are you? You know I don't like you to close on Saturday..."

"Regan, this is Karen. How come the store's closed? Call me."

"This is Detective Fellman from Sheridan police department. Would Regan Calloway give me a call as soon as..."

"Hi, Regan, Derek—could you give me a call?"

"Regan, this is Enid Wharton. Please call me back as soon as you get this."

"Regan...it's mom. Where are you? Your father and I are very worried, honey, please call me back as soon as..."

"This is Detective Fellman from the Sheridan police department. It's very important that I speak to you..."

"Regan? This is Hiram Clauson. What the hell is going on over there? Why was the store closed on Saturday? Call me as soon as you can."

"Regan, it's mom again..."

"This is Bill Wharton, Miss Calloway. I need to talk to you as soon as possible. My mother was hospitalized last night. Call me immediately on my cell..."

"Regan, this is Karen again. I'm really getting worried about you...do you know the police were searching your store?"

"Hey Regan, it's Steve. You okay? Karen's just about flipping out over here and in one more day, I'll be getting worried myself. Give me a call ASAP, doll."

"Bill Wharton again. Miss Calloway, I'm going to have to make some decisions about the business very soon. If you get this message, call me on my cell immediately, or call my mother's house, I'm staying there through Sunday..."

"This is mom, honey, please pick up the phone if you're there..."

"Regan? This is Derek—holy fuck, what is this shit about Veronica? Is she hiding out there with you? What's going on? Would you please call me?"

Interspersed among the messages, especially the later ones, were many hang-up calls, probably callers who had already left messages trying again to see if she would pick up. Regan sat gloomily staring at the answering machine for a few minutes, then went back and made sure she had Detective Fellman's and Bill Wharton's numbers. She set the answering machine counter to zero, and picked up the phone to dial into the store's voice mail. But when she tapped in the numeric password, she only heard a recorded error message—"we're sorry, the password you have entered is not valid." She tried twice more, in case she had inadvertently entered the wrong code, but the result was the same each time. She hung up the phone, apprehension tightening her stomach. Had she forgotten the code, after four years, and was transposing digits—or had Bill Wharton changed the voice mail?

She got up and went to the second bedroom to check her e-mail on the computer. There was much less than she expected—spam, trade mailing lists, e-mails from her parents and some friends that echoed the phone messages: *where are you, what's going on, please reply!* She didn't reply to any of the messages. She had no idea, at least yet, what to say. She thought about calling Bill Wharton's cell and leaving a message, but it was almost 2:00 a.m. She decided she'd call him later in the morning.

She went back to the living room and sat cross-legged on the couch, staring morosely at the answering machine and thinking about everything that had happened tonight since she first awoke in the cold well trying to remember how she had gotten there. *What am I going to do? What will I say to Bill Wharton? How will I explain the funeral home and Veronica—to the police, to Jerry Standish?* And most troublesome of all, the thought that turned her ice cold with fear—*am I really going to live forever like this?* Right now, she wasn't sure how she was going to get through the coming week.

When the phone rang, Regan was so startled, she knocked two throw pillows onto the floor. She stared at the phone as it rang twice more, afraid to answer it. Phone calls at this hour of the morning were never good news. But then, if she had been seen on the way home, this could be anyone from a neighbor to the police. *Or it could be...*she grabbed the phone and pushed the Talk button before the machine picked up.

"Hello?" Her voice still sounded a little husky, at least to her. Sean had been doing most of the talking earlier. She heard her name spoken, in a tone of absolute disbelief. "Yes, Jonathan, it's me." There was such a long silence on the other end of the line that she finally said, "Are you there?"

"Sean told me...that you'd been here. He said you needed to get home."

"Yes, my clothes had about four pints of blood on them, and I really wanted to change. We were uncertain about your plans for the evening."

There was another silence. "May I...may I come and see you?"

"Right now?"

"Yes."

"Sure. You can let yourself in. Just be quiet on the stairs." To her mild surprise, he hung up the phone without saying another word.

She was still sitting in the same position, lost in thought, when she was interrupted by a tingling awareness. *Jonathan.* She raised her head and listened—yes, he was coming up the stairs, even more silently than she had done, but then, he'd had a few more years of practice. She heard the lock click, and Jonathan opened the door and stood hesitantly in the doorway. "Come on in," she said, trying not to sound as apprehensive as she felt.

Jonathan stepped into the room cautiously, closing the door behind him. He stood there looking at her, his expression a mixture of incredulity and confusion, and Regan had to look away from him. He didn't seem revolted, but on the other hand, he wasn't smiling.

"Please don't stare at me," she said quietly. "Have a seat, if you want."

He came around and sat on one end of the couch—perched, almost, he was so tentative. "I didn't think I'd ever hear your voice again. I'd completely given up hope."

"I can understand why. You didn't feel me waking up because Veronica broke the link, with what she did." Regan was quiet for a moment. "It never crossed my mind that I might be coming back. And I had some time to...think about it." Jonathan made a choked sound. "It wasn't your fault."

"It was. I should never have sent you and Sean by yourselves."

"You didn't have any choice. Someone had to go. I shudder to think what would have happened if she'd been recognized at the funeral home, or someplace in town."

"I don't think anything worse could have happened than what did."

Regan looked down at herself reflectively. "Oh, I don't know...look at the bright side, I may not actually be immortal, but I might live long enough to forgive Sean for painting my car cat crap brown."

Jonathan smiled, a little painfully. "He said he didn't have much selection for the color."

"One more thing that's going to be fun to explain to the police, though. I'm just curious, what did Sean tell you? I hope he didn't try to break it to you gently in some elaborate way."

"No, but I almost wish he had. He just blurted it out. I'd been..." he stopped for a moment, as if debating how much to say. "I'd been sitting out in the woods, where the cave is. I'd checked to make sure Veronica was still there, and then I just stayed there for a long time, wondering whether or not to bring her back to the house with me. I almost did."

"Bring her back to the house? Why?"

After a pause, in which Jonathan didn't look at her, he said, "I was thinking that I might just burn the house and her, after all. Send Sean home, or take him myself, and then..."

"Where would you have gone after that?"

He looked up at her. "After that? I wasn't going to leave the house."

She stared at him. "Oh, my god...you can't be serious."

"I don't believe I could have done it. But that's what I was thinking." After a moment, he went on, "I couldn't make up my mind, so I decided to go back to the house and take Sean home. When I came in, the back door was unlocked, and there was this...smell. It was the smell that Veronica was reeking with that night, that awful stench of dead blood. I panicked, I thought somehow she'd gotten out of the chest and come after Sean. But he said, that's Regan you're smelling, Regan's back. I couldn't believe it, but he said to call you. I'm afraid I didn't give him a chance to tell me much more. He said the two of you had talked for a long time, but I have a lot of questions. What happened after you left the funeral home? I'm still baffled as to why I couldn't find you."

Somewhat reluctantly, because she didn't like thinking about it, Regan told him about Veronica's walking away from the house, the argument in the outbuilding and how it ended, and how she had woken up in the old well. "Don't feel bad that you couldn't find it. I'll show it to you—it's practically invisible from five feet away. And you couldn't have smelled anything at the bottom of it. Cold air sinks, the air at the bottom of that well stays at the bottom of the well. And there was the stone cover, too."

Jonathan shook his head in amazement. "How on earth did she know it was there?"

"Rainbow Stone house may seem isolated, Jonathan, but kids who grow up in this town know those woods. There are a lot of make-out spots out there."

"But why did Veronica keep saying that she'd fixed it so you wouldn't come back?"

Regan shrugged. "She may have assumed that I'd never be able to get out of the well, and it wasn't easy, that's for sure. If she did anything else..." Regan paused, not wanting to even speculate. "If she did something else she thought would prevent me from waking up, I recovered from it. She had no way of knowing what would work and what wouldn't."

"As Sean kept reminding me. And all I did was abuse him for it."

"He's the one who wanted to apprentice with a real vampire. But it did sound like you've been a bit rough with him this week. He's still just a kid, Jonathan."

Jonathan looked down uncomfortably. "This past week..." he was silent for a moment. "I haven't let myself think about the reality of your being gone. I just closed my mind to it, and kept looking for you, because if I admitted that you were never coming back, I'd have to face what I'd done to cause that. But after four or five days..."

"You said yourself it could take seven. And for all you know, it could take longer."

"I know. But I wanted it so badly, and I was so terrified of facing the ultimate disappointment, I convinced myself that there was no hope, and I would just have to be strong and realistic and cope with it. The truth is, I didn't feel strong, I hated the reality and I wasn't coping at all."

She sighed. "I'm sorry, Jonathan. I'm sorry I put you through all this. I'm sure it's been pure hell for you and Sean."

"You don't need to apologize for anything, Regan. None of this can be blamed on you."

She looked up at him sharply. "Of course it can. Look at everything I've done to get to this point. I colluded with you, I lied to Hiram, I lied to Veronica. I knew Veronica was suicidal when she stopped by the store that day, she was dropping hints the size of anvils, and I let her walk away. I deserved what she did to me. If it wasn't for me, she'd still be alive. It was my fault, not yours. That night she went out to your house, I should have locked the store and followed her. No, don't tell me I'm not responsible! I knew what was going to happen. I knew it better than you."

Jonathan was staring at her blankly. "Regan," he finally said, "You're making yourself sound like some kind of...fiend. It's just not so."

"Isn't it? What am I now, Jonathan? Look at me. I'm a walking corpse that attacks children and drinks their blood. Can we get more fiendish than that? Oh, you don't know about that yet, do you?" At his blank look, she said, "I followed some kids, teenagers, in the woods between the farm and the house. It was an unintentional detour on my way back. I have a feeling it won't be reported."

She braced herself for his reaction, but all Jonathan said, very quietly, was, "Do we have...a problem?"

"You mean, do we have a body?"

"That would be a problem, yes."

"No. We shouldn't have any...problems. He'll be fine, and he won't remember anything. He's going to have a pretty ugly injury, though. He kidded to his friends about coyotes getting him, his friends will probably remember him saying that."

"We'll see what happens. But I'm not going to condemn you for that, Regan. My god, how could I? Could you get more fiendish, you ask? Well, yes, most definitely. You could, for example, abduct babies from strollers and leave their bloodless little bodies in ditches. You're not going to do that, are you?"

"God, no!"

"Now, see, a fiend would have said, what a wonderful idea. Regan, don't start wallowing in self-loathing. If you keep it up, you'll never be able to stop. You'll have to accept yourself for what you are now."

Regan had pulled her knees up against her chest, and now she bowed her head down against them. "I'm not wallowing in self-loathing. That's the trouble."

"You think you should be?"

"Yes! Jonathan, I look back at what I did tonight, and I keep telling myself I should feel guilty. But I don't. All I can think of is how good it felt, and how sorry I was that I had to stop. The only reason I didn't drain Nick's blood until he died is...I don't even know why."

"But you did stop. Something pulled you back in time, and you obeyed it."

"But I don't know what that was. It wasn't conscience, it wasn't empathy, it was more like...practicality. It wouldn't have been a sensible thing to do. It wasn't necessary. But that wasn't conscience."

"No," Jonathan said seriously. "You don't have a conscience anymore. That's one of the things that's changed now, Regan. You're fortunate to have perceived that so quickly."

"But, what's going to stop me from just—"

"What you have," he said earnestly, "is a sense of principle. That's what you must always remember, and listen to, because you don't have a conscience. Your conscience has been taken away from you now, because you couldn't survive otherwise. You aren't the same person that you were, Regan, and you're not going to be aware of just how different you are in some ways for a long time. You're capable of doing whatever you have to do to meet your needs now, and you won't even think about it beforehand. We walk a perilous balance between doing what's necessary and doing what's right. When we lose that balance...well, look at what Veronica did to you."

She looked at him silently for a moment, thinking that the scenario he was describing was a rather bleak one. "You know, with all that you've told me and Sean about yourself and vampires in general, you still have never answered my question about how you first discovered what you were. You claim you've never killed anyone. Why won't you talk about it? Did your sense of principle fail you then?"

He looked away from her, down at the floor. "I don't like to talk about it because it was a child. A little boy."

"But you didn't kill him."

He swallowed hard. "It was a very near thing. And I would have, if we hadn't been interrupted. I wouldn't have stopped in time."

"You can't be certain of that, though, can you? How can you know what would have happened?"

He shook his head, his eyes distant. "I can't, of course. But...I had been walking, or hitching rides, for three straight days. I was nearly as out of my mind as Veronica by then. I didn't realize until that moment what I had become. Or more accurately, I knew, but I was in complete and absolute denial about it. It just couldn't be true. The dead don't leave their graves, that was nothing but a puerile superstition. Then I ran into this child...literally, he collided with me..."

After a pause, Regan said, "*You* seem to feel guilty about this. Do you have a conscience?"

He looked back up at her. "No. And that's why I understand how you feel. I was so shaken by what I was capable of doing, I didn't drink from a human again for over a year. But I didn't feel guilty. I was afraid of myself, of what I might do, and the consequences it could have. I hate to think about that child because...like you...I didn't want to stop. Perhaps I would have. But it was a *child*, and I didn't want to." There was a long sober silence.

Finally Jonathan, in an effort to lighten the mood, looked around the room appraisingly. "It's not as bad as I feared it might be, after the searches, unless you've done a lot of picking up."

"I haven't been here that long, and I spent most of that time checking my messages and e-mail for the past week. But no, they didn't toss the whole place, so I guess I'm not a suspect in a crime—at least not yet. They'd been all through here, though—checked the computer, listened to the phone messages, even went through the wastebaskets. I wonder what you usually look for when someone's gone missing?"

"Was there anything for them to find?"

"About you? I've been very discreet. I've deleted all our e-mails immediately, and that's all there really would be. Okay, your fingerprints and DNA might be scattered around, but it's not a secret that you've been up here."

"I didn't really mean that."

"There wouldn't be anything else. I didn't have any life. Work was my life. The store was my life. That's all I had—before you, anyway." She stared at the answering machine for a few moments. "I think...life is about to change," she whispered.

He didn't need to ask what she meant. "I called Bill Wharton on Thursday. After Sean told me that he'd been at the store."

"You did? Why?"

"Well, I thought...I realized that his being inside the store was an ominous sign. I thought I would make an inquiry about buying the business."

"You could do that?"

"I could certainly afford it, although I'd have to do some juggling to free up assets."

"But why? What would you want with the store? What if I'd never come back?"

"I knew how important it was to you. I couldn't let it go without even checking."

Regan stared at him, amazed. "I don't know how I'd ever pay you back," she said, humbled beyond words that he would even consider this.

"Be serious. For the utter mess I've made of your life, buying the store would scarcely begin to pay my debt to you."

Regan leaned back, raking one hand through her damp hair in bewilderment. "So...what did he say?"

"Very little. He was not interested in discussing any transaction. I asked him if he'd made other plans, and he only told me to have you contact him."

"He knew who you were—I mean, that you're involved with me?"

"He seemed to know about it, yes. He was...hostile might be too strong a word, but certainly not very friendly." Regan sighed heavily. "Have you talked to him yet?"

"He left a couple of messages. I'll call him later on this morning." Looking at Jonathan's expression, which had an odd half smile, she said, "What are you thinking about?"

"I'm remembering the first time I saw your store. You wouldn't have thought that was a very auspicious first meeting, would you? Have you ever regretted that you didn't call the police that night and turn me in?"

Regan shook her head, staring into the shadowy room. "I should regret it. Look at all the things that would never have happened if I had. Turning you in would have been the ethical thing to do—if not that night, then later on. But I couldn't." She met his eyes. "I wanted you. From the second I first saw you. I couldn't believe that you would be interested in someone like me—this plain, ordinary, boring workaholic, that's all I am. But I wanted you and I didn't care about anything else. I was willing to forgive you anything, and I still don't know why."

"I'm not sure if that's flattering or not."

"It's not meant to be one way or the other. But it's a lot less flattering to me, that's my point."

Jonathan was watching her, still smiling a little. "You couldn't believe I'd be interested in you. Shall I tell you the truth?"

"Absolutely. Lay it on."

He leaned forward a little. "I wanted you...*before* I even met you. And *I* don't know why." She looked up at him, frankly puzzled, and he went on, "I know you think I came to the store that night just to see how much danger you posed to me, and that was certainly part of it. But that wasn't all, any more than you came out to my house the first time just to ask me a lot of curious questions." He smiled. "Workaholic? What is unappealing about dedication and hard work? You call yourself plain and ordinary, but your appearance isn't disagreeable. We're better off not drawing attention to ourselves."

"And what about now? Now I drink blood and have no conscience. Do you still want me now?"

"Regan, how could you even doubt it, after what I've just said? I'm here, aren't I?"

"But you're sitting way over there," she said softly.

He blinked, then without hurrying, he got up and stepped over to her end of the couch and sat down next to her. Before he could move further, Regan unashamedly straddled his lap, so she could wrap both her arms and her legs around him in one motion, and buried her face into the shoulder of his sweater as he tightly hugged her, and they stayed like that for several minutes without moving or speaking. It seemed to Regan that she had been desperate to touch and hold him, for hours, since she'd first woken up. He didn't want to speak or to let her go, and he put his face down into her hair and breathed in its smell as though it were opium smoke, in long deep inhalations. "Oh, god," he said, after a long time. "It wasn't real before now. I saw you and heard you but it wasn't real."

She pulled back so she could look up at his face. "Not me. You were too real. I couldn't get close to you, it hurt so much. That's why I left the house tonight, I couldn't bear the thought of—" she had to stop because he bent down and kissed her. She pulled herself up so she could return the kiss, hard and probing, going hungrily on and on, because now she didn't need to break off to catch her breath. By the time Jonathan broke the kiss he had pushed her down onto her back on the couch, and was half on top of her, pushing up the sweatshirt she was wearing and kissing the bare skin of her stomach. She hadn't bothered to put on a bra when she got dressed, so he pushed up the shirt further, sucking and nibbling at her breasts as she gasped. All her senses were heightened now, so that what would have merely tickled, or even less, before was now just short of painful, it was so intense. She longed to reciprocate, but she didn't want him to stop.

He straightened up for a moment so he could pull off his sweater and toss it aside, and she took off her sweatshirt, which was now bunched up around her shoulders anyway. He stretched back out so that they could embrace and kiss, skin to skin, but after a minute something struck Regan and she broke off the kiss. "Jonathan...wait... I'm afraid..."

"You're *afraid?*"

"I'm afraid we're going to be interrupted."

"It's three a.m."

She couldn't stop herself from continuously moving her hands over the hard muscle and bone of his back and shoulders as she spoke, which did not enhance her argument. "I've been missing for seven days. If someone reports to the police that my car is back, and lights are on here, they're not going to wait until business hours to check it out."

Jonathan considered this for perhaps two seconds. "If they do, they do. You'll tell them you're fine." He started to kiss her again, but she pushed him back.

"I don't think it would be a good thing for you to be here with me, Jonathan. It would look—"

He reached down and undid her jeans and pulled the zipper open. "I'll hide." He pulled her jeans down off her hips, following the exposed skin with his mouth, and she gave up arguing. The sensations were too intense for her to think, and after she kicked her jeans off onto the floor and he got to work in earnest with fingers and tongue, she had to stuff the corner of a throw pillow into her mouth. If the neighbors didn't know she was back yet, she didn't want to attract their attention by waking them up.

When she could finally spit out the pillow, she hooked her legs around Jonathan's waist and sat back up. Climaxing, she found, was the same and yet different than it used to be—just as intense, and yet somehow less purely physical, more like a burst of energy that left her enlivened and restless rather than relaxed. He wanted to just dive into her now, she could tell, but she was interested in something else first. Her preference had some clout backing it up—she was almost as strong as he was, and he no longer had to carefully modulate himself to make sure he didn't hurt her. She pushed him onto his back—not that he was resisting—and pulled his pants the rest of the way off his legs. She stretched out over him on all fours, leisurely tickling his nipples and then his navel with her tongue, as he caught his breath in tight little gasps. He seemed more tense than he had been a moment ago. She trailed her tongue down the long white scar on his abdomen and then, without breaking contact, up the length of his erection to catch the head of it in her mouth. She let go when he half sat up. She looked up and saw him blinking at her, propped on his elbows, as though unsure why he was protesting. But Regan realized what it was.

"What's the matter, are you afraid I'll bite?" she said, smiling wryly. He only shook his head. *I could hurt him now and we both know it,* she thought. *That's something new for him, after all these years...he really has to trust me, now.* The thought made her want to laugh, which she couldn't do with him in her mouth or she actually would bite, without intending it. He relaxed, a little, so she went on carefully enough to signal that she was conscious of her own strength, and after a second he flopped flat with a deep sigh. Regan found that he didn't share her concern about the neighbors overhearing—but at least he was letting himself enjoy it. He tasted different to her than he used to, the way blood now tasted different.

She'd already wondered how sex would feel without all the familiar signals she was used to, sweat and heartbeat and breath. She missed those on one level. But the intensity of both emotion and sensation, and the degree of complete union they could now experience, as if she and Jonathan were not even two separate beings, was entirely novel. And there seemed to be no end to it, she didn't grow weary or bored, and neither did he. She had no idea how long they had been making love there on the couch, by the time they finally stopped. Some of the time they hadn't been moving, but had simply been still, intertwined and interpenetrated, sharing energy and consciousness in a way that she couldn't analyze and couldn't have described. The early morning chorus of birds was well underway outside the drawn shades of the windows by the time they were finally satiated, at least for now. Regan realized that she was feeling sleepy, but she couldn't look forward to any long rest. In just a few hours, she would need to call Bill Wharton, and be prepared for whatever came after.

Slowly and reluctantly, they untangled limbs and hunted around for the clothing that had been tossed in various directions. "I really had better leave," Jonathan said regretfully. "I wouldn't want one of your neighbors to see me, at least not this morning."

"You didn't leave your car parked next to mine, did you?"

He laughed. "It's down the road a ways." His smile faded then. "If you want, I could come with you when you talk with Bill Wharton."

"Thanks. But I'm afraid that wouldn't do anything to improve my situation. I'll let you know what happens."

Chapter 21

At 9:00 a.m., Regan was waiting outside the store, as she had agreed to do in a brief and terse phone conversation with Bill Wharton an hour before. She was dressed in the nicest clothes she had in her closet that still fit her without bagging, gray wool slacks and a matching blazer, over a silk knit sweater that cost new some twenty times what she'd paid for it at a thrift store. She felt a dismal sense of finality in dressing so well, like she had put on her best outfit for her own funeral. She sat in her car and stared morosely at the store, the CLOSED sign turned over on the front door. There was nothing to indicate that Borrowed and Blue was about to become history. She had tried her keys in both doors, just to check, and found that as she expected, the locks had been changed. Of course, she could have gone inside anyway, but she wouldn't have wanted Bill Wharton to find her there, and besides, what would have been the point?

At 9:10, Bill Wharton's Lexus pulled into the parking lot, even its tires crunching the gravel managing to sound impatient. Regan got out of her car, fidgeting with her sunglasses, which still left her eyes dazzled by the bright May sun. Bill Wharton got out of his car, thumping the door shut, and walked around to the front steps. He did not offer to shake hands. Regan had only met him once, several years ago, and had learned then that he did not like her. His opinion of her had apparently not improved.

"Miss Calloway. Thank you for being punctual."

There was an awkward pause, and Regan finally said, "Can we go inside, or did you just want to discuss this standing out here in the parking lot?" Sitting at the little resin table seemed out of character for Bill Wharton, who was wearing a three-piece suit and an Italian silk tie. Besides, the sunlight was hurting her eyes and making it hard to think clearly.

He paused, as if reluctant to let her inside the building, then nodded curtly and took a set of shiny new keys from his pocket. He unlocked the front door, and Regan followed him inside. She could feel a lump forming in her throat at the familiar aisles of merchandize, but at the same time, with a slight shock, she saw the store's interior with different eyes. It wasn't her new state of being, but the effect of being away for over a week, that lent her this fresh perspective. Suddenly, she was startled by how tired, how mundane, how shopworn everything seemed to look. As she followed Bill Wharton back to the office, she felt a sense of shame at the chipped linoleum, threadbare carpets and decades-old shelving, as clean as everything was. *Is this all he saw when he came here?*

When they reached the office, Regan saw the first serious signs of change. The computer was in its usual place, but the file cabinets had been emptied into stacks of storage boxes, and there was a pile of file folders and some new printouts on the desk. Bill Wharton sat in the office chair, looking proprietary and uncomfortable at the same time, and waved Regan to the straight-backed chair by the desk. She sat, slowly.

"I'm sure that neither one of us wants to prolong this conversation any more than necessary. I'll be blunt, Miss Calloway. I'm closing the store for good."

Regan licked her lips, wondering what she could trust herself to say. "Well, I...I had gathered that. Could you explain why?"

"Explain why?" He sounded as though it was an absurd question.

"Mr. Wharton, you're firing me, basically—without even giving me notice. I think I deserve *some* rationale. I've been managing this business for seven years."

"Um," he said. He studied her with a skeptical look for a moment, then said, "Miss Calloway—please take off your sunglasses."

"Oh—" she had forgotten she was wearing them, since she could see perfectly. She took the sunglasses off, blinking. Even the light in the office was too bright. But her eyes adjusted, more or less, and when she looked back up at Bill Wharton, she didn't like the expression on his face.

"You don't look well," he said, making it a criticism, not an expression of sympathy.

"I'm...I've had a rough week."

"I'm sorry to hear that." He swung the chair around to scowl at the computer screen for a moment, then turned back. "I've had a rather rough week, too, Miss Calloway. You knew that my mother was hospitalized on Tuesday."

"Yes, I did hear that, and I'm very sorry. How is she?"

"She's not doing well. She was very distressed by your unexplained absence. This store is extremely important to her, and she relied upon you to keep it running for her."

Incredulous, Regan said, "Are you saying that I'm responsible for your mother's health crisis?"

Bill Wharton opened his mouth, then closed it, and Regan sensed that only some inner sense of fairness prevented his saying *yes*. "My mother is very ill, and she doesn't take proper care of herself, as I'm sure you were aware. Stressing over this business hasn't made things any easier for her, however. Your absence certainly was a contributing factor."

"I'm...sorry, Mr. Wharton. I wouldn't have done anything deliberately to upset your mother that badly."

He stared at her for a moment. "Miss Calloway—this is all moot now, but I feel I have some right to ask this—where the hell have you been for the past week?"

There was a long pause. Regan tried to think of something to say that wouldn't completely destroy her chances of salvaging something from the past seven years of her life. "I—I had a personal emergency come up, very suddenly," she finally said. "It was—an extraordinary situation, I wasn't in control of what was going on. Surely you must believe," her voice became urgent, "that after seven years of running this place alone, that I would never just blow it off and disappear on some kind of binge! Mr. Wharton, don't you *assume* that only something serious would have kept me away? Doesn't your mother assume that?"

"What happened?"

Regan swallowed, hard. "I can't discuss it, I'm sorry. It would violate the confidentiality of other people."

"I see." His tone conveyed what those words usually did. "You are aware that there are some quite astonishing rumors circulating."

"I've...heard a little about that. I just got back, I'm still catching up."

"You can't tell me anything about what you've been doing and why you've been away for seven days with no explanation?"

"I'm sorry, I...I just can't. As you said, it's a moot point."

"You were so out of control that you couldn't use a phone?"

Regan spread her hands helplessly.

"At least you're not fishing around for some excuse. Because quite frankly, after pulling a stunt like this, the only excuse I'd accept is that you were in a coma or dead."

For an awful moment, Regan thought she was going to start laughing, not that anything was funny. "You do know that I was officially a missing person, don't you?"

"Meaning what, Miss Calloway? My mother was the one who reported you missing."

Regan sighed. "Okay. All I can do is say that I'm sorry."

"That's the least you can say. But your disappearing act isn't the main reason that I'm closing this place down. I'm taking my mother back to Atlanta with me. She'll be in a facility where I can supervise her care. I'm afraid that she can't live on her own any longer. I'll be selling the house. Overseeing the operation of this business from a thousand miles away simply isn't feasible for me. Neither of my sisters is in a position to take it over, nor are they interested. We've mutually agreed to liquidate the store."

Regan hesitated, unsure whether she should speak for Jonathan or not. From what he'd said last night, however, she guessed that he wouldn't mind. "Mr. Wharton—there is someone who would be willing to buy out this store, if you're willing to sell."

"Are you talking about Jonathan Vaughn?"

"He told me that he spoke to you."

"Yes, he did. While you were still...missing." Bill Wharton looked at Regan with such a calculating expression that she wondered if he suspected her and Jonathan of plotting her entire disappearance just to maneuver him into selling the store. "Actually, I already had closed a deal by phone when he called me. There's a large-scale dealer out in Ohio who's been interested in buying the store for several years now. I wanted to settle the sale quickly, so I called him and made him an offer that he found very reasonable."

So much for getting a small business loan, I guess... there was only one thing left to ask. "May I request one small favor?"

"And that would be?"

"Could I at least have a letter of reference from you, so I can start job-hunting?"

He leaned back in the chair, studying her. "No, Miss Calloway. I can't do that."

"But—Mr. Wharton. I've been running this store for seven years—seven years! I never had a vacation, I never took days off, except on work-related business, I kept this place running and in the black through the dot-com crash, through the mill layoffs, I ran the whole thing entirely on my own! Don't I deserve *something* for that? I'm not asking for medals, but a letter, one piece of paper, that's all!"

His expression did not change. "I didn't want to get into this. But you're forcing me to be brutally honest. Miss Calloway, I've wanted to close this store for the past four years. My mother wouldn't hear of it. But it's been nothing but a white elephant—for her, for me, for all of us."

"What—what are you saying? Are you saying you don't think I did a good job?"

"Miss Calloway, you've barely managed to keep the doors open. You never took vacations or days off, you say—whose fault is that? My parents ran this business for twenty years. They supported themselves, raised three of us, put us through college and yes, we took a family vacation once per year. You couldn't even manage to hire a part-time assistant so you could have a free day now and then."

"I did just take on an assistant—"

"That high school kid? You must have been paying him under the table, because there's nothing on the books."

Flustered, Regan said, "I was paying him out of my own pocket, until things picked up a little, with him helping I could bring in more stock..."

"Miss Calloway, you barely paid yourself survival wages. And your profits hadn't increased for the last two years."

"Times have been hard, Mr. Wharton, there's been the war, the economy, people don't have the same discretionary income, especially around here—"

"Times were about to get even harder. Not only are fuel prices going up, the building owner is planning to raise the rent thirty percent."

"Thirty percent! For this dumpy little—" she broke off.

"Exactly." He rubbed at his eyes, as though he was tired. "Miss Calloway, I might feel differently—*might*—if you had displayed any real initiative or business acumen as a manager. You could have expanded your merchandise, gone into e-marketing, tried out mail order, done a lot of things that would have involved low overhead but could have boosted the store's profits. Instead, you just let the place ramble into obsolescence, while you amused yourself going to auctions and flea markets and pretending you were a businesswoman."

Regan knew her open mouthed stare wasn't making a good impression, but she was too aghast at his words to think. "How can you...I didn't have the authority to...to make those kinds of changes. I thought about them, I wanted to do a lot of things, but I wasn't the store owner. Your mother didn't want me to change things."

"But you did make some changes. Those lines of crafts you brought in did very well. You should have learned by now that the way to get around my mother, Miss Calloway, is to go ahead and do it and show her the successful results. She'd always have said no when presented with a proposal—that's her way. If you really had what it takes to run a business, you'd know that."

Regan sat in stunned silence. That he was closing the store, she knew; that he would be angry with her for being out of touch for a week, she had expected. But to be told that for seven years, she had been an incompetent business manager and her bosses had never once let on, left her numb with shock. She would have been in tears, except that the hurt was too great for that.

When she didn't speak, Bill Wharton went on, "I'm sorry if it's hard for you to hear this, but I'm doing you a favor. Running a small business is difficult. You don't want to live on the edge of poverty all your life, do you? Get a good job, Miss Calloway—or get married, perhaps." He turned away to straighten up the files on the desktop.

Finally, Regan said, "Getting a good job would be easier with some kind of recommendation letter. How could I tell an prospective employer that I managed this store for so long and couldn't even get a letter from the owners affirming that I was manager and kept the place alive and out of debt?"

He turned back to look at her. "I might agree to that...except for this past week. You won't even attempt to explain what you've been doing. That makes it difficult for me to write a letter of reference, doesn't it? What employer would, under those circumstances?"

Desperately, Regan said, "Mr. Wharton, I feel you're being very unfair. I simply *can't* explain what happened—at least not now. I may be able to, later on."

"Fine. Let me ask you just one question, then. Just one." Regan nodded tensely. "Would you agree to submit to a drug screening?"

Regan opened her mouth, about to reply with an emphatic yes, but suddenly she stopped. *Drug screening—a blood test? What would they find? Is my blood dead? Do I even have blood anymore?* Her sudden confusion was mirrored on her face, and when she looked up at Bill Wharton, he had raised his eyebrows in an unsurprised way.

"That's what I thought," he said quietly.

"Mr. Wharton, you're assuming something that isn't—I don't even drink very often, let alone—"

"Let's not argue about it any more, Miss Calloway. Maybe you aren't aware of how you look." He glanced at his watch and sighed. "I really can't take any more time with this, I'm sorry."

"All right. At least allow me some closure. Wouldn't it be easier for you if I shut down the place for you? For god's sake, I know every inch of it, every knick knack—there are crafters to contact, the website needs to be taken down, there are outstanding accounts payable...you wouldn't even have to pay me, Mr. Wharton—"

"Thank you, but my attorney has arranged for someone to take care of that. And you've kept impeccable records, I will grant you that much. In fact, most of that has already been done."

"But, surely—"

"Miss Calloway, please. I couldn't trust you. Now, do you have any personal items here in the store that you would like to take home? You can get them now, if you want them."

Regan looked numbly around the office. *Personal items...? My coffee cup, the calculator in the desk drawer...* "No. Everything in the store...is the property of the store."

"I believe there is some inventory at your home."

"Yes, there's some overflow stored there. When do you want to get it?"

"The movers will be here on Monday morning. Can they stop at your apartment building first?"

Regan sighed deeply. "Yes. It's a walk-up, they better be prepared to carry everything down two narrow flights of stairs."

"I'll let them know that. They'll have a list. Are there any records on your home computer, or in files at your home?"

She closed her eyes for a moment. "Not the computer. I kept back up records at home, in case this place ever went up in flames."

"I'll need those, too."

"I'll put them together for you." She looked at him bleakly. "Is that all?"

"I believe so. I'll call you if I need anything else."

"Then, thank you for your time." She rose, and he did also—not from courtesy, she guessed, but to escort her out the door. "I hope your mother is feeling better soon."

Regan walked out of the front door and stood by her car for a moment. *Am I forgetting something? What am I forgetting?* She searched her mind carefully but could think of nothing. *Should I go home now? What for?* It occurred to her that she understood how Veronica had felt the day that she killed herself—not that Regan felt suicidal. But she looked ahead to the future—not the next year or the next day, but even the next hour—and all she could see was a blank, featureless wall.

The sun was burning down on her head, and the discomfort finally shook her out of her immobility. She started to open the car door, feeling in her pocket for her keys, when a dark blue sedan turned into the parking lot of the store.

It pulled up on the other side of Regan's car from Bill Wharton's Lexus and a tall man stepped out.

"Regan Calloway?"

"Yes..."

"I'm Detective Fellman from Sheridan Police."

"Oh, yes. I've got one of your cards somewhere...I was going to be calling you this morning. I just needed to meet with—" she gestured vaguely at the store behind her. "How did you hear that I was back?"

"From Mr. Wharton. I'm very glad to see that you're alive and well, Ms. Calloway."

Regan had to stop herself, again, from laughing. "You can close my missing persons case now."

"One down, one to go. Are you all right, Ms. Calloway?"

Regan looked away from him, at the big oak tree across the street. "In any sense that I'm not, it's not a police matter."

"You're certain about that."

"Yes."

"Have you notified your parents that you're safe?"

"Yes. I called them first thing. I'm sorry if I've inconvenienced anyone."

"Can you tell me where you've been for the past week?"

She took her sunglasses off to meet his eyes. "I'm sorry, I can't tell you that. It's personal." She saw his brows crease in a frown, and not because of what she'd said. She put the sunglasses back on. "I need to get going. Is there anything else?"

"Don't you need to open the store?"

"Oh, I don't work here any more."

Detective Fellman didn't look surprised. "I'm sorry. Will you be sticking around Sheridan for a few days, Ms. Calloway?"

"I don't have any plans. Are you telling me not to leave town?"

"I'd appreciate it if you wouldn't."

She looked at him silently for a moment. "Well, I need to be here through Monday, at least. I hope they didn't call you in on your day off just to verify that I'm back, Detective."

"I get overtime. Besides, I never mind being called in when a missing woman turns out to be fine. Can I reach you at home, if I need you?"

She considered. "If not, I'll be at Jonathan Vaughn's. I think you know the number."

"Yes, I do. And he definitely knows mine."

"Enjoy your weekend, Detective."

Chapter 22

She went home, after all, and started returning calls. She was exhausted. The short amount of time she'd been out in the full sunlight had left her drained and overheated, as though she'd been walking across a desert for hours. But she knew that word would start to get around about her return, and she wanted to forestall the calls that would start coming in, not to mention the rumors. After an hour on the phone talking to friends, crafters, and long-time customers, Regan felt she could hardly bear to hear, and answer, the same questions one more time. *But where have you been? I can't get into that right now...are you okay? Yes, I'm fine...Is the store really closing? Yes, he's sold it off and it's closing for good... But how can he do that? Well, he owns it...Can't you buy him out? No, it's too late for that...So what are you going to do now? I don't have any idea...* Regan wondered if she should just change the answering machine message. Only the conversation with Derek was significantly different. He didn't give a damn about the store, which by the time she called him, Regan actually found a bit refreshing.

"What is this story that I heard about you being seen leaving the funeral home with Veronica?"

"You tell me, Derek—I just got back. I don't know what stories you might have heard."

"Veronica's mother is going berserk. Jerry Standish is accusing her of working with you and that Vaughn guy to fake Veronica's death, or steal her body, and sue him for a pile of money."

This must not be out in the rumor mill yet, or someone else would have asked about it. "I heard about the lawsuit and about Veronica being missing, from Jonathan. But I don't know much more about it than that. I've been pretty seriously out of the loop for the last week, Derek."

"Yeah, so I heard. Where the hell have you been?"

"I had something come up, okay? A personal crisis, I had to deal with it."

"And Veronica wasn't with you?"

"No, she wasn't—alive or dead. I'm sorry, Derek. I better not say anything else before I talk to the police."

"I'd call a lawyer, if I were you."

"Thanks for the advice."

He's probably right, she thought bleakly when she got off the phone. *Not that I could afford one...but Jonathan would pay for one, I'm sure.* She hated to ask him. *Maybe I'll wait and see if I'm really going to need a lawyer. I don't want to look guilty going in.*

She tried Hiram Clauson's office number but only got his voice mail, and left a short message.

At least Jonathan was kind enough not to ask her how it went. "Would you like me to come over?" he asked after she gave him a very brief summary of her conversations with Bill Wharton and Detective Fellman.

"Thanks, but this is still sinking in. I just have one more call to make, and I'm going to bed for the rest of the day. I just hope the cops don't bother me until sunset."

She called Sean, and told him that she'd met with Bill Wharton.

"So, how'd it go?"

"Well, we're unemployed."

"Aw, *fuck.*"

"My words exactly."

"Can't you do anything about it?"

"No, the business is already sold—to some operation in Ohio. They're coming on Monday morning to pick everything up in a big moving van. I guess it's all going to be liquidated."

"That really bites."

"I know."

"Hey listen," Sean said after a pause. "Did Jonathan go to see you last night? He told me that's where he was going, but..."

"Yes, he did. I think we straightened everything out. Don't worry, Sean, we had a good talk."

"A talk, right. Um-hmm."

"Now you *stop* that."

"And he didn't think you were revolting or anything, right?"

"Smart-ass."

Sean laughed. "Hey, it's the middle of the day, get some sleep already."

"I'm going to. I'll see you tonight."

She hung up the phone feeling a little better. She turned the phone ringer off, and after thinking about it, she did change the answering machine message: "Hi, this is Regan Calloway, I am back, I am fine, I'm away from the phone right now, please leave a message." She went into the bedroom and took off her clothes, carefully hanging up the slacks and blazer, since who knew what she might need for clothing if she was job-hunting. She took off everything else, crawled into bed, and curled up into a ball under the covers. She didn't need to breathe, so she felt very comfortable nested in that way. She had no idea what sleep in this new state would be like, or if it was sleep at all, in any sense she understood. She knew that Jonathan rested in some way, but she had never asked him for details about it. He appeared unconscious, his body cool, limp and still, but she knew he could be very easily roused from his inactive state, whatever it was. As tired as she was, Regan was reluctant to release herself into unconsciousness. How could she be certain she would wake up? But within a few moments, she dropped out of ordinary awareness into a realm of mists and dreams, like the one she'd lingered in before she revived in the well.

Some time later Regan opened her eyes, and took a few moments to recall where she was and why it was so dark. She listened carefully, and could faintly hear domestic sounds of footsteps and voices and a television from below her, and she could smell cooking food. She identified the smell without feeling any attraction to it. Ground beef, she guessed, and something with tomatoes. She stretched out and pulled the covers off her head and sat up, automatically looking at the clock. It was 6:07 p.m., just about two hours before sunset. She felt much better, although somewhat fidgety and restless.

She climbed out of bed and immediately got into the shower. The sensation of water sluicing over her skin was pleasurable, but what she really wanted was the satisfaction of being clean. She realized that she was starting to gain an insight into how clean Jonathan kept his house. There was something about this state of being that created a continuous need for order and revitalizing. She would never have expected that—it went so against the cliché of the cobwebbed and decaying Gothic castle. But thinking about it now, she vaguely recalled reading about some superstition that you could escape supernatural creatures by throwing seeds on the ground, because the creature would have to stop and pick them all up while you got away. *Vampires, the original obsessive compulsives,* she thought wryly. *God, I certainly hope not.*

When she was dressed, she went out to the living room and pressed the answering machine button.

"Regan, this is Hiram Clauson. I'm glad to hear that you're back. I was starting to fear the worst. Would it be possible for you to meet me some time soon? I have some things to discuss that I don't want to talk about on the phone. Give me a call."

As Regan considered this message, frowning a little, the door buzzer sounded. She went over and pushed the intercom button. "Yes?"

"Regan Calloway? Sheridan police."

Now what? "I'll come down."

Twenty minutes later, Regan was ushered into the interrogation room at the Sheridan police station. Sean had told her what he knew about Jonathan's visits there, but since his accounts were second hand, Regan felt nervously under-informed. Detective Fellman was sitting at the metal table looking at a file folder of paperwork. He closed the folder when Regan entered the room.

"Good evening, Ms. Calloway. Please have a seat."

She sat, reluctantly, in one of the chrome frame chairs. "Should I have an attorney present?"

"Well, I don't know. Are you asking for one?" Regan looked at Detective Fellman silently, and he smiled, although he didn't seem amused by anything.

"I can't think of anything I've done wrong. I guess not."

"I just want to ask you a few questions, Ms. Calloway. I've been grappling with quite a mystery for the past week, and I'm hoping you can help me clear a few things up."

"Am I going to be arrested?"

"I hope not."

"Am I what's called a person of interest, then? And for what crime?"

"I'm not really sure if any crime has been committed. That's what I'm trying to determine—one of the things, anyway."

Regan sighed. "So, what are your questions?"

Detective Fellman studied her for a moment. Finally he said, "Ms. Calloway, do you have any information as to the current whereabouts of Veronica Standish?"

Right to the trick question... There was nothing to be gained by playing completely stupid. Too many people had noticed her leaving the funeral home with Veronica. "I haven't seen Veronica since a week ago, Friday."

"And where did you see her at that time?"

Regan wished she'd been able to think about this more carefully. As she had not, it was best to stay as close to the truth as she safely could. "We parted ways on a road near the edge of town. We didn't exactly part on good terms."

"She was in a vehicle?"

"Not when I left her. But I don't know what her plans were."

"Have you heard from her since then? Phone, e-mail, whatever?"

"I have not." She looked down at the pen in Detective Fellman's hand, and her brow creased in puzzlement—he was drawing small, concise circles on his notepad, instead of taking notes. *Is this being recorded? Or is he just waiting for me to say something worth writing down?*

Detective Fellman was looking at his pad also, and his tone was so casual it was almost labored. "When you went to the funeral home on Friday—did you expect to see Miss Standish there?"

"I had made no plans in advance to meet Veronica Standish at the funeral home." She saw him glance up at her sharply, but she had no idea why he was so struck by her answer.

Detective Fellman straightened up in his chair. "Ms. Calloway, weren't you a little surprised to see Miss Standish apparently alive and well?"

"I certainly was."

"As far as you knew, she was dead."

"Yes, but all I knew was what I heard, and what I heard was passed on third hand, at best. Veronica's family wasn't speaking to me. Veronica herself didn't even get in touch with me until three days after she got out of the hospital, and I had no contact with her while she was there. She stopped by the store for about twenty minutes the day she died—supposedly died, I mean—and did not mention her plans to me then, or I certainly would have done something."

"But you did do something."

"I called her father, yes, because Veronica's mood and some of the statements she made disturbed me...and my assistant, who was there at the time. Mr. Standish told me that Veronica was getting professional help and that was the end of it."

Detective Fellman had stopped doodling and put his pen down. "What were some of these statements that concerned you?"

"She didn't mention suicide, or talk about her medications, or anything blatant like that. She just kept saying that she'd come to some decisions, and everything would be fine, and she wouldn't need my help anymore because she was going to be leaving Sheridan."

Detective Fellman looked down, back at his pad with its chain of little black circles. "Did you believe that Miss Standish was dead?"

"Of course I did, how could I not? There were EMT's and doctors and funeral directors involved, how could that kind of mistake happen in the United States in this day and age?"

"Oh, all kinds of mistakes can happen. So, you went to the funeral home that evening to attend Letty Brownmiller's wake?"

"Yes, I did. She was one of my oldest customers."

"How did you learn about Mrs. Brownmiller's death?"

Regan sensed a trap. Some families didn't place obituaries in the papers. "One of my other customers told me about it. I didn't know she was ill."

Detective Fellman nodded. "What did you think when you saw Miss Standish at the wake?"

"I just about fainted from shock. I didn't know what to think."

"Why didn't you call her presence to the attention of the funeral home staff?"

"I was too stunned. I didn't want to create a disruption at the wake. I took Veronica's hand and led her outside, so I could ask what was going on."

"And did she tell you what was going on?"

"She was very uncommunicative."

"Why didn't you take her to the emergency room immediately to be checked out?"

"Veronica hated hospitals. She didn't want to go."

"So she was communicating well enough to indicate that."

"She was communicating very clearly indeed by the time we parted. Very clearly." Regan could feel herself grimacing at the memory, and tried to smooth her expression, but she could see that Detective Fellman had noticed. He was watching her so intently, he couldn't miss the slightest change in her face.

"You said that she didn't tell you anything about her plans, when she left you."

"Nothing. She seemed very...purposeful. She seemed to have something in mind. She got out of my car and just went walking off. I tried to...to ask her some questions, but..." Regan had to blink, because the memory of Veronica spinning around and throwing her hand off was suddenly so clear, the room around her had momentarily vanished. She realized that she had raised her hand, the one Veronica flung off, from the table top and uncomfortably put it back down. She looked up and saw Detective Fellman leaning back, his expression calculating.

There was a pause, and then he said, "Did she hurt you, Ms. Calloway?"

Regan was completely unprepared for Detective Fellman to take this tack, and for a long moment, she hesitated, not knowing what to say. "In what sense do you mean that?" she finally asked weakly.

"Did Miss Standish have something to do with your being missing for a week?"

Regan looked down, struggling to come up with some reply that wouldn't be exposed later for the lie it was. As the pause lengthened, she could think of nothing to do but evade the question. "I'm not prepared to discuss that, Detective."

He relaxed his intense look a little. "I'm just wondering if you're the one who should be pressing charges, that's all." Regan was silent, and he went on, "If Veronica Standish is responsible for your having been missing—it seems that you're suffering some serious consequences as a result."

Finally Regan said, "This is strictly between me and Veronica, Detective Fellman. It doesn't concern anyone else, and I don't want to get into it."

His eyes narrowed a bit. "That's quite a nasty scar you have."

Startled by the change in subject, Regan touched the scar on her neck before she could stop herself. "So? It's very old, isn't that obvious?"

Detective Fellman flipped open the file folder on the table and unhurriedly paged through the contents. He picked up a photograph and looked at it studiously. "You didn't have it—" he flipped the photograph over to read the back "—three months ago." He skimmed the photo over to her. Regan picked it up, her heart sinking. It was a snapshot of herself, taken at her last birthday in February. Her parents must have sent it to the police when she was reported missing.

"Is it a crime to have a scar?" she said, pushing the photo back across the table.

"It's for you to say if there's been a crime, Ms. Calloway. I'm in the dark here."

"Well, I'm not saying."

Detective Fellman shrugged. "Okay," he said, smiling a little. He replaced the photo and closed the folder. "Do you know a woman named Anita Westfield?"

Regan thought but could not place the name, although Anita seemed familiar for some reason. "I'm not sure," she said after a moment. "Should I?"

"Her maiden name was Copeland."

Copeland...Copeland...where have I heard that... Then Regan remembered. *Veronica Copeland Standish.* "That's Veronica's mother, isn't it? I'd forgotten what her new name was."

"Former wife of Jerry Standish. Are you ever in contact with Mrs. Westfield?"

"God, no. I barely knew her when she was married to Jerry Standish. I haven't seen her or spoken with her for over ten years. Even Veronica hardly ever heard from her, and she never talked about her."

"And you haven't had any communication with Mrs. Westfield lately."

Regan shook her head. "Look," she said impatiently, "I heard the dirt on this one. Jerry Standish thinks that I'm conniving in this lawsuit his ex- has filed—me and Jonathan Vaughn. But it's total bullshit. Any lawsuits that Jerry Standish's ex- has filed, she's on her own. I wouldn't stoop to that kind of crap. And if you think that I've been in touch with Anita Westfield by phone or e-mail, feel free to check my phone records and my computer, any time."

Detective Fellman smiled wryly. "As a matter of fact, we checked both of them, as part of the routine investigation into your being missing. But we can't reveal what we found to the parties in the Westfield lawsuit without a court order from them."

"Is Jerry Standish trying to get one?"

"I believe he is. Just for your information."

Regan slumped back in her chair with a heavy sigh. "I guess I better back up my computer before it's impounded."

"You might want to do that." Detective Fellman considered for a moment, then said, "I believe that's all the questions I have right now, Ms. Calloway. Thank you for your cooperation."

"I'm sorry I couldn't be more helpful," Regan said as she rose gratefully from the uncomfortably hard-edged chair.

"So am I. Do you have any way at all to get in touch with Veronica Standish?"

"I have no idea, but I could try putting out some feelers and see. She was very upset with me, she might not respond even if she got a message."

"If she'd be willing to contact me, it could be very helpful."

"I'll see what I can do."

"Would you like an officer to take you home?"

Regan thought for a moment. She lived a couple of miles from the police station, but she had a feeling that she shouldn't go back home just yet. "Thanks. But I think I'll walk."

Chapter 23

Regan walked north on the broad sidewalk of Main Street, as she had on countless days in the past, in thick summer heat or through misty rain or picking her way around patches of snow and ice with her breath smoking in the winter air. It was nearly 7:30 and the sun was low in the southwest sky, shining long beams through high clouds. *I should be closing out the register now,* she thought. It was still difficult to accept that she would never again unlock the glass paned door of Borrowed and Blue and shove it open with one hand, bells jangling, juggling her lunch pail and a package in her other arm. There had been a lot of changes in the business district of Sheridan in the past seven years, but Borrowed and Blue had been one constant in town. Once a customer—it might have been Letty Brownmiller, now that she thought about it—had remarked that the store would be there long after the town itself was gone. *Well, it was certainly a nice thought.* She paused on the corner of Mill Street, her nose filling with the warm aromas of C & J Pizza. The molded plastic tables and chairs inside the pizza parlor were empty—most of their evening business was take-out. There weren't many people on the street. On Saturday nights, those residents of Sheridan who didn't want to stay home headed to the mall or Providence or Fall River.

She realized she had stood for almost a minute on the curb, lost in memories. She gave her head a shake and strode across the street and on up Main. After she'd walked two more blocks, her attention was caught by a long glossy car parked on the opposite side of Main Street just ahead. She slowed, because the dove gray car was very familiar, its premium low-numbered license plate reading "1852." 1852 was the date that the Standish Mills had been founded. The three-story brownstone building that dominated this side of the block had been built at about the same time—called the Atheneum, it was a private club and restaurant catering to business owners and entrepreneurs. It was luxurious in an understated and Anglophile way, with hand-turned woodwork and polished walnut paneling. It sometimes rented out its function rooms, but membership was still restricted to white Protestants, or so Regan had heard. She knew that Jerry Standish often ate dinner here after he'd been working late, but it seemed odd that his car would not be parked in the gated lot in back of the building. She stepped into the shadowed doorway of the storefront on the corner, which had been vacant since the little pharmacy that occupied it went out of business. She wasn't sure what she was hiding from, or why she didn't simply go on walking. But an inarticulate twinge in the back of her consciousness prompted her to wait.

After a few minutes, without surprise, she saw a familiar figure walking quickly down her side of the street. Although he was still a fair distance away, she recognized the short beard, round glasses and stooped shoulders, clad in a rust brown corduroy jacket. She drew back as the walker slowed and turned to mount the high steps of the Atheneum. Watching him, Regan felt a prickling apprehension run through her body. *What is Hiram Clauson talking to Jerry Standish about?*

She couldn't closely scrutinize the building in broad daylight without being noticed. The Atheneum had a doorman inside the front entrance and a parking valet at the gate to the back lot, and the building would be full of people—a kitchen crew and wait staff, to begin with. Regan turned the corner and walked down narrow Mystic Street, until she reached Elm, the street that paralleled Main and ran behind the Atheneum's parking lot. She walked casually along Elm until she reached an access door in the back of the brick wall of the lot. She put her hand on the door knob and concentrated, feeling the lock tumblers shift and click, noisily, and then she opened the door and stepped into the lot. It was almost full, so there must be some function going on. She scanned the lighted windows of the building. It looked like the main activity was in the second floor dining hall, but the restaurant and private rooms downstairs would probably be busy, on a Saturday evening. *Where's Sean and his electronics when I really need them?* she thought wryly. *Guess I have to do my spying the old-fashioned way...* Taking a quick glance around and seeing no one looking, she crossed the parking lot and trotted past the dumpster and down concrete steps into a narrow well with a door into the basement at the bottom of it. She grasped the door handle, and felt the lock shifting—it was stiff, and for a moment she thought it would hold. Then there was a chunking sound, which she hoped no one heard, and she pulled the door open and slipped inside.

She paused in the dark hallway, listening to the bustle from the kitchen up ahead. Any moment, a chef's assistant or bus boy might come down the hall, so she couldn't linger. There was an entrance to another hallway on the right about twenty feet away, and after a moment she ran for it and ducked around the corner. She pressed herself against one wall, amazed at how calm she felt. Emotionally, she was panicked that she might get caught and aghast at her own audacity, but without the pounding heart, rapid breath and sweating hands that used to accompany fear, the emotion seemed unreal and unimportant. She could focus without distraction on what to do next. She raised her nose and sniffed at the air. It was so rich with scents that she was nearly overwhelmed when she took in a breath, which she now only needed to do voluntarily. Cooking food from the kitchen, garbage, natural gas and hot metal from the stoves and ranges, the odors of the kitchen staff's bodies, cleaning chemicals, dish detergent, a whiff of pungent deodorizer block from the lavatory, dust and decaying plaster. She breathed in deeply. It was almost summer, so this smell would be hard to detect, but in an old building like this one...there it was. Heating oil from the furnace. She went on down the hall, sniffing and following the smell. The hallway made a left turn and then a right, and then a pair of double doors, unlocked with one partly ajar, opened into the furnace room.

She pulled the door closed behind her and stood in the dark room, illuminated only by a glowing red EXIT sign, studying the massive metal burner with its pipes extending up through the ceiling at various angles. The biggest ones, going almost straight up, would lead to the second and third floors. She was interested in the smaller, outer pipes that fed heat to the main dining room and private rooms on the first floor. It had been a warm day, so the burner and the pipes were cool and quiet. She walked over and pressed her ear against the nearest pipe, and listened. Sound, conducted from the heating ducts down the echoing, air filled pipes, was tinny and faint, but by focusing tightly, she could pick out voices. Whether Jerry Standish and his guest were close enough to a vent for their voices to be heard, she didn't know. She caught a man's voice and pressed her ear harder to the gritty sheet metal surface. Phrases faded in and out as the speakers' tone and volume changed.

"...nice little place out past the point there, ever been to Ogunquit? We put in a...forty feet out into the...then that storm two years back..." Regan tried another pipe. "...could be a sweet deal, if the prime doesn't go up...too far out from the highway, anyway. Talk to Jack in the Assessor's office, he knows..." She switched again. This time, she was startled to hear voices she recognized.

"He's offering a very good price, Derek. I don't know why you're trying to monkey-wrench...land won't perc and it'd cost a fortune to sewer. The owner wants to close on it, he's sick of...taxes, especially with the reval..."

"...should think hard about this, dad. With that litigation coming up, Vaughn's assets will...you'll be left holding the bag, and then...could be criminal charges, too."

"...how you know so much about this, Derek. Keep your nose out of...won't help us or...girlfriend. You..."

"I've got...inside information, trust me." Regan pressed her ear so hard to the pipe, the metal suddenly dented inward with a thump, and she jerked back, startled. *Ron Wilson, and Derek—they're talking about Jonathan and the house,* she thought. She put her ear back to the pipe, but could pick up nothing more that was distinguishable. She heard footsteps coming up the hallway outside, and ducked behind the pipes. The footsteps went by without slowing. She went around to the back of the furnace, squeezing in next to the wall, and tried another pipe. Hearing only a mixed buzz of sound, she went to the next. *Bingo.*

"I've got a hell of a lot invested in this, Jerry. My career's on the line at this point—he's got the college trustees asking questions about what I've been doing, setting himself up like some kind of victim. Don't underestimate him." Hiram Clauson's voice, tuned to lecture halls, transmitted clearly. Jerry Standish, gravel-voiced at best, tended to drop off into an indistinguishable rumble.

"...*don't* underestimate him...your own damned fault...stupid enough to use your office resources for private business...I'd have fired you, myself...thinking straight, Clauson."

"I was working on my own time, and it's nobody else's business. They should thank me—they will, when all this comes out."

"...sounds crazy, you know that...put any stock into this vampire bullshit. I never said that."

"I'm not asking you to take it literally."

"You seem to...pretty literally."

"I'm a scientist, I'm keeping an open mind. I've done work with psychotic criminals, Jerry, I know what kind of fantasies they can be prone to. Whether it's literally true or a delusion system doesn't matter—people are being hurt, and that's the point. Your own daughter—"

"I never saw any evidence of that, Clauson."

"There's an emergency room nurse who will testify that Veronica had the same injury as another victim she treated. She'll testify to it in court if you can get Veronica's medical records released."

"But I never saw it."

"Why are you resisting this? You sound like you're on Vaughn's side."

"Hell, no. But Veronica left a letter that gives him a clear alibi for some of those cases you're chasing. Either he's not the only one, or she's lying. And if she's lying..." Jerry Standish's voice had risen considerably.

"If she's lying, that hurts your case. We seem to be working at cross-purposes here. What's more important, getting a predator off the streets or winning a lawsuit?"

There was a silence, and Regan pressed her ear harder to the pipe, mindful of dents, but fearing that Jerry Standish might have left in a huff. Finally she heard, just barely, "No one wants to nail this son of a bitch more than I do, Clauson. But we've got to play our cards carefully. He's a slippery bastard, and he's smart—I'll give him that. We'd have nailed him weeks ago if he was your everyday piece of street scum. Look at the way he's gotten to exactly the people who can hurt us—my ex-, my daughter, that Calloway bitch..."

What can I do to hurt either one of them? Regan thought, startled. The voices were clearer now—it sounded as though the two men, mindful of being overheard, had moved closer to the wall and the heating vent.

"I know why he's after me. I just can't figure out what he's got against you, Jerry. There's not a particle of hard evidence that he's connected to your ex-wife at all, or this lawsuit she's filed."

"He's got to have something to do with Veronica being missing. Calloway does, and he's involved with her. Hell, it's obvious what's going on. There's got to be a way to prove it."

"Did your lawyer get the police to release the information from Regan Calloway's phone and computer records?"

"He's filed. The judge has to rule on it."

"I don't think there's going to be anything there, Jerry." Hiram Clauson's voice sounded thoughtful.

"Have you found anything more on the background checks?"

"Not a thing. I got a copy of his birth certificate, and some school transcripts. Everything else is unavailable."

"Are the documents legitimate?"

"They seem to be. I don't believe it, though. I don't have the wherewithal to fly out west and interview members of his purported graduating class to see if he was really a student there. That's the level we're at now—unless we hire an investigator."

There was another silence. "Two months ago, I'd have done it," Jerry Standish said finally. "But with the pending litigation...these lousy drinks are going on a tab."

Maybe we don't have to worry about electronic surveillance and night-vision technology, after all, Regan thought. *Jerry Standish's assets have been frozen! Thank you, Anita!* On the other hand, she could imagine few things more dangerous than a man like Jerry Standish with nothing left to lose and his honor to prove.

"I think...we have to make some kind of move," Hiram Clauson said slowly.

"What do you mean?"

"I mean—something to put pressure on Vaughn, force him to take some kind of action that will leave him vulnerable."

"That could backfire, Clauson."

"I don't think so. I think we have a potential advantage that Vaughn hasn't had to deal with before."

"You mean Calloway?" Jerry Standish's tone was heavily skeptical. "Don't be so sentimental, Clauson—a man like that uses women like toilet paper. Look what he did to Veronica."

"I'm wouldn't be so sure, Jerry. Let's think about it. Right now, we're out of options. Vaughn hasn't made any mistakes so far. Unless we find some way to throw him off balance, he's not likely to."

Regan listened eagerly for the reply, but this time the silence remained unbroken. Finally she drew back from the pipe, disappointed. The two conspirators must have moved away from the vent—whether they'd left the Atheneum entirely, or just moved to another spot, the remainder of their conversation was out of her reach. Still, she had a lot to think about, and to tell Jonathan. *So Hiram wants to use me to get to Jonathan? Great. What's he going to do? Plant something on my computer? Have me arrested?* She would have to stay alert when she talked to him. *I wonder where Hiram thinks I've been for the past week? I better return his call when I get home.* But right now, she needed to get out of the Atheneum basement without being caught. It was only sunset now and the Atheneum was nearly in the center of town. Crawling out of one of the basement windows would look suspicious, even if they hadn't been covered with steel grates.

She went to the furnace room door and cracked it open an inch or so, and listened carefully. She could hear nothing in the hallway, so she left the room and walked cautiously down the hall the way she'd come. At the corner she stopped and listened; hearing no sounds except distant kitchen clatter, she turned the corner and went on. The next turn was similarly empty, but this was the stretch of hall that she'd ducked into from the entranceway. Up ahead was that junction, and the kitchen sounds and smells were much stronger. There were several doors opening off this hall, and the scuffs on the polished linoleum floor and the wear around the door knobs indicated that these were storage rooms used frequently by the staff. Regan paused. All she had to do was get to the entranceway and out the exterior door. Should she just make a dash for it? Even if she was spotted, she would be gone before anyone got a good look. But as she hesitated, she suddenly heard a young man's voice calling, "Yeah, I'll get it!" It sounded like he'd just left the kitchen and was coming down the entrance hall. She saw his shadow on the floor up ahead, and she opened the door next to her and ducked into the room an instant before he turned into the hall.

Regan pressed against the wall by the door. The young man was wearing sneakers, but she could hear the hard rubber soles making soft noises against the linoleum. Then, to her horror, the door knob started to turn. She grabbed the knob and held it as tightly as she could, which was far more tightly than he could force against. She felt him struggling with the knob. "What the fuck..?" he said, and tried to rattle the door. After a few moments, he gave up, muttering under his breath. The door didn't even have a simple button lock, so he must have been baffled. Regan listened as he retreated back toward the kitchen, then opened the next door down and went inside that room. She turned to follow the sound of his footsteps, and saw the door connecting the two rooms at exactly the same moment that the young man opened it and switched on the light. Dazzled, Regan blinked back at him as he stared blankly at her. She didn't recognize him—he was around twenty and gangly, brown hair under a white baseball cap, swathed in a commercial white kitchen apron. He still suffered from quite a nasty case of acne.

"Who the hell are you? You're not supposed to be in here. Were you—" he glanced rapidly between her and the door, and his voice rose a little in mingled disbelief and anger. "Were you holding that door shut? What the fuck do you think you're doing?"

She could open the door and run, but he had gotten a clear look at her now. "I'm...I'm sorry, I was just...look, I was just trying to play a stupid joke on someone. I didn't mean any harm, honest. I'm really sorry, I thought you were someone else..."

Her humble attitude disarmed the young man at least somewhat. He quickly glanced behind him, and his voice softened a little. "Yeah, well, no one's supposed to be down here but staff."

"I know. I messed up. Don't give me away, okay? I'll just get out of here so I can feel like an idiot in peace. I don't know what I was thinking. I'm really, really sorry. This was a totally stupid idea."

Watching her closely, the young man stepped into the store room, which Regan now saw was lined with heavy utility shelves filled with sealed cases and buckets of kitchen staples, and took a cardboard carton of canned tomato paste from a shelf. "Come on," he said. He stepped back, somewhat nervously, as Regan walked past him into the next storeroom. He switched off the light and closed the connecting door, waving her toward the hallway. "I should report this to the manager," he said dubiously. "My ass is fried if anyone finds out I just let you out of here."

"Well, *I* sure won't tell." She stopped at the hall door, blocking his way.

"Yeah, well, look, lady," he began and then he frowned, hefting the carton under his arm. "Hey, don't I know you?"

Oh, shit... "I don't think so. I don't know you." She was sure she'd never seen him in the store.

He bent forward, squinting at her, as though she was an illegible traffic sign. "Yeah! You're the lady who runs that store—the one who's been missing! Jesus—have you been down here all this time?"

"Don't be silly, what would I have been doing down here?"

"Did you hide that body down here?" His heart rate had doubled—Regan could hear it, and the pungent smell of his sweat suddenly was filling the room. He dropped the carton. "Jesus Christ, I better—"

His voice cut off mid-word as Regan caught him by the throat, moving faster than he could see. She squeezed hard, to keep him from making any noise, and his eyes bulged out. Regan shut the hall door with her other hand and then put that hand on the young man's shoulder and forced him to his knees. That was easy, because he was going into shock—blind fear pulsed off him in shuddering waves, Regan could feel it through her hands. He was not able to reconcile her speed and strength with anything he'd experienced, and he was panicked at being unable to breathe. He was clawing at her wrist with both hands but his fingers might as well have been scratching at steel. His face was turning dark red and he was making horrible gurgling sounds, and Regan feared that she was injuring his larynx. She loosened her grip and he sucked in a great whoop of air. Hastily, she grabbed the back of his head with one hand, clutching a handful of greasy hair hard, and put her other hand over his nose and mouth. "Don't make a sound," she said softly. "One squeak and I'll turn your head around backwards. Got that?"

She didn't think she could really do that, but he did. She felt his head jerk forward in a nod. He was shaking, and then she felt something that startled her—tears, trickling down against her hand where it covered his mouth. *Ah, man, let's get this over with,* she thought, suddenly repulsed by her own actions. At least this one was over eighteen. She pulled his head back by the hair and leaned down, locking her mouth onto his throat. He flinched back away from her, and despite his fear, he couldn't restrain a muffled squeal of pain when she *opened,* the sensation was so unexpected. A gush of blood filled Regan's mouth and she gulped it down eagerly, momentarily overwhelmed by the rush of euphoria it gave her. She let her hand slip off the young man's mouth and he gasped desperately for air, but he was too stunned to cry out. After two more swallows, Regan remembered why she was doing this in the first place, and before the young man could start struggling, she focused her consciousness and blacked him out. His head snapped back, as though he'd been struck by a board, and Regan had to grab hold of the front of his apron to stop his body from crumpling to the floor. She managed to keep her mouth in contact with the wound so blood didn't get all over the white apron. Even though she was reeling from the counter effect of blanking his memory, she had to force herself to stop drinking from him. She took two more swallows and then *closed*, sucking and licking the blood off his skin as she let him down to the floor.

As she crouched next to him, the reality of her position crashed back into her awareness. *Oh my god, now I've done it. What was I thinking? In two more seconds someone is going to come looking for him, and then I'll really be in trouble.* She whirled around to face the door, and listened. There was no sound from the hallway—yet. She put her hand up to her head, unthinkingly raking back her hair, and knocked off her little visored cap that had been pushed almost off her head. As she picked it up, a plan blinked into her mind, and she stuffed the cap into the waist of her jeans. A few moments later, she had dragged the young man's body off to the side of the room and left him stretched on his back, hands neatly folded on his abdomen, at the base of a shelf. She pulled his white baseball cap on backwards, just as he'd worn it, and doubled the apron ties around her waist, the way he had tied them. She took in a deep breath and then opened the hall door and walked swiftly down the hall. She rounded the corner and was almost at the exterior door when she heard an older man's voice shout from the kitchen entry. "Hey, Cal, where you goin'? Where's that paste?"

Without pausing or turning around, Regan waved a hand back at the speaker and shouted, trying to keep her voice low, "Be right back." The light by the exit door was dim, the kitchen noise was loud with hissing fat and clattering pans, and she hoped the chef would be fooled, at least for another five minutes. She didn't hear him speak again before she was out the door. She slammed the door behind her and ran up the concrete steps, praying that no one was in the parking lot, pulling off the apron as she ran. She tossed Cal's apron and hat into the dumpster as she passed it, sprinted to the side of the parking lot and vaulted the eight-foot-high brick wall as though it were a picket fence. It hadn't occurred to her on the way in that she could do this, but Cal's blood was giving her some extra bounce. As she landed lightly on her toes on the other side, it also occurred to her that such athletics would attract a lot of attention if anyone saw her. But deservedly or not, luck was on her side. As far as she could tell, there was no one to witness her jump.

The side wall of the lot faced an alleyway that ran between it and the one-story commercial building next door, connecting Main and Elm. Regan walked down the alley to Elm, turned left, and then turned onto Mystic and headed west, to get away from the vicinity of her crime as fast as she could. Cal's blood was buzzing and tingling through her body, and she kept licking her lips and fingers to get a bit more taste of it, but inwardly she was kicking herself. *It was a stupid thing to do...the shit's really going to hit the fan this time. There's no way this one won't be reported...and I'd just left the police station on foot!* Cal would remember nothing about her, and she could not have afforded to be caught inside the Atheneum. The only hopeful aspect of the whole mess was the Atheneum's solid security. No one was going to be able to figure out how an assailant could possibly have gotten inside, although it wouldn't take a genius to deduce that it wasn't Cal the chef saw leaving. They'd know that as soon as they found Cal, and then found his clothing in the dumpster.

She walked along the side streets that paralleled Main, zigzagging up and down cross streets and choosing the routes with the least number of street lights. As she walked, she recalled Cal's odd question: *Did you hide that body down here?* Evidently, he hadn't yet heard the news that she had returned, but Regan wondered what kind of stories were running through the rumor mill about her and Veronica's missing remains. *One week, and I'm an urban legend,* she thought. Who was making these speculations, and what were people saying about her? *At least,* she thought bleakly, *I don't have to worry about whether the rumors will be bad for business.*

Chapter 24

It was 9:00 when she finally neared her apartment building. Her own windows were the only dark ones in the house. Without knowing why, she hesitated in the shadow of an ancient lilac bush that took up a quarter of the front yard of a small bungalow a few doors down from her building. There was nothing unusual about the street. It was a main thoroughfare, broad and well-lighted, with regular traffic passing both ways. There seemed to be no more and no fewer cars than usual parked by the roadside, and certainly no police cars. But for some reason, Regan scanned the cars carefully, trying to figure out what seemed different about them. Then she caught it.

She walked back the way she'd come until she came to a spot where she could cut through a couple of private yards to the street west of her own, then walked back down that street until she was even with her own building and quickly cut east through two yards again. She paused in the deep shadow of a small house, which fortunately did not boast a dog or a motion-sensor security light. She could see the driver of the silver Corolla parked in front of the house, his attention fixed on her three-decker apartment building across the street. He probably was watching the street, and the side view mirrors, but he was turned entirely away from the house next to him. After a moment, Regan walked unhurriedly down the driveway, went to the Corolla and put her hand on the door latch. The lock button snapped up, and she pulled open the door and hopped into the front passenger's seat, as the driver twisted around to stare at her in shock. The expression on his face was most gratifying.

"Hello, Hiram," she said, shutting the door. "Nice to see you. What are you doing staking out my house, if you'll pardon the expression?"

"Regan—I...of course I wasn't...I was just..."

"Yes, you were. Are you watching over me, or just watching me, Hiram?" He was scared. She could smell it, pungent as a noseful of ammonia.

"I was just waiting for you to get home, that's all. You never returned my phone message, and I wanted to talk to you."

"My apologies. Just as I was playing my messages, I had a visit from Sheridan's Finest. I had to go talk with them."

"Is everything all right?" Hiram asked, cautiously.

"I'm not sure. What do you think, Hiram? Should I be worried?"

He bridled, a bit too much. "Well, how should I know?"

"You must have a lot of time on your hands, to just be sitting in your car waiting for me on a Saturday night. How did you know I wasn't spending the night with Jonathan?"

"I didn't. I didn't realize that was something you'd be likely to do."

"Oh, come on, Hiram. You can't be the last person in Massachusetts to know that we're involved."

He squared his shoulders defensively. "I've been very busy with the end of semester exams and papers, Regan, and I haven't heard much from you for several weeks. I won't deny that I was detecting some mutual attraction there, but I had no idea it had gone any further. I don't keep track of your personal affairs."

"Well, I'm sorry I've been out of touch. There hasn't been much for us to talk about. Have you heard about any more incidents?"

"No incidents have been reported that I'm aware of, and I haven't been contacted by any additional victims."

"So, what did you want to discuss with me, that you couldn't talk about on the phone? Don't think you didn't pique my curiosity, just because I didn't call you right back tonight. Believe me, I intended to. I've just been finding life to be a lot more unpredictable than it used to be."

He looked at her silently for a moment. Regan wished fervently that she had some pretext for touching him, but she knew there was no way that she could get away with "accidentally" making contact with Hiram. He'd realize immediately what she was up to. Finally he said, "May we go inside for a few minutes? I have some things to show you."

"Show me?"

"Yes, that's why I couldn't talk on the phone."

Regan was somewhat surprised that he wanted to be alone with her in her apartment, given the nervousness she sensed in him. Anything he wanted to show her, she could have seen quite well there in the car, but there was no reason to let him know that. "Sure," she said. They both got out of the car. She noticed that he checked the lock on the passenger's door after she closed it, and frowned, but he didn't make any comment. They crossed the street and climbed the two staircases to Regan's apartment, after she had opened the outside door with her key. For one panicked moment, she thought she'd left her keys inside, since she didn't need them any more. *I'm going to have to learn to be careful about how things look to other people,* she thought as she unlocked her apartment door and ushered Hiram inside. He had a leatherette portfolio tucked under his arm, and she wondered what he had brought.

"Have a seat," she said, snapping on the lamps that stood at either end of the couch. The room now seemed over-bright to her, but he glanced uneasily at the shadowed corners and the dark doorways into the kitchen and hall. "There's no one lurking here, really." She sat down next to Hiram on the sofa. "So, what have you got?"

He studied her for a moment before he began speaking. "Do you remember our discussion in the restaurant after the reading with Evelyn Stockard?"

"Yes."

"You recall the things you said about the clarity and depth of the vision you had of the nineteenth century city street? You said that you'd read delusions and dreams in people, and this was distinctly different. You said that even memory was usually not so clear."

"I *said* that. But you made the very reasonable suggestion that, since my entire reading had been much more intense than normal, it followed that all elements of it would be heightened."

"I did make that suggestion. Now I'm reconsidering it. I think I was guilty of rationalizing, and I did you a disservice. You were right: when you perceive dreams, delusions and even memories, your visions are much more fragmented and cloudy. When you perceive something as clearly as that street scene, you can only be tuning into reality."

Regan was starting to feel on very slippery ground. "I'm not sure where you're going with this, Hiram."

"Perhaps you also remember that in that conversation, I proposed a theory to explain our assailant's motives."

"You proposed clinical vampirism, I believe."

"To which you replied that there was more going on here than Renfield's Syndrome."

"What do I know, Hiram? You're the licensed psychologist, not me."

"That's true. But I've started to believe that you were right. There is a lot more going on here than Renfield's Syndrome. I said in that discussion that we needn't be talking about anything supernatural. I'm no longer sure about that."

"Hiram...what the hell are you talking about? You can't *possibly* be suggesting that you think something out of *Dracula* is running around biting people, can you?"

"You were the one who pointed out that every case we had included elements that are extremely difficult to explain logically. The total loss of memory, the way that major blood vessels are apparently opened and sealed in some controlled fashion...I can't explain those elements. I've been doing a lot of research in the clinical literature, and I can't even formulate a hypothesis as to how the assailant is accomplishing these things."

"So you're suggesting the supernatural? My god, Hiram—if you publicize this, you'll lose your tenure and your license."

"I didn't say anything about publicizing it. I agree with you. I don't want publicity, for myself or for the victims. I just want this assailant to be stopped."

"Are you laying in a good supply of wooden stakes, Hiram?"

He smiled thinly. "All the folklore is in agreement that the only certain way of stopping a vampire is by burning the body. A crematorium would do the job."

Regan shivered suddenly, even though she knew Hiram was watching her closely. "Well...leaving that aside, how does any of this connect with my vision of the nineteenth century?"

Hiram undid the fastener on the portfolio and removed a photograph. It was a high-resolution color photocopy, on heavy glossy paper, but the original photograph was a darkened and spotted sepia-tone black and white. He handed it to Regan and she turned it around, puzzled. The photograph showed about fifteen young men, clad in dark suits and seated in three rows, like a graduating class. As she looked at the photograph, Hiram reached over and pointed out one of the figures, in the second row. Regan looked closely at the face he indicated, and her heart sank.

"You see the resemblance," he said, flatly.

"I see *a* resemblance. What is this photograph?" She flipped the page over, but there was nothing written on it.

"Brown University, summer of 1895. It's a group of students who were doing charity work in the poor quarters of Providence. That particular young man... was rather brutally murdered the following year."

"A terrible tragedy. And I suppose some sort of legends evolved about his leaving the grave?"

"No, not at the time."

Regan sighed in exasperation. "I'd appreciate it if you'd cut out all this mystification, Hiram. You think this poor bastard and Jonathan Vaughn are the same person? Just because of this picture? There's a superficial resemblance, but that could be sheer coincidence, or this is some ancestor. Who can say for sure? What was this man's name, anyway?"

"His name was Edward Tillinger. He originally came from South Kingston, Rhode Island."

Regan shook her head. "I don't see the relevance. How did you find this photograph, Hiram? You surely weren't just going through old pictures hunting for someone who looked like Jonathan?"

"You'll see the relevance in a moment. No, the photograph was unexpected. I was in touch with a colleague of mine at Brown who has an interest in local folklore. I was asking him if he knew of any stories or odd events that might have some relationship to..." he hesitated.

"To vampires? Did you actually say that?"

"Only in the academic sense. There were a number of exhumations related to possible vampirism in Rhode Island. This is well known. But my colleague had some intriguing information, information that isn't generally known, even in academic folklore circles."

"About this Edward Tillinger?"

"It seems that three years earlier, he was considering marriage to a young Exeter woman named Mercy Brown. I'm sure you know *that* story. It's in every popular book about vampires, and it's been re-created on numerous television programs."

"Isn't she the one that they dug up and..." Regan paused, suddenly feeling cold all over. "...cut up into pieces and burned?"

"They cut out some pieces and burned them, yes, at least, that was the story."

"But, Hiram. That case was nothing but superstitious hysteria. That poor family all had tuberculosis. Even contemporary writers said so."

"That's what they said, yes."

"And I never heard that Mercy Brown was engaged to anyone."

"I don't believe there ever was a formal engagement. The Tillinger family was quite well-to-do, and they disapproved of their son's infatuation below his station. He apparently fell ill after Mercy's death, but he recovered. His family hustled him off to Providence and enrolled him at Brown. My colleague went to the library archives there and dug out this photograph, just from curiosity, and sent this copy to me."

Regan looked down at the sober faces in the photograph. "And Edward Tillinger was murdered?"

"In September, 1896. But here's where things get strange. My colleague was told this story by his father when he was a boy—it's one of the things that got him interested in folklore and local history to begin with. His father grew up in South Kingston and knew the Tillinger family. In the 1950s, during the post-war building boom, the family donated some land for a new school. Part of the land was a private cemetery, and all the graves were slated to be moved, very respectfully, to a new cemetery on the other side of town. Most of them were Tillingers. When this Edward's casket was being exhumed, it was noticed that the lid didn't seem to be sealed, as it should have been."

"You mean, the casket was empty?"

"Nothing in it but some dirt. Caused quite a stir at the time. The family kept the information quiet, it never got into the news or local gossip. But they accused the town of mishandling their ancestor's remains, and threatened a lawsuit. My colleague's father was employed by the department of public works that was handling the cemetery transfer, and he said that life was pretty unpleasant for a while. Eventually the town settled with the family and they let it go, rather than risk having the scandal become public. But at that time, the connection between the Tillingers and Mercy Brown was brought up, although not to the Tillingers. My colleague says that for years, he was nervous walking alone at night, wondering if there were still vampires lurking somewhere in South Kingston."

"But no one has ever reported vampire attacks in South Kingston, have they?"

"Not since the 1890s. But isn't it a little strange that of all people, Edward Tillinger should mysteriously vanish from his grave: a young man who was personally connected to one of the most famous vampire cases in the United States?"

Regan was silent for a few moments. "It is strange," she said finally. "I agree. That's a very weird coincidence. But there could be any number of reasons for the casket being empty. Someone who didn't like the Tillingers might have been playing a prank on them. Maybe the Tillingers themselves had something to hide—Edward was a suicide, or had some shameful disease, and they didn't want anyone to find out. His body could have been buried someplace else and most of the family never even knew about it. There are rational explanations, Hiram." She handed the photograph back to him.

Hiram took the photograph and slid it back into the portfolio. "I agree. There could be all sorts of rational explanations."

Regan straightened up and looked squarely at Hiram. "You know, I've been seeing Jonathan Vaughn for several weeks now. Don't you think I would know if he had a secret like this to hide?"

She waited as Hiram very deliberately removed his eyeglasses and cleaned them with his handkerchief, then put them back on. He looked straight at her, and his expression was not friendly. "Yes. I would think that. And I do, in fact."

"You think I'm covering up for Jonathan Vaughn."

"I don't know what you're doing with him, Regan, but I think you know more than you're telling—much more. I have no idea how you got sucked into this—whether Vaughn's got some hold on you, or is threatening you, or you're just tragically misguided."

"Tragically misguided? Oh, please, Hiram."

"What I do know is that you haven't even mentioned your recent disappearance. I suppose you won't tell me where you've been for the past week?"

"It has nothing to do with Jonathan Vaughn."

"I find that difficult to believe."

"You may also find it difficult to believe that he was as worried about me as anyone else, and now I'm having to do the same damage control with that relationship that I'm having to do with everyone else. It's really nobody's business, Hiram."

"You mean, it's none of my business."

"Bingo." He continued to look at her steadily, and Regan got up and walked across the room, suddenly overwhelmed with irritation at the pretense of this entire conversation. She knew too much that he wasn't telling her—the trouble he was in with the college, his association with Jerry Standish—and she couldn't let him know that she knew. "Hiram, we never had anything but a working relationship. You can't expect me to confide in you about my personal life. If you distrust me to this degree, we shouldn't even be talking. Why should you believe anything I say?"

He looked slightly wounded at this. "Regan—I care about what happens to you. I've been very worried about you for several weeks now, and I was sick when I heard you'd disappeared. I didn't expect you to turn up alive. I can't pretend to understand all these wild stories about you and Veronica Standish, but whatever's been going on, it's lost you the store and your livelihood. What could have been so important that you won't even venture an explanation in self-defense?"

He certainly sounded sincere. Regan rested her forehead against the fireplace mantel. "I can't talk about it," she said, "because it involves someone else's confidentiality. And I don't mean Jonathan Vaughn's, Hiram."

"Then whose? Veronica's?"

"Don't even bother asking. Unless—" she looked at him with narrowed eyes, and he shifted a bit on the sofa. "Would you answer one question honestly?"

"Go ahead and ask."

She went back to the sofa and sat down next to him, her knees almost brushing his, and noticed that he drew back from her a little. "Have you had any conversations with Jerry Standish about all of this? I'm just curious."

He hesitated, but managed not to look away from her, or stammer, like he did in the car. "No," he said in an abrupt huff. "I haven't been talking to Jerry Standish."

She sat back, regarding him thoughtfully. *He must be very confident that his conversations have been private,* she thought. "You're sure?"

"Why would you think differently?"

Oh, clever psychologist... "According to Jonathan, Jerry Standish is accusing him of treating Veronica badly—something about a letter she wrote before her death. I just thought he might have given you a call—or something."

"He never called me. He wouldn't have had any reason to."

That, I believe, Regan thought dismally. She was sure Hiram had initiated the contact when he learned about Veronica's injury. But now he'd lied to her face, so she knew she was right to doubt everything else he said. He knew about Veronica's injury, and he might know that she had taken Veronica to the emergency room, but he hadn't asked her about it—that alone signaled that he didn't trust her to tell him the truth. And he hadn't asked about her scar, either, although she had noticed him looking at it. "Okay," she said lightly. "It's just a very sticky situation, with this lawsuit and everything. I was just wondering what other complications might be out there."

"You're saying that Vaughn has nothing to do with that lawsuit?"

"I believe that no one but Anita Westfield is named as a plaintiff, correct?"

"I haven't seen it."

Regan sighed. "Hiram, the Standishes have been fighting for thirty years. Any outside parties are superfluous to their private little war. Even Veronica was superfluous to them, and you see what it did to her. I don't know why anyone who knows that family would believe differently."

She saw an expression of doubt shadow Hiram's face. But before he could reply, his cell phone trilled faintly and he tugged it from his jacket pocket and glanced at the incoming number. "Excuse me," he said, and got up to walk across to the kitchen door, where he stood hunched over with the phone tightly to his ear. He was wasting his efforts, since Regan could easily hear every word the caller said. "Hello, Clauson."

"Dr. Clauson? Detective Fellman."

"Yes?" Hiram seemed mildly surprised.

"Are you free?"

"Well, I'm—I'm in a session at the moment. What's the problem?"

"You asked me to call you if there was another of those unusual injuries. We've had an apparent assault here in town."

"Where?"

"One of the kitchen staff at the Atheneum."

"The Atheneum?" Hiram said sharply. "But I was just—" he broke off, glancing quickly at Regan, and lowered his voice. "He was found outside the building?"

"No, inside. They found him out cold in one of the kitchen store rooms. Same as all those others, with that strange-looking contusion on his neck. He's got some other bruising, too. The paramedics said it looked like someone was choking him."

Shit, Regan thought. *I didn't even think about that.*

"Does he remember anything?"

"He doesn't even remember going to work. But he said that he's willing to talk to you. He's down at the E.R., they're running some tox screens and maybe a CAT scan. He'll be there for a while. You can go on down if you want to see him now."

Hiram rubbed his forehead with his free hand—he was sweating, Regan saw. "You said he was *inside* the building?"

"In the basement, yes. That's where the kitchen is. Why?"

"I don't think any of the previous victims has been found indoors."

"At least not the ones who've reported, no."

"How could an assailant get inside the basement?"

"We're trying to determine that. Someone was seen leaving, but the witness thought it was the victim, so there's no description. And it might have been the victim, except that no one saw him coming back in. The only access that isn't visible to the doorman or parking attendant has a security lock. If someone got in that way, they'd have to have a key, or have someone inside let them in."

"Or just have a knack for opening locks," Hiram said slowly.

"He'd have to be good."

"Can I read the police report?"

"Yes. You can come down to the station and see it."

Hiram glanced over at Regan. "Thank you for calling, Detective. I'll be at the hospital in about fifteen minutes."

Detective Fellman sounded surprised. "You're in town?"

"Yes, I'm visiting a client. But I'm wrapping up here." He clicked the phone off.

"What was that all about?" Regan said.

Hiram pocketed his phone and stepped to the coffee table to pick up his portfolio. "It seems that we've had another incident."

"After all this time?"

He looked at her for a moment. "There hasn't been one reported for several weeks, at least not to any of the police departments who would call me about it," he said with careful emphasis. "It does seem odd that there would be one right in the middle of Sheridan. I have to go, Regan. You did say that you didn't want to do any more readings on victims."

"No, I don't. Good luck with this one." Regan stood up uneasily as he walked to the door.

"Thank you." Hiram turned the deadbolt and started to open the door. He paused, staring down at his hand on the doorknob. Then he turned and gave Regan a long appraising look. "Did you walk all the way home from the police station tonight?"

"Yeah. They gave me a ride down there, I walked back. I took a roundabout way home, though—I had a lot to think about. Why?"

"I knew you didn't have your car with you, that's all, and I didn't see anyone drop you off."

"Well, you were pretty focused on my apartment building, Hiram." She meet Hiram's steady stare unflinchingly, watching as his eyes narrowed and an expression of disbelief, then suspicion crossed his face. Abruptly, he turned and left without saying another word.

Chapter 25

I'm starting to get this overpowering conviction," Regan said glumly, "that I should have just stayed at the bottom of that fucking well. Ever since I got out of it, I've done nothing but screw up."

It was almost 2:00 a.m., and she was sitting at the long table in the great room at Rainbow Stone house, along with Jonathan and a bleary-eyed and yawning Sean. As soon she was sure that Hiram had left, she had closed up her apartment and driven out here, paying so much attention to the rear view mirrors that she had almost gone off the road once or twice. She saw no evidence that she was being followed, however. She had told Jonathan and Sean everything that had happened that evening, including every word of the conversations she had overheard or participated in. They had been discussing the implications of it all for hours.

"I'm not going to agree with that assessment, at all," Jonathan said. "You've done quite well, considering how fast you've had to think on your feet. You've only been awake for slightly over twenty-four hours, and you've already fielded two interviews with the police, one with a suspicious Hiram Clauson, and gotten in and out of a very secure building without being apprehended."

"And been fired from my job, lost the business I ran for seven years, attacked two people, and let Hiram know I can open locked doors."

"So, what's on your schedule for tomorrow?" Sean said.

"Be careful, Sean, I could still fit a few things in tonight," Regan said sourly.

"I admit," Jonathan said reluctantly, "young Cal is going to create some complications. I wish that hadn't been necessary."

"God, so do I, but I didn't know what else to do. I wouldn't have done it if he hadn't recognized me. But if he hadn't recognized me, I wouldn't have found out that I'm supposed to have hidden Veronica's body someplace. Nobody mentioned that one when I was calling them this morning."

"Your friends probably don't believe it," Sean said, and then yawned again. When he could, he added, "I heard a couple of kids talking about that in school. But they made it into a big joke."

"Some joke. That would make me guilty of a felony—not to mention conspiracy to defraud Jerry Standish."

"How could they accuse you of hiding a body when the body was seen walking out of a funeral home on her own two feet?"

"They could accuse me of killing her afterwards," Regan said shortly, and Sean frowned.

"There's no need to invent hypothetical problems when we have more than enough real ones to solve," Jonathan said. "I am deeply concerned about Hiram

Clauson. He knows too much, and what's worse, he believes what he knows. Most people won't. The evidence can be right before them, as obvious as a draft horse in a drawing room, and they'll simply refuse to come to conclusions that don't fit their reality. They'll accept the flimsiest rationalizations, rather than have to change their beliefs. That is our greatest protection. But Clauson is that one in ten thousand that we have to fear."

"You know, Jonathan," Sean said, "there's no law against being a vampire."

"There are laws against assaulting people."

"If Hiram had found a shred of hard evidence connecting you with any assaults," Regan said, "he'd have gone to the police with it long ago."

"So you've said all along. But if Clauson watches us, and follows us, and employs others to do the same, with enough determination, he's bound to get his hands on some evidence eventually. We can't co-exist with a Javert on our tails, Regan."

"I know."

"Especially with the advances in technology that make stalking others so easy these days. And especially if he has Jerry Standish financing him. I know what you overheard about Standish's assets, but that doesn't indicate a permanent situation. And Clauson could find other allies."

"If he loses his job at the college, he may have to occupy himself with finding a new one, and he might end up out in California."

"Yeah," Sean said, "but he might also have lots of time on his hands and decide he wants to get even. We'd be better off if he had a job to be worried about keeping."

"Maybe so," Regan said wearily, "But I don't have one, and I don't feel a heck of a lot more dangerous."

They all sat in gloomy silence for a few moments. "I am sorry about the store," Jonathan said.

Regan looked around at the almost empty room. "I don't think it's really sunk in yet. Twice tonight I caught myself thinking that I better get home, because I'd need to be at the store tomorrow. I do need to pack things up for the movers coming on Monday. Maybe it will hit me then." She shook her head. "I don't know what I'm going to do. Can I get a job, and work, when I'm...when I'm like this?"

"Of course you can. But you might not have to."

"But how am I going to live? I mean, pay for rent, for clothes—just because I don't need food anymore doesn't mean much. I still have the same expenses."

"You're welcome to stay with me, Regan. You shouldn't even have to ask."

She looked at him sadly. "I couldn't just mooch off of you. I've been independent since I was eighteen. I'd feel like a kept woman."

"I don't see it that way, but I respect your principles. You know, you could see this as an opportunity—maybe one long overdue."

"Losing the store?"

"Remember what you said that day, about the innovations you wanted to make and couldn't, because Mrs. Wharton didn't trust these new-fangled ways of merchandizing? E-stores, online auctions, even plain old mail order."

"Yes..." she said doubtfully.

"So, why not do that now? You know the field. You've got the contacts—regular customers, suppliers, auction circuits, newsletters, dealers, wholesalers. The store isn't passing on to someone else, it's closing outright—and very suddenly. That's leaving a big hole. You have all your crafters who are losing a distributor. And you've got all your time on your hands. Why wait? Start now."

"You make one heck of a case for it." Regan couldn't keep from laughing at his enthusiasm. "But, Jonathan—a start-up takes capital. I don't have any stock, and no money."

"With a college degree and ten years of work experience in business management, it's hard to believe that no bank would give you a small business loan, and there are government grants, too."

"It might be harder to swing any of those, after Bill Wharton fired me without even a character."

"Then I can loan you the money. No, don't look at me like that, I said a loan. I'll even charge you interest."

"I think it sounds sweet," Sean said, and then he yawned again. "You should go for it, Regan."

Regan was still smiling, but she shook her head ruefully. "It seems awfully risky. And it won't happen overnight. What am I going to live on, in the meantime?"

"I can loan you enough to cover that until you're solvent—just like a bank would. But I can do more than that. Since being independent is so important to you—and that's not a bad thing—I can show you how to build up a permanent financial base."

"What do you mean?"

"I mean a diversified network of assets, investments, funds, under different names, banks in Switzerland, the Caymans, ways of holding real estate, trusts... you know."

"Good lord. Is that how you do it?"

"It's amazing what can be done with money—and it just gets easier and easier as everything goes electronic. Do you know what your net worth is right now?"

"Uhhh...I have no idea, but it's probably a negative number."

"Debts?"

"I kept the credit cards down, because I saw too many people go through that hell. But I still have student loans."

"What's the principal left on them?"

Regan thought, and shrugged helplessly. "I'd have to get out the last bill. I don't look, I just pay them."

"Never been in default?"

"No, my credit rating is okay. I just never had a dime to save."

"Well, we'll see what we can put together. If you can clear even a couple of thousand, we've got seed money to start with."

"But—is this even legal, what we're talking about?"

He smiled, and waved a hand in the air. "Oh—more or less. Don't worry, it can't be traced—not what I'll show you. I've been living on my investment income since 1926."

Regan shook her head in amazement. "Lucky you didn't get wiped out on Black Tuesday."

"Oh, I was hit, but I saw that one coming. I'm still baffled that so many others didn't. But perhaps I take a longer view than the average man. I don't really have a choice."

And now I don't, either, Regan thought. *My parents and everyone I know will be dead someday, anyway, and I'll still be here...just me, and Jonathan...well.* She had to smile. *And probably Sean, the way things are going.* Her smile faded. *And then there's Veronica.*

"Put your records together as soon as possible, Regan, and we'll go through it and see what we've got."

"Wow," Sean said. "Hey, I don't have any debts."

"It's never too soon to start."

Regan ran a hand through her hair in bemusement. "I'll have to do that anyway, to turn over the store records to Bill. But, Jonathan—we don't know what's going to happen with Jerry Standish and all that mess. What's the point of financial planning, if I end up arrested—or if we just have to pull up stakes and run?" He folded his arms, frowning, and Regan gestured around the room. "Do you think I don't know why you haven't done any more with this place than add about six pieces of furniture? You know you don't dare settle in yet, and I haven't done anything to make it easier for you. What difference does it make what my personal worth is, if I'm just going to have to go underground, or change identities?"

"You have a point," he said after a thoughtful pause, "but I still think it wouldn't hurt you to start making plans. If we have to run, that won't slow us down."

Thinking about this, Regan crossed her arms tightly and shivered. "Oh, god," she said desperately, "I'd hate to have to run, Jonathan. Doing time in Framingham would be better than that. At least I'd have visitors, and eventually I'd be out."

"You couldn't, though. You just couldn't. There'd be medical exams, and too many questions."

"What would have happened if I'd gone for a drug screen, like Bill Wharton asked?"

"You wouldn't want to do that. Your blood would test as highly abnormal."

"In what way?"

"Well, for one thing, it's dead. For another, it's missing several critical components. And for a third, it will test with genetic material from people you've drunk from—and animals, too, which would really provoke curiosity."

"You know this from experience?"

"Not all of it personal, but I know it for a fact, yes."

Regan was silent for a moment, gnawing on a thumbnail. "There's something else I thought of too late. If they dusted the doorknobs at the Atheneum for fingerprints, mine had to be on them. What if I'm arrested and fingerprinted? How will I explain my prints being at the Atheneum?"

"You think you're going to be arrested?"

"I don't know what's going to happen at this point, Jonathan."

"Well, I wouldn't worry about fingerprints. We don't usually leave any. We don't sweat. You can be fingerprinted, with ink, and you might leave a print in some soft material, like clay, but your prints can't be lifted from doorknobs."

"I had my hands on Cal, though, and he was sweating buckets. And suppose I left a hair in that hat of Cal's that I tossed in the dumpster?"

Jonathan thought for a moment. "In that case, you might have to run. That would be very difficult to explain." Regan sagged in the chair with a heavy sigh. "You could, of course, risk going back to retrieve the hat. Although if you were caught, you'd *really* have some explaining to do. But I wouldn't even worry about it unless it comes up. Forensic testing is expensive. A police department like Sheridan's isn't going to budget for lab work for anything less than rape and homicide."

"Unless there's a Hiram Clauson lighting a fire under their tails."

"My sense is that Hiram Clauson does not have a lot of clout with the police. It's what he'll do on his own that we have to worry about."

Sean yawned again, and then swayed in his chair so precariously that Regan had to reach a hand out to catch his shoulder and shove him back upright.

"Maybe I better take you home, Sean," Jonathan said.

"Can I crash here? My mom's staying over with her boyfriend again—she hasn't been home since yesterday. I can just sleep on the floor, I don't mind."

"I don't know if that's wise, with everything that's going on..." Jonathan said uneasily.

"You're not going to give me that we don't want you to be involved shit again, are you?"

"Well, no."

"I brought a sleeping bag, I'll just pick the room with the softest floor." He got up, hefted his knapsack, which did look fatter than usual, and trudged out of the room and up the front stairs. "I'm stealing one of your pillows," he called down to them.

Regan smiled wryly at Jonathan. "I guess we're going to be constrained tonight."

"Oh, why would you think that?" He got up and stretched, then walked over behind Regan's chair, and started massaging her shoulders. Regan leaned back, closing her eyes. They had been talking for a long time.

"Don't start anything, Jonathan," she said wistfully.

"I'm not. You just seem tense, and besides, I want to touch you."

"It feels great, but it doesn't solve anything."

He bent down and said softly, "You know, the attic is very roomy, and very private."

She bent her head back to look at him. "Oh, a hard wood floor, how romantic. I don't think—" she had to break off because he was kissing her.

"And you've had a very trying night," he said when he stopped.

"Okay, you've persuaded me. You just have to promise to be quieter this time."

"I promise. If I'm too noisy, you can put a pillow over my face."

"I will. Or something."

Chapter 26

At 10:30 a.m. on Monday morning, Regan was sitting in the shade of the big oak tree across the road from Borrowed and Blue's parking area. She couldn't see much of the building itself—it was mostly blocked by a twenty-four foot Ryder van. She was already well acquainted with this van, since it had arrived at her apartment house at 7:30, with two rather surly young men who had clumped and squeaked up and down the stairs dozens of times with small furniture and boxes of files. They had an inventory list of store property kept "off premises," and they checked it, methodically. They did not make much conversation, and Regan had little to say to them.

It was much cooler than the past couple of days, but sunny with a deep blue sky. Her eyes were burning from the light, despite her new sunglasses, with the darkest polarized lenses she had been able to find. She couldn't force herself to leave and go home, even though she now had quite a bit to do there. Even from across the street, she could hear the continuous metallic thumping of feet and dollies crossing the ramp between the doorway and the truck. The front window and glass door had been covered from the inside with black paper. Regan wondered if Bill Wharton would take the store's sign down. It had been there, repainted numerous times, since the business first opened, and she might have thought his mother would like it as a keepsake. But perhaps not. Enid Wharton was probably not at all happy about the decisions her son was making on her behalf. Regan could see Bill Wharton occasionally, supervising the loading. He must not have planned on doing much work himself, as he was dressed in a suit and tie, just as he had been on Saturday. He must have been hot, Regan thought, but he never even took his jacket off. His car was parked on the side of the building, where the resin table and chairs had been. The loaders were being very thorough. Even the aisle shelves had all been disassembled and put on the truck. There was a dumpster out front, but it didn't seem to contain much except the carpet runners, which Regan agreed belonged there. There wouldn't be anything left inside the building when the truck departed for Ohio except the bare walls and floor.

She wasn't very alert at this time of day, and her mind was rambling through memories: regular customers like Ellen Hayes and Letty Brownmiller, or particularly lucrative sales. It was almost exactly five years to the day since a reporter from the Fall River *Herald* had come to do a profile of her and the store for a weekend feature. "Something old, something new" had been the headline—the bright-eyed twenty-something taking over the little store that was a fixture of the town and "breathing new life into it." Despite what Bill Wharton said, Borrowed and Blue had been about to go under for good when Mrs. Wharton hired Regan. If that hadn't been true, Enid Wharton would have been able to afford someone with more experience, who could have demanded more than minimum and conditional commissions. *And that's still what I was making,* Regan thought morosely. *Maybe Bill Wharton was right.* Deep in gloomy reverie, Regan was startled to realize that someone was behind her, although under other circumstances she would have been aware of anyone approaching long before. She turned sharply, pushing back her cap visor to look up, and then relaxed.

"Sean. You shouldn't be cutting school." Her reproach was automatic. In fact, the sight of Sean, with his baggy khaki shorts, dingy socks falling into his sneakers and skinny calves streaked with bicycle chain oil, suddenly made her mood three degrees lighter.

Sean, who had walked via the trails that cut through the woods, dropped down to sit cross-legged beside her. "I had to come. I knew you'd be here, torturing yourself."

"Well, thanks. I think." They sat in silence for a minute, watching the scene across the road.

"They almost done?"

"Just about, looks like. They've been at it for about two hours. All they had to do was load, Bill Wharton had everything packed. They were at my place first."

"Ohio, huh?"

"Yep. I guess Building #19 didn't want it."

"What's going to happen to it all?"

"Oh, it will probably go to auction."

Sean sighed heavily. After a moment, he said hopefully, "So, are you going to do what Jonathan talked about? The loan, and the start-up?"

Regan drew her knees up and folded her arms on them, resting her chin on her forearms as she stared morosely across the street. "It's a good idea. But I don't know, Sean. There are a bunch of shoes still in the air. For one thing—" She reached back and took a piece of folded paper out of her back pocket, and handed it to Sean. Puzzled, he unfolded it and turned it around to look at the official printed letterhead, his brow creasing. Then he gaped.

"They're *evicting* you? They can't do that!"

"I'm afraid they can."

"Hey, wait a minute. I know something about this. They've tried to throw my mom and me out three times, and they couldn't get away with it. You've got rights. There's this place you can call, up in Boston—"

"Yes, I know, Sean. But that's different. Your mom has a lease, right?"

"Sure—you mean you don't? Why not?"

"It's called tenancy at will. I signed an agreement. Month to month. That's what I wanted."

"Why?"

Regan sighed. "I don't want to explain it all now," she said tiredly. "Bottom line is, your mom gets disability, has a lease, lives in subsidized housing, has a minor child, and has had an open DSS case. I can't claim any of those conditions. My rent is due on or before the fifteenth of the month, and you know where I was on the fifteenth. That's not really why I'm being thrown out, of course. But it's all the excuse the landlady needs."

"Well, that...that really blows."

"Can you blame them? Who wants to rent to a body snatcher? The neighbors probably went to the landlady and said they didn't want a television news van camped out in front of their house, which might happen, if someone got arrested or the lawsuit really got ugly. I suppose I can see their point. I wouldn't like it, either."

Sean glowered down at the eviction notice. "Well, you can stay with Jonathan, can't you?"

"I don't know. I mean, I'd like to think so, but that depends on what happens with all this other crap going on." They both looked up as the van doors were slammed shut with resounding bangs. The two movers came around and climbed into the cab of the van. A moment later, it was pulling out into the road. "Hope they make it," Regan said, trying to sound casual. "Every van I've ever rented has broken down." She watched the van as it headed south toward town, shading her eyes. Then she straightened up. "Sean," she said, quietly, and he looked at her, puzzled. "You better get out of here."

"Why? Hey, look—"

"You're truant from school, and I don't want you to get into trouble. You can't help me if you do." She waved her hand back toward the woods, but she was watching the road, not Sean. Sensing that something serious was going on, Sean got up and faded back down the trail, until he was invisible behind the foliage and undergrowth. Regan could feel him waiting there—she could even hear his rapid heartbeat and breathing. Both picked up even more as the police cruiser pulled into the parking area across the way. Bill Wharton had been about to get into his car, and he turned and watched the cruiser, his hands on his hips. She wondered if he thought she had called and made some complaint, just to make trouble for him. He walked over to the police car and stooped to speak to the officer inside. Then he straightened up and gestured across the road, in the direction of the oak tree. Regan knew he'd seen her sitting here.

She stood up as the cruiser backed around and then pulled across the road and stopped in front of the tree. It was Detective Fellman, she saw, with a uniformed officer she hadn't met. Detective Fellman got out of the car and stood looking at her with his usual impassive expression. "Regan Calloway?"

"Yes."

"You need to come with me, please."

She picked her way down the bank to the shoulder of the road, squinting a little as she entered the full sunlight, which beat down mercilessly through the little cap. "Am I under arrest, Detective?"

"Yes, ma'am." Regan was incredulous to see that he was taking his handcuffs off his belt. "Turn around, please."

She did, overwhelmed with a complete sense of unreality as he tugged her unresisting hands together behind her back. "What's the charge?" The handcuffs clicked shut. She sensed instantly that she could unlock the handcuffs at will, but now was definitely not the time.

Detective Fellman put a hand on her shoulder, ushering her to the back door of the cruiser. The other officer had gotten out of the front seat and was holding the door open. "Conspiracy to commit fraud, and aggravated assault."

"*What?*"

"You have the right to remain silent..." he began, and Regan let him finish reciting the Miranda rights, amazed that it sounded just like it did on television—except that it wasn't corny at all in real life.

She sat motionless and silent in the back seat of the police car as it passed through Sheridan, reflecting that her emotions were probably a bit different than those of ordinary suspects. They were powerless, handcuffed in the back seat with its bulletproof Plexiglas shield and handle-less doors. Her immobility was self-enforced. She could have unlocked both handcuffs and doors and fled at any time, and even had the police resorted to shooting at her, she suspected that bullets wouldn't stop her, although she wasn't quite sure just what they would do. But she felt that she had to cooperate, as far as possible, because if she broke and ran at this point, she would have to keep on running and never stop. She wasn't prepared to do that yet, not before she knew more about what was really going on. *I wonder who I'm accused of assaulting? Cal at the Atheneum? Or are they trying to pin all the incidents on me?* She didn't think she had a solid alibi for a single one of them.

At the police station, she went through booking, with an electronic fingerprint reader and digital photographs. The fingerprint reader was a surprise. Regan wondered if Jerry Standish had made an anonymous donation, as she didn't recall any such purchase coming up at town meeting. She turned over her purse, keys, sunglasses, hat, and even her shoelaces to be dropped into a manila envelope. "Is there someone you want to call?" Detective Fellman asked her. She called Jonathan.

"I heard," he said when she greeted him. Sean had called him, semi-panicked. He had seen her handcuffed and ushered into the cruiser but had not been able to overhear what was said. "What do you want me to do?"

"Do you know any attorneys?"

"There is someone I can call, but..." he hesitated, aware that their conversation might not be private. "She's only familiar with my *business* affairs." In other words, Regan interpreted, she knew nothing about the vampire side of her client's life.

"I understand. Will she take a criminal case?"

"If not, I'm sure she can refer someone. Are you at the Sheridan police station?"

"Yes, but, I don't know for how long. If I'm arraigned on any charges, I'm sure they'll take me to Fall River."

"You're going to be arraigned today?"

"I don't know, Jonathan. They haven't told me anything. Maybe the attorney can find out what's going on. They'll have to let me go if I'm not charged and arraigned, anyway."

When she finished the phone call, Detective Fellman asked, "Do you want to make a statement?"

"I have an attorney coming. I have nothing to say until then."

One of the officers led her down the back hallway to a holding cell, which was empty. He slid the cell door shut and left her alone. Regan walked to the side of the cell and sat heavily on the bare steel shelf that served as a seat or bunk. She could hear the buzz of phones and an occasional voice from the station's offices. There was a lot of soundproofing, but it wasn't perfect, and she could discern some phrases and sentences. But nothing she heard carried any significance for her. It was general police station business, and Sheridan was a quiet town on a Monday morning. After a while, fatigue and the hour caught up with her, and she curled up on the bench and dropped into her resting state, although somewhat uneasily. There was a camera monitoring the cell, and the officer on duty might wonder if she was very still for too long. But the worst that would happen is that they'd come and check on her, and Regan felt too drained by now to stay awake.

She started bolt upright when the cell door clanged open, and squinted at the officer in the doorway, shading her eyes with one hand. The cell was dimly lit, its overhead bulb protected with a steel mesh cover, but even that much illumination dazzled her for a few moments. The officer said, "I called to you three times—for a moment there, I thought you weren't breathing. You okay?"

"I'm fine," Regan said, her mind starting to clear after her sudden awakening. "What time is it?"

"About one-thirty. Your attorney's here."

"Oh." She stood up, wiggling her feet more securely into her unlaced shoes, and followed the officer out of the cell and around several corners in the warren-like back hallways of the station. The officer stopped and buzzed open the door to a small interview room. This room had a two-way mirror, and a camera monitoring it, and a small metal table bolted to the floor, with lightweight folding chairs on each side. Seated in one of the chairs was the attorney, a sturdily-built woman in her forties wearing a tweed skirt and dark blue jacket that clashed so desperately, Regan winced at the sight of them. The attorney rose from her chair and extended a large thick hand. She was several inches taller than Regan.

"Kate Delaney," she introduced herself as she snapped Regan's hand up and down in one shake. She had a serious grip.

"I'm Regan Calloway," Regan said, flexing her fingers as they sat down. Kate's graying light brown hair was permed in tight curls around her head, and with that and her heavy flat-heeled shoes, she looked as though she should have been striding down a country lane with at least four spaniels bounding happily after her. Her hazel eyes, however, were keenly intent as she looked Regan up and down.

"You don't look like you're up to aggravatedly assaulting anyone," she commented cheerfully.

Regan just smiled. *That's probably what Cal thought,* she thought wryly. *And speaking of which...* "Who am I supposed to have assaulted?"

"You don't know?"

"They haven't told me a thing."

"They haven't questioned you? You didn't make a statement?"

Regan shrugged. "They knew you were coming. Hey, I watch TV—I wasn't going to open my mouth until you got here."

"Good girl."

Regan leaned across the table, her hands clasped tightly in front of her. "All right, can *you* tell me what's going on? How could I be arrested without the police questioning me? What am I being charged with? Okay, conspiracy to commit fraud, I think I know what that's about. But aggravated assault?"

Kate opened a leatherette folder that was sitting on the table in front of her. "A warrant was issued for your arrest at Fall River court. That's why you weren't called in by the police first—although you have talked to Detective Fellman a couple of times, haven't you? I have some notes here from him—"

"He made notes?"

"Brief ones. They're part of the file. As far as this warrant goes—it's a piece of shit. There's not a present participle of hard evidence anywhere in it. Any judge more conscious than Terri Schiavo will toss it into the nearest shredder."

"But...how could someone even get a warrant like that issued?"

"Oh, it happens all the time. In this case, my guess is that someone bought it—more or less."

"Someone can *do* that?"

"Well, maybe not blatantly. It's usually more along the lines of, someone makes a 'donation' to the right cause, someone else does them a favor...all very civilized." She looked at Regan's expression and smiled grimly. "Dear innocent. Welcome to jurisprudence in Massachusetts. You're not really surprised, are you? Based on what I'm seeing here, who *might* do that kind of thing?"

"Well, duh, I guess," Regan said gloomily. *I'll bet there are a couple of judges who eat dinner at the Atheneum occasionally.* "But what would be the point? If the charges are that worthless, isn't this all a waste of everyone's time?"

"Well, no. For one thing, it gets you off the street for a while—if getting you off the street serves someone's purpose. I don't know how it could, but maybe you can think of something. Or it could be an attempt to intimidate you, or someone else...scare you into doing something you might not do otherwise. Or it could be just plain harassment, although that's hard to prove. You'd have grounds for some legal action, in that case."

Regan drew back in her chair, pondering this. "What, exactly, does the warrant say? I mean, does it specify exactly who I'm supposed to have assaulted, and when?"

"Yes..." Kate flipped through some papers. "Let's see—April twenty-second, 2004—Veronica Standish."

"*What?*" Regan stared open-mouthed. She had assumed that the warrant might have named Cal, based on the fact that she had been walking through town at the same time that he had been overcome by something at the Atheneum, and that Hiram Clauson would have had something to do with that. She also had half-expected to have been connected with any or all of the other incidents. But Veronica?

"You seem very surprised." Kate had been watching her client closely, and her expression was calculating.

"Surprised! I—I can't believe that anyone would—Veronica! Veronica was my best friend!"

"You dropped her off at the emergency room, it says here, at six twenty-three a.m. on Friday, April twenty-third, in a debilitated state with injuries to her neck and mild contusions...never made a report to the police, never called her next of kin, evaded the questions of hospital staff—it says—left her at the hospital and had no further contact with her...hmm. Miss Standish refused to offer any explanation for her medical state and...appeared to be withholding information from hospital staff who questioned her, it says." She turned over the page. "Subsequently...Miss Standish indicated in a written communication to her father that defendant was instrumental in events leading to her hospitalization...no details here as to instrumental in what way."

That fucking letter, Regan thought desperately. *What the hell did Veronica say in that thing?* "And that's evidence to charge me with assault? Veronica didn't accuse me of assaulting her in so many words, did she?" *What an irony that would be, considering the fact that she killed me!*

"That's hard to know, without seeing the written communication they refer to. Do you know what they're talking about?"

"Yes, I do. Veronica wrote her father a letter, just before she...well, before she did whatever."

"You're sure of that? Have you actually seen it?"

"No, but Veronica told me about it, and Jerry Standish told Jonathan—and it sounded like Jerry Standish's attorney had read it. I don't doubt that it exists. The issue is just exactly what it says. Can we subpoena it or something?"

"We could try, if you go to trial. Do you want to do that?"

"No!"

"Unless you need the letter for your defense, her father has no obligation to reveal its contents—and obviously he's refused to show it around, up to now."

"Jonathan asked to see it and was told no, at least. Doesn't that sound fishy to you? They could be claiming that it says almost anything."

"They'll have to put the letter where their mouth is eventually, if they intend to use its contents as evidence. Withholding it now may not be fishy, just strategic on their parts. Of course...Veronica Standish herself would be free to tell the world what she wrote, or to recant every line of it, if she wanted to." Regan sighed heavily. Kate was watching her face closely. "Is Veronica Standish alive, Regan?" Regan looked up at her sharply. "I've heard all the rumors—that she committed suicide, that she walked out of the funeral home with you, that she's been hiding out at your friend Jonathan's house, that you buried her body out in the woods—"

"Good *god.*"

"And I noticed that you said she 'was' your best friend."

"We had a rather serious falling out, to say the least."

"Over what?"

"Not about my assaulting her, that's for sure."

"Over Jonathan Vaughn, maybe?"

Regan looked down at the table. "That was part of it," she said after a moment.

"He's cute--not worth a crime of passion, but I suppose that's a matter of taste. So, Veronica *is* still alive."

How do I answer that? Regan thought helplessly. "She wasn't dead the last time I saw her. I certainly didn't hide her body anyplace, I can tell you that much." *It was the other way round, counselor.*

"Any way you can get in touch with her?"

"I'm sure as hell going to work on it." Regan looked up at the attorney, and felt a surge of annoyance to see her wearing the same small smile that she had seen on Detective Fellman's face. *What? What are these people thinking?* "You'll be the first to know, I promise you." Wanting to take control of the conversation, since she couldn't control anything else, she added, "What does the warrant say about the conspiracy to commit fraud charge?"

"Oh. Well." Kate turned over another page. "That's even more vague than the assault one. And the two charges are almost contradictory, since this one states that you're working with Anita Westfield and Veronica Standish to extort money from Jerry Standish by filing a frivolous lawsuit and forcing him to settle. There's no mention of why someone you allegedly assaulted would turn around and share a haul of loot with you."

"Because she's afraid of me?" Regan said sarcastically. "You could make a case for Veronica trying to extort money from her father, though, if you don't know Veronica very well."

"Do you think that's what's happening?"

"I know that's not happening." After a moment, Regan said, "It doesn't say that the three of us are allegedly collaborating with Jonathan? That's what Jerry Standish accused him of, or so he says."

Kate flipped through the pages and shook her head. "If that's in the mix, it's not mentioned here."

"So what happens now? Do I still have to be arraigned?"

"Fraid so. You could plea *nolo contendere*, but I wouldn't advise that. Plea not guilty and I'll file a motion to dismiss. I want to do a bit more digging, make sure they haven't got something else up their sleeves. But I don't think so."

"Can we do that today?"

"It's too late to get on the docket today. I'm afraid you're stuck here for the night, if you can stand it."

Regan looked around the small room and sighed. "I always wondered what goes on down here at night. My tax dollars at work and all that."

"Tomorrow you can tell me. I'll be here by eight, we'll go over to Fall River and punch this through. Can you make bail, or will Jonathan Vaughn take care of that?"

"Jonathan probably will. Could you call him?"

"Sure."

"Do I still need to make a statement for the police?"

"No, and don't. They know better than to try and question you without me. Don't talk to anyone, period. There have been way too many off-the-record discussions going on, as far as I'm concerned."

"Can I read that complaint before you leave?"

"Yes, but it doesn't explain anything we haven't talked about."

Back in the holding cell, Kate Delaney's card in her jeans pocket, Regan sat on the metal bench brooding. *One thing's for sure: they've got me off the street—and away from my apartment. What's going on out there? Is this all Jerry Standish, or did Hiram have some way of getting that warrant issued? Do they think Jonathan will confess to something to help me? Is my apartment being searched? And for what?* But her thoughts only tied themselves into knots.

Chapter 27

H and me that box, will you, Sean? Thanks," Regan said.
"Shit, they really made a mess. How can they get away with that?"

"They had a search warrant. I'm just glad I backed up the computer and gave the disks to Jonathan."

This violation had appalled Sean more than anything else. "Do you get your hard drive back?"

"Don't know. I guess some forensic computer analyst is trying to find everything I deleted. I don't know how long that takes and whether I'll even want the drive back. They're going to be disappointed."

"What do you think they were looking for in here?"

"Oh, everything from evidence that I've been communicating with Anita Westfield, to Veronica's actual body, I imagine."

Jonathan said, from the next room, "That's everything from the kitchen."

"Great. Let's take a break for a minute."

It was Tuesday night, about 8:00. Jonathan had brought Regan home from Fall River court that morning, after paying her bail. The assistant D.A. at the prosecutor's table had appeared bored to death, while the judge had flipped through the complaint and muttered something under his breath that would probably get a defendant threatened with a contempt citation. The case was continued to June 28th. Kate had asked for personal recognizance but was denied, because of the assault charge. The bail was minimal, but Regan still couldn't have made it, as much as it galled her to have to let Jonathan post it for her. "Don't worry," Kate had told them as they left the courthouse, "this will be tossed right out. I've already filed the motion."

They'd gotten back to the apartment house and were met by Mrs. Ferreira, breathless and flushed. "I want you to know," she said, before Regan had even gotten out of the car, "that you've caused more problems than I've seen in all my years renting out these apartments. In thirty years, the police have never been here. Never! I'm going to bill you for the damage, missy."

There was no actual damage, but Regan could understand why Mrs. Ferreira might have assumed otherwise. The whole apartment was a shambles and from the looks of things, the search team must have made quite a bit of noise, turning over furniture and carrying things out. They hadn't sliced open any of the sofa cushions, but they had turned over all the mattresses and broken the lock on one of the glass-fronted bookcases.

She didn't have to be out of the apartment until the 31st, according to the eviction notice, but Regan couldn't see staying any longer after this. It didn't feel like home any more, and Mrs. Ferreira and the neighbors would doubtless make her life miserable. She had rented a small van, and all afternoon she, Jonathan and Sean had carted furniture downstairs and hauled it over to Rainbow Stone house. If they had to flee altogether, it could all just stay there. Knowing the owner, he would probably wait a couple of months and then rent the house as "furnished." There were now only a few dozen recycled liquor cartons filled with books, clothes and kitchen wares, about one more vanload, and Regan would hand over her keys and be done with the place. The landlady could clean it, as far as she was concerned.

Regan and Jonathan sat on cartons, while Sean sat cross-legged on the bare wood floor, nursing the end of a two-liter Mountain Dew. "So long, pathetic old dump," Regan said, her eyes roving around the room. Stripped of furnishings and rugs, it was clear that the hardwood floors she'd loved so much could have used a sanding and refinishing twenty years ago. The buff-colored walls, untouched since a quickie latex paint job before she moved in, were darkened with soot from the fireplace and Regan's beloved candles. The ceiling was grayed and blackened in patches, and a crack ran up the wallboard above the mantel. The edges of the floor were lined with dust balls. "The holding cell at the police station looked better than this. I am going to miss the fireplace, though. How many apartments have those?"

"Rainbow Stone house has eight of them," Jonathan said.

"None of which I'd so much as strike a match in, mind you. God only knows what's in those chimneys."

"I know a kid in school, whose dad cleans chimneys," Sean said helpfully.

"Great. Get his name," Regan said, and sighed heavily. "Like it even matters. We're not going to be able to stay there."

"Why not?" Sean sounded startled.

Jonathan said, almost at the same time, "Don't be pessimistic, Regan. From what I've heard from you and Kate, Jerry Standish and Hiram Clauson are tilting at windmills. If they keep it up, we'll have legal grounds to retaliate. Jerry Standish doesn't want to be the defendant in another lawsuit."

Regan only shook her head. "I don't want to make any assumptions, Jonathan. It's only by pure chance that I found out that Hiram and Jerry Standish are working together, and I get the feeling that each of them has a completely separate agenda. There's a lot I don't know about what Hiram's up to, and what he knows, and who else he's working with. He's been on this vampire-hunting thing for a while now. I overestimated his trust in me. He knew what was going on the day after I met you, when we went out to Hong Kong Delhi."

"Couldn't you find some way to read him?" Sean said. "And then maybe erase his memory...I mean, I don't know, what's the use of having these powers if they're no good when you're in trouble?"

Regan smiled grimly. "Powers, as you call them, are only as useful as your resourcefulness. They all have limits. I learned that from reading comic books."

"So did I," Jonathan said, but he looked very amused.

"Oh, come on, you guys..."

"I wish I could read Hiram. God knows I was trying to think of some way to sneak around and do it on Saturday night. Trouble is, he knows me too well. He was very careful not to let me touch him even accidentally. I have to maintain contact, too. I just couldn't do it—he's too paranoid now."

Sean pondered darkly. "Maybe we could dope him somehow?"

"I don't know how. And anyway, it's hard to get meaningful information from people who are sleeping or unconscious. I might get a lot, and I might just get dream mumbling, and I can't control or predict which it is. And I can't ask the person to cooperate to make it easier."

"What if you made him forget about it afterwards?"

"I can't do that without leaving a big ugly mark, and that would give away the whole thing, not to mention, give Hiram another piece of evidence to use against us. Besides, you mean hold him down and force him? He'd just block me, if we tried that."

Sean sighed heavily. Jonathan said, "I've been wondering if there was any way you could get something from Jerry Standish."

"If you can think of a way I could touch Jerry Standish for an extended period of time without raising his suspicions, I'd be happy to try it. He doesn't believe that I'm psychic. But he sure doesn't like us. I can't imagine his even politely shaking hands. I doubt he'd agree to a friendly back rub."

"Ew," Sean said. "I guess you couldn't erase his memory, either."

"Not with Hiram keeping an eye on him. He knows about Veronica's injury, too. I don't know what he'd think, if he got up in the morning and saw that thing, but I don't want to open that can of worms."

"No, definitely not," Jonathan said.

"You know, I really don't get something here. I thought these guys had it out for Jonathan, didn't they? So why are they after Regan now? What happened to you?"

"Oh, that's easy," Regan said.

"Ah, fuck, you know I hate it when you say that—"

"Well, sorry! It's all strategy, Sean. The whole time that Hiram and I were interviewing people, the one thing he was desperate to find was hard evidence connecting any of them in any way with someone who could have attacked them. Well, now he's got evidence. When I took Veronica to the hospital, I was the first person who suddenly had a suspicious connection with one of those weird injuries. Stupid me, it never even occurred to me how it would look, when I left her off and neither one of us explained what had happened to her. And suddenly I make a more plausible suspect than Jonathan. I'm not sure I have an alibi for any of the attacks. All I did most nights was close the store and go home."

"Ok, Veronica, I can see. But does he really think you've been attacking people all along?"

"I don't know," Regan said. "I really don't."

"If he really thinks Jonathan is a vampire now, does he think you are, too, after you disappeared for a week?"

"I have a feeling he does. Just what, exactly, he thinks that means is another question, though."

"Is he going to try and find some way to prove it?"

Regan opened her mouth to answer, then hesitated, and shook her head with a troubled frown. "I don't know what he could do, that would provide proof."

"There are a lot of things," Jonathan said. "And there are different standards of proof. Proving to his own satisfaction is one thing, proof that would be accepted officially is another. But all he needs to do is show evidence of guilt, for one of the incidents. He doesn't need to prove that we're vampires to do that."

"And all he needs to do is connect me solidly with Veronica's injury, and he then can claim I must be responsible for all the others, just because they're similar," Regan said. "And anything I said during a reading that would seem to point elsewhere would just have been my way of deflecting suspicion and creating red herrings. Oh, Hiram could make a very clever case, I know he could."

"Not to mention," Jonathan added, "that any accurate details you described in a reading would suddenly serve as evidence that you must have been on the scene, as far as a skeptic is concerned."

"So, Jonathan's completely off the hook, then?"

"I have Veronica to thank for that."

"Exactly," Regan said. "Jerry Standish is depending on whatever Veronica wrote to him in that letter, to bolster his case that his ex-wife's lawsuit is a conspiracy. If Jonathan is responsible for the incidents, then Veronica lied about being with him at the times they occurred. I seriously doubt that was her intention. Protecting Jonathan wasn't her goal. But if any of the letter is false, then all the rest of it could be false and Jerry Standish's case falls apart. That's where he and Hiram are acting at cross-purposes."

"Which doesn't matter, if they still both get what they want," Jonathan said.

"God. This fucking letter must be longer than *The Lord of the Rings*. What could she have said in it that's giving them so much ammunition?"

"Well, there you have it," Jonathan said. "We need some way to find out what's in that letter. I've been wracking my brains, but...we're fighting half blind without that."

"Well, shit. You guys can open locks. Couldn't you just steal it? Or even get in and read it, and put it back, so no one would know?"

"I probably could," Jonathan said. "Where is it?"

"Uh...well, how should *I* know?"

"Exactly. I can't break into every possible location, hunting for it."

"But this Green guy, old man Standish's attorney, he doesn't know there'd be anything suspicious about Regan touching him. Maybe you could find out from him where the letter is."

"If he knows," Regan said, "He probably wouldn't agree to talk to us in private, because of conflict of interest. And we can't erase his memory, for all the same reasons. Anyway, I bet that letter is in a safe deposit box in Fidelity Bank, or in Attorney Green's office safe. We might get to it, but we probably wouldn't get out free and clear. And then we'd have even more charges to flee from."

They were silent for a few moments. "Fuck," Sean finally said, his shoulders slumping. "If only Veronica had told you more about what she said, that night." He looked up suddenly. "Is there any way you could read—" he broke off. "No, no, no, let's not even go there." There was another silence then, as Sean took a long swig of his Mountain Dew. Regan and Jonathan sat quietly on their cartons, looking at each other. After a few moments, Sean noticed this and glanced between them, then straightened his shoulders, putting the bottle on the floor with a loud thump. "You guys better not be thinking what it looks like you're thinking."

Neither Regan nor Jonathan gave any sign that they had even heard him. "There's only one person now who can cut through the crap and solve all this mess," Regan said finally. "Or most of it, anyway." Jonathan looked away from her then, down at the scuffed floorboards at his feet.

"You can't be serious! Jonathan, for god's sake, tell her what we're dealing with here! You know what she was like!" Sean's voice had gone up at least a minor fifth.

Regan ignored him. "Jonathan..." she said, and he looked up at her. "We were going to have to face this eventually. We couldn't have just left her there indefinitely, and we certainly can't leave her there if we flee. Now we need her."

Jonathan looked at Sean for a moment, then back at Regan. "I have to agree that Sean's concerns are well-founded. What makes you think that we can control Veronica now?"

Regan was silent a moment, but consciously, she was extending her awareness out of the room, touching a formless, tormented presence that she could just barely feel, outside of dreams. "I think..." she said slowly, "...that things are going to be very different now."

"You're connected to her," Jonathan said, as though realizing it for the first time.

"You didn't see her in a normal state. I mean what her normal state would be as a vampire, not what she was like in life."

"In life...her normal state was erratic, to say the least."

"But that's changed now, too. Jonathan, have you ever completely drained a human being of blood? Drained them until they died?"

Jonathan stared at her. "No. I've never done that."

"But you can imagine what it would feel like, to drink that much blood."

Jonathan was quiet a moment, a look of distaste on his face. Then his expression changed. "She was high."

"Exactly. That's what you saw, you and Sean. Once, just once, not long after

I moved back down here, Veronica got totally wasted on coke. She acted just exactly the way she did when you and Sean caught her. In fact, that was the first time she was arrested, and she ended up hospitalized for two weeks. Veronica was on overload when you saw her, Jonathan. But she had nowhere to go but down. And that's where she's been since then, especially since I woke up. Can we control her now? She was never easy to control. But we can talk to her now. What she'll agree to, I can't say."

Sean waved his hand in the air. "Can I just...please say something?" They looked at him, and he went on, "Do you remember what she promised to do, the minute she got loose? I mean, I don't want to sound all self-centered here, but she did say she was going to kill me, about fifty different ways, right? Doesn't that count for something? Do you guys care if I get killed?"

"Of course we care," Regan said. "But Veronica also promised Jonathan that he'd never get me back, and she was blowing smoke out her ass about that, wasn't she? Come on, Sean. You never saw any of your friends getting high?"

"Well, yeah..."

"Never got high yourself?"

"Well, sure—I mean, I'm no stoner or anything..."

"And people who are high never talk a lot of bullshit?"

Sean opened his mouth and then closed it. "Okay, okay. But this was different. I mean, fuck, Regan! She'd just ripped *your* throat out! Forgive me for believing she would do the same to me!"

"I forgive you. That night, she probably would have. But now I'm asking you to trust me." She looked at Jonathan. "I'm asking you both. Trust me. Things have changed."

This time, it was Sean and Jonathan who exchanged looks. "I do trust you," Jonathan said finally. "But you didn't see the way she was that night, for hours, Regan. She raved for hours. It seemed like she would never stop."

"Excuse me. I did see her the way she was that night. Remember who she was with before she got to you. Do you really think *I'm* naïve about how dangerous she could be? I'd be the last person pushing to let her out of that box, if I wasn't sure that she's not going to be like that now." Jonathan hesitated, and Regan said, "What's the alternative, Jonathan? She can't stay where she is much longer. The next house the police will be searching is yours. We both know that. She'll be found. We've got to do something with her. What do you suggest?"

Jonathan swallowed, hard. "Sean thought..." he said hesitantly, glancing at Sean, "that we should just burn her, box and all."

"I'd still vote for that," Sean said.

"And where would you find anyplace hot enough to do that, and leave no remains that could be identified?"

"The funeral home has a crematorium."

"Oh, right," Regan said. "Now there's a place that no one is keeping an eye on these days. And cremations take hours, Jonathan. We couldn't break in and hang around that long, at Burgos or any other funeral home." As Jonathan frowned down at the floor, Regan leaned towards him. "We need her, Jonathan. *I* need her. I don't want to go underground for the next sixty years."

"You don't know what she'll say, Regan. She might not help at all. She might make things worse. She could tell the police where she's been for the last eleven days, for instance."

"She can't do that without exposing what she is. And I could tell the police what she did to me, if it came to that. I've got the scar to prove it."

"Aw, come on," Sean said, "the cops will throw all of us out the door for being nut jobs."

"Which might be one solution to our problems." There was a pause then. The television in the apartment below was turned on, on higher volume than usual. They needed to load these last boxes and leave, before it got so late that the neighbors complained.

"All right," Jonathan finally said.

"No! It's too dangerous!"

"It's okay, Sean," Regan said. "We won't let her hurt you. If you're right, and she's still out of control, we can do what you want, and get rid of her. We won't have any choice."

"You think eleven days in that box will have improved her mood any? Because I sure don't."

"We'll see," Regan said.

"Shall we do it tonight?" Jonathan said.

Regan considered. "Yes. Let's do it right away. I don't think our adversaries want to give us time to regroup. Now they've gotten me arrested and evicted from my apartment, so they know we're off-balance. They also must suspect that we might pack up and flee, Jonathan, knowing your history. God only knows what they'll hit us with tomorrow. We've got to hit back first, if we can, or at least be ready."

"Doesn't that make it even more likely that someone will be watching us tonight?" Sean asked.

"You're our electronics expert. Jonathan and I will be able to find anyone who's near the house. The woods will make it hard for someone to be watching from a distance, even with night-vision technology. You can do the best sweep you can after dark. Beyond that, we're just taking our chances. But we're running out of time."

"Here's hoping this place wasn't bugged," Sean said gloomily.

"You're the one who swept it."

"I know, but I couldn't get into the attic, or the apartment downstairs."

"Well..." Regan stood up and stretched. "If it is, we'll find out. Let's finish up here."

Chapter 28

They got back to Rainbow Stone house a little after 9:00, after returning the empty van to the rental station and leaving its keys in the night drop-off box. Before they released Veronica, there was a practical problem to solve. She would be hungry, after eleven days, and that would make her mood and behavior more unpredictable. They would have better luck handling her, Regan pointed out, if they could think of some way to get some blood for her. This proved to be a tough puzzle to solve. They were discussing it in the car after they returned the van.

"I hope no one thinks I'm going to volunteer."

"We wouldn't ask you, Sean," Regan said patiently. "For one thing, Veronica doesn't seem to have the hang of *closing*. She's going to need some remedial lessons."

"Not that either of us couldn't take care of that, if need be," Jonathan said.

"Oh, can we *close* a wound that someone else has *opened*?"

"Listen, guys! Moot point, all right?" Sean's voice was a bit higher than usual. Jonathan chuckled.

"I was only speaking hypothetically. But your answer is yes, Regan, at least conditionally."

"That's interesting...but anyway. What about the dairy farm?"

Jonathan shook his head. "I try to space out my visits there, and even then it's risky. I have to go in the daytime. All the livestock are put into the barns after sunset, and they have dogs. Besides, there's a difference between just getting a drink, which takes less than a minute, and collecting blood in some kind of container. It wouldn't be easy at all." But he looked thoughtful.

"We couldn't steal some?" Sean asked. "Maybe the hospital?"

Regan sighed. "It would be very difficult to get in and out of a hospital undetected, and their blood is inventoried. And if I'm caught pulling any stunts like that while I'm out on bail, I'll be remanded."

"I think I have an idea, though," Jonathan said. "The dairy farm isn't the only place that has livestock. There are quite a few people who own animals around this area. Horses, ponies, goats, all kinds of things."

"But won't we face very similar problems anywhere else? Everyone has sheds and barns for their stock, especially with all the problems in this part of the state with feral dogs and coyotes. They'll have motion sensor lights, dogs and security alarms, too."

"Not to mention guns," Sean added.

"In most cases, that's true. But I have seen a few small operations that aren't so well equipped. It's just going to take me some time to get there, get the blood without being caught, and get back."

"You want to do this alone?"

"I think the fewer people, the safer. It will be tricky enough to pull off, as it is."

When they got to the house, Jonathan found two plastic containers with wide mouths and screw-on lids among Regan's kitchen wares. He filled one with ice from his refrigerator's freezer, and embedded the smaller container in the ice. "Don't be concerned if I'm not back for a while. I'm not going to take any unnecessary risks."

After he left, Sean and Regan went outside and searched the area around the house for any sign of surveillance. Sean was hampered by the darkness, but his electronic detectors found nothing suspicious, and he saw no LED's shining among the trees. As far as Regan could see, smell or hear, there was not another human being closer than the farm. They took a long time, partly because it was a way of diverting their thoughts from worrying about Jonathan and thinking about what lay ahead. When they finally could do no more, they came inside and sat in the great room, saying very little. Regan sat upright in the chair that faced Jonathan's computer, watching the screen saver but lost in her own thoughts. Sean sat hunched over at the end of the table, growing steadily more tense as time passed.

Jonathan returned about a half hour past midnight, carrying the plastic container which now sloshed and rattled with ice-filled water. "I'm sorry I took so long. I had to wait for the owners to fall asleep. Are we ready?"

Regan rose from her seat. "Yes," she said. Sean looked up, swallowing hard, and said nothing. But he rose as well and followed Regan and Jonathan mutely as Regan led them through the kitchen and down into the basement. "I think it would be easier to bring the chest in through the bulkhead, don't you think?"

"I agree. She'll be easier to contain down here, too, if...if there are any serious problems."

"You know," Sean said, as Jonathan unbolted the bulkhead and pushed the doors open, "maybe I shouldn't be here. It'll just make things more complicated, right?" His voice was shaking a little and he was still standing on the fourth step of the stairs.

"I want you to stay with us, Sean," Regan said. "In case things do go wrong, I don't want you out of my sight."

"Aren't you the one who's so sure everything will be okay?"

Regan looked at Sean steadily, and he looked down. "Just in case. Come on, let's go."

They walked in single file up the steps and out over the back yard, where the grass was already almost six inches high after April's copious rain. The air was crisp and cool, and the crescent moon was low and yellow in the western sky. Crickets were chirping now, and in the distance they could hear a dog barking up at the dairy farm. Jonathan led them along the almost indistinguishable path through the woods in back until they came to the granite outcropping. Sean had to wait while Regan and Jonathan pushed through the brush and moved the boulder that partly disguised the entrance to the tiny cave in the rock. Jonathan dragged out the wooden chest, and then he and Regan each took an end of it and carried it back to where Sean was waiting. They set it down there for a moment and all three of them stood looking at the chest. It seemed too small to hold a person, especially one as tall as Veronica. There was no sound from the chest.

"Do you think she's dead, dead for real I mean?" Sean whispered. Jonathan just shook his head. Regan knelt and placed her hands flat on the top of the chest, then leaned down and put her ear to the wood, listening. Then she stood up.

"Let's get her back to the house," she said briskly.

It took about ten minutes to carry the chest back to the house, down the steps and into the basement. They set down the chest, and then Jonathan went to the barn and returned with two hammers, two crowbars, and a large heavy ax, which he leaned carefully against the bulkhead steps. Then he swung the bulkhead doors closed and bolted them. Sean paled at the sight of the ax, but he didn't ask what it was for.

Working at opposite ends of the chest, Regan and Jonathan used the flat ends of the crowbars to pry the nailed lid of the chest up about an inch. They hammered down the lid, which left the nail heads protruding above the wood. Then they pulled the long framing nails out, one by one, with the hammers. After almost two weeks in the damp cave, some of the nails made screeching noises as they pulled free of the wood. Sean, sitting on the bottom step below the bulkhead, hugged himself more tightly as each complaining nail was pulled free. When all the nails had been removed, Jonathan raised the lid of the chest. He and Regan both pulled back slightly at the smell of the air that puffed over them.

Veronica was in exactly the same position that she had been after Jonathan so unceremoniously stuffed her into the chest eleven days before. She was absolutely still and her face, where it wasn't stained with dried blood, was so white it almost glowed in the dim basement light. There were patches of slippery dark green mold growing on moist spots on her clothes and skin. After a moment, Jonathan took hold of the chains and lifted Veronica out of the chest, stepped back and laid her on the floor. He bent to unhook the chain, but Regan raised her hand to stop him.

"Gag first," she said softly. She knelt by Veronica's head, leaned down and spoke her name. Then Veronica moved for the first time. Her fingers curled slightly and then opened again. Regan worked loose the duct tape on Veronica's face and pulled it free. She untied the rope around Veronica's head and then tilted her head back and carefully slid the wooden gag out of her mouth. It was shining and wet with deep marks from Veronica's teeth. Regan tossed it aside. Veronica's tongue slowly emerged from her mouth. It looked very dark as it slid over her lips, which were almost as white as the rest of her face. "Now chains,"

Regan said. Jonathan bent down and unhooked the end of the chain. As the tension was released, Veronica drew in a deep breath of air and then let it out in a long, soft moan. Regan and Jonathan had to lift Veronica's body and tip it toward each other as they unwound the chains, and at this Veronica's eyelids fluttered, but she still hadn't opened her eyes. As her arms and legs were freed from their bindings, however, she slowly stretched them out, flexing her hands and feet. Regan, remembering how limber and fit she had felt after a week motionless at the bottom of the well, doubted that Veronica would need long to recover physically. She glanced once at Sean and saw that he had one hand over his mouth, almost gripping it, but he didn't move or speak.

When all the chains had been removed, Regan and Jonathan sat back and waited. Veronica rolled over so she was crouching on her knees and elbows, her forehead pressed to the hard earth floor of the basement. Finally she raised herself so that she was kneeling upright, and then, at last, she opened her eyes. She didn't look at anyone, but stared dazedly at a point on the floor about a yard in front of her. After a minute or so, she straightened her back and sighed deeply. She slowly raised one hand to touch her hair, which was matted with dried blood and hanging in blackened strings around her face. The blood-soaked blue dress was torn in numerous places from Veronica's struggle against the chains and one sleeve was almost entirely detached at the shoulder.

Regan moved so that she was on one knee facing her friend, who did not acknowledge her presence. "Hello, Veronica," she said gently. Veronica slowly raised her head to look at Regan, then squeezed her eyes shut and turned her face away. Regan waited a moment, then reached out and turned Veronica's face back towards her. "Look at me." Veronica stared back at her, her eyes narrowing as though she expected a blow. "Do you understand now what's happened to you?"

Finally Veronica opened her mouth and said, "Yes." Her voice was a raspy whisper that was barely audible even in the silent room. After a moment, she said, "But I don't know why."

"These things can all be explained."

Veronica bowed her head. Then she looked up again. "I thought you were dead." To Regan's amazement, a tear was trickling slowly down her cheek. "I'm sorry, Regan."

Regan tilted her head, studying Veronica with bemusement. "Why were you so angry, Ver? Why did you wake up with so much rage?"

Minute by minute, Veronica was returning to a more normal state. Her voice was already stronger. "I didn't want to be here. I didn't want to see you, or anyone, ever again. I thought it was over. I couldn't stand it, that it wasn't over."

"Do you feel that way now?" Veronica, after all, had had eleven days with absolutely nothing else to do but think things through.

Veronica closed her eyes, but she shook her head slowly. "I'm stuck with it. I know that now. That's my punishment for killing myself. I'm in hell." She opened her eyes. "I'm so hungry," she said, almost in a moan. "I know he's here. I can smell him."

"Who? You mean Sean?" Regan heard Sean suck in a gasp, but didn't glance at him.

"I can't even look at him. Oh, god, I said such horrible things, Regan. I did such horrible things. I didn't mean to kill you. I didn't know what I was doing."

Regan looked down for a moment, touching the coils of chain at her side with her fingers. "I think, Veronica, that at this point we're going to consider everything even."

"I thought you were going to burn me. I didn't ever think I'd see the light again. Why did you let me out?"

"There's no reason you have to stay in that box if you're going to behave yourself. Actually, we need your help, Ver."

Veronica looked bewildered. "My help?"

"But first, we have something for you." Regan gestured to Jonathan, and he got up and went to the stairs and took the smaller container from its ice water bath. It was filled now with dark liquid. He handed the container to Regan, who unscrewed its lid and offered it to Veronica. She leaned forward and sniffed, then took the container with both hands. She took a sip, swallowed, and wrinkled her nose.

"It's cold," she said, but she began drinking, and continued without stopping, her head falling back, until the container was empty. Then she put her hand inside the wide mouth and cleaned the remaining blood off the inside surface with her fingers, licking her fingers off, until there was nothing left in the container that she could reach. Only then did she hand the container back to Regan. "I feel better now," she said, and sighed.

Regan saw Jonathan and Sean exchange looks and knew what they were thinking. Would the euphoria of blood tip Veronica back into an irrational state? But there was no evidence of that. "Give me your hands, Veronica."

For the first time, Veronica smiled faintly. "Are you going to read me, Regan?"

"Are you going to block me, Ver?"

"I can't block you anymore, don't you know that?" She stuck out both hands as though she expected to be handcuffed. Regan took hold of them, and Veronica clasped Regan's hands tightly. Regan closed her eyes, and had to suck in a breath, because for a moment she could feel chains biting into her flesh, holding her rigidly motionless, while a hard spike of ash wood filled her mouth and throat. *Eleven days she suffered through this...* but Regan pushed past that, focusing on what her friend was feeling and thinking now. There was no rage or confusion or paranoia, only a gentle bubbling sense of euphoria from the blood she'd just drunk, and that wouldn't last long. Behind that was nothing but a flat gray expanse. Veronica's psyche now made Regan think of a quotation from Gertrude

Stein: *There is no 'there' there.* But Veronica's vampire state had nothing to do with this. Regan let go of Veronica's hands, suddenly overwhelmed by sadness, for the first time since she'd heard the news about Veronica's suicide. *She hasn't really come back at all. She killed herself, and at the core of her being, she's still dead.* How could Veronica go on this way? How could they ask that of her?

"Do I pass inspection?"

Regan, shaken out of her reverie, looked up quickly. "One hundred percent. Maybe you'd like to wash up a bit, Ver? Then we can all have a talk, and fill you in on what's been going on."

Veronica spread her hands and looked down at herself, grimacing as she realized, for the first time, the condition that she was in. "Where are my clothes?"

"I have no idea, but I imagine your parents packed up your condo. I can loan you some things." They both stood up, Veronica just a bit stiffly. She looked around the room, and when she saw Sean and Jonathan, she ducked her head away quickly and didn't speak to them.

"Are we going back to your place?" she asked Regan hopefully.

"Unfortunately, I've been evicted from my place—"

"What?"

"I'm living here for now."

"What happened?"

Regan almost laughed. "We'll take it in chronological order, Ver." They all filed up the stairs, Sean trailing the rear. In the kitchen, Regan said firmly, "You better take Sean home, Jonathan. Sean, if you cut one more day of school, your mother will be furious, and the school might report it to DSS."

Sean made no protest. Jonathan hesitated. "Are you sure..." he broke off, as if unwilling to even invoke the possibility of another disaster.

"Yes," Regan said firmly.

Veronica turned and looked at Sean and Jonathan for the first time. "I'm not going to hurt anybody," she said, her voice quavering.

"Besides, she can't now. I can defend myself. Sean, all you're going to miss is a long boring recap of stuff you already know."

"No prob," Sean mumbled.

"Well..." Jonathan paused, and then shrugged resignedly. "I'll be back as soon as I can. Come on, Sean."

Veronica cleaned up very nicely, as Regan told her humorously. The only clothes Regan had that fit her were leggings and a large sweatshirt, but even those took on an air of elegance on Veronica's tall frame. Washed clean of blood, dirt and the funeral home cosmetician's sausage curls, her pale blonde hair flowed in shining ripples down her back. Her skin had the flawless translucence of a baby's. Even her hands were smooth and unmarred, and looked younger trimmed of their false nails. Regan's shoes were too small for Veronica's long narrow feet, but she pronounced herself perfectly comfortable barefoot. "I'm just going to move to Greenwich Village," she said after studying herself in the bathroom mirror.

It was closing on four in the morning before Jonathan and Regan finished telling Veronica everything that had happened since the 10th, and answered her many questions. Never much of a reader at all, Veronica had far less context for understanding vampirism than Regan or Sean, and it took extensive and careful explanation to overcome her confused misconceptions. But she finally seemed to be comprehending it all, and even more important, accepting it. Regan had insisted that Jonathan tell Veronica what had happened the night she had driven out to his house. Veronica recalled nothing of that afternoon or evening, but she did remember the injury on her neck.

"Didn't you wonder about that, after everything I told you?"

"Well, of course I did, but...I was so sure that you would have done something, if it was the same thing. I never saw one, you just described them."

"Didn't the hospital give you one of Hiram's cards?"

"Yes, they did. But..." she shrugged. "I didn't want to talk to anyone. I lost the card up at the place in Haverhill, anyway, I think I just threw it away."

"That explains the seventeenth victim, though," Jonathan said.

"Yes. But I knew that when I overheard that conversation between Hiram and Jerry Standish."

"I can't believe they're saying *you* attacked me! How could they think that?"

"Well, what else would they think? You wouldn't explain, I wouldn't explain, and I brought you in. But since we're on that general topic, Ver..."

"What?"

Regan sighed. "We need to talk about this letter."

"Letter? Oh. That letter."

"*That* letter. Right."

Veronica folded her arms and studied the tabletop. She was blushing, but more subtly than she would have done in life. *It's a counterfeit blush,* Regan thought, remembering Jonathan's words. "Well...what about it?"

"We need to know what you said in it, to begin with."

"Well, I..." Veronica was looking anywhere but at Jonathan. "It was all stuff I made up! Up in the hospital. I was on every medication you can think of, things I'd never even heard of before. I guess I just...I don't know, I think I believed it then. I wrote it like a diary, and I got myself all worked up. It all seems so stupid now. I was reading it to my therapist up there. I don't think she believed it, really."

"But...what did you *say,* Ver?"

Veronica bowed her head and shrugged. "Well...you know...sort of, fantasies..."

After a short pause, Jonathan said wryly, "I think we already have the gist of it, from what Ted Green and Jerry Standish told me. We don't have to pry the exact details out of poor Veronica."

Veronica ventured a timid look at him. "Did you see the letter?" she asked in a small voice.

"No one has seen this letter, except your father and his attorney. It's a complete mystery." Veronica visibly relaxed.

"But," Regan said, "if either of us goes to trial, for anything, that letter is going to end up being subpoenaed and probably read in court."

"Oh, *god!*" Veronica gaped at them. "Oh, no, you *couldn't!*"

"It's not our choice, Ver."

"Attorney Delaney will request it as part of her discovery, first thing," Jonathan said. "She'll have to, Jerry Standish is relying on it for a huge part of his case."

"But...how do we stop that?"

"Well," Regan said, "the only way to destroy the letter's value as evidence... is for you to recant it."

"You mean...tell everyone that I was lying?" Regan gave her a look, and she cleared her throat. "I mean, tell everyone the truth."

"It's not a question of everyone," Jonathan said. "So far, only a few people even know about it. If you admit that nothing in the letter really happened and you wrote it...well, say you wrote it as part of your therapy and believed it at the time...then there's no reason for it to go further. You can claim copyright of your own letter, you know. No one else has a legal right to publish or reproduce it in that case."

"Is that true?" Veronica asked in amazement.

"I think so," Regan said, "*if* the letter is not evidence in a criminal or civil trial."

Veronica folded her arms and leaned back in her chair, one knee crossed as she tapped her bare foot against the leg of the table and considered. Finally she said, "What do you think my father is going to say when he sees me? He thinks I'm dead, doesn't he? Or does he? I'm still confused about that."

Regan and Jonathan looked at each other, and then Regan shrugged helplessly. "We aren't sure what he thinks. He thinks I'm colluding with your mother to sue him, but I don't know if he's convinced that you really walked out of the funeral home with me. He might think we stole your body and rigged someone up to impersonate you. I don't know *how* we're supposed to have done that..."

"That's so ridiculous! And I just can't *believe* my mother is suing my father! Wasn't that fucking divorce enough?"

"Maybe this is her revenge for his getting custody," Regan said cynically.

"Yeah, like she wanted me. She didn't give a fuck." She scowled down for a moment, and then squared her shoulders. "So, what do I do, just pick up the phone and call my dad? Sure, why not? I'll call him right now, give him the shock of his life, hello dad, it's me, back from the grave. Mom can take her fucking lawsuit and shove it right—"

"Whoa, whoa, whoa, Ver! Yeah, you can contact your father, but let's just think things through first. You can't tell him the truth."

"Well, no, of *course* not. But—"

"We all need to get some kind of story put together, and it should be as simple and as close to the truth as possible. And we need to figure out some way of verifying where we say you've been for the last week and a half, in case anyone checks the story out."

"But...how can we do *that?*"

Regan looked at Jonathan inquiringly. "Jonathan? Can we hack the records for some hotel or retreat center or something?"

Jonathan appeared to be deep in thought, and he glanced up, blinking, at the question. "No. I mean, yes, we could do that, but it would be much too easy to expose if anyone took the effort. I have another idea."

"Which is...?"

"I...know someone. Up in Maine. I think she'll be willing to say that Veronica was staying with her." He looked up at the two women's bewildered faces. "To get away from things, you know. Look. It's very simple. You woke up in the funeral home and met Regan. Just like she told Detective Fellman, you wouldn't go to a hospital and went storming off on your own because you were so furious that you'd been declared dead. You went up to Maine to stay with this friend of yours. We can fill in the details about how and when you met her, and Regan can verify that part. You had no idea what was going on down here until Regan finally tracked you down, and now you're back to straighten everything out. You're still upset, mind you. You're not about to be one bit more cooperative or forthcoming than you have to be. And that's not much. You're a lucid adult and you haven't done anything wrong. You don't have to submit to medical exams or answer questions or explain yourself in any way. If anyone gets pushy, you just start talking about the lawsuit you're going to file." He sat back and folded his arms with a self-satisfied look. "How does that sound?"

Regan was trying to find some holes in this plan, just because he looked so smug, but she couldn't. "I guess that sounds...pretty good."

"But, how am I ever going to explain why for a week everybody thought I was dead?"

Jonathan spread his hands in a so-what gesture. "Since when is that your problem? You were unconscious, you don't know how all those professionals screwed up. You're the victim here. You don't owe them tests, explanations, apologies or anything else. It's not up to you to cover their asses for them."

Veronica pursed her lips, thinking about this. "Okay. Then how did I get to Maine?"

"On the bus. You can buy a bus ticket with cash, and claim you lost the stub. They don't keep records like airlines. And you can catch a Greyhound bus to anywhere in Fall River."

"So I walked to Fall River?"

"You hitchhiked. Plenty of men would stop to pick up someone who looked like you on a dark road at night, don't you think?"

"And how did I get back here from Maine?"

"Your friend drove you down."

"Who *is* this person?" Suddenly Regan remembered something, a detail from her long meditation on the barbed wire ball. "Is she...one of us?"

Jonathan looked at her seriously for a moment and then inclined his head. "Yes."

"The one you met here?"

His smile broadened. "Very good."

"But how can you be so sure she'll do this?" Veronica said uneasily. "You haven't even talked to her."

"Is this one of those favors you're calling in?"

Jonathan looked down, still smiling. "It's not a simple quid pro quo. We're old friends. I'm sure she'll help. She's a good soul. But she may want to talk to you, and see a picture of you."

Veronica hunched her shoulders. "God...I'll feel like such a newbie. She doesn't have to know everything I did, does she?"

"She's going to be very entertained by this whole story." He chuckled dryly. "I can imagine what she'll say."

"I guess it makes sense, though. I'd been kicked out of my condo, I'd been declared dead, I sold my car to this used car dealer in Fall River—"

"Oh, is *that* what happened to it?" Regan said.

"I sold it for two hundred dollars and threw the money down a storm drain so my father wouldn't get it. Stupid, right?"

"Hey, who am I to judge? But there's your bus money, if we need to explain where that came from."

"I bought a bus ticket and went stomping up to Maine. Okay. So, when can we talk to your friend?"

"She keeps the same hours we do. I'll call her right away."

Veronica stared at him for a minute and then shook her head. "It's like...a family or something, is that it? We're all some kind of family?"

"In a way. Or tribe, maybe. But the four of us here, we are a sort of family. We didn't choose each other, but we have to trust each other."

"Are there other...families?" Regan said.

Jonathan hesitated, then nodded. "I was sort of unusual, being so solitary."

"Well," Veronica said, "I'm going to get that letter back from my father. And I'm going to burn it. God, I'm glad you didn't see it."

"I don't know why. I'm feeling very disappointed that I missed all that, actually." He was grinning.

Veronica covered her face with her hands, and Regan said in exasperation, "Jonathan, would you stop it!"

"What? I'm sure it's tame compared to what people put on their blogs these days."

"Be that as it may...don't you have a phone call to make?"

Still grinning, Jonathan pulled the strongbox forward and started searching for the phone number.

Chapter 29

At around 9:00 Wednesday morning, Jonathan, Regan and Veronica drove to the Sheridan police station and asked to see Detective Fellman so they could let him know that Veronica was back. Regan thought this would be preferable to a phone call. Detective Fellman betrayed only a brief moment of surprise when he first saw them, but after that listened to their story with the same detached expression that he always seemed to wear.

"Is it correct to assume that none of you wants to prefer any charges against each other?" he asked. When he was assured this was the case, he thanked them for coming in. But Regan had an additional request.

"I was wondering if you could check Veronica's fingerprints." She knew the police had them on file. "Just in case there are any questions about her identity. I've heard some rumors that it was an impostor seen leaving the funeral home."

"We can do that." The electronic fingerprint reader confirmed that Veronica was indeed who she claimed to be.

"Have you gotten in touch with your parents, Miss Standish?" Detective Fellman asked as they were about to leave.

"We're going to do that soon," Veronica said. She had been a bit stiff with Detective Fellman throughout the discussion, which was understandable given her past experiences with the Sheridan police department.

"*God,* I would hate to play poker with that man," Regan said when they were back in the car. "What is he *thinking?* I would kill to get a chance to read him! What do you think it would take?"

"Be careful what you wish for," Jonathan said quietly. Regan, suddenly realizing what she had said, was silent.

They went back to Rainbow Stone house, where Jonathan called Kate Delaney. He gave her a brief version of the cover story that had been agreed on earlier that morning. "Are you available for a meeting with us and the Standishes this afternoon?"

"For this, I'll clear my calendar."

"I'll have to talk to Ted Green and have him arrange a meeting time, then I'll call you." He clicked off and called Ted Green's office. Jonathan had intended to leave a message for a return call, but the secretary asked him to hold and after just a few seconds, the attorney was on the line.

"Mr. Vaughn, what can I do for you?"

"Good morning, Mr. Green. I'm calling because I'd like to arrange a meeting with you and the Standishes—that is, Jerry Standish and Mrs. Westfield."

There was a pause. "That might be problematical, Mr. Vaughn, under the circumstances."

"I understand, but the circumstances have changed somewhat. *Miss* Standish would like to have a meeting with her parents. We'll be bringing counsel, by the way."

There was a long silence. "Miss Standish..." Ted Green said finally.

"That is correct. She's just gotten back from a trip out of state. Her friend Regan Calloway tracked her down, with some difficulty."

"Miss Standish has her own counsel?"

"Yes, we're complicating things. Just how complicated they'll get depends very largely on Mr. Standish and Mrs. Westfield. However, I can promise you that Miss Standish would like to talk over her concerns. Regan Calloway and I will both be present, as well, for reasons I don't think I need to explain. Would you like to speak to Miss Standish?"

"Is she there?"

Jonathan pushed the mute button on the phone and turned to look at Veronica. "He knows your voice, doesn't he?"

"Of course he does, he's my dad's lawyer, every time I was in trouble that's who my dad called. He wouldn't come himself, he'd just send Mr. Green, esquire." Jonathan handed her the phone. "Hello, Mr. Green."

"Miss Standish..." Regan and Jonathan could hear his voice clearly. His evident stupefaction was most entertaining. "Are you all right?"

"Well, I am now. No thanks to my father and a million other incredibly stupid people."

"Where have you been, Miss Standish?"

Veronica glanced uncertainly at Jonathan and he gave her a quick shake of his head. "I'll explain everything when we're all together. Both my parents, and me and Regan and Jonathan. And all our attorneys, so you'd better have a big conference room. Oh, and since my father *and* my mother will be there, you probably will want to remove all the breakables and frisk everyone at the door."

There was another short pause. "Can I reach all of you at Mr. Vaughn's home number?"

"Yes, you can, due to the fact that thanks to all the *shit* that has been going on, Regan and I are both homeless, and we're staying out here in this dump now."

Ted Green cleared his throat uncomfortably. "As soon as I've gotten in touch with your parents, Miss Standish, I'll give you a call. It may take a little time..."

"But you're going to get right on it."

"I'll get back to you as soon as I can."

Veronica clicked off the phone, scowling.

"Veronica, you are in cracking form today," Regan said wryly.

"I hate him."

"I think you just hate the fact that your father used him as a stand-in," Jonathan said sympathetically.

"Isn't that enough? Lawyers are whores, anyway."

"But sometimes useful. Try to be polite to Kate Delaney, at least. She's on our side."

"Of course she is, you pay her." Veronica looked down at herself and made a sound of distaste. "I can't wear *this* to meet with my parents! I don't even have any shoes." She'd worn a pair of Regan's flip-flops to the police station. "Isn't it going to look awfully weird that I supposedly have been in Maine all this time visiting this alleged friend, and I don't have anything to wear?"

"You left with no clothes, no credit cards, and barely enough money for your bus ticket," Regan said reasonably.

"But I'd have found *something*..."

Regan looked at Jonathan. "She has a point. It's not like we have to keep her in hiding, is it? We've already been into town."

"Well, no," Jonathan said. "I'd just rather clear things up with her parents before too many other people find out that she's here. Your being back, Veronica, is going to create a certain sensation, I hope you're aware of that."

"Besides, Veronica, you have no money and I don't have much. You can't ask Jonathan to keep both of us, can you?"

"Who knows, I might expect some favors in that case. Especially now that I know how imaginative you are."

Veronica's cheeks pinked with that counterfeit blush. "Of course not, I didn't mean...I forgot about not having money."

"Yes, well, you never saw that as a requirement for shopping." Regan sighed. "I imagine it's going to take Mr. Green a couple of hours, at least, to get hold of everyone and coordinate this meeting," she said, getting up from her chair, "and they can damn well wait for us. Come on, Ver, I know a couple of thrift shops around Fall River. We can pick you up some things and be back by one or two. No, don't worry, you can pay me back sometime..."

"Right, maybe after I sue both my parents," Veronica said sullenly as she followed Regan to the door.

"That's one option among many."

One of the richest and cheapest sources of interesting used clothing Regan knew was a weekly thrift shop in the basement of a Methodist church, and Regan found a few things for herself while Veronica sighed and tsked through racks and tried on shoes. As they emerged from the alleyway between the church and the parish hall, Regan was startled to hear someone call her name.

"Regan Calloway? That's right, isn't it?"

Regan turned and peered at the speaker. The midday sunshine dazzled her eyes even though she was wearing sunglasses and it took her a moment to recognize the thin woman who had spoken to her. "Mrs. Stockard. Hello, how are you?"

Evelyn Stockard smiled a little wanly at this question. "There's not a simple answer to that...but with luck, I'll be okay." Seeing Regan's puzzled look, she said, "I was just telling Jim that I wished I could get in touch with you somehow.

I called that Dr. Clauson, and he said that you two aren't working together anymore. He wouldn't give me your number."

Filing this information away to examine later, Regan said, "Why did you want to get in touch with me?"

"To thank you, actually. For possibly saving my life."

Then it clicked. "You went for a physical. I honestly didn't think you would."

Evelyn looked away for a moment, her smile crooked. "I wasn't going to. But Angie's high school did one of those antique road show days as a fundraiser for the sports teams. I took mom's figurine in and had them look at it. When they told me what it was worth, well...I thought maybe I'd take your other piece of advice, as well."

"What happened?"

"Good news and bad news. I'm having surgery next week, and I'll be on chemo after that. But my oncologist says my prognosis is very positive, because we caught it so early. If I'd waited until I had any symptoms, even a cough, my chances would be much worse."

"I certainly wish you the best, Mrs. Stockard. Chemo is never easy."

"I know. I've seen several people go through it. And I'm trying to quit smoking, see?" She pushed up the short sleeve of her cotton knit top to reveal a nicotine patch.

"Good for you."

"Jim and Angie are being very supportive. Actually, Angie's being a little *too* supportive—" Evelyn laughed. "I didn't realize how much they wanted me to quit. It's been that much harder, of course, being out of work and everything."

"Out of work? Because of your medical situation?"

"No, I was let go."

"What? Seatech *fired* you? No...not because of what happened! They couldn't."

Evelyn smiled cynically. "Oh, they couldn't say it right out. But I heard through the grapevine that management thought I'd made the company look bad. I was back at work on Monday, but I had a performance review come up, they gave me unacceptables in half the categories and I was fired the next day."

"Ah, man, that *sucks*. But I can relate. That just happened to me."

Veronica had been standing by listening to the conversation with more interest than she usually displayed. "Sounds just like something my dad would do."

"This is my friend Veronica, Mrs. Stockard." They exchanged pleasantries. Evelyn Stockard did not appear to recognize Veronica from the photo in the Fall River *Herald*, but Veronica, like Regan, was wearing sunglasses and a hat, and despite these was still shading her eyes with one hand and squinting at Evelyn's sunlit face.

"I've seen your name in the paper a few times," Evelyn said to Regan. "It sounded like you were having some problems."

"Oh, well...stuff happens."

"Anyway..." Evelyn looked at her watch. "I'm temping, that why I'm in Fall River today. I don't want to get back late from lunch. But I am glad I ran into you, Ms. Calloway. If there's ever anything I can do for you, I'd like to know. I mean that."

Regan looked at Evelyn speculatively for a moment. "You know...what I'm supposed to say, when you tell me that, is something like, oh, don't mention it. But the truth is, Mrs. Stockard, I just might need you to do me a favor sometime. I wonder if you'd mind giving me your phone number?"

"Of course." Evelyn dug in her purse and pulled out a little pink plastic folder with a pad of paper inside, and scribbled her number on one of the sheets.

"Thanks." Regan put the paper in her handbag. "Unfortunately, I just got evicted from my apartment—"

"Oh, my god."

"—so I don't really have a phone number I can give you, but I'll try to keep in touch."

"What in the world has been going *on?*"

"Way too much excitement. I hope things are going to be settling down a bit. Good luck next week, I hope things go well."

At 3:30, Jonathan, Regan, Veronica and Kate Delaney arrived at Ted Green's office. They had been conferring for two hours at Rainbow Stone house, where Kate had already been waiting when Regan and Veronica returned from Fall River. "'Bout time you girls got back," she'd remarked when they came in the front door. Jonathan's plan was to keep their own demands as simple as possible, but Kate warned them that they shouldn't be too confident. "We don't know what they might be going to throw at us. Be careful what you say and be prepared to hear anything."

"What *could* they be going to say?" Regan asked, genuinely bemused. "They can't possibly have been expecting this."

"We don't know what they've been expecting, do we? I have a personal rule never to assume anything." Regan had a strong suspicion that Kate did not believe a word of their cover story, although that begged the question of just where she did think Veronica had been.

They all filed into Ted Green's conference room and sat along one side of the mahogany table. Facing them were Jerry Standish, an avuncular-looking gray-haired man who was introduced as Cyrus Stuart, Anita Westfield's attorney, and Mrs. Westfield, Veronica's mother. Regan looked at her with interest, as she had not seen the former Mrs. Standish in over a decade. Anita Westfield had Veronica's pale blue eyes and over-thin frame, although she was not so tall. Like her daughter, she ruthlessly bleached her honey blond hair, but Anita's hair was expensively permed and styled, and her clothes were severe but costly. She was deeply tanned and her skin was older than her years. Regan noticed that she wore a small gold cross on a delicate gold chain. *Lucky there's nothing to that superstition or half of us would be fleeing the room,* she thought, and suppressed an amused smile. She needn't have worried that anyone would notice. Veronica's parents were staring at their daughter with such intensity that they wouldn't have glanced at Regan if she'd danced on the table. When Veronica walked in, Anita put a hand to her mouth, tears welling in her eyes. Jerry Standish appeared to be battling with such conflicting emotions, rage chief among them, that his face was a rigid mask.

When everyone was seated, Ted Green, wearing a somewhat stunned look, said, "I'd like to thank everyone for responding on such short notice. Perhaps we should make introductions..." The three attorneys introduced themselves and their clients. Ted Green then said, "Since Miss Standish has requested this meeting, I suggest that you, or your counsel, begin."

Veronica had agreed that as long as Jonathan was paying Kate Delaney to be there, it made sense to let their attorney do the talking, at least to start with. Kate looked around the table, pointedly meeting the eyes of everyone on Ted Green's side, until she had their undivided attention. "I hope we can keep this fairly brief. Before I get to our main points, I'd like to remind everyone here of a few facts. Miss Standish has absolutely no legal obligation to reveal her whereabouts since Friday, May fourteenth, or her future plans. She is an independent adult and has committed no crime. I will say that her whereabouts and her identity can both be documented. It's Miss Standish's decision whether she will choose to respond to any such questions. She has a demand of her own, however, which is the purpose of this meeting."

Kate paused significantly. Recognizing a cue, Ted Green said, "And what is Miss Standish's demand?"

"We would like the letter that she mailed to her father returned to us."

"Now, wait a moment," Jerry Standish began.

"You may not use the letter in any way without Miss Standish's permission, and she revokes all such permission. Not only that, she recants in full the contents of the letter, and will say so publicly."

"Are you saying that everything you wrote was a lie?" Jerry Standish said to Veronica.

"I made it all up. Every word of it, for my therapist up at the hospital. They had me on tons of drugs and I believed it was true when I wrote it. But it's all bullshit. I hadn't even met Jonathan when I said half of that happened." Anita sucked in a little gasp at the vulgarism, although even at thirteen, Veronica's language had been colorful.

"Miss Standish is very concerned that this letter will be used in some way contrary to her interests, or the interests of people she cares about," Kate said. "So, we want it back. Moreover..." she opened her briefcase and removed a set of papers. "We would like a signed statement to the effect that not only the original, but all copies that may have been made, including electronic, digital or audio, have also either been turned over to us or destroyed."

Jerry Standish leaned over and muttered to Ted Green, who straightened up and spoke. "Ms. Delaney, you stated that Veronica hasn't committed any crime. I don't want to sound harsh, but she did attempt suicide, and not only caused her immediate family significant distress, she also incurred some expense to the taxpayers of this state. By Massachusetts law, persons with suicidal ideation can be remanded to psychiatric care involuntarily. The letter may contain information relating to that."

Before Kate could respond, Veronica said tartly, "Who says I attempted suicide?"

"Well, you left a note." Ted Green sounded as though he thought this was a ridiculous question.

"I didn't say I was committing suicide in the note, did I? I'd written that note for the realtor, that's all. I just said I would be out of the condo by the fifteenth for the new owners. Did I say I was going to kill myself?"

Jerry Standish opened his mouth and closed it again, his face reddening. "You took an overdose of pills, Veronica. We found the bottles."

"I didn't take all those pills. I flushed them." Veronica looked at Regan. "Sorry, Regan. I did it again. Those meds were messing with my head. I'd had it." Regan just shrugged and smiled weakly. Veronica looked back at Ted Green and Jerry Standish. "Can you prove I took the pills? There was never an autopsy, or I wouldn't be sitting here. Go ahead, prove I took them."

"What do you mean, you did it again?" Anita Westfield looked appalled.

Veronica turned and gave Regan an urgent look, and Regan said uncomfortably, "Veronica told me that she flushed all her medications a few weeks earlier, before she went to Haverhill."

"That's why I had that breakdown. It had nothing to do with Jonathan, or anyone else. And I told the emergency room nurses that and my therapist in Haverhill, too."

"Oh, honey," Anita said. "Why did you *do* a thing like that? Don't you know—"

"Mom, just don't even go there." Veronica fixed Jerry Standish with a look that should have left second degree burns. "But I see why I ended up at a funeral home instead of a hospital. You came in, saw the pill bottles, and immediately thought, oh, there goes my pathetic, useless, psycho daughter, she's taken an overdose and killed herself. So no one even bothered to check, they just zipped me into the body bag and whisked me off—"

Both Veronica's parents reacted simultaneously, interrupting her.

"Oh, *Veronica*..."

"I think that's a very unfair characterization, young lady—" Jerry Standish had paled slightly and he looked, if Regan could have believed it, almost hurt. Anita Westfield was nearly in tears, pressing her delicate lace-trimmed handkerchief to her mouth.

"But technically accurate, I'm sure," Kate Delaney said dryly.

"You were taken straight to the emergency room. We were told nothing could be done."

"As a matter of fact," Kate Delaney said, "We have the E.R. records here. We went to the hospital and Veronica signed a release form for them." Kate removed the records from her briefcase. "According to these, the examining physician noted a few anomalies in Veronica's condition, specifically a lack of rigor mortis."

"He did sign the death certificate, nevertheless," Ted Green said.

"Well, we spoke to him—"

"After he picked himself up off the floor," Veronica interjected.

"Well, yes, although he follows the news like everyone else. He indicated to Veronica, and yes, I know this is hearsay because I doubt he'd be willing to say it again, that he felt a certain pressure to sign the death certificate. He had the feeling that Mr. Standish was eager to arrange for a full autopsy."

"Aren't I lucky that my identification said that *both* my parents should be notified if anything happened to me, and that the police found that. I'm sure mom wouldn't have heard from you, dad, until it was all over and done with."

Anita had turned to glare at her ex-husband, but Jerry Standish was looking down at the table, and for a change, his expression was not angry. "Someday, when you have a child, Veronica, and god forbid, you're faced with making a decision like that, maybe then you'll understand just how hard it is to do." He looked up at his daughter. "Do you think that was easy for me? Do you think being called by the police, and having to identify your body, and call the funeral home, and tell the doctors what they should be doing, was easy? For that matter, do you think it was easy for me to tell you that you needed to be responsible for your own life, do you think that was easy?"

Anita said hotly, "I think we all know how easy it is for you to be cruel, Jerry, you've never had any problem—"

"Oh, shut up, Anita! You walked out of Veronica's life twenty years ago and left me with an adolescent girl who was off the wall, you didn't seem to have any trouble doing that—"

"Oh, you don't think so? Would I have left her with you if I'd had any choice—"

"And the minute she's dead you come charging in here with your goddamned bible-thumping holier-than-thou—"

"As if you didn't do everything you could to cut me off from her, you wouldn't even call her to the phone when I—"

"Leaving me alone with her when I had a business to run, where the hell were you when Veronica needed you?"

"Good question, mom," Veronica said loudly. This stopped the argument just long enough for attorneys Green and Stuart to get their clients' attention.

"Let's keep to the main point," Kate Delaney said. Her expression was sober but her voice had a certain lilt to it. "Are you going to relinquish that letter, or do we need to get a court order?"

Ted Green glanced at Jerry Standish, who raised his eyes in a look of exasperated acquiescence. "We'll give you the letter," Ted Green said.

"And all copies?"

"No copies have been made. Yes, we'll sign the form." He got up and left the room, with a nervous glance behind him as though he feared a melee would break out if he left Jerry Standish alone with present company. His concern was groundless. Everyone sat in stiff silence, pointedly not meeting each other's eyes, until he returned with the letter, which had been in his office safe. He handed it to Veronica. "Here, Miss Standish."

"Make sure all the pages are there," Kate Delaney said. Veronica glanced uneasily at Jonathan and slid the letter out of the envelope. It consisted of fifteen pages of white lined notebook paper covered on both sides with handwriting, in several colors of ball point pen ink. The writing was so ragged, as though Veronica had been trying to write the whole thing on her lap in a car, that Regan wondered how Jerry Standish had managed to read it. Veronica went through the pages carefully, as her cheeks grew pink, carefully checking to be sure no page was missing. Then she hastily refolded the letter and stuffed it back into the envelope. She cleared her throat self-consciously. "It's all there."

Kate Delaney pushed the form across the table to Ted Green, who read it, signed it, and handed it to Jerry Standish, who signed as well after a heavy sigh. "Thank you," Kate said as Ted Green slid the form back to her. "I believe we're done here, is that right, Miss Standish?"

"Pretty much. Although I did want to ask whether I could at least have my clothes back, and some of my other things, and especially, my financial papers, the bills and stuff? Because seeing that I'm going to be entirely responsible for myself from now on, I'm going to need to find a job, and I've got some credit card bills to pay off."

Ted Green looked at Jerry Standish. After a moment, Jerry Standish said, "I paid the credit card bills out of the proceeds from the condominium sale. You can owe me for those. Your records are here, Ted's been handling that for me. The rest of the contents of your condo are in storage. If you want to arrange for them to be picked up..." he shrugged.

"We'll do that," Jonathan said. "I assume we can go through Mr. Green for that?"

Jerry Standish nodded. "Veronica, could I just ask...where the hell have you been all this time?"

"I went to stay with someone I know in Maine. I was too angry with everyone here to tell anybody where I was going. I had some cash hidden from selling my car, and I just went. You don't know her, but I'll give you the name and number if you want to call her and check."

"That's not necessary."

"Oh, really?" Veronica raised her eyebrows. "You sure have been acting paranoid about all this, dad, accusing Jonathan of driving me to suicide, accusing Regan—my best friend!—of assaulting me—I'm surprised you believe me. Should I believe you? Or have you got some other charges and lawsuits all ready to go as soon as we walk out of here?"

"I believed your letter," Jerry Standish said hotly. "You're standing here and I believe that. I just can't understand how in hell you could have walked out of that funeral home after all that time."

"Neither do I. But it's going to stay a big fat mystery, dad, because if you think for one second that I'm going to let any doctors or scientists or investigators get within fifty feet of me after *that* happened, you're out of your mind. I'm leaving here and becoming a Christian Scientist after this, because there's nothing like being declared dead to destroy your confidence in the medical profession. It's not like other people haven't woken up after being declared dead, anyway, I can send you the Internet links if you want to see some stories."

"But—"

"I didn't take an overdose, I don't know what happened, and I don't want to know. I just want to get on with my life now, and to be really honest, mom, dad..." Veronica paused and gave each of her parents a hard look. "From now on, I don't want to talk to either of you anymore. Let's just stay out of each other's way, one hundred percent. I think we're all going to be so much happier if we do that."

Anita gasped audibly. "Oh, *honey,* how can you *say* that?"

Veronica all but rounded on her mother. "Honey? *Honey?* What's with this honey shit, mom? For twenty years, I've heard your voice a couple of times a year! Do you realize this is the first time I've set eyes on you since my wedding? Twelve years! I'd forgotten what you *looked* like!" She leaned back, her eyes narrowed. "You've wrecked your skin, you know. Haven't you ever heard of sunscreen?"

Regan couldn't help feeling a pang of sympathy for Anita, even though she could see the justice in what Veronica said. *God, she looks just like Veronica when she cries,* Regan thought as a tear slid down Anita's trembling cheek.

"All right, Veronica," Jerry Standish said heavily, "If that's what you want. I can't say that I didn't prepare myself for this reaction when I gave you the ultimatum I did. Maybe when you're older, you'll understand my reasons better."

"Who knows, dad. Maybe I will. Oh—" Veronica looked back at her mother. "That reminds me. You can stuff your lawsuit, mom. No one had anything to do with my leaving that funeral home and disappearing except me, so you don't have anything to sue about."

"We'll be discussing that matter privately," Cyrus Stuart said.

"I'm sure you will. But then, I guess it is none of my business, isn't it?" Veronica straightened up in her chair and looked to either side. "I think *now* I'm ready to go, right?"

"Just a moment," Jerry Standish said, causing most of those present to look at him in genuine surprise, partly because of his tone of voice. He was sitting back in his chair, his hands steepled, with a dark brooding look on his face. "Mr. Vaughn," he said, and paused.

Jonathan glanced at Regan and Veronica. "Yes..?" he said after a moment of silence.

Jerry Standish seemed to be debating whether he wanted to go on or not. Finally he squared his shoulders. "Do you know a man named Hiram Clauson?"

Anita and Cyrus Stuart looked puzzled, but there was silence on the other side of the table. "I've met him."

"You know him, don't you, Ms. Calloway?"

"Only professionally, and not for very long."

Jerry Standish nodded. "He was the one who called you, wasn't he? I mean about this...investigation he had the two of you doing."

Where is this going? "Yes, he was, as a matter of fact. About two months ago, out of the blue. We'd never had any previous contact."

"Picked your name out of some news stories, isn't that right?"

"Well...I was involved in a very high profile case, Mr. Standish. I'm not sure Hiram ever said exactly where he heard about it. There was a book."

"I know, I read it."

Regan blinked in surprise. "Why are you asking me about Hiram Clauson, Mr. Standish? We're not working together anymore."

"Yes, I know." There was another long pause. "I hate to feel like I've been played for a sucker. But I'm wondering now if that's been going on."

Regan looked at Jonathan and cleared her throat. "What do you mean, Mr. Standish?"

"This Clauson. He called me up, right after the news came out about Veronica. Said he had some information that might relate to what happened, information about you, Mr. Vaughn. I'd just gotten that letter, and..." he sighed heavily. "I wasn't thinking straight. Anyway, we met a couple of times, and..." Jerry Standish shook his head. "All kinds of nutcase crap. Vampires, he was talking about. He claimed he meant it in some kind of clinical sense, but I sure didn't get that from the way he talked about it. All I cared about was finding out what happened to my daughter. I listened to him because I thought he had something that I could use to get to the bottom of that. But now, I think he was just taking me for a ride, hoping to get me to fund some kind of...vampire hunting team. I couldn't finance a cup of coffee, or who knows what the hell he'd have dragged me into."

"A vampire hunting team?" Regan stared at Jerry Standish, aghast. "He had other people involved?"

"He didn't come right out and say it. But I got that idea, yes." There was another pause, and then Jerry Standish shrugged. "That's all. But I'd watch my step if I were you, Mr. Vaughn. This Clauson is a few sandwiches short, in my opinion."

"I appreciate the heads-up."

"Just out of curiosity, Ms. Calloway, where were *you* for an entire week?"

Regan, who had been thinking about what Jerry Standish just told them, looked up at him, and smiled grimly. "Through the looking glass, Mr. Standish. Yes, I know," she said, at the look on his face. "Life's a bitch, isn't it?"

"I hear you'll be job-hunting, too."

"Actually, I'm looking at a start-up, I think."

"Good luck."

"Mr. Green, if you could get my financial papers for me," Veronica said as she got up. Regan, Jonathan and Kate Delaney all got up as well.

"Gentlemen, Mrs. Westfield, thank you for your time and cooperation," Kate Delaney said. The four of them left the conference room, with Ted Green following to get Veronica's papers for her. There turned out to be several boxes of these, since Veronica had never been very organized, and had just stuffed her old bills and records into storage cartons from Staples and put them on a top shelf of the bedroom closet.

When they were all in the car and on their way back to Rainbow Stone house, Kate said, "All right, Miss Standish, you've got your letter. You'll be getting your belongings. What else should we be worrying about?"

"The charges against Regan?" Jonathan said.

"Will certainly be dismissed, especially now. In fact, with this new information, I'll file a second motion. But we'll have to wait for the judge to rule on it."

"Meaning I still need to stay out of trouble, if I don't want to be remanded."

"Yes, although I'm not sure what you might want to do that would be a problem."

Regan was staring moodily out the window, thinking about the look on Anita Westfield's face as Veronica left the conference room. "Well...I promised my folks I'd go up and see them. They had a pretty rough time while I was missing."

"Out of state?"

"Vermont."

"You're on bail, not on parole, Ms. Calloway. It shouldn't be a problem as long as you don't miss your scheduled court date."

"You should go," Jonathan said firmly. But Regan just shrugged unhappily. She couldn't say more in front of Kate Delaney.

After Kate had left, Veronica dramatically crumpled the letter into fifteen balls of paper and burned each one in the wood stove.

"There go your alibis, Jonathan," Regan said ruefully.

"There was nothing in there I couldn't say in person. If you need an alibi, Jonathan, I'll vouch for you."

"I appreciate it. I'm just not sure our problems are that simple now."

"You mean this Dr. Clauson? Yeah, what's going on with that?"

"I don't know, but I have a bad feeling about it," Regan said. She looked around the room suddenly. "You know, I wonder where Sean is. Isn't he usually out here by now, Jonathan?"

"Yes, he is. You're right. This is the first day he hasn't been out here in a week and a half."

"I think he's scared of me," Veronica said sadly. "And I can't blame him, the poor kid."

"But still..." Regan was starting to feel a deep disquiet. "I can't imagine that he wouldn't at least call, from a safe distance, to find out what's going on. He must be dying of curiosity."

"Should we call his house?" Jonathan said. "I didn't have the sense that Sharon Neeson distrusted us, after all."

Regan reached for the phone, and suddenly stopped. "No," she said, not clear where her certainty came from, but suddenly sure that they should not call. "I think calling would be a bad idea. Sean will get in touch when he can."

Chapter 30

At about 6:00 p.m., Veronica, Regan and Jonathan were sitting around the long table, discussing how Veronica should get in touch with their friends, or whether she even wanted to. After the confrontation with her parents, Veronica was becoming somewhat despondent.

"I don't know...maybe I should just leave town. I can't face explaining to everyone, over and over again, what supposedly happened."

"You should have been me, calling fifty thousand people about the store. I just wanted to put a new message on my answering machine and unplug the phone."

"The store. God, Regan, I still can't believe it. You *were* that store."

Regan dropped her head down on her folded arms for a moment. She hadn't rested since Monday night in the Sheridan police station holding cell. "I should have seen it coming. I knew Bill Wharton didn't like me. Even if I hadn't disappeared, I suspect things would have turned out just the same. Maybe Bill would have given me a reference, but that's all. He wasn't about to sell the place to me. He had that buyer lined up ages ago."

"I think you're probably right," Jonathan said.

The cordless buzzed, and Jonathan picked it up. "Hello?" He straightened in his chair. "Sean. Where are you?" Regan immediately sat up. She and Veronica could easily hear Sean's voice on the other end of the line.

"I'm home. I only have a couple of minutes, but I wanted to call you fast, in case you wondered where I was."

"We *did* wonder. Is everything okay?"

"I think it's going to be. Yeah, it should be. It's just kind of weird right now. I've got to sort of lay low for a couple of days. That Clauson guy filed a 51a on my mom." Regan gasped.

"Why? Because of you being out here so much?"

"I guess. Because of me being out there so late at night, and missing school. Thing is, I'm over sixteen, and my grades are okay. DSS closed my mom's case a few months ago, and they don't want to open it again. But they've got to investigate the report, so...I better keep my nose really clean. If I get put in foster care, my mom will start drinking again." Regan and Jonathan exchanged a bleak look.

"Sean, it's fine. You just cooperate and focus on school."

"Look, it'll be okay. Regan gave me a job, for god's sake."

"I know. If DSS wants to talk to us, they're welcome to. We have nothing but good things to say about you."

"Thanks, that'll help. How are things going with, uh, Veronica?"

"She's fine. We met with her parents today—"

"You *did?*"

"—and I think we've settled all of those issues. But it's a very long story."

There was a sound on the phone line, like a slamming door. "Look, I better go," Sean said hastily. "I'll talk to you soon." He hung up.

Regan stared at Jonathan, a hand over her mouth. "Oh, my god."

"I can't believe Clauson is retaliating against Sean."

"He's not," Regan whispered. "He's splitting us up, Jonathan." Then she pressed both hands against her mouth as an even grimmer possibility occurred to her. "Or...getting Sean out of the way, so he can..."

"What?" Veronica said, wide eyed. "What do you think he'd do?"

Regan could only shake her head in disbelief. "I don't know."

"Are we safe here?"

"I don't know!"

"Do you think," Jonathan said slowly, "that he knows that Veronica is back?"

"How could he know that?" Veronica said.

"If he tried to call your father," Regan said, "he just might. And that might have pushed him to something desperate, although he would have to have filed the 51a before this afternoon, for DSS to already be investigating today."

"But the whole town has been talking about Veronica and you leaving the funeral home together, ever since the news stories about the lawsuit."

"I know. Hiram mentioned it on Saturday night."

Jonathan said, "Do you think we should try to get in touch with him? Force some kind of confrontation?"

Regan gnawed on a knuckle as she thought about this. "I just don't know... I'm not sure we have any advantages, Jonathan. If we make any moves, we'll just be giving him more ammunition."

"What does he want?" Veronica said.

"Proof," said Jonathan.

"I'm not sure about that anymore, Jonathan." Regan shivered. "I think...I think he wants to kill us."

"Weren't you the one who said how principled he was? Remember?"

"A month ago, yes. But that was before Saturday night. That was before I overheard that conversation in the Atheneum. That was before he sat there in my living room telling me that the most reliable way to kill vampires was burning them, and that a crematorium would do the job."

"He said that?" Veronica's voice higher than usual. "Would he burn down the house?"

Regan hesitated. "Not unless he was sure we couldn't get out. He wouldn't risk it otherwise. No, I just don't see him doing something so crude. He's much more methodical than that. Still..." she looked around the shadowy room with its wide pine floorboards and cracked plaster walls. "I don't think we should all be sleeping at the same time."

"Then we shouldn't be here at all," Jonathan said.

"But where are we going to go?" Regan stood up and paced halfway across the room, suddenly furious. "Hiram must have talked to Derek. My god, why didn't I even think of that?"

"What's Derek got to do with any of this?" Veronica said, startled.

"Hiram sat right at that table at Hong Kong Delhi and saw how jealous Derek is of Jonathan. That conversation I overheard at the Atheneum, Ron Wilson accused Derek of trying to monkey wrench Jonathan's buying this house. Derek said he had inside information. That's got to be it. And I'll bet Hiram talked to Mrs. Ferreira, too. That's why I got evicted! He knew I'd move out here."

"So he's trying to get us all in one place?" Veronica looked appalled.

"I'm sure he's trying to limit our options, anyway. Damn him to hell! I'm not going to let him win. I don't want to go underground. We've got to find some solution to this."

"And what solution can there be?" Jonathan asked. "Regan—"

"We've got to outthink him somehow."

"I know you don't want to go into hiding, Regan, but that may be our only way of being safe. We have time on our side, don't forget that. In a few decades, Hiram Clauson will cease to be a problem. He'll be dead."

"And so will my parents," Regan said sharply. "And what if he does start some kind of group, or organization? What if he leaves notes and documentation? What if he finds a few young people like Sean, who aren't on our side? Jonathan, listen to me," she went on urgently, cutting Jonathan off as he tried to speak. "The world has changed now. It's changed completely in just the last ten years. Look at what Sean could find on the Internet. It's not going to be so easy to stay out of sight anymore. It won't be too many years before webcam surveillance and DNA data banks will be the rule, not the exception. Retina scanning and thumbprint ID will be everywhere, no one will sign their name anymore. If we're going to live in the world at all, we've got to find other ways of solving problems, not just hiding and running away. You *know* that, don't you?"

Jonathan stared at her and finally spread his hands helplessly. "Yes. You're right. But what do you suggest we do to solve this problem? Kill Clauson?"

There was a heavy silence in the room. Veronica was looking from Regan to Jonathan, open mouthed. Finally Regan said, "It's him or us."

"I won't do it."

"Jonathan, he's threatening all of us. He's threatening *Sean,* for god's sake."

"We don't *know* that. What we know is that he's upset about the assault victims he's interviewed and he wants the assailant to be stopped. That's what he told you, isn't it? How does that make him different from Detective Fellman?"

"So you're saying what, that his heart's in the right place, so it's okay? Jonathan, he stood there and lied to me."

"You lied to him."

Regan stared at Jonathan incredulously. "Because I *had* to! Why are you *defending* him?"

"I'm just saying that we aren't exactly innocent victims, Regan. Let's leave aside the fact that everything Clauson believes about the assaults is true, in the first place. There's been a lot of lying going on, on all sides. I certainly haven't told the truth to many people. Suppose you had reported me right at the beginning? I'd have disappeared, and you and Veronica would both still be alive. But if I had been as ruthless then as you're suggesting we be now, I would have killed you that first night in the store, before you had a chance to tell anyone else about me. Would that have been preferable?"

Flustered, Regan said, "This is all moot, Jonathan..."

Jonathan sighed and got up from his chair. "Regan," he said, walking to where she stood. "Do you remember the conversation we had about conscience?"

She looked down. "Yes."

"We have to be so careful, Regan. That line is so easily crossed, because there's no instinct there anymore. If we cross that last ethical line, we leave humanity behind forever. We'll become exactly the fiends that you feared you were. Killing must be the last resort. And I have yet to be in a situation in which there was no other solution whatsoever."

Regan shook her head. "This might be it, Jonathan. This is an obsession with Hiram. You haven't talked to him."

"I'd like to. I certainly want to, before we do anything more drastic. Don't you think he deserves that?"

"I suppose so..." Regan sighed, defeated.

"I understand how frightened you are." He put his hands on her shoulders and she looked up at him glumly. "But consider how disoriented you're feeling. Since last Friday, you've lost your store, which was the total focus of your life, lost your home, and you were arrested and lost, at least temporarily, your freedom. I understand that you don't want to lose anything more. But drastic actions won't improve things. You've got to trust that I know what I'm talking about."

"I do."

"If I've made it sound like I abandoned everything and ran at the least provocation, I apologize. I've sweated it out through worse than this, and sometimes it paid off, and sometimes I barely escaped. But either one was preferable to murder. I've seen a lot of killing, human beings killing other human beings, especially in those first years when I lived by stealing. I never got used to it. Blood is too precious to waste."

Regan pulled away from Jonathan and walked back across the room to sit heavily in her chair. "Even if we run, Hiram's not going to give up. We'd have to go to...Fiji or someplace, and that's not so easy to do post-nine-eleven. Cyberspace is opening up, and real borders are closing. And what about those other vampires you've talked about, Jonathan? Your friend in Maine, the other ones you said were here in Massachusetts—if we don't clean up this mess, we'll be leaving them in danger, too. It's not all about us." Still standing where she'd left him, Jonathan folded his arms, frowning darkly. Regan turned toward the front of the house and the road, listening. "I'm surprised there aren't already news teams knocking on the door, if Hiram has heard about Veronica."

"Reporters? Why would Clauson do that?"

"Just to keep us off balance. Make us feel exposed, restrict our movements, make us feel less secure...heck, Jonathan, if I were Hiram I'd do that myself. Unless he has some reason of his own not to attract the attention of the media. He did tell me he didn't want publicity for himself or the victims."

They were all silent then. Veronica was staring down at the floor, her forehead creased in a frown, as though she was suddenly realizing that her problems were more extensive than she'd even begun to imagine. Jonathan came back over to the table and sat down in front of his computer, but he stared at the screensaver unseeing, his arms tightly crossed. When the cordless phone buzzed, they all jumped. Jonathan stared at the phone for a moment as though he expected it to explode. Then he recovered and picked it up. When Regan heard the faint voice on the other end of the line, she felt a prickling sense of horror over her whole body.

"Hello, Jonathan."

Jonathan sat motionless in the chair. "Hello, Hiram. What can I do for you?"

There seemed to be a great deal of background noise on Hiram's end of the conversation. "I just heard that Veronica Standish is back in town." His voice was light, casual, and unconcerned. "I'm sure that must be a great relief for you and Regan."

"Yes, it is. We had some trouble tracking her down."

"Amazing, how hard it can be to locate someone, and then it turns out they were practically in your own back yard the whole time." Jonathan looked sharply at Regan, who put her hand over her mouth.

"Well, you know what they say about people who don't want to be found."

"Indeed. More than four hundred thousand adults are reported missing every year, I think Regan once told me. I always wonder what could possibly happen to that many people."

"How did you hear about Miss Standish? We're not exactly planning to hold a press conference, after all she's been through."

"I quite understand that. I heard it from the Sheridan police, actually. I've been talking to them about some other matters. That's why I'm calling you, in fact.

"Oh?"

"Well, I'm calling you and Regan, since this is the only phone number I have for her now. Is she there, by the way?"

Jonathan glanced at Regan, who nodded vigorously. "Yes, she is. Did you want to speak with her?"

"Please."

Jonathan handed the phone to Regan. "Hello, Hiram," she said, trying to keep her voice steady.

"Hello, Regan. I understand that you've been having a very rough week. I'm so sorry."

"Oh, well, shit happens, Hiram. I probably would have had to move anyway, being unemployed, and my attorney is confident that the charges against me will be dismissed. They all seem to be quite frivolous and ungrounded, to begin with."

"I'm glad to hear that."

"By the way, did you get to talk with the victim on Saturday night? The one you were going to go see when you left my place?"

"Yes, I did."

"I was just curious, did you find out anything new? I did say that I might consider another reading if there was justification."

"As a matter of fact..." Hiram paused significantly. "That's one of the reasons I'm calling. I was wondering if you would be free to meet with me for a talk."

"What—you mean right now?"

"I'm in town now, so, yes, if it was convenient for you. I'm calling from Hong Kong Delhi, in fact, we could meet right here. I have a table."

"Well, I—"

"I'd like Jonathan to come too, if he's free."

Regan looked up at Jonathan in confused alarm. "You want to meet with both of us? In the middle of Hong Kong Delhi?"

"What's the matter? You and I have met there many times. Would you prefer someplace more isolated and secluded? I've never seen that house, I've heard that it's quite remarkable."

"No." Regan realized that she'd spoken too quickly, but she hadn't been able to restrain herself. "No, you don't have to drive all the way out here. It just sounds awfully noisy there right now, Hiram."

"Yes, they're having their Wednesday night all-you-can-eat buffet, the place is packed," he said cheerfully. "But all the better not to be overheard, don't you think? Can you two make it?"

"Just a moment." Regan put the phone on mute and looked at Jonathan. "You said you wanted to talk to him."

"Yes, but..."

"It's not like we have any other way of finding out what he's up to. We might just as well talk to him now as wait for him to spring something on us."

"All right."

Regan clicked the phone back on. "We'll be there in about fifteen minutes, is that okay?"

"Perfect. I'll see you soon."

As Regan put down the phone, Veronica said in alarm, "Are you leaving me here alone?"

Regan glanced at Jonathan. "Well...do you want to come? If there's anyone we know there tonight, they're going to have some kind of reaction when they see you come walking through the door. Are you ready for that?"

"I don't want to sit here by myself. What if something happens? What if a news crew comes by? What if the phone rings? What if you didn't come back?"

Regan looked at Jonathan, who shrugged. "She has a point. Strength in numbers and all that, I guess."

"I don't know what Hiram could do in the middle of a crowded restaurant."

"I don't either. Maybe he thought we'd feel safer meeting him there, and we'd be more likely to come."

"Which raises the question of why he'd think we wouldn't feel safe meeting him. You'd think he'd be the one who'd feel nervous."

"He certainly doesn't seem to, does he?" Jonathan said thoughtfully. "Well, we'd better go."

Chapter 31

They had trouble finding a parking space at Hong Kong Delhi. The Wednesday night buffet was very popular. No one appeared to recognize Veronica when they entered, but their friends tended to drop in a little later in the evening. Regan told the hostess that they had come to meet Hiram Clauson, and she directed them to a booth on the farther side of the dining area, away from the buffet. Hiram was sitting where he could see the door, and he raised a hand in cheerful greeting when he spotted them. It looked like he'd had some food while he waited for them, and he had a half-finished drink in front of him. Jonathan and Veronica closely followed Regan as she threaded a way between the tables to the booth, where the three of them all squeezed in on the side opposite Hiram.

"Ah, it's all three of you," he said jovially. "Excellent."

"All three of us?" Regan said.

"You know what I mean. Welcome back, Veronica. You've been sorely missed."

Veronica shifted uneasily. "Thank you."

The waitress came to the table, and Regan thought they should order something, if they were going to sit here. She and Veronica ordered Mai-Tai's, while Jonathan ordered a margarita. "I've always had a taste for lime," he said.

"I'm certainly curious as to what you wanted to talk to me about," Regan said when the waitress had left. "Our last conversation was somewhat confrontational, as I recall."

"I'm sorry you felt that way. Did you fill in Jonathan on what we discussed?"

"Yes, as matter of fact, she did," Jonathan said.

"And what did you think?"

Jonathan looked at him steadily for a moment. "I think you're a very clever man, Hiram. I'm a bit surprised that you'd be so quick to jump to the conclusion you did. I said I lived in Rhode Island the night we first met. In fact, my family genealogy in that state goes back some two hundred and fifty years. I wouldn't be surprised if I resemble an ancestor or two. I wouldn't be surprised if you turned out to have an ancestor doppelganger, either. Would that make you and he one and the same?"

"There doesn't seem to be a record of you in Rhode Island. I'll bet Regan told you that, as well."

"Yes, I did."

"I changed my name for reasons I prefer not to make generally known. But I told Detective Fellman why, when he called me in for questioning. You really seem to have made an avocation out of me, Hiram. With all the time you must have spent on this, I can't help wondering when you get your work done. Isn't teaching a full course load rather demanding?"

"Oh, yes, that. The truth is, I'm not going to be teaching for the foreseeable future."

"You're not?" Regan said, startled.

"I seem to be on suspension. The Board of Overseers has begun a proceeding to revoke my tenure."

"I'm sorry to hear that," Jonathan said. "I've heard that it's not easy to revoke tenure. It requires some rather serious allegations. You weren't using your office computer for anything inappropriate, were you?"

"I didn't think so," Hiram said, taking a sip of his drink, "Although someone else apparently had quite a bit to say to the Board about my leisure time activities. It's a bit ironic, really. It's not as though I've been breaking into buildings and assaulting innocent victims."

"Unlike some people you could name, you mean?" Regan said. Hiram gave her a long steady look. The waitress came to the table with their drink order, and paused a moment, as though she wondered whether she was interrupting something. Regan gestured to her impatiently, and she put the drinks down hurriedly and left. *I guess this conversation doesn't seem a little tense or anything, does it?* Regan thought, beginning to feel irritated. "So, just what did you learn on Saturday night when you left my place in such haste to interview that victim?"

"Nothing new."

"Did you try hypnotizing him?"

"I established four months ago that hypnosis isn't effective in these cases. You know that."

"But that isn't what I asked. Did you try hypnotizing him?"

"Why does that concern you? If you were so curious, you could have come along with me to the interview."

"Did you try to hypnotize him?"

Hiram took in a breath, then said, "No."

"I don't believe you."

"Why would you think I'd lie to you, Regan?" Regan took a sip of her drink and for a moment was completely distracted. She hadn't tasted alcohol since she'd awakened on Friday. The intense poignancy of the tart fruit juices almost made her mouth pucker, and the alcohol burned her tongue. She realized that Hiram was watching her closely, his eyes narrowed. To make things worse, Veronica was also watching her and now picked up her own drink and gave it a suspicious sniff. Hiram said, "There's nothing wrong with your drink, is there?"

"No." Regan gulped down the mouthful quickly, trying not to grimace.

"I imagine most things taste a little different now, don't they?"

Regan put her glass down so suddenly, some of the pink liquid sloshed onto the table. "Hiram, you have *no* idea." The little smile he was wearing faded, which goaded Regan to continue. "Trust me, you don't have a clue what you're screwing around with here."

"Why don't you tell me?"

"Why should I? You've done nothing but lie to me. Jerry Standish told us this afternoon that you've been meeting with him for two weeks. On Saturday you flat out denied that you'd talked with him."

"I can't be held responsible for what Jerry Standish sees fit to say."

"Oh, so now *he's* a liar?"

"That's bullshit, you know," Veronica said. "My dad has plenty of faults, but I don't think he's ever told a lie in his life. Brutal honesty is more his style."

"There you go," Regan said, "One of you lied, and Veronica says that it can't be her father. Whereas you, Hiram..." Regan leaned back and eyed Hiram speculatively. "Are you wearing a wire, by any chance?"

"What?"

"A wire. Microphone. Are we being recorded?"

"No, of course not."

"That's the logical next step, isn't it? You've lied through your teeth to me, you've investigated Jonathan, you got that warrant issued on phony charges so my apartment could be searched—"

"That wasn't me."

"You've interfered with Jonathan's plans to buy the house—"

"Where are you *getting* this stuff, Regan?"

"Tell me, Hiram," Regan leaned towards him across the table. "Just how high does Derek Wilson rate on the suggestibility scale? I'll bet he's right at the top, isn't he?"

"You hypnotized *Derek?*" Veronica said.

"Oh, this is ridiculous. Regan, I think you're approaching clinical paranoia here."

"Oh. I'm crazy, am I?" Regan said softly. She reached across the table. "Take my hand, Hiram." He pulled back, staring at her hand as though she was holding out a rattlesnake. After a moment, Regan withdrew her hand and sat back herself. "You know, you never have shaken hands with me, not once. And here I just thought you were respecting my boundaries. How obtuse of me."

"You always avoided shaking hands, Regan, and I understood why. Now you're making my respect for you sound sinister?"

Regan took another sip of her drink, which was less of a shock on the second try. "It's funny how seemingly innocent details can take on a whole different meaning when you look back on them in the light of new information, isn't it?"

"Yes, I'd agree with that."

"So tell me, Hiram, do you think that Jonathan broke into the Atheneum last Saturday and assaulted that victim?" Hiram was silent, looking at her, and Regan met his eyes steadily.

"No, I don't."

"Oh, good, the truth at last. So, who do you think did?" *Go ahead, let's hear you say it.*

Veronica and Jonathan were both watching Hiram intently. He looked at their faces, then at Regan, then down at the tabletop. His expression was enigmatic. "You should be much more careful than this, Regan. I'm not holding you entirely responsible, you know."

"Where's your evidence, Hiram? Jerry Standish isn't going to fund your little investigative cabal, you know." Hiram looked up at her sharply. "You're on your own here. But you've been talking with, how many police departments is it? And after all these months, you still don't have a particle of real evidence."

"Yet. That doesn't mean there isn't any to be found. Sometimes you just have to start thinking in an entirely different way."

"Is that what you're doing, Hiram? Is that why you filed a 51a on Sharon Neeson?"

Hiram straightened his shoulders. "I'm a mandated reporter, Regan. I didn't feel that Sean was being properly supervised. I was only thinking of his best interests."

"You didn't think his association with me and Jonathan was very healthy, is that it?"

"With the hours he was keeping? No."

"Mandated reporter only applies when you're seeing the victims professionally, anyway. You just wanted to get Sean away from us."

"If you say so."

Regan sighed. "Don't you think this has gone far enough?"

He raised his eyebrows slightly. "Far enough?"

"You're losing your job. You're crossing ethical boundaries. You are *obsessed*, Hiram. I said that weeks ago, after Evelyn Stockard's interview. How much more are you going to sacrifice to this crusade? It's pointless."

To her surprise, Hiram started to laugh. "Oh, Regan. What have *I* sacrificed? Compared to you, nothing at all. You really don't get it, do you? This has nothing to do with crusades. This isn't about me. It's not even about justice for the victims. It's about setting things back the way they should be. I haven't even begun to make sacrifices. Not like you and Veronica, here. You've lost everything—and I mean that literally."

Looking at his face, Regan suddenly felt a chill. "Hiram...you have sailed right off the edge of the horizon here. You really have."

"Oh, no." Hiram shook his head, still smiling. "You know better than that. I've just had to face the fact that consensual reality is no longer my reality."

"And just how would you set things back the way they should be?" Jonathan said quietly. "Hypothetically speaking, that is."

Hiram's smile twisted. "I haven't solved that problem yet. I'm not sure it will fall to me to handle that. I may simply be the messenger."

"Just be careful, Hiram," Regan said. "If I learned anything in Gardner, it's how much people hate to have consensual reality challenged. Messengers who try it tend to get placed on locked wards, among other things—and it doesn't matter if they're proven right or not. At least do yourself the favor of learning from my mistakes."

"Oh, I am, Regan. Learning from your mistakes, that is. More than you realize."

Before Regan could reply to this, their conversation was unexpectedly interrupted. From some distance away, a familiar voice cut through the babble of conversation like a klaxon. "Oh, my god! Oh my *god!* It's *Veronica!*"

They all turned to look, as did almost everyone in the restaurant, although Regan and Veronica, at least, didn't need a visual to identify the speaker. There stood Karen, her jewel-tone and black print dress making her as conspicuous as though a spotlight was on her, be-ringed hands pressed to both her cheeks. Steve was standing slightly behind her, and in contrast to Karen's expression, he merely looked bewildered. "What do I do?" Veronica said in a tone of near panic.

"You wanted to come," Regan said urgently. "We better go say hello." They both got up hastily and made their way between the tables where Karen was standing, too overwhelmed to approach them further.

"Yes, I'm back, Karen," Veronica said. "I was only—" but she was cut off as Karen flung her arms around Veronica in a voluminous and somewhat motherly hug.

"I can't believe it," she kept repeating, "I can't *believe* it! Do your parents know?"

Regan was watching Veronica uneasily as she attempted to answer Karen's questions over their friend's continued exclamations. Veronica appeared to be controlling herself well, although she did put her nose into Karen's hair and sniff deeply before Karen disengaged to pull back and look up into Veronica's face. Regan had actually been somewhat surprised that Veronica hadn't reacted more obviously to the atmosphere of the crowded rooms, but perhaps she hadn't been taken off-guard to find that a restaurant full of people smelled, to her, just like a restaurant. That wasn't quite as disorienting as Regan's experience of having a courtroom full of people smell just like a restaurant. Steve was talking to Veronica now, and the people at tables around them were displaying an open interest in the scene. Regan could hear remarks around her to the effect that some customers had realized who Veronica was from the newspaper photos. There was a rising excitement percolating through the room. Hiram and Jonathan had come up to where they were standing now, having left money for their food and drinks in the booth. The two men had taken different routes between the tables, and Regan abruptly realized that Hiram was standing close behind her, smiling at Karen and Veronica, while Jonathan was moving around a table closer to the doorway.

Karen looked past Regan and saw Hiram. "Dr. Clauson! Isn't this amazing? I can't *believe* it!"

"It certainly is. And I'm sure the whole story is even stranger than any of us imagine."

"Well, I'm not going to try and explain to the whole restaurant, Karen," Veronica said. There was a sudden loud clanging from the kitchen entranceway, and Regan, startled, glanced in that direction. Two busboys, distracted by the commotion in the middle of the dining room, had collided. The dining room manager started to harangue them in Chinese as they noisily picked up fallen trays and plate covers. As Regan turned back from that mishap, she was suddenly immobilized by a combination of almost overwhelming sensations, right in the center of her abdomen. There was a blinding pain, a nauseating feeling of penetration and a dull thump, like a blow. Suddenly she couldn't breathe in, and she half doubled over, registering what she was feeling but utterly confused as to the cause. Then she saw that Hiram was stepping back from her, withdrawing his empty hand as if he had been holding something.

"I'm sorry, Regan," she heard him say, very calmly. She could feel the front of her sweater getting wet, and she groped at her abdomen, still unable to straighten up or breathe in. Her fingers found something long, hard, and warm, extending straight out from her body. It felt like plastic, with a wavy or ridged edge, and when she gripped it and pain seared straight through her body from front to back, she realized, incredulous, that it was the handle of a knife. Before all the implications of this knowledge could sink in, Karen screamed and the sound was so excruciating, Regan thought her eardrums must be bleeding.

"Oh my god! Oh my god! Stop him, he's stabbed Regan!"

Complete pandemonium erupted in their immediate vicinity and spread outward through the whole dining room with terrifying speed. People were getting up from their seats, shoving chairs back on the carpeting so that the chairs tipped backwards onto the floor. There were screams coming from everywhere. "Does anyone have a cell phone, somebody call the cops," Regan heard unfamiliar voices saying, and there were people on either side of her now trying to get her to lie down on the floor. "Hold that guy, don't let him go, did you call the cops? What's the address here?" Lying down was absolutely out of the question, and Regan shoved an older man away from her, harder than she meant to, so hard that he stumbled and fell against a table. "Jesus Christ," she heard him say. The other helper was pushing some wadded up table napkins at Regan's stomach, evidently intending to apply pressure to the bleeding, or at least staunch it around the knife handle. Although a wide patch of her sweater was soaked now, there was not too much blood, and Regan took the wad of cloth away from the helpful hand and put it against the wound. By now a scrum was blocking the door, including a number of parents trying to get their children out of the restaurant. The air was filled with the shrill sound of children crying and wailing questions. Two men stood on their chairs bellowing ineffectually at everyone to stay seated and not panic. Regan sank down on one knee, covering her head with her free arm, the chaos and noise hurting her more than the knife as long as she didn't move. She realized Jonathan had taken the place of the helpful customer and was kneeling next to her, but she couldn't straighten up and look above her to see what Veronica was doing.

She felt Jonathan's hands on her shoulders, and he said, so quietly that only she could have heard him, "Regan, just don't move. You'll be okay." She appreciated his reassurances, but she didn't need them. She knew that he was right—and that was exactly the problem. *This is why Hiram wanted to meet us in a public place, jammed with people...sometimes you just have to start thinking in an entirely different way...haven't even begun to make sacrifices...evidence, my god, when the paramedics get here, he'll have his evidence...* She tried to straighten up. *Oh, god that hurts...*

"It's okay, Regan, it's okay," she heard Steve saying. "The ambulance is on the way, Regan, just stay calm, you'll be all right, don't pull on the knife. They'll have to get it out at the hospital...oh..." he stood up and went to see to Karen, who had just sunk into a vacated chair with a moan when she heard what he said. Regan knew that Steve was right about not pulling out the knife, as far as standard first aid went, but she had to speak, and she couldn't do that without air in her lungs. She wrapped her fingers around the knife handle and gave it a little tug, releasing the blade about a half inch. Pain shot up, down and to both sides from the entry wound, so intense that for a moment all she could see was a field of white, but the pain faded back, and then, *oh mother mercy,* her diaphragm unlocked and she could take in a breath. From the reduced noise level, she could tell that many of the customers had gotten out of the building. Regan straightened up a bit more. Veronica was crouching in front of her, both hands clamped over her mouth, her eyes wide. She wasn't sure where Hiram was—had he gotten away? But she wasn't concerned with Hiram now.

"Jonathan," she whispered, "we've got to get out of here. We've got to get out before the paramedics get here. We've got to do something."

"I know." There was no way they would get outside unhindered with so many people around them. Everyone still inside the room was grouped around Regan and Jonathan where they crouched on the floor. But Regan had thought of something.

"Veronica..."

"What?" Veronica, who had clearly heard what Regan had just said to Jonathan, moved closer to them.

"Veronica...sprinklers, remember?"

"Sprinklers...yes! And then run?"

"Quick, Veronica, oh god—" she could hear sirens, still so distant that only she, Jonathan and Veronica were aware of them, but they only had a few minutes left. Veronica stood up and faded back through the tables. No one appeared to pay any attention to her at all. "Get ready," Regan whispered to Jonathan, who seemed uncertain what was happening. "You'll have to pull me, run like hell—" Suddenly, much faster than Regan had expected, the overhead sprinkler system turned on and began deluging them with water. The main overhead lights went off, the emergency lights went on, a deafening horn started beeping, and the room erupted into screams, shrieks and curses as those remaining dove under tables or ran for the doors. Jonathan instantly pulled Regan to her feet and ran, hauling her with him, out the front door along with a tangle of people. Regan tried to carry her own weight as much as possible, but every motion was agony and she could hardly move her legs. Jonathan fortunately seemed to have no trouble at all dragging her with him, moving at least as fast as a normal person could run full tilt. He pulled her through the parking lot to the car, thrust her into the back seat and dove into the driver's seat, as Veronica, who had joined them halfway across the lot, bounced into the passenger's side. Regan could only half curl up on the back seat, her teeth clenched. The pain was unimaginable, and every bump of the car as Jonathan started the engine, drove straight forward over a grass verge and then over the curb and into the street, felt like she was being stabbed all over again.

She couldn't help making sounds, and she heard Jonathan's desperate voice from the front seat, "I'm sorry, Regan—"

"Drive! Just drive! Not the house! Not the house!"

"No, not the house."

"Then where are we going?" Veronica's voice was a panicked squawk.

"*Anywhere!* That we can get this fucking thing *out!*" Regan gasped. The car made the sixth or seventh squealing turn and Regan almost slid off the back seat onto the floor.

"*Careful*, Jonathan," Veronica said.

"I want to make sure we aren't followed, that's all. It's still full daylight. We'll need someplace where we won't be disturbed."

"But—*we* didn't do anything *wrong!* Regan can refuse treatment for *anything* as long as she's conscious, I *know* about this."

"Yes, but I don't want to have to handle that now."

About fifteen minutes later, Jonathan pulled the car over on the side of a narrow unpaved road in the heart of the state forest north of River Road. They weren't too far from where he had left Veronica's Mazda a month earlier, but this tiny road turned off of Proctor and wound through thick underbrush until it narrowed to a footpath and finally vanished altogether. Jonathan and Veronica got out of the car and Jonathan stood listening for several minutes. It was just about sunset, but the sky was overcast and the woods were already dim with twilight. There were no sounds coming from closer than a distance of several miles except the evensong of birds. Finally Jonathan opened the back door of the car. "Come on," he said apologetically, "best not to leave any more blood in the car than we have to." He pulled Regan upright, as she hissed through gritted teeth, then lifted her out of the seat and let her down on the ground by the car, her back braced against the rear tire. Regan closed both hands around the knife handle and started to pull, but it was an awkward angle, and at the pain, which went straight back through her body as well as radiating out from the entry wound, she thought she would pass out.

"I can't do it myself," she said in a gasp.

Jonathan had fished the gory wad of napkins from the back seat and he knelt down and pressed them into her hands. "You'll need these. Try not to make too much noise, sound carries a long way in these woods." He grasped the knife handle firmly. Veronica gave a soft little squeak and looked away, a hand over her eyes. Jonathan hesitated. "I'll try to be quick, but—"

Regan put the wad of cloth over her face. "Just shut the fuck up and pull." Grimacing, Jonathan braced Regan's abdomen with his other hand and then yanked out the knife. Regan, who was biting down on the napkins, could only make a hoarse grunt because the pain was too intense to breathe or move. Blood welled from the wound and soaked into her lap, and Jonathan hastily pulled the napkins and Regan's hands down and pressed them hard against her stomach. That hurt too, but gradually, the pain was lessening. Jonathan remained patiently as he was, and after about five minutes, Regan was finally able to take in and release a long deep breath and relax somewhat. At that point, Jonathan eased the pressure on the cloth and then carefully removed it. The wound was no longer bleeding, although it looked like any exertion at all would break it open again. Regan let her head fall back against the side of the car, closing her eyes. "How long will I will be out of action?"

"At least a couple of days. And...you will need blood."

"Great. How will I ever...oh, fuck."

Veronica had moved to sit cross-legged on the ground next to Jonathan, and now she picked up the knife and turned it over in her hands. It was a hunting knife, with a wide, five-inch blade, new, very sharp, otherwise unremarkable. Hiram would have had no trouble concealing it. He might have simply tucked it into the waist of his pants. He'd been wearing his rust corduroy jacket. "He thought he could kill you with this?"

"Oh, no," Regan said. "That was never his intention. He was sure he *couldn't* kill me with this, or he'd never have done it. My being dead wouldn't prove a thing."

"And this was all about proof," Jonathan said.

"But—lots of people get stabbed without dying."

"Veronica," Regan said quietly. "I'm already dead. And if the paramedics had gotten there and started trying to take my vitals...it would all have been over."

"So...what are we going to do?"

"I don't know," Regan said despondently. After a silence, she said, "What happened to Hiram, anyway? Did either of you see if he left the restaurant?" Both Jonathan and Veronica shook their heads. "I heard someone say something about holding that guy, not letting him go. It sounded like some customers were restraining him."

"I wasn't looking at anyone but you," Jonathan said.

"Me, neither. But Dr. Clauson didn't try to run away or anything after he stabbed you. He just sort of stepped back, like he wanted to see what would happen. It was like..." Veronica crossed her arms and shivered. "It was like he was performing some kind of experiment. He didn't look like he cared that it hurt you at all."

"If he got out of the restaurant," Jonathan said, "he'll be picked up by the police very quickly. Karen and Steve knew him, and the Sheridan police know him very well. Unless he planned ahead to go into hiding...but I don't think he's done that. I doubt that he expected us to get out of the building before the paramedics arrived. He was going to be right there to proclaim the truth, with trained witnesses and medical technology to back him up. He knew he'd be arrested."

"He said it at the table, about making sacrifices. He's only the messenger," Regan said.

"Thank god the Hong Kong Delhi has a sprinkler system. Many smaller places don't."

"Oh..." Regan carefully pushed herself back so she was sitting up straighter. She was regaining some of her strength. "There's a story about that, the sprinklers date back to some previous use of the building."

"Well, I'm in awe of you two for coming up with that solution, and under that degree of duress. I'll admit, for a few moments there you lost me, I had no idea what you were about to pull."

Regan chuckled, then winced. "That's because you weren't here for our wasted youth. One of the really big pranks from high school...Jarrod got probation for that, didn't he, Ver?"

"No, he got six months in DYS. He was already on probation."

"It was a different restaurant—"

"Someone was talking about seeing this movie where a character triggered the sprinkler system by holding a cigarette lighter under one of the sprayers."

"So Jarrod said, what do you think would happen if you took one of these Sterno pots, the ones they put in the middle of the pu-pu platter trays—"

"When no one was looking he stood up on his chair and poked the pot up at the sprayer, and the Sterno stuck to the metal, like a lump of clay or something."

"And bingo," Regan said. "The whole sprinkler system went on. What a mess."

"You mean, you just did that same thing in Hong Kong Delhi?"

Veronica shrugged. "Those little Sterno pots were all over the room. Everyone was staring at you and Regan."

"Thank god you're so tall."

"Lord," Jonathan said after a moment. "I hope no one saw you."

"I hope so, too, because I think people were taking pictures. I thought I saw flashes."

"What? Pictures of me?"

"I saw that, too," Jonathan said grimly. "That's the trouble. Everyone has cameras now. They've got digital cameras or those little disposables, or camera cell phones. A few people took pictures of Veronica, before Clauson pulled out his knife."

"Well..." Regan said after a moment, "There's no way we can just deny this happened at all. Pictures wouldn't prove how badly injured I was, or even that the knife was real and not just a fake handle. But we need to come up with some kind of cover story. What are we going to say, to explain why we left the restaurant and didn't wait for the paramedics?"

"Veronica had a valid point, that lucid adults have a right to refuse treatment under almost any circumstances. Homeless people frequently do so," Jonathan said. "We can claim that you weren't that badly injured, that you were treated on a confidential basis by a private practitioner. Veronica was just misdiagnosed as being dead for a week, as far as anyone else knows, remember what she said about becoming a Christian Scientist. It will only be an issue if we need medical documentation to press charges against Clauson. And that's the rub. The more our story covers for us—"

"The more it lets Hiram off the hook."

"Assault with a deadly weapon?" Veronica said. "Come on, he'd be in deep shit even if he'd missed."

"But not deep enough," Regan said. "He might be able to make bail on that charge, if I'm not hurt badly enough to be in a hospital."

"And if he's at large, he might try something like this again."

"Not might, Jonathan. He will. He's not going to stop now. If he had the slightest lingering doubt about what he believed, it's gone. We may have escaped public exposure, but he's got his proof. In sterling."

"When can we go back to the house?" Veronica said morosely. "Do you think it's safe?"

"It's safe if Clauson's in custody. But we need to stay out here long enough to create the illusion that Regan's getting medical attention somewhere."

"We can't find out what's going on without access to a phone," Regan said. "I wish you'd gotten that cell phone, Jonathan..."

"The price of procrastination. I'll get one tomorrow. For now, we'll just need to be patient. It's still quite early in the evening. We can stay here for a while and then try going back to the house and finding out what we can."

At around 3:00 a.m., they cautiously drove out of the state forest and back to Rainbow Stone house. By now they were all exhausted, but Regan especially could barely stay awake. She and Jonathan had both been up and active for nearly forty-eight hours, and while they didn't require sleep in the same way as

living people, they did need rest. Veronica had now been awake since her release
from the chest and was bored and frustrated sitting in the woods. The wester-
ing half moon glowed eerily through clouds at first, but the clouds thickened
and began spitting rain a little after midnight. Except for that, the night was
dark and quiet. When they returned to the house, Jonathan surveyed the yards
carefully, listening and smelling for evidence that anyone had been there, for
any reason. It would not have been unreasonable for the police or one of their
friends to have come looking for them out of concern, given their disappearance
from the restaurant. But he detected no sign of visitors or intruders, and they
all entered the house through the back hall, after Jonathan put his car inside
the barn and locked it.

Jonathan called the Sheridan police department, and was told by the officer on duty that Hiram Clauson had been placed under arrest that evening
and was currently in custody awaiting arraignment. He would not give them
any further information due to confidentiality policies. "I'm sorry we haven't
been in touch sooner," Jonathan said. "We've been very busy getting medical
attention for Regan Calloway."

"I understand, sir. How is she?"

"She'll be all right, but she won't be able to come down to the police station
and make any kind of report."

"We wouldn't expect that, sir. We've gotten a detailed report of the incident
from several witnesses. There's been some concern that no one knew where Ms.
Calloway had gone."

"With all the chaos, I'm afraid we panicked and made some fast decisions,
rather than wait for the ambulance. Ms. Calloway preferred to seek non-con-
ventional medical care."

The officer seemed to accept this without further comment. After that call,
Jonathan left a message for Kate Delaney, asking her to let them know when
and if Hiram posted bail. "Let's get some sleep," he said tiredly when he hung
up the phone.

"Where should I sleep?" Veronica said.

"My bed's not set up yet, but you can just use the mattresses on the floor."

"Okay." This quick acquiescence convinced Regan that Veronica must be
tired indeed.

Jonathan double-checked the locks on the doors, although Rainbow Stone
house was hardly secure. Anyone who wanted to get inside would only have to
break a pane on one of the eighteen ground floor sash windows, none of which
had storms. Of course, most of them would have demanded a crowbar or small
explosive charge to open at all. "We won't have to worry about Clauson for the
next six or seven hours, at least," Jonathan said as they went upstairs.

"At this point, Jonathan, I don't even care, I'm so wiped. If he wants to
break in here and drive a stake into me, he can go ahead. It couldn't hurt worse
than the knife did."

Chapter 32

It was Friday afternoon before Regan felt strong enough to stay up and be seriously involved in a long discussion about their situation. Jonathan had helped Veronica retrieve her furniture and belongings from the storage unit across town the day before, and Sean came out to work on moving the furniture inside, or so he had explained to his mother. "What about the DSS investigation?" Regan asked worriedly when Sean appeared at the door. Her two housemates were upstairs measuring rooms.

"Oh, that." He shrugged disdainfully. "We heard that it will be found unsupported. We just didn't get the letter yet. I don't think it hurt us when that Clauson guy went nuts just a couple of days later. I've actually got permission from my mom to be here, so it's cool. I've got to be home by ten, though."

"Well, I'm sure Jonathan and Veronica will appreciate another strong back. I'm afraid I'm not quite ready for heavy lifting yet." At Sean's quizzical look, she pulled up her jersey as far as the wound on her stomach.

"Oh, *yuck.* Is that still really hurting? It looks horrible."

"Yes, it still hurts, and I have to be careful about exerting myself. It made quite an impression on Detective Fellman when he came out here yesterday to take a statement from me. That was the most...discomposed I've ever seen him."

"Didn't he think it was weird that you weren't in a hospital? You don't even have stitches."

"We told him that I'm getting alternative medical treatment. Hey, that's my right. Jonathan's going to hack some kind of documentation. Detective Fellman even took a picture, for the case file. At least no one can claim the whole stabbing was faked somehow, just because I'm walking around."

"I guess vampires don't heal as fast as...uh..."

"As in the movies?" Regan smiled wryly.

"Hey, it's not like I believe that shit, but that mark Jonathan left on me healed up pretty fast."

"I know, I'm teasing you. No, it's not healing as fast as it might, if...well, under more ideal circumstances. But then, you should have seen the knife. I'd show you, but the police have it now."

"Was it silver, or blessed, or something?"

"No, it was just a regular knife—I didn't read anything special from it. I think Hiram bought it in a hardware store."

"What's happened to him, anyway? I heard the cops arrested him, and he didn't even try to get away. Just stood there waiting for them, with this little smile."

Regan shivered at the image he evoked. "He was ordered in for twenty days psychiatric evaluation at his arraignment. That's to establish if he's fit to stand trial. I doubt that he'll go for an insanity defense. But I don't know what he wants."

"He stabs you in the middle of a Chinese buffet with a million witnesses staring at him, and they won't say he's insane?"

Regan snorted. "It's a *joke*. Hiram used to do mental health assessments for the Department of Corrections. Even if he didn't know half the DOC personally, he sure knows exactly the right things to say."

"So, if he passes his evaluation, then what? You think he'll use his trial to blow your cover, tell everyone about you and Jonathan and Veronica?"

"No," Regan said grimly. "I think he'll make bail and disappear. That's what I'm scared of. When I say disappear, I don't mean he'll go far. He'll just drop out of sight."

Sean considered this with concern. "So...what are you going do?"

"We're still discussing our options. We've got a breather, at least. I don't know what the permanent solution will be." There was a short gloomy silence. Regan knew that Sean was wondering if she, Jonathan and Veronica were going to disappear themselves, but was afraid to ask because he didn't want to hear the answer.

After several hours of carrying furniture, Jonathan and Veronica returned the rental truck and picked up a sub sandwich for Sean at C & J Pizza on their way back. Regan would have to wait a while for her own meal. "Jonathan's been bringing me cold blood...cows, goats, I don't know what all it is. But it's not human, and it's never enough. That's why I'm not healing as fast as I should," she told Sean as they sat alone at the table in the great room. "It's all so complicated. I never thought about how the logistics would work, I never expected this to happen at all. And now there are three of us. We all can't just...drag someone into the bushes every couple of weeks, can we?"

"Can you share? I mean, drink from the same person?"

"Jonathan says there are vampires who do, and I guess if we were really careful...it's not like we need that much at one time. I don't know...the idea gives me the creeps. I suppose I'll have to get used to it." She sighed. "Jonathan thinks that if he can buy the house, and if we get enough of the land with it, and if we can actually stay here, we'll raise our own stock."

"Sounds like a great solution to your problem."

"That's a lot of ifs, though. And it doesn't help us now."

The four of them talked about the events of the past week for several hours. They agreed that Jerry Standish was no longer a concern, now that Veronica had turned up and his ex-wife's lawsuit had been dropped. However, it appeared that these same events, and the loss of both a funding source and a potential ally, had only exacerbated the threat posed by Hiram Clauson—or so Regan argued, at great length.

"I'm not disagreeing with you, not after Wednesday night," Jonathan said patiently. "I just wish there was some way we could find out what his real objectives are. I know there's no hope of your reading him."

Regan shook her head sadly. "If he was conscious, he'd block me. I don't know how I could maintain contact without his being aware of it. I suspect he's so guarded now, that he has blocks set up that would be effective if he was drugged or sleeping."

"Do you know where he lives?" Sean asked. "Maybe you could get inside his house and try reading some of his stuff."

"I thought of that. But there are a lot of problems there. One major issue is that Hiram obviously expected to be arrested. That means he expected his home to be searched, and he might have expected that as a result of that, I would have access to some of his things."

"So he'll have cleared everything out that he believes could be readable," Jonathan said.

"He just knows too much about what I can and can't do, and how it works, Jonathan. I'd be nervous about breaking into his house, anyway. Thanks to my being so stupid, he knows we can open locks—or he knows I can, at least. I wouldn't be surprised if he'd left his house booby-trapped somehow, or at least with spy-cams like the ones Sean used. On top of that, the Bridgewater cops are probably keeping an eye on his place. And his car's been impounded."

"He's finished with his psych eval on June seventeenth, isn't he?" Veronica said.

"Yes. We've got two weeks to figure out what we can do, because unless the judge will agree to remand him, I think he's going to jump bail."

Sean said, "Can't we tell the D.A. that we think that?"

"And how are we going to explain why we think Hiram would jump bail, and why that's a concern for us?" Regan said. "You can bet he'll have said all the right things to make himself sound remorseful and rooted to the community. And we can't exactly ask for police protection, can we? The last thing we want is the police keeping an eye on us—any more than they already are."

"How come we didn't get a restraining order?"

"Because, Sean, in Massachusetts you can only get restraining orders against intimate partners, family members or people you lived with," Veronica said. "Trust me, I'm an expert on that topic."

"So, some crazy person that you never had sex with runs you through with a knife, and might come after you and do it again, and you're shit out of luck?"

"That's about right," Regan said.

"That's really fucked," Sean muttered.

"An opinion you share with many. However, I have come up with an idea for possibly getting some information from Hiram without his knowing." She looked around the table. "Hiram has no idea that Veronica and I ran into Evelyn Stockard in Fall River. And Evelyn Stockard has offered to do us a favor."

"What kind of a favor?" Jonathan looked dubious. "The poor woman is about to have surgery, Regan."

"All I need is something in Hiram's handwriting, something he wrote without realizing that I might be able to access it. You see, that's one thing Hiram doesn't know. When it comes to psychometry, at least my gift for it, handwritten papers are in a special category. If Evelyn can send a note to Hiram in the hospital and get something back from him...I can get some information from it."

"Like what?" Sean asked.

"I won't know that until I get hold of the paper."

"Didn't she say she'd asked Dr. Clauson how to get in touch with you, though?" Veronica said. "It seems like he'd be suspicious."

"Not if she says the right things. I think she'll be willing to go along with it. Remember, Evelyn said he wouldn't give her my contact information. Hiram will want to protect her if he thinks I'm trying to locate her. There'll be some turnaround time, having her send the note and then getting an answer."

"And if he doesn't answer her?" Jonathan said.

"Let's keep brainstorming. Maybe we'll come up with a better plan. But I'm going to give Evelyn Stockard a call."

Summer had finally arrived by June 14th, after the long, wet spring. That morning, Regan drove to Fairhaven to meet with Evelyn Stockard, who had called to say that she had received a reply from Hiram Clauson. Evelyn had only been home from the hospital for four days, and she looked tired and even thinner than that first night in April when Regan and Hiram had come to interview her. But there was a lightness in her attitude that was new. When Regan entered the small living room, she immediately noticed the lack of cigarette smell.

"I see you're staying away from the ciggies."

"You better believe it. I think Angie searches my purse when I'm not looking."

They sat down, Regan in one of the armchairs and Evelyn on the sofa. "Mrs. Stockard, I don't want to take up much of your time. I can't tell you how much I appreciate your doing this, with everything else going on right now. I would never have asked if we hadn't had such a time constraint."

"Oh, heavens, I was happy to do it. After what I read in the papers about his stabbing you? I just couldn't believe it. When I think that I let him right into the house, with Angie here and everything, I get cold chills. Anything I can do to help keep him locked up is no favor at all, believe me."

"I don't think you need to have any worries that Hiram would have hurt you or your family. Trust me. This was personal."

"And you have no idea why?"

"That's exactly what I'm hoping to find out from the note."

"Well," Evelyn picked up a small envelope from the low table in front of the sofa. "Here it is. It just arrived on Saturday." The envelope was neatly addressed and bore a rubber stamp stating that it had been mailed from a Department of Corrections facility and its contents had not been reviewed by DOC officials. Evelyn held out the envelope, but Regan hesitated.

"Have you opened it?"

"No, I didn't. I thought it might interfere with your reading."

"That's very good thinking. In this case, however, it wouldn't do much harm unless you wrote on the note. Would you do me a favor, please? Would you open it?"

"All right." Evelyn slit open the envelope with her thumb and extracted the single sheet of lined paper. There was about a paragraph of writing on just one side, in what appeared to be thick soft felt pen.

"Hold it up, I just want to see if it's his handwriting."

Evelyn complied. "Is it?"

"It certainly looks like it." The handwriting was larger and a bit more ragged than usual, but that could be meds, stress, or...*who knows, maybe he really is losing it.* "What does he say?"

Evelyn turned the page back around and scanned it, pursing her lips. "He says I shouldn't contact you in any way, and he also warns me about several other people...wasn't Veronica the name of that pretty woman who was with you in Fall River?"

"Yes, I'm not surprised he'd say that. Mrs. Stockard, could you just fold that up and put in back in the envelope? I want to make sure I have optimum conditions when I read this. Thanks." Regan held her purse out and Evelyn, looking as if she was stifling a giggle, dropped the envelope into it.

"This all seems like one of those John Grisham novels."

"I'm afraid this is the level we've fallen to, unfortunately. Just exactly what did you write to Hiram, by the way?"

"Just what you said. I kept it short and said that you'd been trying to contact me and I was very worried, and I wanted his advice about what to do. I said that I didn't understand what happened but I was sure he had some reason for it, especially after that fit you had the night the two of you were here. I wished him the best in clearing his name. Jim read it, and he was convinced."

"Your husband read it?"

"Of course, I wasn't going to do this behind Jim's back. Besides, he'd have wondered what was going on, if this had come in the mail while I was in the hospital. But don't worry, Ms. Calloway, Jim is on your side as much as I am. He just would never come out and say it."

As Regan got up to leave, she said, "How did the surgery go, Mrs. Stockard?"

"Well, it's never a walk in the park, as they say. But my oncologist said the pathology report was even better than he hoped. He's very optimistic."

Regan looked at Evelyn soberly for a moment and then reached out toward her. "Give me your hand."

Evelyn caught her breath. After a moment she reached out and clasped Regan's hand. Regan closed her eyes, feeling Evelyn's fingers trembling against her own. But her mouth curved into a smile.

"Oh, yeah," she said quietly. "Yeah...you'll be just fine." Evelyn let out her held breath almost in a gasp.

"You're not just saying that?"

"I've never been so happy to be proved wrong, Mrs. Stockard. I guess you surprised me. But you stay away from those cigarettes."

"Don't worry. Are you all right? Your hand is so cold."

"Oh..." Regan had forgotten about that. "I'm okay. I'm just...really hungry, that's all."

"Oh, I'm sorry, can I get you something?"

"No, no," Regan said hastily. "That's okay. I'm still not eating regular food since the stabbing, you know...thank you again, Mrs. Stockard. I hope this is the last time I intrude on you with my problems. But remember: this never happened, you never saw me, and I never got this letter from you. Agreed?"

"Absolutely. I'll make sure Jim understands."

"Please. You don't need to be involved in any of this from now on, Mrs. Stockard. Get well and enjoy your life."

"Good luck," Evelyn said as Regan left.

As it neared midnight that night, Regan sat in the kitchen of Rainbow Stone house, wanting a place with a different atmosphere than the great room with its clutter of computers and papers. She had set a dozen candles and small oil lamps on the table and the cracked and warping linoleum-topped counters. They filled the room with soft yellow light and deep shadows, making the open shelves of the cabinets look bottomless and sinister. Regan recalled seeing those shelves filled with big glass jars of brown rice, mung beans, hand-ground corn meal and organic herbs. Now they didn't even contain dust. Neither the hour nor the illumination had any mystical significance. Regan had just wanted to wait until there was less chance of being interrupted, and she found the soft light soothing. She wished she wasn't so hungry, as that was somewhat distracting. With three of them to provide for, however, they needed to stagger their visits to the outlying farms, and they had agreed to stay away from humans until after the situation with Hiram Clauson was resolved. Regan's stab wound had completely healed without even leaving a scar, but she still seemed to get hungry faster than Jonathan or Veronica.

Sighing, Regan firmly pushed thoughts of food and blood from her mind and relaxed in her chair, consciously grounding and centering her consciousness. When she felt as focused as she could be, she picked up the envelope from the table in front of her and slid the letter out of it. The minute she touched the paper, she felt a chill of anxiety in the pit of her stomach. She spread the note out on the chipped and scored wooden surface of the table without making an effort to read what it said. She did look at the signature, which certainly seemed to be Hiram's.

For a long time she sat at the table, her bare toes scuffing at the worn vinyl floor, her fingers running slowly over the lines of writing over and over, until they were stained black with felt pen ink despite barely touching the surface of the paper. Thoughts and images and emotions and words flicked and faded in and out in her consciousness, as she suppressed her own reactions and focused entirely on collecting information from the impressions. After a while she pushed the paper away and folded her arms tightly and simply sat and thought, reviewing what she had absorbed and putting it together. It was almost one in the morning by the time she folded the note and replaced it in the envelope. She got up and walked out into the great room. Jonathan was working at his computer; Veronica had picked up some low-paying clerical piecework to bring in some money and was unenthusiastically fussing with that. They both looked up at her expectantly when she walked into the room. Regan sat in one of the vacant chairs, one hand to her chin, brooding darkly.

Finally, Jonathan said, "Were you able to learn anything?"

"Oh, yes."

There was a pause, in which Jonathan and Veronica looked at each other uneasily. "So...how bad is it?"

"By any means necessary," Regan said quietly.

"What?"

"That's what he's thinking. It's his motto, his mantra. By any means necessary. But he doesn't have a specific plan."

"Are there other people helping him?" This had been particularly worrying Veronica.

Regan took in a breath. "No. At least, I'm fairly certain there aren't, *yet*. He plans to try and recruit helpers, though. I'm quite certain that he plans to skip bail. I'm conscious of the fact that I might be projecting that, because it's what I expected him to do. But it fits with everything else. He's not going to allow himself to be incarcerated. He's letting go of everything—his job, his house, he doesn't care. His marriage broke up years ago, he has no children, he's not close to any of his family—I knew all that already. He hasn't been happy with his career or his job for a while. I'd inferred that already, too. I suspected from the start that he was hoping to get a book out of this whole thing. But now...he has much more than that. Now he has a cause."

"Which is what?" Jonathan said. "Expose us? Prove we exist?"

"To start with."

"Kill us?" Veronica said.

"I think so. He definitely wants to stop us, and I don't think he believes that we can be kept in custody. Well, he knows about the lock business, anyway. I'm sure he assumes that if I can do it, we all can." She paused a moment. "He is targeting Sean."

Jonathan looked at her sharply. "Are you sure of that, really? I know how much you fear that."

Regan shook her head. "No, I'm not *sure*, Jonathan. I'm not that sure about anything I read, ever. It's always probabilities and possibilities. It can always be colored and influenced by my own expectations or mental blocks or fears. But in this case..." She trailed off, and the other two sat waiting for her to finish her thought. "He knows Sean is our weakest link. Or more to the point, *my* weakest link. He thinks Sean may be a vampire too, but if not, Hiram certainly thinks that we're grooming Sean to join the tribe, maybe in a year or so. In any event, he doesn't appear to see Sean as an innocent to be rescued."

"What do you think Clauson might do?"

"That, I don't know—probably because he doesn't. He was genuinely thrown by the fact that we got out of the restaurant before the paramedics arrived. He did not expect that. He'd planned that whole scenario very carefully. I think he expected more helpful bystanders to rush in and interfere with our leaving. He didn't anticipate that people would be so frightened that they'd just want to get out of the building, especially the families with children. He knew that he'd be arrested, but he expected to be vindicated to some extent when I was exposed by the paramedics. So now, he's having to rethink things, and his plans are somewhat nebulous. But I'm sure he's thinking of using Sean against us in some way—and if he has to sacrifice Sean, that's what will have to happen, as far as he's concerned."

Jonathan stared down at the tabletop, his face grim. "I don't want to believe what you're saying, Regan, but..."

"Does any of this really seem all that implausible? For god's sake, Hiram wouldn't have gotten this far if he wasn't tenacious, to say the very least. I know, I lost enough arguments to him—starting with the one about helping him with the investigations to begin with. God, he just wouldn't take no for an answer! And now he's past giving up, because he's invested too much. He'll have lost everything for nothing if he can't stop us, one way or another. And that's without the moral and ethical crusade. When we were still doing interviews, he was talking about people being hurt. The night he stabbed me, he was talking about putting things back the way they should be. Do you hear an escalation there, or is it just me?"

"So what do you suggest that we do?"

Regan's expression tightened. "I've already said what I think we should do."

Jonathan sagged in his chair, looking hopelessly up at the ceiling. "It just seems that we're being too hasty. What has he done to deserve execution? That's what we're talking about, isn't it?"

"What has he *done?* Maybe if you were the one who'd had a five inch long steel knife shoved through your liver, you'd be less ambivalent."

"I've survived worse."

"I'd rather not, thanks." Regan put her hands over her eyes, feeling exhausted. "Do I have to go over it all again? Hiram won't stop, even if we disappear. He will recruit assistants. Once he does, they'll be galvanized into fanaticism if anything happens to him. He knows enough now to be a danger to other vampires. The only alternative solutions I could even imagine would be if we could somehow erase his memory of the entire last six months, or persuade him to see our point of view sympathetically. Do you believe either of those is possible?"

Jonathan hesitated, as if he was trying desperately to think of some way they might be. "No."

"Jonathan—if I may borrow a phrase from you, remember your Shakespeare."

"It's not at all the same thing. At least with revenge, as doubtful as it is, there's a concrete wrong in the past to be avenged. Drastic action to prevent something that may or may not happen is quite a different matter."

"But if we don't act, we may end up with just about as many bodies as the end of *Hamlet*."

"You keep saying 'we,' Regan. Are *you* prepared to take a life? In cold blood, do you really think that's something you could do?"

Regan didn't look away from his hard stare. "Yes. I'll do it. And I'll do it alone. You don't have to help me."

He was silent for a moment, studying her with a small frown, as if he suddenly found her appearance changed but wasn't sure how. "You realize that just a few weeks ago, you could not have said that and meant it."

Regan looked down at the tabletop, thinking for a moment of what her life had been like only a few weeks ago. It seemed like months had passed since the night she had first met Jonathan in the store and her world had turned inside out. "I do realize that. After Nick, and Cal...how could I not? And didn't you explain to me why?" She looked at Jonathan's troubled expression for a moment and sighed. "Is this going to change things between us, Jonathan?"

"What do you mean?"

"I mean, will it change how you feel about me. Am I going to be unclean somehow, so you won't want to be around me anymore?"

"If I said yes, would that affect your decision?"

Regan thought for a minute about what it would mean, if Jonathan pushed her away, perhaps left without her. The prospect made her feel desolate. But then she imagined how she would feel if he, or Veronica, or worst of all Sean, were harmed or exposed or killed, and suddenly it was as though a searing flame passed over her body. "No. If that's how you'll feel, then I'll just have to accept it. I won't let it stop me from doing whatever I have to do."

There was a silence. Veronica was looking apprehensively between the two of them, and Regan could understand why. Where would Veronica be if her new family split up like her birth family had done? But Jonathan finally sighed. "It won't change things. I don't know what could, really. But at least I know where your priorities are."

"Protecting all of us. That's where my priorities are, Jonathan. It's that simple."

"There's still the possibility that Clauson will be remanded. Kate has been working hard on the prosecutor in charge of the case. The problem is the judge, not the D.A.'s office."

"I know. If Hiram is remanded, we won't have access to him, anyway. But he can still communicate with others from prison, and potentially get some kind of alliance underway. There are countless gangs and criminal groups whose leaders run the show from inside prison almost as well as out."

"Oh, I'm definitely aware of that."

"And even if he's convicted, from our perspective he won't serve that much time. He might cop a plea, too, and get even less. Remand just gives us a little more time, it doesn't solve a thing."

"Do you have a plan?" Jonathan asked quietly. "It better be a good one. We'll be very high on the suspect list if Clauson is obviously murdered."

"I have some ideas. But I'm still thinking about it. I'm hoping it won't look obvious."

On June 17th, they all were at the court in Fall River for the hearing on Hiram's psychological evaluation and the judge's decision on whether to grant bail. Hiram was brought into the courtroom in shackles by a uniformed court officer, which was rather a shock, but was evidently standard procedure given the charge against him. His attorney had been talking to the A.D.A. handling the case and with Kate Delaney, who was appearing as a victim advocate for Regan. Hiram gave Regan, Veronica and Jonathan the briefest of glances, just enough that they knew he had seen them, and immediately looked away.

As Regan had predicted, Hiram had passed his evaluation with a clean bill of mental health, and made no attempt to plea insanity or mental defect. His plea was recorded as "not guilty." The A.D.A. requested remand.

"On what grounds?" The judge had heavy jowls and red, vein-shot cheeks and an expression that suggested he suffered badly from acid reflux. His inflection and tone of voice when he looked at the A.D.A. was considerably less friendly than when he spoke to Hiram's attorney. Regan wondered if there was some personal history there or if the judge simply didn't like female lawyers.

"Your honor, the victim fears for her safety, given the irrationality of the crime against her. She was attacked without warning in a public place before witnesses, and she is not eligible for a 209A against the defendant. Dr. Clauson has no local family, has lost his job and has just sold his home. It's obvious that he is a flight risk."

"Your rationales contradict each other, counselor," the judge said sourly. "If the defendant is a flight risk, he can't be a threat to the victim, and vice versa. Which one is it? Mr. Whitlock."

Hiram's attorney rose. "Your honor, my client sold his home in order to raise the funds to post bail and pay his legal fees. He has limited resources which will quickly be exhausted, and he anticipates taking menial work somewhere to support himself until trial. Remand would be an even greater hardship on him than the court has already imposed by placing him in custody for the mental health evaluation. My client is an educated professional of some standing. He made no attempt to evade arrest and has been completely cooperative. We are confident that he will be exonerated at trial."

The judge grunted. "Bail is set at ten thousand dollars cash or bond, and the defendant is ordered to have no contact with the victim before trial." He gave the gavel a bored thump.

"That's it?" Veronica whispered to Regan, appalled. "He walks?"

"All he has to do is post his bail, and he's on the street," Regan said, watching as Hiram's shackles were being removed over by the court's side door. Attorney Whitlock was talking to him in a rapid, clipped voice.

"Did we know that Clauson had sold his house? Kate didn't mention it."

"Well, *I* didn't. I didn't pick that teensy detail off the note. He must have taken a big loss or had some private contact to sell that fast in this market."

"What do we do?" Veronica said in a panicked whisper, as Hiram and Attorney Whitlock left the courtroom.

"There's nothing we can do," Regan said helplessly. Kate Delaney came down the aisle to where they were seated, spreading her hands in an exasperated gesture. She motioned toward the courtroom doors, as the next case on the docket was being called. All four of them went out into the lobby and huddled near the wall.

"Well, you heard."

"Is he going to be able to get his car back?" Regan asked.

"I doubt it. But that doesn't mean he won't have some clunker to get around in. George Whitlock makes it sound like Clauson will be washing dishes in a diner and walking to work with a lunch bucket in his hand. But if Clauson's got house money, he can buy and register a car before the day is out."

"Which means we won't know what he's driving," Jonathan said grimly.

"You do have a no contact order, at least."

"Yeah, and I've got an old T token here, too, and I can tell you which one is worth a buck."

Kate sighed. "I'm sorry. The stuff that comes through Fall River court...I have a feeling the judge didn't take this case too seriously."

"I'd like to see how seriously he'd take it if someone put a knife in him," Regan said heatedly. Kate shushed her urgently.

"Careful how loudly you say that, Ms. Calloway. I hear ya, but they get about two knifing cases a week in here, hon. Let's just take this a day at a time, all right? Now we've got a continuance to August third, we'll just have to stay on it."

"August third," Veronica moaned, sounding like a child who had just been told that the last day of school had been rescheduled to that date.

"That's not too bad as these things go," Kate said. "Look, I'll be staying in touch with the D.A.'s office, and I'll keep you informed if anything comes up. If you have any problems at all, call the police. That detective up there, Fellman, he seems to be sympathetic to you. Right now, I'm afraid that's all you can do."

In the car on the way back to Sheridan, Jonathan said, "Well, Regan? He's out and he has money. Have you decided to go through with it, and how?"

Regan was silent a long time, staring out the car windows, thinking unwillingly of the last time she'd ridden this stretch of highway in a passenger's seat. *He's such a rationalist...could everything I read from the note be wrong? He was confident he wouldn't kill me with that knife. And he was right.* "Let's keep an eye on him. He's going to be moving into a new place and starting new routines, anyway, I'd need to know something about that. Now that school's out, we can keep a closer watch on Sean, too." She sighed. "Maybe you were right. I was just panicking."

Chapter 33

For some time, things did seem to be quiet, and Regan began to wonder if her fears had been groundless after all. Her court case was dismissed, and Jonathan got back the bail he'd posted. DSS sent Sharon Neeson a letter informing her that the 51a report of possible abuse or neglect had been investigated and found unsupported. The only thing that made Regan nervous about this was the knowledge that Hiram, as the reporter, would also receive a copy of the letter. But Jonathan pointed out that DSS probably didn't have a current address for Hiram Clauson, and in any event, the letter contained nothing that Hiram would be able to use. Regan just hated the idea that Hiram would be reminded of Sean in any way. Despite a lingering suspicion that they wouldn't be able to stay in Rainbow Stone house, Veronica and Regan arranged their furniture in different parts of the sprawling building, just so that they would be able to function. Regan was developing a business plan for a web-based second hand retail store, while Veronica had gotten a more lucrative work-at-home job doing medical transcription on the computer and kept herself busy at that. Ted Green had worked up a payment plan for her to reimburse her father for the credit card bills, and Veronica had agreed to sign it. They even met Karen, Steve, and Derek for drinks a few evenings, although not at the Hong Kong Delhi which was still closed for repairs following the sprinkler mishap. Daily life had returned to such a level of normality, in fact, that it made Regan uneasy. She kept thinking of Jonathan's word: *counterfeit*.

She continued to wonder if Hiram was attempting to form, as Jerry Standish put it, a vampire hunting team. But according to Kate, who was keeping in touch with Attorney Whitlock, Hiram was working two jobs in Bridgewater, doing very little socializing, no longer had a cell phone, and, as far as anyone knew, had no computer at home. He'd always used his office computer prior to his tenure revocation. With his investigative software, Jonathan did some snooping to see if he could find any record that Hiram Clauson had an Internet service provider, cell phone account or broadband service on his phone line. He found none of those, and only basic cable going to Hiram's tiny apartment in downtown Bridgewater. "But that doesn't prove anything," Jonathan admitted. "He could have signed up for service under a false name. He could access the Internet at the public library. And if he wants a cell phone, he can buy one of these Tracfones like mine in any CVS or Wal*Mart. They're untraceable." He was somewhat relieved that he could find no vehicle registered to Hiram in the DMV records. But Regan was not soothed by this.

"He could register a vehicle under someone else's name, or not register it at all. Or rent one, any time he wanted."

Sean came out to the house most days, and at his persistent request for things to do, Jonathan set him to working on the outside yards, where the grass was now over knee high in back. There was also some discussion of getting Sean his driver's license. Sharon Neeson had never had the money to pay for driver's education classes, and as Sean said, more sad than sarcastic, "let's face it, would *you* want to be out driving with my mom?" To Regan's amazement, Veronica offered to take on this project, and Sean accepted her offer. It seemed that Veronica was trying to make up for having started off her vampire life by threatening to gruesomely murder Sean. Regan was just a little nervous about their being alone together, given Veronica's history and the degree of stern self-denial about drinking that they all continued, from necessity, to practice. But at least Veronica definitely understood how and when to *close* now.

One night at the end of June, Veronica answered the cordless phone and then handed it to Jonathan. "It's your friend from Maine." He took the phone with a quizzical look.

"Hello, Diana."

"Jonathan. I thought I'd call you and see how things have been going. I put a news feed on the Fall River *Herald* and I saw that little mess you had at the Chinese restaurant down there. Is everything settled down now?"

"Well...it seems to be, but we're still keeping close tabs on this Hiram Clauson."

"So, there are still three of you? And *only* three of you?"

He smiled reluctantly. "Correct on both counts, so far."

"I would have e-mailed you, but for some reason, I thought perhaps all this shouldn't be committed to writing. What exactly happened?"

Jonathan related the story. When he finished, there was a thoughtful silence.

"Do you really want to stay there? You sound like you're getting pretty settled in. You said something about buying the property, back in May."

"Well...I've run into a snag there. The owner doesn't want to sell to me, apparently. I made an offer and he's rejected it."

"You think this Clauson fellow soured the owner on you?"

"Yes, I do. My attorney's been pursuing it, but the trouble is—she's my attorney. There's just so much she can do."

"Give me the information and I'll look into it. If you want."

"What do you think she could do?" Regan said curiously after Jonathan had hung up.

"With Diana, anything goes. But at least the owner won't have any idea she's associated with me. And she has fond memories of this place, too."

"The hippie house," Regan said, smiling. "You know, I'm sorry I missed it."

"A couple more people and we will have a commune here. Maybe we can restore Rainbow Stone Junction to a shadow of its former glory."

They had gorgeous weather for the Fourth of July holiday weekend: warm, sunny, and not too humid, the nights drenched in moonlight. Sheridan always had town fireworks in the park by the river, funded in part by the Standish Mills. Due to their continued notoriety in town, the three residents of Rainbow Stone house chose not to attend the public events, although they could see the fireworks well from the attic windows of the house. Sean, however, told them that he was planning to go to the concert and fireworks on Sunday night, and then stay close to home to keep an eye on his mother. Holidays were always a challenge for people trying to maintain sobriety. It sounded safe enough even to Regan—the Sheridan Fourth of July celebration was attended by hundreds of people and was virtually SRO down by the riverside.

The following day was the Monday holiday. It dawned overcast and muggy, with rain expected later in the day. All three of the Rainbow Stone denizens went to bed as sunrise approached, but Regan found that she was restless and couldn't sleep. She wasn't sure what was bothering her. It wasn't the weather. None of them were troubled by weather conditions or temperature anymore, although as Jonathan said, the other side of that advantage was that they no longer enjoyed temperature variations, such as the languor of summer heat or the bracing nip of a brisk autumn day. There was only one thing now that would make them feel warm. But Regan couldn't complain about being impervious to Massachusetts' summer humidity.

At around 9:00, she finally gave up on trying to rest, got dressed and came back downstairs, thinking she would get some more work done. She was just booting up her laptop computer when the phone rang, and she almost let it go to voice mail, since typically no one was awake to answer the phone at this hour. But she was so conditioned to grab the phone fast at the store, she couldn't stand to sit and listen to it ring, and she picked it up before voice mail did.

"Borrowed an—I mean, hello."

"Hello, is this Regan?"

"Sharon?" Regan felt a sudden jolt of alarm.

"Yes, it's Sharon Neeson. I was wondering if I could talk to Sean."

"To...Sean?"

"Yes, he's out there, isn't he? He didn't come home last night and I figured he must be with you. He practically lives out there now, anyway."

"He didn't..." Regan suddenly couldn't speak. *It's nothing, it's nothing, it can't be...* "I haven't seen him, Sharon. He told me that he was going to go home after the fireworks, we didn't expect him."

"He did? That little shit...I'll just bet he got wasted last night with some of those voke school kids. How many times have I warned him..."

As Sharon Neeson ranted on, Regan looked desperately around the room, as though Sean might be crashed in a corner sleeping and she hadn't noticed him. She'd have smelled him the moment she came downstairs if he'd been anywhere on the first floor, but she tried to disregard that. *He does have a key... maybe he rode his bike out here late...or early....* "Are you absolutely sure he didn't come home? You checked his room? Maybe he just stayed out really late and snuck back in."

"I've looked *everywhere*. That worthless little fuck, doesn't he know better yet? Another report to DSS and he'll be in a fucking group home, I thought he was shaping up..." Regan winced at the torrent of abusive language, even though she could hear the fear in Sharon Neeson's voice.

"Sharon...Sharon, just calm down. I'm sure he's fine. Look, I'll check around here and make sure he's not crashing anywhere, and if I find him, or he shows up, or I hear from him, I'll make sure he calls you."

She got off the phone and went to wake up Jonathan. She was trying to keep her composure, but by the time she was halfway up the stairs, she was running.

Within five minutes, Jonathan had pulled on some clothes and come downstairs. "He might have gotten picked up by the police for underage drinking or rowdy behavior, if he was with a lot of other teenagers."

"In that case he would have called his mother, or us."

"We don't know that Hiram Clauson has anything to do with this, Regan. We've been keeping tabs on Clauson as much as we possibly can and he hasn't done a thing to raise suspicion—"

"He wouldn't! Don't you think he knows that we'd be watching him? He'd have to be a complete idiot not to assume that. And one thing that Hiram is not, is an idiot."

"What's going on?" Veronica's voice, somewhat sleepy, came from the bottom of the stairs, and then she drifted into the room, barefoot and wearing only an oversize T-shirt.

"Sean's mother called," Regan said tautly. "He never got home last night."

Veronica put both hands to her mouth, her eyes widening. "Oh my god..."

"Let's just not panic." Jonathan raked a hand through his disheveled hair. "Even if our worst fears are true, we've got to be able to think clearly, or we'll be sure to commit some blunder we'll regret."

Veronica went over to the table and poked around among the stacks of papers and various computer components until she located the phone base.

"What are you doing, Ver?"

"This records, doesn't it?" Veronica's tone was cool and business-like. "I mean, if a call comes in, you can record while you talk."

"It does," Jonathan said. "I don't use it, because I have the Verizon voice mailbox, but..." His expression was somewhat impressed.

"Good. Because I bet we're going to get a call," Veronica said, folding her arms. The sound of birds singing in the woods around the house outside was jarringly incongruous against the tense silence in the dim room.

"Should we call the police?" Jonathan finally said softly. "Or would his mother do that?"

Regan shook her head. "Sharon Neeson is too afraid of DSS, I doubt she would call the police. She's probably going to go out and look around the riverside park and ask any kids she sees if they know where Sean is. Anyway, a kid Sean's age can't be listed as missing this soon. He'd likely be assumed to be a runaway, especially with his history."

"Yes, but...given recent events, and his association with us..."

"Then the police will be watching us, too, Jonathan. What can they do, after all?"

"Don't call the police," Veronica said quietly.

For several minutes they all stood mute and motionless. Finally Jonathan went to his computer, brought it out of standby mode and checked his e-mail, just to see if there was anything there from Sean. He met Regan's querying look and shook his head. "I think Clauson has gone off-grid. That's why we haven't found any records. He's not using false names. He's closing all his accounts entirely."

"And that means..." Regan couldn't finish her thought.

"It means you were right all along. He's going to run."

Regan closed her eyes a moment. *With Sean? Or after...no, no, no he couldn't, he just couldn't...* The cordless phone buzzed, and she had to stifle a small scream. She stared at the phone as it buzzed a second time.

"Get it, Regan!" Veronica hissed, her finger poised on the base unit's Record button.

Swallowing hard, Regan picked up the cordless. She knew who it was before she pressed the Talk button. "Hello, Hiram." Veronica pressed Record silently.

"Good *morning*, Regan," Hiram's voice was effusive. "I'm sorry to get all of you up at this ungodly hour, but I'm sure you've been waiting to hear from me."

What is this, has he got spy-cams in here? Regan thought, scanning the corners of the room frantically. "What makes you think so, Hiram? Frankly, none of us ever wants to hear from you again."

"Oh, now, that hurts my feelings, Regan. After everything we've shared."

There was a sudden crackling noise in the background, with a voice in it, and Regan abruptly understood. *A police scanner. Sharon Neeson must have called...so Hiram knows she called us.* "So, having gotten us up, just what exactly do you want?"

"I'm sure you're worried about your little protégé, Sean. I'm calling to let you know that he's with me."

"We had guessed that, actually."

"I'm sure you did."

"Where are you, Hiram?" Hiram didn't dignify this question with any answer except a short laugh. "What do you *want?*" Regan repeated, trying to keep herself under control.

"I want Jonathan Vaughn to turn himself in."

"Jonathan—" Regan jerked around to stare at Jonathan, horror struck.

Jonathan had straightened up, but his expression was unreadable.

"I want him to go to the Sheridan police station and make a full confession. Everything he's done, and exactly why. The *whole* truth, and he's to show them proof."

"What makes you think that Jonathan would do that?"

"If he doesn't, I'll kill Sean." Hiram said this in the same casual, almost cheerful tone.

"Hiram, you *can't!* In the name of god, Sean's just a kid! How can you possibly justify this? No one's been killed!"

"Oh no? I count at least two murders so far. Vaughn killed you, didn't he? And he killed Veronica Standish. Young Sean is better off dead than what Vaughn will make of him. You know that as well as anyone, don't you, Regan?"

Regan was so stunned by what Hiram had said she couldn't think of a reply. She knew better than to try and argue with him. "And what about me, then? What about the Atheneum?"

"You and I will discuss that later. You keep insisting that Vaughn isn't a monster—fine. This is his last chance to prove that you're right. Show me that he'll put this boy's welfare ahead of his own and I might start to believe you."

"So, when do you expect Jonathan to do this, right now?"

"Ideally. You have until noon today. That gives you, let's see, two and half hours. I think that's plenty of time for you all to come to the right decision. I *will* know whether or not he's gone."

"How will you know whether Jonathan's told the police everything or not?"

"Because he'll see to it that I do. Everyone will know."

"You're talking about media publicity?"

"Of course I am. Really, Regan, what else would you expect?"

"And then you'll let Sean go?"

"After Vaughn has made his confession, then I'll get back in touch." At those words, Regan suddenly felt as though a fist had slammed into the pit of her stomach.

"Let me talk to Sean. Is he conscious?"

"He is now. He's still a bit groggy." There was a pause, then Regan heard Sean's voice, a little slurred, as though he was drunk.

"Regan?"

"Sean, are you all right?"

"Yeah, I don't know where I am, he's put tape over my eyes..."

Regan didn't realize she had swayed until her hip struck the edge of the table, and she had to catch herself. "That's okay, Sean—"

"Don't do it!" Sean's voice sounded strained, but urgent. "I'm not scared, Regan. Don't do what he says."

Hiram's voice came back on the phone. "I wouldn't take his advice, if I were you. Don't tell the police about this phone call. Do exactly as I say, or I will keep my promise. No more games, Regan. You won't survive the next time. After this, I will no longer regard you as a victim. Twelve noon. I'm watching." The call clicked off.

Regan slowly set down the phone on the table, feeling as though she had been struck a brutal blow from behind and it was still taking effect. She looked up at Jonathan. "He doesn't know where he is, because his eyes are taped," she said calmly. She looked down at her hands, pressed against the tabletop, and it seemed that she was looking at another table, in another room, eight years ago. There were men all around her, and on the wood-tone Formica in front of her were a child's sweater decorated with Winnie-the-Pooh and balloons, a small pair of pink socks, a plastic bag with blood soaked panties...images were flashing in her mind like blinding strobe lights, the Exacto knives lined up on a tray in a perfectly straight row, the hooks set into strategic points in the walls and ceiling, little girls with silver duct tape over their eyes and binding their wrists, but not over their mouths because he used their mouths...she backed away from the table, bumping into the chair behind her, trying to get away from the images, the horrible sounds and smells, and there was a tiny, stiff hand in her own, ice cold, fingers clenched in agony. Regan sank to the floor with an incoherent sound, her hands over her head, and then Jonathan was next to her, his arms tightly around her.

"Regan, don't do this, hang on, Sean needs you, this isn't Gardner, he's still alive..."

"Breathe, Regan," she heard Veronica say on the other side of her, and suddenly Regan almost had to laugh. Then she was sobbing. But the room around her slowly became clear again and the horrible flashing images had stopped.

"Oh, god, what are we going to do now?"

"Regan," Jonathan's voice was low and serious. He let go of her and cupped her face with his hands, and in his eyes was the look of mingled pain, shame and anger that she had seen when he'd called her out to the house to help him with Veronica. "I can't do what he asks. I just can't."

"I know you can't, Jonathan," Regan whispered. She saw the look of genuine surprise on his face, and knew he had been prepared for this to be the end of their connection, forever. "I understand. You can't expose all of us to save Sean. But it wouldn't matter. Even if you do exactly what Hiram wants, he'll kill Sean anyway."

Jonathan swallowed hard. "You really think that?"

"I *know* that. You heard him. Sean is better off dead than one of us. Hiram will kill him and make sure he doesn't come back. And he knows exactly how to do that." Regan hugged her knees and shuddered. "And then he'll come after us."

Veronica slowly stood up and walked around the table. "Let's listen to this phone call." Her voice was cold and firm. Looking up at her, as she wiped tears off her face, Regan recalled that flat gray expanse she had felt when she read

Veronica, after they had released her from the chest. *Maybe that isn't such a curse, after all...* Veronica clicked the Play button. Regan had to steel herself to listen to the conversation again. "Don't pay attention to the words. Listen to what's in the background. Is that a police scanner?" She paused the playback. Regan nodded. "Then they've got to be here in Sheridan, if he's using a scanner to listen to Sheridan police."

"But he could be in a van, Veronica, which means he could move constantly and be almost anywhere," Jonathan said. Regan got up and moved closer to the table, the faintest flicker of hope returning to her.

"Well, let's listen." Veronica played the call over once, then twice. "No, I don't think they're outside, and I don't think they're in a car." She looked up at Regan and Jonathan's amazed expressions. "What?"

"I didn't know you were such a detective," Jonathan said.

Veronica looked down at the phone base, smiling faintly. "When I was a teenager, I was always calling my dad and pretending to be places I wasn't. After I got caught a few times, I started to pick up some valuable tips about how you can tell where people are calling from. It's actually pretty obvious. Jarrod taught me a lot about that. Anyway." She cleared her throat. "All right. He's in town. He's indoors. He must be someplace where he won't be found or heard by accident. And...he must be someplace where he can destroy a body. That narrows down the options." Her face grew distant. "I'll just bet..."

"What?"

"It's just a feeling, but..." Veronica played the call again. Regan was listening so intently to the spaces between the words that she didn't even hear the speakers' voices now. "There. Right there, do you hear that?"

"I—I don't know what you're hearing, Ver..."

Veronica fast forwarded and played a few seconds of recording again. "*That.* I know that sound."

To Regan, it was a barely audible double thump, a bit like the sound of car tires going over a speed bump. "What is it?"

"It's something the main generator does, I'm not sure exactly why. It makes that noise every two minutes. They're in the mills."

Regan stared. "The *mills?* The Standish Mills? But how is that *possible?* How would Hiram get in?"

"It's not that hard to get in. The mills are closed for the holiday today, remember? There are a couple of security guards, and the front gate is locked, but there's a way to get into the boiler room. The building is more than a hundred and fifty years old, and there's nothing valuable down there. There's a side entrance near the river. If you have a key, or just break the lock, you're in. I used to take my boyfriends in there to make out."

"What, in a boiler room?"

"It was like doing it right under my dad's nose. They didn't complain, they were getting laid, weren't they?"

"And how would Clauson know about this?" Jonathan didn't look entirely convinced.

"One of said boyfriends wouldn't be Derek Wilson, would it?" Regan said shrewdly.

"Yes, it would. In fact, he kind of liked doing it."

"But a boiler room, why would Hiram—"

"There are incinerators down there. Two big ones, up at one end. They're really old, but they're still used, mostly for scrap wood. Technically, we're not supposed to be burning them anymore, but..." Veronica shrugged.

"How would Hiram get there, with Sean?" Regan asked, trying to control the cold horror that was almost making her nauseated.

"That's another clue. There's a path running along the river from the park all the way down along the side of the mills. He could walk, he wouldn't even need a car or a van to attract attention. I'll bet kids were going up and down that path all last night, in the dark—no one would even have noticed. All the druggies go down there. That's what happened every time I went to the fireworks on the Fourth, anyway." Veronica walked across the room and back, gnawing on a fingernail. "I'll just bet...this Dr. Clauson went to the fireworks last night to see if any of us was there. I'll bet he looks different. All he'd have to do is shave that beard off. And Sean never even met him, did he?"

Regan looked at Jonathan. "No, I don't think he ever did. And there was no photo of Hiram in the papers after the stabbing incident."

"You know Sean's always nursing a can of that camel piss he loves so much, that Mountain Dew. That stuff would hide the taste of anything. I'll bet Dr. Clauson slipped him a roofie or something. Then when Sean could hardly walk, he offered to help him get home."

"I don't know, it sounds like a rather far-fetched scenario," Jonathan said.

"No, it doesn't. That sounds exactly like Hiram," Regan said slowly. "Subtle, manipulative, simple, and opportunistic. What would he have to lose? In a big crowd like that, with his appearance disguised, maybe a small knapsack or something...if he spotted any of us, he'd just get lost fast. But he was probably pretty confident that none of us would be at a big public event like that—and he was right. If he didn't see Sean, he'd go home and try again some other time. God, for all we know, this is his tenth try, and that's why things have seemed so quiet all this time."

"So what do we do?"

"Let's go and get Sean," Veronica said staunchly.

"But...what if you're wrong, Veronica? This is excellent guesswork, but Clauson could be somewhere else entirely."

"Sean will be just as dead whether we sit here or go to the mills," Regan said desperately. "We might just as well try looking there, as do nothing."

"Well...we better finish getting dressed, then." Jonathan still looked uncertain.

"Right, but you're not going with us, Jonathan," Veronica said.

"I'm not? And why not?"

"You need to go to the police station. No, not to make a confession. You need to tell Detective Fellman what's happening."

"But—

"She's right, Jonathan. I'll bet he's got a spy-cam set up watching the police station entrance. All he'd need to monitor it is a cell phone. That's why he's so sure he'll know whether or not you've gone in."

"Didn't he say not to tell the police about the phone call?"

"I'd say we're not obligated to stick to any bargains here. Just don't mention that we taped it. We can't play that recording for the police."

"Well—"

Regan said, "Jonathan, use your own judgment as to what you say. But you can't send the police to the mills until you hear from us, because we can't get caught there." She and Veronica were both halfway to the stairs. "Thank god you reactivated your cell phone, Veronica. Can we get in that entrance without Hiram knowing it? He might have it booby-trapped somehow, and if he thinks we've found him, Sean's dead meat."

Veronica paused on the stairs to give Regan a disdainful look. "Silly girl. It's the Standish Mills. I'm Veronica Standish. We're going in the front door."

"But, isn't there a security guard inside the front door?"

"Of course there is. And he's not even going to remember seeing us."

Chapter 34

Jonathan dropped Regan and Veronica off at the end of a side street near the river, about a half mile north of the park. "Don't say you know where Hiram is until we call you," Regan said. He looked very uncertain but tersely agreed. Regan and Veronica walked quickly along the twisting, uneven trail that led through high reeds along the riverbank. The smell of the river, whiffs of chemicals and sewage mingled with the fishy, muddy odor of water, was heavy in the warm muggy air, and there were visible clouds of gnats, mosquitoes and may flies hovering above the reeds. "Veronica," Regan said quietly after a few minutes. "Do you think that maybe this is...too easy?"

"You mean, that he's expecting us to come after him and has set a trap?"

"Yes. What if he calls the house again and gets no answer? He'll know that only Jonathan went to the police station. He knows your father owns the mills. We're guessing that he found out about the boiler rooms from your boyfriend. Do you think he'll suspect that we've worked out where he is?"

Veronica tossed her hair back impatiently. "He might. Do you have a better idea than this?"

"What if he's got explosives or something, maybe he's rigged up a bomb."

"Don't you think we could smell that?"

"It depends what it is. I don't know what plastic explosive smells like, and nitro doesn't smell at all."

They slowed down, as they had reached the beginning of the park, and the trail, although still running through reeds, was visible for the length of the public area. "Regan, you're worrying too much. If this Dr. Clauson was going to rig a bomb in the mills, he'd have to have been carrying everything to do that with him. The Fourth of July security people check bags and things for that. It would look too suspicious."

"I suppose." Regan ducked her head as a jogger went by on the paved running track up above them. The jogger had iPod buds in her ears and didn't give them a glance. "It's just that...that would be one way of destroying a body, wouldn't it? Not to mention that it's a pretty reliable way of destroying us."

Veronica stopped walking for a moment, thinking about this. Then she sniffed dismissively. "In that case, he wouldn't need to be near an incinerator, would he?"

"But—"

"We're wasting time, Regan."

They cut up from the trail to the south end of the park. Ahead, across a short, wide street, was the north end of the mill complex. The mill yard, running back from the street along the side of the building, was bounded by a heavy chain-link fence, its wide double gate closed and locked. There was a small booth by the gate where an employee monitored truck traffic in and out while the mill was open, but it was empty now. The north end of the building had no barrier or fence, but directly abutted the cracked concrete sidewalk. Three broad shallow granite steps led up to a heavy set of double doors painted green. The employee parking lot ran the length of the mill complex on the opposite side from the river, and beyond it ran the exit ramp from the highway. The parking lot was also nearly empty. But it was the vehicle parked just inside the yard, behind the locked fence, that brought Regan to a stop.

"Veronica...isn't that your father's car?"

Veronica looked and shrugged unconcernedly. "Yep. He *would* be working today."

"But—"

"He'll be up in his office, Regan. He doesn't wander around the buildings, checking the dust on the windowsills."

"But won't security call him for anything unusual—like you walking in?"

"When he works off hours, he doesn't want to bothered, usually. Come on."

"*Wait* a moment." Regan caught her friend's arm. "Veronica, let's not rush in and do something stupid—just because you're hungry."

Veronica turned and stared at her almost angrily, then she sagged. "Okay, okay. But we've only got until noon, Regan! What more we do we have to think about?"

"Does this complex have security cameras? We can't blank out a video-tape."

Veronica shook her head. "Maybe up in the administrative office, because that's the only place where there's money, or anything valuable at all. Dad doesn't monitor his employees, and he wouldn't shell out for an expensive system. He always said ten cameras couldn't beat one alert pair of eyes. That's why he hires security."

"Not even the front door, though?"

"No, I'm sure of it. What are people going to do, anyway, run off with eighty-pound spools of nylon?"

"What if Hiram's got a camera set up outside here?"

Veronica scanned the area around the street, unconsciously stepping closer to the tree next to them as she did. There were not a lot of likely locations for a spy-cam. The trees were fully leafed out, there were no utility poles closer than either corner and the facade of the building was flat, weathered red brick. It would have been difficult to rig a camera without being caught. "We'll have to take our chances. Come on, Jonathan must be talking to the police by now."

They crossed the street and quickly climbed the steps to the double doors. "I used to have a key for these," Veronica said. "These doors are open days when the mill is." She took hold of the heavy door knob and paused, her brow furrowing.

There was heavy clunk from inside, and she pulled the door open. They quickly stepped inside, and Veronica closed the door behind them almost silently.

They were in a long dark hallway. Regan was immediately reminded of the basement of the Atheneum. About thirty feet ahead of them light spilled from a doorway on the right, and shone through the slats of a Venetian blind that covered a wide window into the hall. The linoleum tile floor gleamed underfoot. "That's the receptionist's office," Veronica said quietly. "When she's not on, the security guy sits there." They both paused, listening. The building above them was utterly still, and the only sound was faint music from a radio, the soft whirring of an electric fan, and a rustling noise, like newspaper pages. Regan had feared that there might be more than one person in the office—worst case scenario, Jerry Standish—but if she listened very carefully, she could hear breathing, and just barely, a heartbeat, from one individual. Veronica glanced at Regan, then she banged on the wall loudly with her knuckles and called, "Hello."

They heard a chair scrape back suddenly, and the security guard appeared in the doorway. Suddenly the hall lights came on, and Regan winced, her eyes dazzled even though she still had her sunglasses on.

"Oh, man, you scared me, Miss Standish. You must have let yourself in." The security guard wasn't armed, Regan noticed, although he was wearing a light blue uniform shirt with the security firm logo.

"Sorry. I thought you might be doing rounds and not hear the buzzer." Veronica walked confidently to the doorway and Regan trailed behind, noticing that the guard was giving her an interested look. He must have seen her picture in the papers. She was more well-known after being missing for a week than she had been after seven years as the manager of Borrowed and Blue.

"Did you want to talk to your father, Miss Standish?" The guard was automatically reaching for the phone on the desk.

"No, no, you don't need to bother him. I was just wondering if you'd noticed anything suspicious going on in the building during your shift?" Veronica had followed the guard into the office, and Regan paused in the doorway, feeling that it would be a bit crowded in there with three of them. She looked around the room carefully, seeing three desks, an intercom base unit and multi-line phones, but no cameras or security monitors.

"No, should I have done? Suspicious in what way?"

"Any signs that someone might have gotten inside, like unlocked doors, broken windows, things like that?"

He was frowning, as though disturbed at the thought that he might have missed something. "I haven't noticed anything like that. Is there something I should check?"

"We heard a rumor that someone might have gotten into the boiler room, maybe last night after the fireworks. Is there any maintenance work going on today?"

"No, there's not. In fact, we're short handed upstairs today, someone called out sick. But I've been doing the rounds every hour. You think someone's down there?"

"You haven't gone down to the lower level at all?"

"Not yet. Sounds like I should."

"It might be a good idea. You wouldn't go all by yourself, though, would you?"

He stiffened his back a little. "That's my job. It'll be my ass on the line if someone's messing around down there and I didn't even notice it." He turned to the desk and picked up a nightstick, which he slid into a holder on his belt, and a cell phone. "If I run into a problem, I'll call the cops." He turned toward the door, and Veronica stepped up very close behind him, almost bumping into him.

"Kill the lights, Regan." Regan snapped down the switches on the wall next to her and the office and hallway were immediately plunged into total darkness—at least as far as the guard was concerned. For Regan, it was as though she was seeing through a thick, dark gray fog, in which the guard himself glowed with ghostly radiance.

"Hey, what are you—" was as far as he got, before Veronica caught him from behind, one hand tightly over his mouth, locked on to his neck and *opened*. He made a huffing sound of pain and outrage through his nose, pulling at her wrists with his hands. It must have been a great shock to him that she was so strong. He was no taller than Veronica but broad-shouldered and beefy and probably outweighed her by seventy pounds. None of this made him anywhere near her equal, but he was trying to kick, so Veronica blanked his memory. His body jerked once and then he went as limp as a sleeping cat. Without losing a drop, Veronica sank to her knees, letting him fold up with her. Regan leaned against the door jamb, watching with mild interest as Veronica's hazy form grew brighter to her vision. She was getting warmer as she drank.

Abruptly, Veronica *closed* and straightened up, letting her head fall back with an expression of complete bliss. After several seconds she drew in and released a long sigh. "Oh, *god,* that feels good. My fingers have been cold for weeks and weeks. They just never get warm."

"Yes, I know." Regan's tone was more sardonic than she intended. Her stomach was cramping. Veronica blinked, and she looked at Regan, then down at the motionless figure of the guard, still cradled in her arms like a *pietà*.

"Oh..." She sounded abashed. "Do you want some?"

"Well, not *now*, you've taken enough already. We better get going, Ver. Let's not leave him lying on the floor, though." They each took one of the guard's arms and lifted him into the desk chair. With a little careful arrangement, they balanced him with his head on his folded arms on the desk, as though he'd dropped off for a nap.

"Did I blank enough of his memory?"

Regan put her hands on the guard's temples. "You sure did. My god, I hope he remembers his name." She glanced up at Veronica and added, "Better too much than too little, though, it's safer that way."

They left the office and Regan followed Veronica as she made her way without hesitation through the maze of dark hallways. They passed through three large rooms filled with machines for processing fibers and looming fabric, all of them quiet and still, although lights glowed on many of their control consoles. At the end of the last room they went down a steel staircase, stepping as silently as they could. Veronica undid the lock of the heavy door at the bottom of the stairs and they entered the lower level. There was a strong smell of oil. They were standing in a vast dark space, almost the length of the building, with a low ceiling by comparison with the floor above, down which ran a row of massive boilers, turbines that produced steam and electrical power for the machinery upstairs. On a normal day, this room would have been filled with a roar of sound, but today only one of the boilers was operating, for power. Even so, Regan realized with dismay, it would be difficult to hear any sounds that might reveal where Hiram and Sean were, and the reek of oil would make smell problematical, as well. But they did have their ability to see in the dark, and it was nothing down here if not dark. Regan's eyes searched the dense gray fog and saw no brighter patches that would have given away a warm body, even in hiding.

Veronica gestured at a set of heavy double doors some ways down the wall from the door they'd just come through. "The incinerators are in there."

Regan drew in a shuddering breath. "Let's go take a look."

They walked silently along the wall to the double doors. One of the doors was ajar about three inches, emitting a draft of slightly warmer air, and no light was on inside the room. Regan reached out and touched the door. Someone had opened it recently, she perceived, but not with any particular purpose—only checking the room. She tugged the door open just enough to step inside. It was completely quiet and the incinerators appeared damped down and almost cold. They had not been burning recently, and Regan could not see or smell any evidence of a human in the room, alive or dead. She went back out and pushed the door closed as far as she'd found it. "Where is this back exit that you talked about?"

Veronica beckoned and they walked along the stained and gritty concrete floor, past one boiler after another, until they were almost at the end of the room. Veronica pointed out the door in the exterior wall there. It was closed, but Regan regarded it suspiciously. Then she pointed to something near the top of the frame. "Veronica, look at that." She kept her voice pitched softly enough that even standing next to her, only another vampire could have heard her, and Veronica followed her cue.

"What is it?" Veronica stepped forward, craning her neck to look, but Regan caught her elbow.

"Don't touch the door. Step back. It's some kind of sensor."

"You mean a motion sensor?" Veronica froze.

"I don't think so. It would already have picked us up. But I'm sure it will trigger if the door is opened or touched." Regan prayed she was right. Hiram could have bought a motion sensor at any big home improvement store.

"My god, when you talked about booby-traps—"

"I don't know what this would do. Let's not find out." She knelt down to examine the floor closely. She could smell fresh mud. There were footprints on the floor, and bits of trampled grass and reeds. The footprints seemed to turn to the right, away from the staircase she and Veronica had come down. "What's down here?" She pointed at the wall about twenty feet away. "More rooms?"

"Yes...small ones, they're mostly empty. It's too damp down here from the river for storage, and there are rats."

"Rats!"

"They don't bother people. But they'll chew things, so you can't really store anything down here."

Regan straightened up and looked along the width of the wall. There were four doors. "Are these rooms interconnected, or are these doors the only way to get in?"

Veronica stood staring at the doors. "I can't remember."

"Does any of them have another way out? If the sensor on this door was triggered—what would someone in one of these rooms do?" But Veronica could only shake her head. Regan walked stealthily toward the nearest door, looking at the floor to see if the footprints could be tracked that far. There appeared to be faint prints leading to both of the nearer two doors. She studied their frames. If there was light behind either door, no crack showed, even at the bottom. She also couldn't discern any sign of a wire or sensor. But in darkness this complete, her night vision ability only went so far. Details of inanimate objects that were all roughly the same temperature weren't very clear. It was like trying to watch a very snowy television picture, only much darker.

Veronica came up to stand next to her. "What should we do?"

After a moment, Regan stepped back a few feet, motioning Veronica to follow her. "Jonathan once said...in a cat and mouse game, the loser is always the one who panics first. Let's just wait, and listen."

"It must be getting close to eleven."

"I know." Regan could hardly believe that it had been less than two hours since she had gotten the phone call from Sharon Neeson.

They waited. The single active boiler, about halfway down the room, rumbled away. About every two minutes, some mechanism above the boiler made the dull metallic double thump that they had heard in the background of the phone call. There was no other sound. Each two minute interval felt like an hour to Regan. Was Sean even still alive? Had Hiram left when Jonathan entered the police station, was he now miles away, while she and Veronica stood here and stared at the doors to empty rooms? Her stomach clamped down in another cramp, and she regretted not taking some blood from the security guard when she'd had the chance. *Just a little drink, it wouldn't have killed him...* She started at a tiny sound to the right, and glancing over beyond the nearest boiler, saw that Veronica had been correct about the storage problem. There was a rat, scurrying along by the wall. They had been so still for so long, it had felt safe to venture out. *Hey, he's got blood...* It was very tempting. But, no. *He'd probably get away, I might make a noise chasing him, and we need to stay right here.* Her mouth was watering. Then Veronica touched her arm and Regan was snapped back to attention. There was a voice coming from one of the two doors—Regan thought it was the second one.

"Well, Sean, Vaughn's been at the police station for a while now. What do you think he's telling them?" It was Hiram's voice. Regan turned her head sideways, straining to hear, but could not detect a reply from Sean. There was silence after that. Was Sean dead, had Hiram just been talking to his corpse the way one might talk to an animal or a photograph?

Regan decided to risk trying to learn more. She walked forward until she was within a foot of the second door, reached out, and touched the door with her fingers. No alarm went off and there was no sound from inside the room that suggested anyone had been alerted to her presence. She closed her eyes and tried to gather impressions from the door. Then she walked to the first door and did the same there. She started, jerking her hand back, when she heard something inside the room. All she could clearly discern were unhurried footsteps and a few small noises like objects being moved. But suddenly, with a chill, Regan thought she knew what was going on. She went back to where Veronica stood. "I think Sean's in the second room. There must be a connecting door. It sounds like Hiram is packing up his stuff—the police scanner, and whatever else he has. He's got charley bars bracing the doors." She jerked around when she heard Hiram's voice again.

"All right, Sean. Stand up. You need to come with me now."

"Why?" At the sound of Sean's voice, Regan felt a burst of relief so intense it was like physical pain. She swayed on her feet, even as she felt Veronica clutch at her arm with emotion equal to Regan's own.

"We're going to the other end of the building."

"Is it noon? It's not noon yet, is it?"

"Ummm...when I said noon, I didn't mean it that literally. You see, it really depended on what Jonathan Vaughn did. I can't say that I'm surprised."

"But he went to the police station, didn't he? You said you saw him."

"Yes, he did, and that's why I think I need to be moving on now. Get up, Sean."

"Why should I? What if I don't?"

"Then I will have to tape your mouth, tie your feet and drag you. Don't think I can't. I was practically carrying you most of the way here last night."

"Then you can do that, you cocksucker. Why would I do anything to help you?"

Hiram chuckled, and Regan felt as though her hair was standing on end. "I suppose I can leave you here while I get things ready. Are you sure you wouldn't like another drink of this? It will make it much easier."

"No! Get that shit away from me."

"Suit yourself. But I think..." he trailed off, but the clear sound of tape being pulled from a roll was audible. "There. Not that anyone could hear you, but you're getting just a bit too frisky." Sean didn't answer. Regan heard the sound of the charley bar being unlocked, and she gave Veronica a hasty push. They both ran for the shadow of the nearest boiler, reaching it just as the door opened. Light spilled out into the room, and Hiram emerged, shining a tiny penlight so he could make his way in the dark. He was clean shaven and his hair was shorn very closely to his head, and the round eyeglasses had been replaced with steel-rimmed aviator frames. He looked so different, Regan wasn't sure she would have recognized him in broad daylight. He had a much weaker chin than she would have guessed. As he went on down the long room, Regan said to Veronica, "Go check on Sean. Let him know we're here—but be careful. Don't untie him and don't touch anything."

Veronica opened her mouth to protest, then stopped and nodded. As she went toward the door of the room where Sean was waiting, Regan trotted, then ran, the other way. Hiram was now opening the double doors to the incinerator room. As Regan reached the last boiler, he snapped on the light, and Regan, dazzled for a moment, stepped quickly into the shadows to the side of the doorway. "Now let's see..." she heard Hiram say, and then she heard one of the incinerators being opened. A hot, rather unpleasant smell drifted out through the doors. She moved close enough to peer through the crack by the door frame and saw Hiram gathering up scrap wood, pieces of crates and pallets, and heaving them into the incinerator. Although the fire inside had burned down to coals, flames quickly leapt up. Regan could see a sort of hopper on the side of room, with sides more than six feet high. It looked like combustibles came down a chute from the floors above, and the hopper was nearly full. Watching Hiram stoke up the incinerator, to burn Sean, as coolly as he would start a camp fire, Regan felt rage filling her entire body. She thought that she could have torn Hiram into pieces, starting with his individual fingers and toes and working her way in, and felt only a fierce joy in doing it. But nothing like that was going to happen. When Hiram went back to the hopper for another load of wood, Regan stepped into the room and pulled the doors shut behind her with a solid thump, and then locked them. Hiram whirled around, wood clattering to the floor.

"My god," Regan said quietly. "You actually look surprised. I guess that sensor on the door was just in case kids or homeless people wandered in, was it?"

Hiram slowly straightened up. "I suppose I should have expected you to find me. I wondered why Vaughn went to the police station alone."

"If we were strictly literal about it, you only said for Jonathan to go."

"I suppose that's true." Hiram glanced from side to side, looking, Regan knew, for an exit, or a weapon, or something he could use to weasel his way out of this situation. "I'm sure the police are on their way."

"No, they're not. They will be. But not just yet."

She watched his face as the implications of this dawned. "You're going to kill me, is that it?"

"You don't think you deserve it? Drugging and kidnapping a teenager? Holding him hostage? Threatening to murder him, with the full intent of doing so? Blackmailing Jonathan, and cheating, besides. Sean was doomed no matter what Jonathan did. There are states where you'd get the death penalty for this, Hiram."

"In that case, it would be justice. What you're doing is vigilantism, Regan. Don't flatter yourself."

Regan savored those words, an unwilling smile curling her lip. "Oh, Hiram. You're so...*good*. To think that I let you manipulate me the way I did." She started walking slowly toward him, and he backed away from her. "There are so many questions I'd love to hear you answer. When did you hypnotize Derek Wilson, and how? What made you so sure that you wouldn't kill me with that knife? When did you first suspect that I'm a vampire, too? How long have you been planning this, and stalking Sean? But I'm resigned, Hiram. You'll take all that with you to your grave. We agreed at the very beginning, some mysteries are never explained."

His face was getting very white. "That's not true. I'll tell you anything you want to know."

"I'm not interested enough in your lies to let you buy the time with them. And I have no intention of giving you another chance to publicly expose us. No high-profile trial and media spotlight for you." He suddenly broke and ran, cutting around between the further incinerator and the hopper. When he got past the incinerator, Regan was already standing in his way. He stopped with a yelp and stumbled back toward the wall. "Don't make me chase you around the room. It's pointless. The door's locked."

"So what are you going to do? Tear out my throat and drain my blood? I'm sure that will be a treat for you." His voice was cracking.

At the thought, Regan's stomach cramped hard, and she ran her tongue over her lips. "A *treat*? I wouldn't drink one drop of your blood. I'd choke on it." She walked toward him again, and when she was a yard away, he made a hoarse sound and tried to run back toward the hopper. This time she caught him, grabbed the front of his shirt and slammed him back up against the wall, hard enough to knock his breath out of him. She lifted him off his feet for a few seconds, to make sure he knew how strong she was. "Just give it up and stop fighting, Hiram. It's over. I don't want to leave marks on you, like I did with Cal. That was a mistake."

"Then you admit—"

"And he's just the only one you know about. God, look at you. You're not even as brave as Sean, are you? Well, don't worry, you're not going to suffer. I'll make this quick. I don't even want to take the time to try and read you."

"What are you going to do, then?" He was shaking uncontrollably, and Regan wondered if he was going to pee himself next. She stepped up close to him and bent toward his face, as he strained back away from her.

"Don't be afraid, Hiram," she breathed into his ear. "All I have to do is touch you." She let go of his shirt and put a hand on either side of his neck, over the veins, pressed lightly for a moment, and *opened,* on both sides. Then she stepped back quickly as twin fountains of blood bubbled from his neck and began to soak his shoulders and chest. For a moment he looked confused, as though he didn't know what was happening, then he put his hands to his neck, trying to stop the flow of blood. Instantly his hands were soaked red, and warm fluid ran between his fingers and spattered on the floor at his feet.

"What...what did you..." he sank to his knees, and still the blood poured out of him. All the front of his shirt was drenched deep crimson now and it was soaking into the top of his pants and forming little pools on the floor where blood was splattering from his hands. Regan backed further away from him, holding her hands away from herself, although there was very little blood on them. *Not one drop...not one...* Hiram was gasping for breath, his face the grayish color of putty, but his lips were turning blue. Then he fell forward, sprawling onto the floor. Two streams of blood immediately began to snake over the grimy concrete. Regan stood motionless, listening as Hiram's breathing grew more labored and slower, while his rapid heartbeat became thready, then irregular. Finally both stopped, and there was no sound in the room except the rustle of flames from the open incinerator door.

For several minutes Regan stared down at Hiram's still body on the floor, his blood already coagulating where it had collected in hollows. Finally she remembered that Veronica was waiting, with Sean. She looked at her hands, the ends of her fingers stained red, thinking vaguely that she would have to be careful about touching anything. She turned and walked to the door of the room and unlocked the doors, then realized that the incinerator was still open. She went over to close it, feeling the heat of the flames on her face. Suddenly she reached inside and scooped up a handful of red hot cinders and scrubbed at her hands with them as though they were soap, not even flinching at the searing pain, until the skin on her fingers was burned scarlet and black and starting to crack open. The smell of her own charring flesh was sickening, but the blood was gone. She slammed the incinerator door shut and pushed the latch into place with her elbow, wishing that she could scream but knowing that if she started, she wouldn't be able to stop.

She left the light on and the door to the incinerator room open, and walked rapidly back to the small room where Veronica was sitting with Sean. It seemed to take a long time to get there, and her hands burned as though they were still in the fire. The pain was so intense that she felt faint. Veronica looked around with a gasp when Regan appeared in the doorway.

"God, Regan! What's been going on? I tried to explain to Sean that you said to wait...where is...is Dr. Clauson..."

"He's dead."

Veronica looked confused, and Regan knew that Veronica could perceive that she was still just as hungry as before they arrived at the mills. "What did you...I mean..."

"I'll tell you about it later."

"Oh my *god*, what happened to your hands?"

"*Later.*" Regan knelt down by Sean's chair. His eyes and mouth were still taped, his hands were tied with plastic ties, and Hiram had fastened him to the old broken office chair with a heavy belt so he couldn't move while the incinerator was being stoked. Seeing him like this, Regan felt again the surge of blind rage that had almost overwhelmed her as she waited outside the incinerator room, but she thought of Hiram's body lying among streams of blood and her rage vanished. "Sean," she said urgently. "We have to leave you here and call the police. They'll find you, but it can't look like anyone else has been here. You understand why, don't you?" He nodded violently, and made a muffled sound that might have been the words *I understand* spoken through duct tape. "Don't be scared. You're safe now. The police will be here very soon. I know you'll know what to tell them, Sean. Everything, except leave us being here out of it, right? Hiram left you alone here and never came back." He nodded again. "I promise, we'll see you really soon."

Chapter 35

Regan's hands were not very functional. She asked Veronica to look through the small nylon daypack that Hiram's things were in, hoping that he hadn't had his cell phone in his pocket. Veronica found the phone and dialed the house number, letting it ring until voice mail answered. Then she and Regan left, giving Sean one more reassuring pat on the shoulders as they did. Veronica pulled the alarm off the exit door. It proved to be nothing but a cheap battery-powered gadget that buzzed if the door was opened. She and Regan pulled the door shut behind them and locked it, and Veronica pitched the alarm into the middle of the river. They walked back along the path, wary of being seen, as it was now close to lunchtime and there might be more people in the park. But it had become even muggier and more overcast, spitting a few drops of rain, and they saw no one. When they had walked almost as far as the spot where Jonathan had dropped them off, Veronica turned on her cell phone and called Jonathan's phone. He was still at the police station, and with a most convincing simulation of barely controlled panic and hysteria, they told him, and then Detective Fellman, that they had gotten another call from Hiram Clauson, he had revealed where he was and had made statements indicating that he was going to kill Sean and himself. "I wish I could be there to see the look on my dad's face, when the S.W.A.T. team gets there," Veronica said after she'd terminated the call.

Regan and Veronica walked back to Rainbow Stone house, since it would be difficult to explain how they had gotten to the police station without a car. Veronica knew the shortcut through the woods that Nick had mentioned to his friends, and they took that way, which cut a couple of miles off the walk and reduced the chance that they would be seen. Regan half expected there to be police cars and reporters at the house waiting for them, but all was quiet. They got back at about the same time that the police recovered Sean. Jonathan called them to say that Sean was at the hospital, Hiram's body was being removed from the mill building, and Sharon Neeson was making a bigger fuss over her son than she probably had done since the day of his birth.

"Jonathan shouldn't be dealing with all this alone," Veronica said after the call. In response, Regan held up her burned hands.

"How will I explain these?"

"Why won't you tell me what *happened*, Regan?" Regan had barely spoken on the long walk home.

"I just can't. You go, take my car, go ahead. Just say I'm too upset to face anyone." With some protests, Veronica finally accepted her keys and left.

Regan could not recall when she had felt so drained, even after the stabbing incident. But she didn't want to sleep, at least not in bed, and she didn't want to be down in the main part of the house answering the phone or monitoring the news on the Internet, like Jonathan would have been doing. She wandered the house for a while and finally settled up in the attic, where they had all watched the fireworks over the river just the night before. The attic was clean and spacious and dim and had bats, all still sound asleep. Sunset wasn't until 8:22 p.m. She sat on the floor near one corner, her back against the wall and knees drawn up, her hands curled loosely against her chest, listening to the birds in the woods outside and trying to ignore the continuous throbbing pain of her burns.

Veronica and Jonathan returned to the house by around 6:00. After some time, Jonathan came up the attic stairs cautiously, perhaps thinking she might be sleeping up there. "I was just a little worried," he said when she turned to look at him. "I wasn't sure where you'd gone."

"I left all the doors open for a clue."

Jonathan walked over to her and hunkered down, looking at her with concern. "Yes, I finally figured that out. I'm afraid I've done all the clue-solving I want to be bothered with for a while."

"No shit," Regan said tiredly. "How is Sean?"

"He'll be fine. They're going to keep him in the hospital at least overnight. He wasn't harmed physically, but Veronica was right, Clauson drugged his soda. The bottle was still in the room with the drug in it. They're running tests on it, and on Sean, just to make sure they know what he might have been given. And they're going to bring a trauma counselor in to talk to him."

"Did you see him?"

"Yes, I did. He asked why you weren't there, though. He's worried about you."

"About me?"

"He wondered what Veronica was talking about when she asked what happened to your hands."

"Oh. That. Yes, I guess he would have heard her say that."

After a pause, Jonathan said quietly, "I'm wondering, too. May I see them?"

She looked at him for a moment, then extended both her hands towards him, palm up. He winced at the sight. All the burned skin had peeled off her fingers and the upper palms of her hands, and she'd lost six fingernails along with it. But already the thinnest tissue of new skin was starting to form, covered with weeping drops of sticky fluid. "It's not even going to scar, is it?"

"No, but you're not going to be able to use them for a couple of days." He hesitated. "I saw Clauson's body, so I know what you did. You don't have to tell me the details. But how did you burn your hands?"

Regan folded her hands back against her chest. "They had blood on them, so I washed them. With cinders from the incinerator."

"You found the answer to Macbeth's question," Jonathan said softly.

"I wasn't going to drink from him. Not one drop." Regan's stomach clenched painfully, and she closed her eyes. "I'm so hungry," she whispered despairingly.

"I'll get you something, later tonight."

Regan smiled faintly. "Oh good, cold blood in plastic. Yummy."

"I'm sorry, it's the best I can do."

"I know. Forgive me, I'm going to be a bitch as long as my hands hurt this much."

"Nothing is as bad as burns, not even for us. Soaking your hands in ice water will help deaden the sensation."

"I suppose acetaminophen doesn't have any effect on us, does it?"

"I'm afraid not. But at least you'll heal much faster than you would have in life. Until then, you'll just have to suffer."

"That's what I get for being a drama queen. What do the cops think happened to Hiram?"

"Well...granted, the scene did have some puzzling aspects. I think they're assuming it was suicide, but there wasn't anything he could have cut himself with. And then there's the security guard upstairs. We may need to be prepared to answer some more questions. But I got a feeling this afternoon that Detective Fellman believes Clauson may have been responsible for all the reported incidents he knows about."

Regan blinked and then suddenly laughed. "Now that is truly ironic."

"Detective Fellman knows that Clauson was in the Atheneum when Cal was attacked, for one thing. Jerry Standish told him that today. And the security guard at the mills is another one that could be most easily connected with Clauson. But I don't know if Fellman is definitely concluding that."

Regan leaned her head back against the wall. "Oh, god, I want to read that man so badly, I can taste it. I have never met such a sphinx in my life. And he's wearing a wedding ring, damn it. I couldn't even ask him out and finagle a good long kiss."

Jonathan looked amused. "Keep working on it, maybe you'll come up with something. Ask Veronica to help you."

"Veronica? Why?"

"I've come to the conclusion that between the two of you, there's nothing you couldn't solve, resolve or get around. You two together are like an unstoppable force. I'm frankly feeling just a bit intimidated."

Regan stared at him, ready to laugh but stopped by the look on his face. "You're not joking. Oh, god. Well, you should tell her that. She could use the self-esteem boost."

"Maybe I will." He sobered. "You got to the mills just in time, you know."

"I know. I'm trying not to think about it."

Jonathan looked down for a moment, as if he was debating whether to continue. "When the police went through Clauson's bag, they found...a garrote. A

knotted cord, with loops at the ends. That's what he was going to do—strangle
Sean, and then burn his body."

"Oh, fuck, do I really need to hear this, Jonathan?"

"Veronica told me that she saw the cord when she was looking for Clauson's
cell phone, but she didn't say anything about it because she didn't want to upset
Sean...or you."

Regan made an incoherent sound and put her forearms over her face, shuddering. "Please, Jonathan, I can't bear to even imagine what—"

"I'm telling you this, because I don't think you should feel regrets, not for
one second. If the police had been the ones who found Clauson and Sean, they'd
have killed Clauson, if they thought they had to, rather than take any risk of
Sean being hurt."

"Hiram said that was justice, and what I was doing was vigilantism."

"What you were doing was defending someone you love from imminent
death. Even the law makes allowances for that."

Regan sighed. "I certainly hope the law's tolerance will never be tested in
this case."

"I don't think we'll have to worry about that. After the stabbing incident,
no one is going to be exclaiming that they'd never have believed Clauson could
do such a thing. There are going to be a lot of people coming forward to testify
about how unbalanced he seemed to be."

"And unfortunately, a lot of attention being paid to the general topic of
vampires."

Jonathan folded his arms. "You know, you are the worst person for seeing
the glass half empty."

"I am not! My hands hurt, and I'm starving."

"Would you like me to leave you up here in peace, or would you like to come
downstairs and soak your burns in ice water?"

Regan glowered at the middle of the room for a second. "Ice water."

"Well, come on, then."

Sean's narrow escape not only made headlines in all the major Massachusetts
newspapers and news shows, it made national news, as well. Little Sheridan
had its fifteen minutes of fame, or at least notoriety. Regan had prepared herself
for the likelihood that Sharon Neeson would blame them for Sean's being in
danger and object to their having any contact with him. But Sharon was effusive
in her gratitude for their part in Sean's rescue, and as soon as he was out of the
hospital, Sean was resuming his visits to Rainbow Stone house. He complained
bitterly about his trauma counselor and pestered Veronica to continue with their
driving lessons.

Sean was there one evening in the second week of July when Jonathan's
friend from Maine called again.

"You know, Jonathan, I am getting a much clearer picture of why you have
to disappear so often. How do you get yourself *into* these things?"

"I don't know, Diana. I must just get bored. But I expect life is going to be much less exciting now."

"That's what you said the last time we talked. But look, I'm very glad your young friend wasn't hurt. That sounded like a very close call."

"Too close."

"I've got some news for you, by the way. About Rainbow Stone house."

Jonathan straightened up in his chair. "Is the owner going to sell?"

"Indeed he is. To me."

"You're buying it?"

"Well, he just wouldn't budge about you, Jonathan. He's afraid you're starting some kind of cult, apparently—"

"What?"

"Don't shoot me, I'm only the piano player. Someone fed him a real line of bull and he believed every word of it. He's eighty-three years old and living in a gated retirement community in Florida and he's a little out of touch. He's also gotten some pretty good offers from developers. Did you know that the dairy farmer filed for an injunction to stop the land from being used for a 40B complex? I guess Sheridan doesn't have enough affordable housing."

"No, Derek Wilson conveniently neglected to mention that one."

"Quite right, since he would have been breaking confidentiality to tell you. But I topped all the developers' offers and the owner is going to sell."

"So...are you going to re-sell to me?"

"Are you kidding? Jonathan, if I sell you that property, the next thing I know you'll disappear for twenty years and show up in Nepal. In fact, I'm going to raise your rent."

"Oh, thank you very much."

"Look, it's for the best. There's less chance that anyone will try to investigate our arrangement if you're paying close to market rate."

"Does this mean if the furnace blows up, we call you?"

"You can *call,* Jonathan." Diana chuckled. "You have carte blanche to restore, renovate and otherwise improve the property any way you want. I'll see to it that the lease is written that way. Derek Wilson from Wilson Realty will be calling you about signing the new lease in a couple of weeks."

Jonathan pondered this for a moment. "Well...thank you, Diana. You're probably right, this will be for the best. You'll have to come down and see the place after we've done some work on it."

"I will. I'm dying of curiosity. I was amazed to hear that it was still standing. You know, if there are three of you, and you're planning to stay a while, you should talk to Johanna."

"We're not that close to them, Diana."

"She might not agree with that, given that I'm sure she follows the news, too. You ought to let her know your status, anyway."

"Well..."

"It's up to you." Diana's inflection clearly conveyed that evading this courtesy call would be most unwise.

Jonathan sighed heavily. "You're probably right." Listening closely to this exchange, Regan wondered who Johanna might be. From Jonathan's expression, she must have an intimidating personality.

When Jonathan terminated the call, Sean, Regan and Veronica were all looking at him expectantly.

"So, you're in?" Sean said. "This means you're staying here for good?"

"At least it means that we won't be evicted from the house. We may be able to stay here for quite some time, anyway."

In the beginning of August, Jonathan went to Wilson's Realty to sign the new lease. Regan went along with him, hoping to have an opportunity to ask Derek Wilson a question that was still bothering her, even if it was moot at this point. But she was spared the need of bringing up the topic herself.

"Boy, that was crazy about that Clauson guy, wasn't it," Derek said as Jonathan read over the lease. "I just can't believe that I let him hypnotize me."

"Well, Hiram was a certified hypnotherapist, I don't think there's any question about that," Regan said diplomatically. "How did it happen that you did a session with him?"

"It was two sessions. He stopped into the office here after that night when we all met at the Hong Kong Delhi. I had this big presentation I was giving in Boston, and I was sweating it. I hate having to talk to crowds, I always fumble around and make an ass out of myself. Clauson said that hypnosis could help with that and offered to give me a couple of free sessions. It sounded like a deal, especially when he told me what he usually charged. Now I feel like a complete idiot."

"Why did Hiram come into your office to begin with?"

Derek crossed his leg and leaned back, frowning. "I don't know. I can't remember now." He shrugged. "I don't think it was anything important."

Regan and Jonathan exchanged looks. "Did it work? For your presentation, I mean," Jonathan asked.

"Oh, yeah. It worked great. I was amazed. That's why I didn't...I mean, I would have seen through that Clauson guy a lot sooner if he hadn't gotten my confidence like that."

A week later, Regan came downstairs in the early afternoon to find Sean sitting alone at the table in the great room. She was the first one up, and she was surprised to see Sean who usually did not come out to the house when they were all still sleeping. He seemed to be brooding darkly about something, and his greeting when he saw her was muted. Regan went to the table and sat down, watching him reflectively. He had grown about an inch this summer, and his shoulders were a little broader, but he was never going to be tall. He'd sprouted the embryo of a mustache over the past weeks and now Regan could see a fine shadow on his cheeks, as well. *Why doesn't he have a girlfriend?* she thought fondly. But in high school, being short, nerdy and shy obviously was still a lethal combination. *I'll bet he does much better in college.* Sean's MCAS scores had been fine, but he hadn't taken the SAT's or college boards yet, and Jonathan was coaxing him to think more ambitiously about his future.

Sean didn't say anything more, so Regan just let him brood and booted up her computer. Jonathan came down a few minutes later. He rarely stayed in bed long after she got up, and Regan suspected that he got lonely without her.

"Hello, Sean." Jonathan also sounded mildly surprised to see him.

"Hi," Sean said. When Jonathan had sat down at the table, he went on, "I'm sorry I'm bugging you so early. I've got something to talk to you both about. It's going to sound pretty weird, but...just hear me out, okay?"

Regan glanced at Jonathan, who was giving her a somewhat cautious look. "We're listening."

Sean took in a deep breath. "Okay, it's like this. My mom had a really hard time after that whole kidnapping thing. She, well, she fell off the wagon. Big time. It's been brutal."

"God, Sean, I'm sorry to hear that. You never said anything."

"I was hoping she'd pull it together, before, you know, before DSS got called in again. I really tried to cover up for her because I knew how scared she was about that."

"DSS, the axis of evil," Regan said dryly.

"No fucking shit. Well..." Sean sighed heavily. "Be careful what you wish for, because my mom's decided to sign herself into rehab."

"Rehab?"

"Yeah. She's gotten into a residential treatment program. Six months, up in Chelsea. She'll have to give up the apartment."

"Sean, my god, what are you going to do?"

"That's just it. That's what I'm getting to here." Sean pressed his steepled hands to his mouth for a moment. "See, there's no open case right now. So my mom can sign papers giving legal guardianship to anyone she wants. There's no relatives or anything, my mom doesn't have any family, and my dad's been gone for years. Actually, we're pretty sure he's in prison out in Kansas. So the thing is, she really likes you guys. She thinks you've been a good influence on me. She'd sign guardianship over to you."

Regan gaped. "She'd...she'd make me and Jonathan your legal guardians? Sean..."

"Not both of you, but probably you, Regan, because she's known you a long time, and everyone in town knows you. Hey, it's a no-brainer, as far as she's concerned. If she doesn't pick a guardian, then DSS will step in, and they'll probably put me in foster care, because I'll be homeless."

Regan stared at Jonathan. "But that means you'll be living out here."

"My mom says I already live out here. But yeah, it'll be that or a cardboard box in the park." He flushed. "I don't want to sound like I'm inviting myself in, but...look, it's only for six months. And in just eight months I'll be eighteen and on my own, no matter what happens. I just don't want to have to move away from here and not see you guys, and be in some shitty foster home again. If I live here with you, I won't have to change schools."

There was a long silence, during which Regan tried to stifle a hysterical laugh at the complete surreality of Sean's request. *If Sharon only knew...!* But compared to what Sean had grown up with, living at Rainbow Stone house with three vampires was a wholesome improvement.

"Well, I'd have no problems with it," Jonathan said. "It's a big house."

Regan flung her hands in the air. "If the court agrees to it, I'll sign," she said.

"Are you guys serious?"

"Have your mom call me, Sean," Regan said. "Lord, we're going to have to start buying a lot more groceries."

Sean's face was breaking into an incredulous grin. "I was scared shitless to even ask you."

"I don't know why. Your mom is right, you do already live out here. God, we wouldn't let you get sent to foster care if we could help it, Sean. You're family." At the expression on Sean's face, Regan said, "Oh, stop looking at me like that, my heart is breaking here."

"Thanks," Sean said, a little hoarse.

"I hope you know what you're signing on for, Sean," Jonathan said with exaggerated sternness. "If you think we've been a pain in the ass about your schoolwork before now—"

"Yes, you're getting three parents. And we're going to expect you to make us look good."

"Yeah, right," Sean said, rubbing his hand back over his hair and grinning sheepishly at the tabletop. Then he got up. "Look, sorry to meet and run, but I'm going to go talk to my mom right away."

"When does her program start?" Jonathan asked.

"September first, and she's got to stay sober. It's going to be rough, she'll have to pack up the apartment and everything."

"Tell her if there's anything I can do to help out, I'll be there," Regan said.

"Thanks, I will." Sean headed for the front door and was almost running by the time he got there.

Jonathan and Regan stared at each other, momentarily speechless. "That's it," Jonathan said finally. "We do have a commune."

"Or a cult."

"Maybe Sean would like to re-paint the mural on the barn door."

"I bet he would." Regan sat with one hand over her mouth, smiling helplessly down at her computer. "Good lord. Did I just say I'd be Sean's legal guardian?"

"Yes, you did."

"What in god's name will I say to my mom about this?"

"Congratulations, it's a boy?"

Regan put her hands over her face. "I am crazy, aren't I, Jonathan? Completely crazy." She looked up at him, and he grinned back at her.

"Yes, you are. Starkers." Then they both were laughing.

LaVergne, TN USA
17 August 2009
154984LV00012B/30/P